WILDCHILDS

eugenia melian

A NOVEL

FSB
FASHION
SPHINX
BOOKS

Published by Fashion Sphinx Books, San Francisco / Madrid
eugeniamelian.com

GIRL FRIDAY
PRODUCTIONS

Edited and Designed by Girl Friday Productions
www.girlfridayproductions.com

Editorial: Emilie Sandoz-Voyer, Amara Holstein,
Laura Whittemore, Carrie Wicks
Interior Design: Rachel Marek
Cover Design: Shawn Stussy
Cover Image: Dara Allen and Fernando Cerezo III, photographed
by Ethan James Green and styled by Dara Allen

ISBN (Paperback): 978-1-7325477-0-4
e-ISBN: 978-1-7325477-1-1

First Edition

Printed in the United States of America

For a man from Passaic—with simple needs, simple desires

CHAPTER 1

The FedEx employee looked Iris up and down as he handed her the thick envelope. *¡La gringa está bien guapa!* Supercute gringa!

Used to people's stares, Iris flashed him a sweet grin and looked at the name tag on his uniform. "*Muchas gracias . . .* Fulgencio."

Heart racing, Iris walked out of the store to sit in her Chevy pickup. *I should wash you, Chevy, I promise, when it rains.* She tore open the package, knowing all too well that a lawyer's FedEx would mean either something terrible, or something even worse.

It was early May in Northern California and five years into the drought. There was dust and gravel where once were lush lawns, burnt brown wisps of wild grass replacing the flower hedges. Here and there cheerful terra-cotta planters held decorative succulents in an attempt at urban landscaping. Day after day the sun burned bright in the blue sky. Dry. Scanning the horizon every morning for rain clouds had become a habit and talk about saving water a necessity. *Another day in paradise,* Iris thought. She looked around to make sure that she was alone. No one was a stranger in La Arboleda.

Iris locked herself inside the truck, praying for privacy, and did not turn on the AC. *It's so unecological, I hate it.*

As drops of sweat trickled down her face, she rubbed them off with her sleeve, concentrating on the documents. Tears started to roll down her cheeks, merging in rivulets on her neck. Iris wept. She was loud, noisy. She started to shake, her body out of control; sobs rattled her slim shoulders, jarring her face and ribs. Then, she was spent. There were no more tears left in her. She looked up into the mirror and dabbed at her red eyes and runny nose with the back of her hand. From the glove compartment, she took an old paper napkin. The green-and-orange logo from Taqueria El Molino made her smile for a second. After blowing her nose, she fixed her hair into a semblance of a ponytail, turned on the motor, and opened the windows. Still stunned, she forced herself to snap into the present with a quick rundown of her mental checklist. Her phone alarm rang. "Shit! Lou!"

Racing down the side streets of La Arboleda, she made it to the light just as it turned red. "Fuck! Fuck! Fuck!"

In her head, she heard Lou telling her off: *Yo! Potty mouth! Don't swear, Mom!* Drumming on the steering wheel, she waited for the light to turn green while she watched other moms in their shiny SUVs. Beige moms, perfect moms, soccer moms, trophy moms, cookie-cutter moms, rich MILFs dressed head to toe in Lululemon.

Do these women EVER get out of their yoga pants? Since when are yoga pants a proper outfit? Where do they think they are going in those bloody Cayennes and Range Rovers? To cross the fucking Sahara? You're only going to Whole Foods, for God's sake. Dude, next time you get your knickers in a twist about climate change, just remember that you drive a fucking SUV when you really don't need to.

Lost in her thoughts, she half jumped out of her seat when a dusty station wagon pulled up next to her and honked. Recognizing her friend Maca, she waved out the window.

"Hey! Iris! 'Sup, yo? Jeeeeeeez, you look rough! Shitty day?" Maca looked at her with a worried expression and made a call-me sign as the lights changed and they both drove forward, side by side.

The thought of talking to Maca made Iris feel better. Earth mother and ex-commune hippie, Maca was one of those women who smelled of fresh-baked bread and cookies. Unlike most of the mothers she met at La Arboleda County School,

Maca did not care about working out or fancy yoga pants, hair salons, lifestyle magazines, or mani-pedis. Gregarious and outspoken, Maca was always available for a good laugh and a consoling hug. After the school run, they had spent so many mornings sleepy and bleary-eyed, drinking mugs of coffee in Maca's chaotic kitchen.

"Dang! We look like dogs' dinners!" Iris would say. And they would explode with laughter, comparing who looked worse.

"What time do you think Pauline woke up to get ready for the school run? Squeezer looked like she was going clubbing! Did you check out her makeup? I mean, come on! To do the school run at eight a.m.? In La Arboleda, not Las Vegas! What was she thinking?" Maca asked.

"I think she's banging Andrea's husband, for real," Iris said. And with this they laughed until their sides hurt, thinking of bald and boring Mr. Sullivan with that foxy slut Pauline. Then they would drink so much coffee that they'd get the jitters and laugh some more.

Iris found comfort in those early-morning sessions of silly girly gossip. Like her, Maca was a single mother, who struggled to raise her two boys on a small salary, their realities different from the majority of parents at La Arboleda County School. Maca's placidity radiated peace, unlike some of the high-strung moms Iris met at the school: nervy, high-maintenance women who self-medicated and needed to go to therapy if they got lost shopping at Saks.

Cheered up by the vision of Maca's grinning face and plump arm waving out of the car, Iris braced herself, quieted her mind, and prepared for her daughter, Lou.

La Arboleda County was a small public high school on the outskirts of town. A rustic one-story wooden building with sunny rooms and few students, dense oak woodland and grassy meadows surrounding the campus and soccer fields.

Lou was so lucky; one day soon, Iris knew her daughter would miss all this. *I will miss all of this. I don't want my baby to grow up.* Iris got in line behind the other cars and turned the motor off, scanning the entrance for her daughter. This was the moment of the day she loved the most, waiting by the gates, watching the gaggle of kids being herded into their respective cars by their moms. Shouts, calls, laughter, kids, so many kids, moving in shrieking shoals. Short shorts, tiny T-shirts, and Uggs. Long shorts, Giants baseball caps, Warriors tees.

Then she spotted Lou.

Like Iris, Lou was tall, slim, with an athletic frame, and unlike the other teens at school, her body language was not languid and floppy but tight and tense; she moved graciously and silently like a fawn, unmistakable in Iris's favorite tattered Sex Pistols T-shirt, Converse, and frayed hoodie. Silky black hair framed a pale freckled face with piercing gold-green eyes, salient cheekbones, and full lips.

It was hard to tell Iris and Lou apart. It was also impossible not to stare at the striking pair like exquisite creatures that had landed in La Arboleda in a spaceship. Iris was in her late thirties but looked like a feral teenage boy, her uniform consisting of skinny black jeans, scuffed Chelsea boots, and a black T-shirt or indigo shirt. Her messy black hair was chopped off bluntly to graze the jawline. Wispy bangs and a dimpled chin were her only outward signs of femininity. If Iris had been an animal, she would have been a black panther.

Iris's features were unusual, slightly masculine but sensual in their ambiguity. Her strong, tanned face needed no makeup; her penetrating dark eyes were framed by equally dark and thick eyebrows.

Reserved, she preferred the company of her two closest friends and her daughter, and avoided most social occasions. Iris did not do well in crowds. She hated the probing and curiosity of the other parents at school: *Why did a girl like you end up in a place like this?*

Iris loved living in La Arboleda, her home of the last eleven years. *What's not to love?* A small rural town of two thousand inhabitants in a hidden valley near Sonoma, La Arboleda had been famous at the beginning of the century for its apples and eggs. Now, profitable vines had replaced most of the orchards, and old farms were being turned into small mansions with manicured lawns where no children played. Empty streets, silent cul-de-sacs. La Arboleda kids were investments, too busy with private dance, sports, and music lessons. Kids too busy becoming their parents.

In La Arboleda, young couples from Silicon Valley and San Francisco had displaced the farmers, poets, writers, artists, hippies, and cowboys. With them also came the weekend hipsters playing farm or vineyard owners in their organic compounds, breeding fancy chickens, and selling their artisanal breads, coffee, and jams at the local grocery store.

Not only was the demography changing fast but also the landscape and the values of the town. Iris now spent many parent meetings quarreling about empty causes: *Organic kale smoothies at the cafeteria?* Check. *Why can't my daughter bring her iPad to class?* Check. *Only one school trip per year? What about skiing trips?* Check. On and on they went, oblivious to the fact that some parents could not afford organic kale, let alone an iPad or an increase in school fees. Most of the time Iris, Maca, and a few other parents sat together at the back of the room, trying to ignore the obnoxious demands, then went home feeling wiped out and defeated.

The world is changing and I hate where it's going. I've been there, I've done it all before, and it's not a good place to be stuck. Some things do not bring you happiness.

"Mom, yo! Mom?" Leaning against the pickup truck in deep thought, Iris had not noticed her daughter standing right next to her. *God, she is beautiful!* In desperate need of comfort, Iris tried to wrap her arms around Lou, who drew away.

"Mom, are you okay?" Lou asked, a hint of concern in her voice, then added with unexpected roughness, "What's the matter with you? Everyone's looking at us."

Iris climbed into the Chevy and stared ahead. Her eyes stung behind her sunglasses.

Lou sauntered off to a group of teens who turned in Iris's direction and whispered, frowning and giggling. Finally, and with a dramatic eye roll, she made her way back toward the truck and climbed in noisily. "Dude! You know I hate hugs! How could you do that in front of everyone!"

Iris ignored the rant and turned to face Lou. She took off her sunglasses. "It's Gus, he's dead . . . he . . ." Her voice broke. Unable to finish her sentence, she started the truck and backed out of the school pickup lane. As they drove in silence she clenched the wheel until her knuckles turned white. *Say something, Lou, say something, please say something nice.* Lou opened the window and stuck her head out. Eyes closed, she let the wind whip her hair and smother her face.

"For God's sake, Lou! Stop that right now! Aren't you going to say anything?"

"Mom, say *anything*? Like, what? You want me to say what *I feel*? I don't feel anything; *you* tell me *how* I should feel!"

Iris slammed on the brakes and pulled to the side of the road. Shutting off the engine, she turned to face her daughter. "He was your father, Lou."

"My father? MY FATHER?" Lou shot a look at Iris from the corner of her eyes. "I never met *my* father, *my father* did not give a shit about me, he made me and that's about all. I hate Gus, my father, whoever that may be, whoever this guy was."

"Lou, calm down, stop shouting."

"Why? Why should I calm down?" Lou raised her voice even more. "It's all your fault."

"My fault?"

"Yes, yours. I hate you for not marrying my father, I hate you for making me fatherless. I hate you for all the times I've had to fill out an application with *Name of father? Occupation?* I hate you for all the times I had to lie and tell everyone that I had a father who loved me and was waiting for me, somewhere. You have *NO* idea, *NO* idea what it means to not have a father, so don't tell me *how* I should feel."

"Your father loved you, baby," said Iris. "It's complicated."

Lou stared ahead, refusing to look at Iris: "Yeah, right! Loved me! How could you say that? Did he call you? Did he ever ask you about *me?* Did he? Or are you just talking out of your ass?"

Part of Iris wanted to yell at her daughter for using foul language, but she let it go. Her daughter's hurt and anger must have been brewing for a long time. Stung, she blurted out, "Stop this, Lou. Stop this right now. Your father, Gustavo de Santos, left you his estate."

Iris started the ignition and drove up the hill.

CHAPTER 2

Iris and Lou made the rest of the trip in silence. Lou chewed on her nails and glared out of the window. The tension in the confined space became unbearable. Iris longed for the days when Lou was a sunny and open child who grew up trusting everyone. What had happened?

While living in New York with her parents after her escape from Paris, Iris had believed that those days would last forever and that she could have a semblance of a family life while she recomposed herself, bit by broken bit, one piece at a time. Lou had become her raison d'être, the only purpose of her existence.

Lou was five when they had moved from New York to Northern California after Iris's parents were killed in a car crash. Iris had relived those days hundreds of times in her head; it seemed that tragedy followed her everywhere.

Now, driving up the steep Mount Cerro Negro, she let go of dark thoughts to take in the beauty of the landscape. As she always did on the climb, she rolled down the windows to let in the overpowering scent of eucalyptus and pine.

Massive moss-covered redwood and oak trees lined the steep road up the mountain. Round white boulders and craggy rocks that had been named by Iris and Lou—the Old Man, Princess of Passaic, Leila, Master Gatekeeper—stood guard silently, like faithful valets at the beginning of the unpaved road leading to their home, followed by two tall carved wooden totems, which marked the entrance to the property.

As she took the final bend, Lou forced open the truck door, unable to stand one more minute in her mother's presence—"I'm outta here. Stop, Mom, stop *now*"—and she sprang out like a wild animal, dropping her school books on the driveway and sprinting toward the tree house at the end of the pond.

Iris took a deep breath and looked past her house for Chuck's pickup. *Where are you? Please, please be there; oh God, this is going to be a long one.*

Iris collected the pile of books lying on the dirt road, not wanting Chuck to drive over them, then emptied the mailbox. Bills, coupons, junk mail, a slutty and irritating *Sylvia's Secret* catalog were all dropped into the recycling bin. She kept the envelope from Blitz.

Opening the door to Lou's room, Iris could not help but smile when she saw the black-and-white Patti Smith poster hanging over her daughter's bed. Patti in a leather jacket, the zipper open and her chest bare. A present from Gus in their Paris days, which Lou had immediately claimed, even though she was but a child. Next to it, another poster: a close-up of workers'-rights activist Cesar Chavez. In a tangle of clothes on the bed was a beaten-up guitar she had found at a garage sale, Iris's old Nikon F3 camera for her photography class, and a pile of drawing pads filled with sketches. On the floor, Iris's chessboard.

Tough punk chick, this one. She dropped Lou's schoolbooks on the bed.

Dusk began to fall and Lou was still in her tree.

Standing underneath, Iris called up to her, "Wanna talk?"

Lou lashed out. "Talk to whom? To my tree?"

"Baby, please, we really need to have this conversation. I'm going to LA in two days."

Lou let out a long sigh and made her way down the trunk of the massive oak. Chuck had built the tree house for Lou when they moved onto the property a few years back, and it had become her security blanket. Lou had turned the small structure into an extension of her bedroom, covering the floor with Navajo rugs, frayed corduroy beanbags, a battery-powered lamp, and piles of books.

Rancho Dos Casas was but a few miles away from the town of La Arboleda, but they could have been on another planet. Iris had chosen it for its seclusion. At Dos Casas she had the space and peace of mind to work on her sculptures uninterrupted, her contact with people limited to Chuck and Maca, or to the brief and cordial encounters with other moms during her school runs. Most of the time no one left their cars, and the interaction took place through their windows:

"Call ya!"

"See ya!"

"Howzit going?"

"Are you okay?"

"Love ya!"

"You look *amazing*. Did you do something to your face?"

This suited her fine. Iris did not need other people to be happy, but she was beginning to think that her daughter was not as content with their lifestyle as she was.

"'K, Mom, what?" Lou said, glaring at her.

Sitting across from her at the kitchen table, Iris pulled out the lawyer's letter from the FedEx envelope and fixed her eyes on Lou's.

"Lou, your father left you his photographic estate. That means everything: all his editions, negatives, prints. Until you are twenty-five, I will be the executor of the Gus de Santos trust. I know this sounds abstract to you, but maybe one day you will feel connected and proud to be his daughter."

"Connected? Why did you keep me away from him? How could you do this to me, Mom? Do you realize what you've done? Do you? Why didn't he want to meet me? Or did he? And now he's dead?" Lou's voice sounded sad and tired.

"Your father had been sick for a long time, but nobody knew. I didn't know myself, Lou. I guess he didn't want to cause me pain. We broke up before you were born and I moved from Paris to New York to live with Grandma and Grandpa; I've told you all this already. Gus moved around the world. Looking for something? Running away from something? I have no idea what."

Iris gazed out the window. Lou grabbed a pencil and chewed on the tip.

"These were the days before the internet. We had no social media, and people could just disappear and reappear at will. I'd heard through friends that he was living in LA, then New York. After that he went off the radar and reappeared in Berlin. Artists do that, they're afraid of being fastened. They're free spirits. Somewhat tortured spirits, but free. I sort of followed his whereabouts through his work, through his editorial publications . . ."

"Did *you* try to contact him?" Lou said.

"No. There were issues—"

"Like me? I was your *issue?*" Lou asked, hiding her head under her hoodie while she doodled a geometrical pattern on the white paper covering the kitchen table.

There was a long silence except for the scratching of Lou's pencil.

Then Lou continued talking without lifting her gaze from the paper: "Why does your stuff, *your* problems with Gus, have to affect my entire life? I will never meet my father now."

Lou stopped scribbling and wiped her downturned face with her sleeve. "It's wrong, maybe, but I feel nothing toward him."

"I'm sorry, Lou. I'm so sorry, baby."

"Why are you going to LA, and can I stay at home while you're gone? I don't want to be schlepped off to Maca's, I starve there. I hate her vegan stuff and her fermented cabbage and her composting worms; they stink, it's all so gross!"

"I have to meet Gus's lawyers for a lot of paperwork. A container arrived with his belongings. It could take two or three days. You can't stay here alone."

"Makes no difference. Even when you're here, you're not *here* here. Also, Chuck is right nearby. I can get the bus to school and make my own meals. Nothing new, if you think about it, and Taco can look after me too," said Lou, referring to Chuck's beloved sheepdog.

Iris's voice was firm. "You cannot and will not stay in this house alone. Period."

Lou lifted her head. Never one to give up easily, she insisted, "When am I getting my driver's license? And why do we live here anyway? Can't you live in town like all my friends' parents and do your sculptures there? Why do you have to drag me out here into the sticks? I'm sixteen, Mom. I don't have a real life here."

Catching sight of the letter from Blitz, Lou started opening it. Snatching it back, Iris said, "A check. Royalties. And none of your business."

"Mom, when are you going back to modeling?"

"That's never going to happen," said Iris as she got up to make herself a coffee.

"Why? Blitz is constantly asking you to come back. I hear the messages they leave on the house phone, looking for you. Someone from a Hollywood casting agency left a voicemail recently, wanting you to audition for something. I gave you that message too. You don't even get back to them, and they've called twice. It's fucked up!"

Iris turned toward Lou. "For God's sake! Stop swearing!"

Lou crawled back into her hoodie.

Iris busied herself with the coffee. "Those days are behind me, Lou. I want to go back to art school. I want to get better at sculpting and one day make a living out of it so I don't eat into my savings."

"But why, Mom?"

rare weekend at home with her mother when Ludo was away, taking care of his import-export business. Sharing Delfine's bed, Iris would bury her face in the pillows and inhale her mother's heady Joy de Patou, happy just to stare at her while she slept, looking at her resting face devoid of all tension, relishing that moment when her mother's guard would be down, mistaking this for serenity and affection.

Some afternoons Iris would come home and Dionne Warwick would be playing on the stereo, a sure sign that her mother was in a good mood. Floating around the living room in her favorite midnight-blue-and-gold caftan, Delfine would hold her daughter's hands and sing her favorite song, "I'll Never Fall in Love Again."

Alas, Delfine's good moods never lasted very long.

When Iris was a child, Delfine had repeated over and over to her, *"Why did I ever get married? Never ever get married, Iris, you hear me?"* As flamboyant and exotic as Delfine was, Iris's father was a quiet and down-to-earth businessman from Passaic, New Jersey, resigned to live in a foreign city in order to enable his wife's successful career. With the sacrifice came also a kind of compromised understanding between husband and wife, which allowed them to carry on with their lives in separate ways. Iris was the product of this strange couple that had very little in common but appeared to live the most wonderful of existences. Even Iris had been fooled.

Iris never realized how emotionless Delfine's behavior toward Ludo was until she started staying over at her friends' homes and saw their parents interacting with respect and warmth.

Ludo's daily escape had been the small garden he tended at the back of the *hôtel particulier* where they lived. Here he would meet Iris after school, and together they would weed, prune, and fuss over his spectacular roses, dahlias, and kitchen herbs.

"*Shaineh madela*, are you going to Mathilde's birthday party on Sunday?"

"No, Papa. Mummy's taking me on Mr. Edmund's shoot."

Ludo turned toward Iris, his watering can dripping all over his shoes. "But don't you want to see your best friend?"

"Yes, but Mummy says she's 'teaching me the business.'"

Ludo shook his head and muttered, "Delfine and her damned magazine. It'll be the death of us."

"What, Papa?"

Ludo turned away. "Nothing, honey."

He bent over the herb bed, inspecting it closely. "Look at the aphids on your chives, sweetie pie! We'll buy some ladybugs to get rid of them . . ."

"Papa?"

"Yes, darling?"

"Mummy also says that I'm her 'calming goat.'"

"Her what?"

"If a horse is nervous, you give him a calming goat. He lives with the horse in the same stall. Mummy had calming goats and nervous horses on the estate in Lectoure. I am Mummy's own calming goat."

Ludo burst out laughing and hugged his daughter.

Outside this little piece of urban nature, Iris grew up surrounded by ephemeral beauty and brain-numbing frivolity, and she observed its devastating consequences at a prudent distance, far removed.

Ma ché carina questa bambina! What a cute little girl!

Ma guardala! Sembra una bambola! But look at her! She looks like a doll!

Perched like a toy on her mother's knees in the front row of the Paris shows, Iris had gotten her full dose of fashion culture and lots of attention. Photographers would go crazy when Delfine brought her gorgeous baby daughter to a *défilé*, and Iris found her true calling: *When I am a grown-up, I want to be a designer or a model.*

With no sense of decorum and impervious to her presence, designers would gossip with her mother during their endless boozy sessions in her elegant home on rue de Varenne or at the Hemingway Bar in the Hotel Ritz, Delfine's favorite HQ.

"*Oh non, non, mon Dieu!* Not la Comtesse de la Casse. I abhor it when she comes to fittings . . . *she does not wear underwear!* Maybe this is better because when she does, it is saggy and ugly. How can you wear ugly underwear to an haute couture fitting in my *maison?*"

"And *cette conne*, that cunt, of Marie Pierre *du Modes!* She is old, old—you understand? She has no fucking idea how to run her team, and her magazine looks like *merde.*"

"I heard she's having an affair with her husband's boyfriend!"

"Well, she better have fun while it lasts, *chérie*, because, and do not quote me, she is going to get fired soon and no one will hire her anymore because her husband lost the Chanel account. Also she takes a lot of pills, so she is becoming a bit *crayzee.*"

On and on they went, oblivious to the fact that their conversation was totally inappropriate for a child, even giving Iris nightmares on many an occasion.

Delfine's young assistant, Joan Hutley, was brought in *in extremis* to babysit on nights and weekends when there were urgent changes of plans, as was often the case.

Unlike everyone else at the *Revue* office, Joan was not the rich daughter of a titled Parisian family working for a meager salary while living at home. Joan did not wear pearls, black crewneck cashmere sweaters from Aux Laines Ecossaises, starched white shirts from Old England, and shiny Repetto ballerina flats like the other young *Revue* slaves did. Joan was the daughter of a literature teacher at the American University of Paris and an overweight housewife with bad teeth and thick varicosed legs. Iris was mortified for Joan the day she brought her parents to a fashion show and introduced them to Delfine. Iris saw Delfine tense up as she maneuvered them away from her circle of dashing front-row friends. A PR assistant with a clipboard hurried over and removed them to the standing row in the back. Joan never spoke of the gauche *incident*, and Delfine never extended an invitation to Joan's parents again.

In the twelve months that followed the episode, Joan underwent an expensive and painful transformation: she groomed and waxed her brows, got braces and veneers on her teeth, colored her mousy hair a dark shade of auburn, and did electrolysis on her forehead, arms, and legs. She toned her body with hours of excruciating planks, replaced her food intake with coffee, low-fat yogurts, and cigarettes, and took diction lessons with a speech coach until all traces of her plebeian elocutions were forever wiped out. On the days she had to babysit, Joan would show a delighted Iris the needle scars on her bikini line and armpits.

Iris winced as Joan said, "Yes, it hurts like hell and then you have a thousand blooming scabs that itch and take forever to fall off . . . but now I could be stranded on a deserted island and will never grow shaggy pubic hair! Now I will always be bikini ready!"

Iris nodded, pretending to know what shaggy pubic hair was but not having a clue.

Iris admired Joan working two jobs in order to pay for her transformation, toiling late into the nights as she translated English to French for a school textbook company.

As the years went by, Joan ditched her proletarian accent and began to talk like Delfine, articulating with the same languid, long-drawn enunciations. Joan had dieted herself into a sample size, which did not flatter her body type but conformed to the *Revue* prototype. After a couple of years spent looking for a style, she began to dress like Ada Shaffer, *Revue*'s fashion director, in tight, sexy, form-fitting copies from high-street shops instead of the high-end brands from Avenue Montaigne that she couldn't afford. What Joan lacked in dash, she made up for in knack. Fashion loves a Cinderella story, and the industry slowly welcomed her as she honed her craft in Delfine's shadow.

"International Editor at Large." Iris was eleven years old when Delfine, after twenty-two years of absolute reign in Paris, was demoted and banished to a small job with a big title in the New York office. Iris was shocked. Not because of what it meant for Delfine—she was too young to grasp the consequences of the humiliation and how it would slowly destroy her mother—but because she would be separated from Joan and the office employees: her real family, besides Ludo.

By leaving behind a legacy, Delfine had fought for immortality. The day she received a copy of *Revue* with a slick Hollywood star on the cover, she knew that her legacy had been crushed. Ada had taken over as editor in chief, and Delfine's opinions didn't count anymore.

Now, in California, Iris dreamed of giving Lou a solid family structure where she would feel secure and loved, but she didn't know how to do it.

As she walked toward the corral, Taco nuzzled her hand with his wet nose and licked it, nibbling on her fingers.

Leaning on the fence, she called gently and clicked her tongue like Chuck's Mexican farmhands, Edgar and Conrado, had taught her. Chuck's four rescue mustangs came out from under the shed, ears twitching, recognizing the noise.

"Hey, Flako, how are you, big boy? Bandida . . . shhhhhhh, good girl . . . gently, gently. Speedo . . . beautiful Speedo, I miss you guys . . . when are we going for a ride? And how is Fang? Wanna scratch?" Iris loved these wild animals, whose spirits remained unbroken in spite of having been adopted and tamed a few years back. Chuck didn't choose them individually, they were just Lot 17 on their way to the slaughterhouse. Conrado and Edgar said that Señor Chuck had special powers with animals, that he was a horse whisperer. The mustangs were devoted to him.

Iris liked to come to the corral when Chuck was working on them, patient and kind but firm. Chuck was lucky in that they were quite docile most of the time. He had made them rideable and trusting.

Chuck taught Iris and Lou how to ride as soon as they came to live at Dos Casas. They were naturals, especially Lou, who liked to ride bareback with just a sheepskin and a leather string, hanging on like a monkey. Some of their happiest moments were spent on long rides with Chuck, Taco, and Conrado up Mount Cerro Negro, the noble animals in harmony with the humans.

Dos Casas had a distinctive smell of hay, horses, coyotes, and jasmine. Iris had never smelled a coyote, but Chuck had made her a furry coyote hat that smelled earthy and peculiar. Jack, the drifter, had shot it the day he found it in the chicken coop with four dead hens at his feet.

Slapping Fang on the nose as he tried to bite her, Iris heard Chuck's pickup turning into the driveway. After waving to him, she climbed over the fence and stood in the huddle of horses, hugging Fang's neck and burying her nose in his hide, inhaling the odor. Edgar had taught her to do that, and to look for the velvety spots on their muzzles and behind their ears. *"Horses smell sweet,"* he always said. She agreed.

"Bones! What's up, gorgeous?" Chuck leaned on the fence.

"Urgh, horrible day, Marlboro Man," Iris said, as she untangled herself from the dusty animals and walked toward him.

She was happy to see her neighbor and landlord. His wide and kindly smile, twinkly blue eyes, tanned handsome face, and tall frame were always a welcome sight after spending days on end talking to no one except her daughter, Lou.

As if reading her face and the crooked smile she pulled for him, Chuck gave Iris a bear hug. "Are you okay?" he asked.

Iris smelled vetiver and lavender as well as leather soap, horses, and wood smoke on his clothes. She closed her eyes, let herself drift for a moment.

She wants me to be more engaged with the world, move to a city, take up a glamorous job, model again . . . she wants to feel proud of me. She's too young to figure out that a normal life can be a happy life, you know? To her friends, success is measured by how much money you have made and not by what you have accomplished. She's being influenced and brainwashed into thinking that life is about fame and power. So, life is sex, celebrity, having fun, and doing dangerous things. It sounds like such a cliché because it *is* a cliché. Deep down she really is a kid, a naive country kid, regardless of who she pretends to be with her friends. I'm scared of exposing her to a world that she's not ready for. This stuff coming up, the LA stuff, is hard to fathom."

"She's a teenage girl, Iris. What do you expect? I'm so happy I have boys. Boys are black-and-white. I could not take the mood swings of hormonal teen girls, the unpredictable behavior, the weird mental games, the passive-aggressiveness . . ."

Iris laughed.

"One minute they want to plunge a fork into your jugular and the next they are showering you with kisses and drawing hearts all over the fridge. The daily turbulence . . . exhausting."

"That's my Lou. But it's not *just* that, Maca. It's also that I think she doesn't trust me."

"Lou is very smart. Talk to her about you and your ex. What she lacks in maturity, she makes up for in intuition."

"Maca, I was thinking . . . my parents didn't have an adolescence. They were children and then they were encouraged to marry and to quickly have a child, and have jobs and responsibilities. That was what their generation did. I feel that our kids, Lou's lot, are eternal adolescents, carefree and looked after until they're ready to go off on their own, which in many cases is never. I was working at seventeen and living alone in Milan and Paris, unchaperoned. It was the end of my innocence, and I want to protect Lou from that for as long as I can. How do I explain to her that her father fucked with my mind, and also that he was a drug addict who most likely kept her away because he didn't want her to see him in that condition?"

"Shit. That's depressing. I'm sorry, Iris, I had no idea."

Maca cut herself another slab of homemade bread and slathered it with honey.

Iris threw her napkin at her. "Macarena Vallow Aguado, focus, *please*! I need advice."

"But I *am* focused. Iris, are you having a middle-age crisis at thirty-seven? Where does all this confusion and doubt come from?" Maca asked.

"What do you mean? I'm happy sculpting and living at Dos Casas. I know what I want, I want this normal life. I don't want to change anything."

"Hah! Your *normal* life? Define *normal*, please. You're not fucking normal; you were a fucking top model and still look like one! Your childhood was not normal, nor was the modeling . . . so now you're done with fabulousness and you want Lou *not* to want some of that? It sounds like *you* are what you're scared of."

"Rubbish! Explain."

"Well, in my humble opinion you're overthinking everything. Get in your truck, drive to LA with Lou, be strong and take your meetings, and then *que será será*. You think that Lou is a child, but she understands things, she's open, she questions everything; she needs to be there with you. You're talking about her father here, your past and *her* future. You're getting priorities muddled up with excuses. Maybe you'll find your calling. You always loved photography, as has Lou—she's so talented. Who knows? Just don't close those doors before you even open them. You can do anything you want in life, why these doubts?"

"There are things I *do not* want to tell Lou."

"Like about that vacant look in your eyes that you have sometimes? Until you do, until you're totally transparent with her, nothing will change. She's not stupid. She has a well-developed bullshit radar, she's watchful . . . you guys are going to spend the rest of your lives fighting like cats and dogs."

"I know," Iris said.

"Be fearless, be honest with Lou, she'll respect that. Oh, and don't throw away your coffee beans, please, they're for my composting worms."

CHAPTER 5

The next evening, Chuck invited them to a barbecue, and Lou brought her best friend, Amy Sachs, for a sleepover.

Also invited was Jack the coyote shooter, a drifter who lived in the old toolshed by the barn. Chuck had taken pity on him, the only homeless man in La Arboleda, a thirty-five-year-old Iraq veteran and one of those hapless souls that had been exploited and then forgotten by the system.

Jack was a good handyman and earned his keep with dignity, living with next to nothing because he claimed he had all he needed. Always deep in a book in his spare time, he never talked about his family or past, even on the monthly drive to La Arboleda public library with Iris and Lou. He once told Chuck that he was from San Diego, but that was about all.

Jack was also good with a gun. When wild boars destroyed Chuck's vegetable garden, Jack hunted them down and shot an old male. The carcass sat in the freezer, and no one, apart from Jack, could bring themselves to eat it, partly because it was so stringy and tough but also because they were sad for the stupid boar. Because of Jack's love of hunting, Iris learned how to make hare pappardelle and mustardy braised rabbit with carrots.

Chuck and Jack played chess most evenings on the porch, and it comforted Iris to know that she and Lou were not alone when Chuck was away on one of his book tours.

The dinner table was set outside under an immense oak tree covered in pendent Spanish moss, which cut surreal shadows in the moonlight. Lou and Amy were deep in conversation with Jack about living without a television set or internet, something unfathomable and strange to the two girls.

"Thank you for having this dinner, Chuck. I feel good knowing that this"—Iris made a sweeping gesture with her arm—"awaits us on our return, and by *this* I also mean you. You make us feel welcome."

"Count on it; it's no big deal, Bones. We'll miss you, won't we, Taco?"

Iris smiled and turned to look at him, a strange feeling in her heart.

"I'll be glad when the trip is over."

"Take your time. It's a lot for Lou to assimilate. She's lived without a dad all these years, and now she has to confront his life and death in a lawyer's office, of all places."

Iris's throat tightened and tears pricked her eyes. She turned away from Chuck's gaze and faced the floor.

The words *life* and *death*, so definite.

Gus is dead. My Gus, my love, my life, my companion, my friend, my teacher, my bad boy, my angel of darkness, my man, my poet. I will never see you again, ever. This is it. This is for real? You are gone? I still feel your lips on my face, your caresses on my skin, your tongue in my mouth, your sex against my body, your hand on my breast. I sit on your hips and look down at your solemn face as I make you come. My heart explodes. You close your eyes, and your long black hair makes graphic shapes on the pillow. I take a strand out of your mouth. You bite my hand and hold my wrist, hurting me. You look so happy. Then you look sad. "Mi niña, mi niña Iris," you say. "What are we going to do?" you ask.

I don't know. In my heart, you died years ago.

Lou and Amy sauntered over. "Mom, can I show Amy your model pictures, please, please, pleeeeeease?"

Iris wiped her tears, and as she got up to take the girls to her office, she heard Chuck's voice calling out, "Bring them out here, Bones. Jack and I want to see them too."

CHAPTER 6

"Road trip, *yee-haw!*" Lou bounced up and down in the truck, clapping and hooting.

Is this demented child mine? What is her problem? Iris smiled at her daughter. *There will be a before and an after LA, that's for sure.*

It had been a while since they'd gone on one of their road trips, something that they used to enjoy doing often.

At the turn of every sharp curve, they would shout out their joy at being alive, blown away by the sight of yet another hidden valley, another damp, mossy forest of towering redwood trees, another cliff, the Russian River, a cove, and always, at the end, the Pacific Ocean.

Nothing prepared you for the immense nature, the massive open spaces, and the sense that you were perched on the westernmost part of the world and the last sunset of the universe.

Watch for whales, it's that time of year. And otters, seals, pelicans, dolphins, sea lions . . . how blessed we are.

Lou was the perfect traveling companion. When the freeway got boring, she would take a book out of her backpack and read quietly. Lou had never been a needy, jumpy kid connected to the world through a Dre headset.

They hit the road early and drove through the Sonoma valley toward San Francisco.

The trees were full of buds, some beginning to bloom, and the fields emerald green. Brown, woody grapevines lay exposed among a sea of pink milkweed and yellow wild mustard flowers that the monarch butterflies feasted on. Beyond the hills covered in orange poppies and through the massive oaks one could see the farms and estates that lined the valley.

Fruit trees of every type displayed thick clusters of blossoms: pink, white, red, purple.

As the sun came out, Lou had sat silent, taking in the beauty of the landscape. Stunned by the rain of petals blowing in the wind from the thousands of blooming trees, she whipped out her camera and took pictures through the open window.

Iris welcomed the time they would have together before their LA meetings.

After driving over the Golden Gate Bridge and as soon as they hit 101 South, Lou connected her iPod. Warren G's "Regulate" came on, and they sang along at the top of their lungs.

After scrolling through her playlists, Lou turned off the iPod and twisted her body around to face Iris. "Mom, why did you really split up with Gus?"

Iris paused before replying.

"He lied to me. We had a terrible misunderstanding, things broke beyond repair, and then it was too late."

"Why too late?"

"Gus was acting crazy. He became a danger to himself. He hurt me very much, baby. He broke my heart. I left Paris and went to live with Grandma and Grandpa in New York. Then you were born," Iris said and glanced at Lou.

"Did *he* know when I was born?" Lou looked at Iris from the corner of her eye.

Iris did not reply.

"Mom?"

"Probably not for a few years at least. I stopped all contact with him and with his Paris posse. It did my head in, and I needed to keep away from all that while I raised you. Also Grandma was not herself and was going through bad times. Grandpa was all I had, but he was suffering too. I did not want to bring the specter of Gus into their home, you understand?"

"Mom, was Grandma sick? I would have loved to know her properly, she was so royal looking. I looked at your press clippings of her, and the obituaries . . ."

"Grandma lost it when she was relegated to New York. Can you imagine what it was like for a French lady of that standing going from a huge office full of orchids, scented candles, and assistants in Paris to a tiny cubicle without a window in an ugly building in Manhattan?"

Iris looked at the road ahead of her. Lou was silent.

"Was she fired?"

"No, just made irrelevant in a sneaky corporate way because it was cheaper to keep her. She lost all the props that she was used to, the things that gave her status: the town car, her driver, the parties . . . goodie bags, sample clothes, restaurant expenses—she became trivial, she was powerless, she was made unimportant. It was heartbreaking for Grandpa and me to watch. Grandpa was loyal to Mum, he treated her with a lot of respect."

Lou shot her a look. Iris had a firm set to her mouth.

"That's so sad for Grandma. Why did she continue to go to work? Why didn't she stay at home with Grandpa and you and me?"

"I don't know. Grandpa was working long hours, running his family's company. They were successful worldwide liquor importers. He was happy to be back in his beloved city where he had many friends, and happy to be near his big, noisy Jewish family. I was glad for him because I saw him in his element. He thrived. But Grandma wanted nothing of his life, she wanted hers back. Grandma could not let go of the fashion world, it was all she had—that's what she believed. Papa and I were not enough for her. Her fashion-editor job was what had defined her. At least that is what she thought. By then they had drifted apart too much."

"Why didn't they have a life together if they were married to each other? Why did they have separate lives?" Lou asked.

"I guess they were not made for each other. They were not really in love when they married, but *their* parents arranged it. That is how it's done in some families. Grandpa's family's company in New York imported Grandma's family's Calvados. Grandma's titled family was property rich but cash poor. Grandpa was wealthy, successful, and charming, so her family paired them off. As soon as they were married, Grandma changed his name from Louis to Ludo; she said Louis was too 'Passaic, bounderish.' Grandpa used to joke about it, but I'm sure it hurt him."

"That's horrible, to change Grandpa's name like that . . ."

Iris nodded, her eyes fixed on the road. "I think it was more than the name."

"Mom, did they meet my father?"

"No."

"Why?"

"It just didn't happen, baby."

"The whole thing sucks, and my father sucks big-time too. I hate him more each day."

Lou ended the conversation abruptly and clammed up like she often did, full of anger and frustration at the fucked-up adult world. She picked up her book and turned to look out of the window. As she drove in silence, Iris forced herself not to shoot a stinging remark to her daughter. *I wish it was that simple, I wish it was black-and-white, but there's a lot of gray. I come in peace today. Let's make this part of the trip special for us.*

Iris remembered her own father from her teenage days in New York. Ludo had been a gentleman of habits, and on Saturdays he liked to put his Mets cap on and take his daughter to Katz's Delicatessen on Houston. Over matzo-ball soup, blintzes, chopped liver with onion, and a towering pastrami sandwich, they would talk about Iris's new school. Inevitably the conversation would always become about Delfine.

"Papa, are we ever going back to Paris?"

"Do you miss it, sunshine?"

Iris shrugged. She took a bite of her sandwich, and slices of pastrami fell on her plate. She put the sandwich down.

"Mummy cries a lot, you know?"

Ludo wiped his mouth with a paper napkin. "She does? I never see her cry."

"Yes, Papa. When she comes back from work, she sits at her vanity table and 'takes off her face,' her makeup. I can see the tears on her cheeks."

"Does she talk to you?"

"No."

"Tell me the truth, Iris."

"Well, yes, sometimes she says mean things about you."

"Sometimes? Or all the time?"

Iris had looked into her father's sad eyes.

"All the time."

As she drove in silence, Iris remembered many things about Delfine's fall from grace, in particular the way that she became fixated with beauty, only wanting to be in aesthetically pleasing environments, with aesthetically pleasing people.

Does beauty have healing powers?

Instead, Iris yearned for the company of her adoring aunts, Ludo's sisters, neither elegant nor chic enough to adorn Delfine's living room or grace her dinner table. Iris had missed Paris and her school with all her heart, but her mother refused to be drawn into that conversation.

"Oh, Iris, toughen up, you'll get used to it. We all get used to everything in the end," was all she said.

When Iris had come back from Paris after three years of modeling abroad, she was shocked at how Delfine had let herself go. Not only had she put on a lot of weight and did not bother to dye her gray roots anymore, but their home was shabby and run-down.

The Christmas tree did not come out that December, nor did the fragrant vats of candied fruits, nuts, and orange peel that Delfine used to make her elaborate Christmas fruitcakes.

Gone were the fresh bouquets of peonies and camellias, the Floris candles, the Elnett hairdos, and the ruby-red nails and lips.

Delfine's eagle eyes that had never missed the tiniest details, like when the scarlet china teacup was not paired with the Georgian silver teaspoon, were now dull and unfocused, as she spent most evenings in a loose housedress and slippers, staring at the television while poor Ludo dreamed of being elsewhere.

When Iris had fled Paris and had gone back to live with her parents, she was an ailing, broken creature in need of help. Delfine never asked her any questions and would have been incapable of giving her the emotional support she needed, so Aunt Nicole and Aunt Julie had taken over, making sure that Iris felt welcome in New York.

Trying to let go of those painful memories and the gloomy vibe in the pickup, Iris turned on the radio and hummed to Janis Joplin's heart-wrenching "Summertime." *Jeez, just what I need right now.*

"They must be so hot," said Lou, gazing out of the window at the rows of produce pickers bent under the broiling sun in the fields of Salinas. "It's like in the movie *Song for Cesar*, but this is not a movie." The tone of her voice became pensive. "I'm sorry, Mom, for being a brat. I'm so lucky to be born me and not to be there picking cauliflower all day. I'm sorry."

Iris nodded. Lou went back to her book.

When they reached the winding bends at Paso Robles, Lou closed her book and looked at Iris. "Mom? Tell me again how you started modeling. That story is so dope."

"Again?"

"Yeah, it's been ages since I heard it. I've forgotten chunks of it."

Iris smiled. Like small children that can watch the same movie over and over again, Lou loved listening to Iris tell her the story for the one hundredth time.

"I was almost seventeen. Father had taken me to Barneys to choose a dress for Cousin Roberta's wedding, and a scout from Blitz came up to me and gave me her card. I called them, and after classes I went to the agency with my closest buddy, Angelica. A few months later I graduated from high school and was on a flight to Milan. I never went to college. That's not cool."

"Were Grandma and Grandpa stoked?"

Iris was silent. *Stoked? Batshit is more the word.*

Delfine had sat at her vanity table, staring at her reflection in the mirror. She had dabbed makeup remover on her ruby lips with a cotton disk, wiping the color off.

Iris looked at her mother as she went through her evening routine.

"Mummy, can I go to Milan? Blitz said they would put me in a flat with six other girls. Nothing's going to happen to me."

Delfine turned to look at Iris, her mouth now devoid of color. "I can't deal with this. Ask your father."

Iris went to the living room and plopped herself on the sofa next to Ludo. The Mets were playing and Delfine would keep to her room.

"Papa, can I go to Milan and Paris with Blitz?"

"Iris, we have this conversation every single day. You're driving me bananas. I already told you no. What did Delfine say?"

"She said to talk to you. I really want to go, Papa. After Milan I can go to Paris, Joan's in Paris. I love her, she always took good care of me."

Ludo turned toward his daughter and, lowering the volume on the TV set, he sighed. "Only, and really only, if you promise to me that you will go to college after you get bored of this modeling thing."

Bored? I'll never get bored. "Yes, of course, Papa. I promise."

"Won't you miss us? You'll be homesick, you'll see, cutie-pie."

"I'll miss *you*, Papa, heaps and heaps and heaps."

Ludo had put his arm around his daughter and had pulled her toward him. "My oh my, you're a big girl now, aren't you?"

Iris looked at the changing landscape as the miles flew by. Lou watched her closely. "Were you sad? Were you, like, heartsick all the time?"

"Yes, it was horrible. In the beginning I cried nonstop. I missed Grandpa and Aunt Julie and Aunt Nicole. They called me every week, thank goodness for that. I thought I was tough and mature, but I was just a lost kid in the middle of a bunch of other lost kids, trying to act like a grown-up and make a living instead of being sheltered and guided by caring adults, which is what I really needed at that age."

Lou looked pensive and chewed on a strand of hair. Her forehead was furrowed. "How was your flat? Did you have a nice room?"

"The models' flat in Milan again? The pits. Eleven girls in two large bedrooms with bunk beds; two small, gross bathrooms; and a disgusting kitchen where no one washed their dishes. Everyone smoked in bed, and there were piles of dirty laundry everywhere. It was just awful. But the *pensione* was even worse."

"No, Mom, I mean Joan's place in Paris."

Iris laughed. "*Again?* Joan had known me since I was a baby. She worked for Grandma. When Grandma was exiled from Paris, Joan was promoted to fashion director at *Revue*."

"Joan must have been so sad to see you and Grandma go."

"I'm sure she was, but she benefited from Grandma's departure."

"What do you mean?"

"She was her assistant for eleven years, but when Grandma left, she became fashion director. Anyway, that's how this world goes. Joan then moved into a big, funky apartment in le Marais, an old gnarly area on the Right Bank. It was bohemian and playful and also sexy and feminine, not at all like where I had lived across the river, which was grand and formal. It felt good to live at Joan's; do you get what I mean?"

Lou nodded, chewing on her hair.

"Was Joan like your mom then?"

"She was like my older sister. I'll always be grateful to her. She looked after me like a sister would. Her flat was the place I went back to every day and felt safe. My night-light. Unlike my mother. Let's say that Delphine was kind of aloof and did not check in with me very often.

"I had a beautiful room in a mezzanine that overlooked the courtyard and a big magnolia tree. I especially liked it when the *concierge*, Madame Perrot, shouted. She shouted all day; she shouted at people, parked cars, dogs, cats, Monsieur Perrot, the garbage bins, the postman, our bikes. Everything and everyone got yelled at.

"*'Non mais ça va pas la tête?'* 'But are you stupid? What is wrong with you?' *'C'est à qui le biclou?'* 'Whose bike is this?' *'Les poubelles, vous pouvez faire attention a mettre vos ordures DANS les poubelles?'* 'Put your garbage INSIDE the bins? Duh!' Her words are still engraved in my brain. I loved listening to her venting in the courtyard. It was like my alarm clock: eight a.m. and BINGO!, off she went."

Lou piped in: "*Dans les* bloody *poubelles!*"

Iris laughed. "Every morning I crept out, hiding to avoid her disapproving looks through the curtains of the *concierge loge*. She made me feel guilty all the time. She once told me I was dressed like a *clocharde* because I was rocking a Comme des Garçons sweater with holes in it.

'Mademoiselle Iris?'

'Oui, Madame Perrot?'

'Why is your sweater full of holes?'

'Because I like them. I like the holes.'

'If Madame Joan is not capable of darning them, then I will do it. Ce n'est pas possible that you walk around looking like a homeless person.'"

Lou chortled.

"How could I explain to her that the holes were intentional and that the sweater cost me half a year's lunch budget?" Iris smiled thinking about it. She glanced at Lou. "And that's it, baby."

Lou prodded her thigh. "Oh, come on, gimme a break. Tell me more!"

"Don't nudge me when I'm driving!"

Fearing a fight of epic dimensions, Iris sighed and continued. "I explained what go-sees were, right?"

"Yeah, Mom, go-see him, go-see them, go-see that agency ... I know what a go-see is."

"So I would go to my agency to get my go-sees for the day, and the list of castings, if there were any. Some days I did four or five go-sees, other days it was insane and I did ten, thirteen. One go-see every half hour with thirty minutes to get there, no matter what.

"Often at the go-sees they would make you wait two or three hours, sitting on the stairway, then they looked at you for five minutes and would say rude things about you to your face like *'Oh no, too fat. I'll tell your agency. You'll never fit in the clothes. Why did your agency send you? I mean, what size are you? Two? Oh, non non non, this season we did size one, sorry, chérie. You're pretty. Next!'*"

"That is *sooooo* gross," Lou said, whipping her hair out of her face.

"Yes, disgraceful to treat young, fragile girls like that. I could see chunks of their souls falling off. You already felt so insecure as it was, imagine how much worse they made you feel. We were like, *'Do they want me to shave off some hip bone?'* I sort of had a thick skin, I could take it better than most of the others, maybe because I was used to some of my mother's friends saying awful things about people. Very personal stuff. Mean gossip.

"I never really paid attention to all that. After a while it went over my head. In my mind, they were sad people with no lives outside the industry, like they felt they were in some exclusive club or something."

"So they thought that they were special?" Lou said.

"Yes, that's it. Special, untouchable, privileged, above the law, above morality. Fashion attracts a lot of people without principles or consciences, people who feed off those who are easily blinded by the shiny bits.

"Some girls were less strong, so they were really affected by the comments. They were far from home, they had no one to guide them, to watch over them. Some bookers are lazy, negligent, they don't talk to the girls, ask them how they're doing. Instead, they give them pills to lose weight and they don't check on them. The girls start going out every night, they get into trouble, they do things with bad people that they trust . . ." Iris's voice trailed off.

Lou looked at her mother. "Did all the girls speak French?"

"Are you kidding? Very few girls arrived speaking French, but they had no choice! They had to learn it and learn it fast. First thing you must figure out is how to get around the city by *métro* and bus, and how to ask for directions. Also, if you spoke a bit of French at castings, they liked you more."

Lou nodded.

Iris continued. "I would put on a pair of sneakers and run from one end of the city to the other for ten or twelve hours a day, eat a ham-and-cheese baguette in the *métro*, and when I arrived at a go-see I would slip into a pair of high heels and catwalk in, the picture of confidence, even though I was trembling inside."

"Say *sandwich*, please, Mom?"

"*Une baguette gruyère jambon beurre, s'il vous plait.*"

At this, Lou howled with laughter and, imitating her mother's accent, said, "*Merci, mademoiselle, tout de suite.*"

Lou continued. "Did you have model friends?"

"Yes, a few. I ended up making friends with the ones I met at the castings over and over again, or with the girls in my agency. Our bookers sent us all together to the same places. Inevitably we bonded, for survival purposes. We shared a cab or a flat, then had someone's shoulder to cry on when it got tough. Sometimes we were scared of going on certain go-sees alone . . . photographers that had bad reputations, our bookers did not warn us, but we knew . . . so we went in pairs when we could."

"Scary."

"Yes, very scary."

"Who was your best friend? Like best *best* friend?"

"My friend was a model called Saskia. She was Dutch. She was bonkers in a good way, a brawler. She swore a lot, she was very funny and afraid of nothing. She was tall and strong, she protected me. Once she got into a fistfight with a guy at a party. She whacked him in the face and split his lip. There was blood everywhere. I loved her."

Lou howled with laughter.

Iris gave her a side-glance. "Sound familiar?"

"Were there any American models?"

"There were a few Americans at Blitz. It was the end of fashion's love affair with grunge and Nirvana's music. At school in New York there were a few pale, skinny punk girls full of angst, and that look, the Goth look, seeped into fashion. In Paris, designers and photographers were looking for chameleons—girls who could look edgy, urban, and tough, but five minutes later look glamorous and chic. I got lucky because I had the look they wanted."

"What was the look, Mom?"

"More than a look, it was a mood. There were many things happening, they were exciting times for fashion. Off the top of my head and quoting the titles of some of Joan's shoots: 'Cool Britannia,' 'Japanese Designers,' 'The Minimalists,' 'Bohemian

Avant-Garde' . . . I fit into all those. Most American girls looked too healthy and too happy.

"The English were the hot new girls too. They had this emo thing going on, with buzzed heads, piercings, and tats everywhere. Designers liked to put them in haute couture. It was pretty great, actually."

"Like Kate Moss? I *love* Kate Moss."

"Don't we all! Kate was part of what the irresponsible tabloids called the 'heroin chic' lot, remember those Calvin Klein ads? She's like this tiny, skinny waif with no boobs and she models underwear. Brilliant! This was a few years before I arrived, and right after the reign of the supermodels. So first came Kate and the waifs, and that really paved the way for the grungies like me. And after that it was about glamour and looking rich or looking intelligent, understated, and chic."

"Why do you call them irresponsible tabloids?"

"Because they glamorized drugs with that term. There's nothing chic about heroin."

"Did Gus do heroin?"

Iris hesitated for a beat and stared at the road. "I don't know, baby. A lot of people in the industry did. Many died."

Lou chewed her bottom lip for a couple of miles.

"Were you friends with Kate?"

"No, we booked shows together, but she was already famous when I started. I had a different gang. Younger, which in model years means decades younger. Many of the girls I was with were from eastern Europe: Russia, Ukraine, Poland . . ."

Lou was mesmerized. She stared at Iris, her lips parted. Spellbound.

"There was a big wave of those girls arriving in Paris. They could finally get temporary visas, so they came in droves. They were stunning, with high cheekbones, Slavic and exotic features, tiny frames and the longest legs. Many of these young girls came from rural environments and had whole families to support by age seventeen. Agency scouts combed beauty contests in remote villages and discovered such incredible faces . . . Nadja, Katja, Olga, Dasha, Karolina, Darja, Lena, Jordanka . . . these girls were so hungry and driven that when we collapsed at the end of the day they would still do a few more go-sees.

"So many beautiful girls started, so few made it . . . you see, Lou, it's not just about beauty, you also have to have personality . . . and be tough. With some girls, there was very little going on behind the eyes . . . girls with bigger personalities had more of a chance."

Lou nodded.

"Every night, in Joan's flat, I wore my only pair of high heels and practiced my catwalk, especially the full turns— those were bloody hard. I also devoured her fashion magazines and books. I studied every single page, I looked at the model, her poses, her attitude. I wanted to know what tricks she had pulled to make herself more beautiful, how she had used the light. I searched her constantly changing expressions, which is what makes the supermodel." Iris grabbed Lou's water bottle and took a swig. "I wanted to get into the model's head and find out what narrative she was following, how she acted to a given story. And I imagined what the photographer had told her. I approached modeling in an artistic way, but I was also very professional about it."

"Wait, Mom. Stop the story one sec. I wanna take pictures. I love those huge rocks!"

Lou grabbed her camera and started shooting the landscape as it flew by her window. Iris smiled.

"Tell me about your first shows, please, Mom."

"My first big casting was for John Galliano's show. I was terrified. There were hundreds of us at the casting. He made us run in stilettos and huge crinolines; he was so nice and so caring. To put us in the mood, he said, *Imagine that you are a Russian princess: you are running away from your castle, the wolves are howling, you are frightened.'* So, we played the part and tried to be actresses and also feel the clothes, make them move dramatically, give them life. I remember this nasty Italian top model called Mafalda, she made me trip on the catwalk, superbitch, and Kate was there, she was Galliano's muse."

"Wow, *Mom*! Did you get the job?"

"No, not that show, but I did do other shows with John later. It helped that I lived with Joan because all she talked about was fashion. She was obsessed by it, so I really got into the zone. I knew all the photographers' names, the designers, the trends. Hanging around my mom's office when I was a kid had helped because it gave me the background knowledge and set the bar high. Fashion was a thing of great beauty and art to me. I looked past the ugliness of the people that are in the business for the wrong reasons, and I embraced the creativity and the wonder."

Lou mouthed *The wonder*...

"My big break was when I booked the first Balenciaga show under its new designer. The clothes were black, and the silhouettes were unlike anything I had worn before. It was my first high-profile show, as well as that of an unknown Brazilian model called Gisele."

"Gisele? She started then? With you?"

"Yes, baby."

"How long did it take to become a top model?"

"Normally it took forever, five or seven years at least. If you made it, if you were the one in a thousand. First, they sent you to Japan to make money for the agency and learn the trade, cut your teeth doing lots of well-paying but ugly catalogs. Then you were shipped off to Milan, which was the worst and most hated place to be for a model. You made no money but booked better editorials and advertising. In Milan, the modeling agencies were run by playboys, and if you could not find a bed in a model flat, you lived in a revolting *pensione* with a bunch of other starving, broke, desperate girls surrounded by horny sharks, middle-aged Italian dudes who lived at the bar of the

"Ludo—Grandpa—taught me that when everything was going bad, you could always count on books and nature to heal your grief, to ground you. I spent many hours with him in his garden in Paris and on his little terrace in New York. We also read together. We did not need to talk. He gardened and I watched. We shared books. He soothed himself like this. Delfine made his life very difficult in the end. That's why I moved to Northern California. Nature. I was at the hairdresser's and they had a *National Geographic* magazine with an article on rural America. There were beautiful pictures of La Arboleda. It's that simple."

Mother and daughter stared at the gray ocean, lost in their thoughts. The motion of the waves had a calming hypnotic effect. Here and there a pelican floated among the thick beds of brown seaweed. Gulls flew low over the swell. Two seals chased each in the surf.

"And you? What do you want to do? You drive me crazy telling me what *I* should do, so what about *you*? What are your dreams?" asked Iris.

"I want to be a model."

"A *what*?" Iris jumped up from the bench to confront her daughter.

"A model. I want to be a model."

"Why on *earth*? You've heard me tell you over and over again how hard it is, how unkind, how difficult. Are you out of your mind?" Iris snapped at her.

Lou's green eyes narrowed as she glared into the sun at her mother, a ball of fury.

"You don't care about what I do, you only care about what I shouldn't do. Have you even looked at my pictures? I also have my own website, but you've never discussed it with me . . . do you give a damn?"

"Lou, I . . . I didn't know. Why didn't you tell me? You yelled at me once for 'snooping' on you on Instagram; you even blocked me for months! You never tell me anything anymore.

If you're so serious about photography, why don't you apply for a scholarship at Cal Arts? Or what about Stanford? We discussed Stanford, remember? A long time ago, I know it was a dream of yours . . . you could get a scholarship, you're that smart. Anything but modeling. I won't let you. That's the end of that," Iris said.

"Whatever, Mom." Lou leaped up and strode toward the inn, her head and shoulders hunched against the wind.

CHAPTER 7

Walking behind her daughter, she could not help but stare. Lou was a sylph, lingering in that space suspended between girlhood and womanhood. One minute she was caught in the beauty of her long and lissome body, the way she held herself so straight, her exquisite poise and grace, while the next she was a mass of taut nerves and strung-out graceless gestures. *I love her so much. Why can't we talk? Why can't we figure things out?*

Lou stomped ahead, kicking at the occasional shrub with her army boots, her spindly legs and narrow frame floating inside her favorite military parka. In the past six months, Lou had shot up in height and blossomed, seeming unable to control her gangly body, uncomfortable with her new femininity and beauty. She shoved her fists in her pockets and pulled her hood over her head.

Back at the inn, Lou went inside her room, locked the door, and turned on the TV.

Lying on her bed, Iris pulled out her computer and logged into the Iris de Valadé Instagram page. As she expected, there had been no activity since Lou set it up for her a couple of years before. Feeling guilty, she went to Lou's handle, @lou.de.santos, and clicked into her daughter's feed.

She had 83,617 followers? What on earth? Iris scrolled through hundreds of beautiful pictures that Lou had taken. Trees, boulders, sunsets, the ocean, flowers, Chuck's horses, Taco, Edgar, Conrado, Jack . . . and then picture after picture of Iris. Her face was beautifully lit and framed, her body lithe and graceful, a photographer's dream. With every shot of Iris #mom

#irisdevalademodel came dozens of comments and hashtags: #stunning #irisdevaladecomeback #legend #fashionhistory . . .

The last photograph was a ravishing close-up of the two of them taken the week before by Chuck. Iris and Lou vamped for the camera. The first comment was *Ms. Newman, please contact our New York office. @r13denim.*

I guess it was bound to happen sooner or later.

CHAPTER 8

The offices of Hunt, Marshall, Cook took up the thirty-fourth floor of a modern tower on Wilshire Boulevard. Iris sat with Lou in the waiting room, assimilating the British feel of the place. The dark wood-paneled walls, deep leather armchairs, and warm lights contrasted with the glass-and-steel façade of the building. On one wall was a framed photograph of the Queen in a pink chiffon dress surrounded by her army of corgis. On a second wall hung a cricket bat signed by Sir Gary Sobers. On low coffee tables were piles of crisp new magazines: the *Spectator*, *Tatler*, and the *World of Interiors*.

"Would you like a cup of tea while you wait, madam?" asked the receptionist. She turned toward Lou. "Coca-Cola, perhaps?"

Lou was despondent and failed to react. Holding her daughter's hand in hers, Iris said, "Are you sure you want to go through with this? You don't have to, baby, it's all right."

Lou squeezed her mother's hand. "It's fine, Mom, it's cool. I can handle it."

Fifteen minutes later they sat at the long mahogany table in the conference room. Across from them were Andy Marshall and Matthew Cook, Gus's business managers and lawyers.

"We are so terribly sorry about your loss, Miss de Valadé, Miss Newman. No words are adequate, really. Frightful shock for us too, I might add—this took us by surprise . . ." Andy Marshall's tone was sincere. Gus had been their client for many years.

Andy Marshall fiddled with his silk cravat and continued. "If you will bear with me, I should further explain: I received a phone call in the early-morning hours from the Charité hospital in Berlin. The doctor was extremely upset, and all I could make out was—if you will forgive me—'Gus de Santos dead, *Herr* de Santos dead, *mort*.' Having reviewed and paid all his bills over the years, we were privy to the knowledge that he had a serious illness. Frankly, his doctor's invoices were astronomical at times. But we never discussed it. Mr. de Santos—as you know, of course—could be the most private of persons.

"Matthew had to fly to Berlin to identify the body and deal with the papers at the consulate. He was cremated in Berlin."

"What did he die of?" asked Iris, her eyes filling up with tears.

"It was liver cancer, I'm afraid," replied Matthew Cook.

Iris stole a glance at Lou, who looked straight ahead, her face still and expressionless.

"I am sorry. I suppose we should have suspected that something was going on," said Andy. "He had been acting strangely of late. There was the motorbike license, of course—and we know how much he hated having to drive—and the scuba diving lessons, particularly challenging given his claustrophobia. And he emailed asking if I would like to adopt his adored cat, Virgil, then without waiting for my reply, he put Virgil on a plane with his assistant.

"Honestly, I'm somewhat gutted that I missed all the signs. I should have seen that he was living his life fully to the end, flaming out in big style. He was also working maniacally: the output of these last years has been phenomenal. You may know that he was preparing a major exhibition at the Victoria and Albert in London, through the Royal Photographic Society. The V&A show would be very prestigious."

Andy took off his glasses and rubbed his eyes, then paused before putting them back on. "We will, I'm afraid, need your review and approval of the wording of the obituaries we intend to submit to the *Guardian* and the *New York Times*. I fear that soon we are going to be inundated with requests for retrospectives, editorials, and inquiries about sales . . ."

"Where is Virgil?" asked Lou. Her voice was barely a whisper.

CHAPTER 9

The entire day had been one long blur of legal documents to read, decipher, and evaluate. On the table in front of her was more homework to get through, all of it urgent. Spreadsheets of the inventory and its locations; spreadsheets of gallery editions that were for sale; artworks that were on loan; accounting Excels from Gus's galleries in Los Angeles, New York, and Berlin.

Marshall and Cook were in the process of doing a first evaluation of the value of the estate, as well as quantifying its future potential. Iris had no idea that Gus had been so prolific in such a short period of time. He was only forty-four when he died.

Iris had observed Andy Marshall and Matthew Cook at work all morning and understood why Gus had remained with the same firm for such a long time.

Andy Marshall was in his early sixties, a dapper, old-fashioned British gentleman with a reassuring but restrained demeanor. Matthew Cook was in his late forties, and unlike his older associate, he had an attractive devil-may-care glint in his eyes. Both men were meticulous and thorough, helping Iris sift through the information without a hint of impatience or condescension.

Assessing for the first time the significance of what was required of her, Iris sat in the conference room and stared in dismay at the sea of files they had prepared for her. Curious at first, Lou soon lost interest in the technical details and retreated to the back of the room with her book.

During their afternoon tea break, Matthew Cook took out a sheaf of papers that were covered in fluorescent sticky arrows and said, "We have an issue, Miss de Valadé. At best, it is a little annoying; at worst it might prove . . . not inconsequential."

You gotta love the understated way the Brits give bad news, thought Iris.

"Please call me Iris. Iris Newman. De Valadé was my professional name, my mother's family name." Iris looked into Matthew Cook's eyes and smiled. Matthew held her gaze for a few seconds, then looked down at his desk and began to shuffle his papers.

"Quite. Of course. My apologies, Ms. Newman. Right. As you know, the will names you as executrix of the estate. As executrix, you are to distribute to the de Santos family half of the annual net profit yielded by the estate. Of course, that presumes that there should be net profit, but that is an entirely reasonable presumption, given your good management in the past. As you have seen, the remaining half is to be split between your daughter and yourself.

"However, the addendum contains a proviso, and I quote, 'On condition that Iris de Valadé completes the estate and recovers the missing material that was left behind in Paris.' Ms. Newman, should we refer to these pieces as 'the Paris archive'? We are under pressure from Mr. de Santos's family to distribute the proceeds of the estate to the family, failing which they threaten to initiate legal proceedings. The grounds for such an action are not entirely clear, of course, but I would assume they might allege incapacity—that, when he executed the will, Mr. de Santos was of unsound mind, i.e., he was too ill to know what he was signing." Matthew Cook paused.

Iris groaned under her breath. She sat up in her chair, her back stiff as a rod. She stared at the expensive linen cloth of Matthew Cook's navy-blue Savile Row suit, trying to make sense of what he was saying. Her attention was wavering. She clasped her hands in her lap.

Matthew Cook took off his reading glasses and put them down slowly on the table. "We are to meet the family tomorrow at the facility where Mr. de Santos's personal belongings are being stored. Nothing has been touched since his studio manager sent the container from Berlin. Everything is as Mr. de Santos left it. We do not know the full nature and extent of the contents of the storage container, apart from the list of furniture and some boxes and trunks listed as *personal*. My strong recommendation is that you arrive there a couple of hours in advance of the family so you can perform an inspection.

"The will permits you to take what you want; the rest you can give to the family. But I recommend that you keep any personal notes and sketches as part of his art legacy. The artwork itself, including the different print formats, along with all negatives, are in a separate art storage. That will be our next destination. Mr. de Santos included a check written out to you for future expenses. As soon as you have recovered the Paris archive, there will be another sum that will be used to start the Gustavo de Santos Foundation."

"Did Mr. de Santos leave me a letter?" Iris asked.

"Not that we are aware of," said Matthew Cook. He cleared his throat.

Iris slumped slightly into her chair and gripped the armrests. Andy Marshall took out a white linen handkerchief from his pocket and dabbed his forehead.

Matthew Cook continued. "We must stress to you that it is in your interest to act quickly to recover the Paris archive; you never know what might happen to those negatives. Mr. de Santos's main gallery has passed on to us their current files, and they are all urgent, I'm afraid. The Thames & Hudson monograph has been put on hold until further notice, and we are going to have to field requests from museums and collectors. The sooner we resume the work, the sooner you will be able to fully protect the estate's interests."

"And what would happen, Mr. Cook, if I refused to comply with the terms of the will, and do not take any part of the estate?"

Lou raised her head from her book and shot Iris a look.

"That's entirely your choice, of course, but I suspect you may rethink that course of action once you meet the family. We have had what I might euphemistically refer to as the pleasure of having Mr. de Santos's brother, Nicolás, here in person last week, as well as umpteen phone calls from him, on an almost daily basis. If I may say so, I do not think you will want to just turn over the estate to him. Without being too indiscreet, let's say he shows no indication that he fully appreciates the cultural and intellectual value of the collection. To be blunt, my sense is that he would seek to dispose of it immediately, without regard for his brother's legacy."

"Dispose of it? You, you mean sell it off?" Iris stammered.

"Yes, as is, the whole physical archive and the copyright. Apparently, Mr. de Santos's brother already has an eager buyer in Paris with whom he has been emailing. Being that Mr. de Santos's galleries have been selling very few and very carefully chosen editions of his work, unless the presumed buyer is extremely professional, a flooding of the art market with many pieces at once would render Mr. de Santos's work worthless and his name damaged in a very short time. Which would, of course, be a real shame.

"Otherwise and as of now, the estate will stop releasing editions. When the supply stops, prices will inflate."

"And what does the Paris archive consist of?"

Andy Marshall harrumphed. Taking out a separate list from his folder, he said, "If I may be so bold as to step in here. Excuse me. Allow me to quote: *The Paris Archive: all work produced in Paris between October 1995 and March 2002. The archive is currently in the possession of my ex-agent, Clemente Campisi, Campisi SARL, 252 rue de Rivoli, Paris 75001. Mr. Campisi has no rights over my archive.*"

At the mention of that name, Iris's stomach cramped and she started feeling very cold.

"Mr. Marshall, Mr. Cook, would you mind if we call it a day and meet tomorrow morning at the storage?"

"But of course. I say, Ms. Newman, are you all right? If I may, you do look somewhat pale."

Iris's voice faltered. "I'll be fine, thank you. It's been an emotional day. I think I just need to lie down in my hotel room for a little bit."

CHAPTER 10

Iris drove up Wilshire toward Santa Monica Boulevard and then changed her mind. She took Sunset Boulevard west to the Pacific Coast Highway and drove along the ocean, windows down.

It was five in the afternoon and packs of surfers all along the Malibu coast were straddling their boards, waiting for a wave.

She parked the car at Malibu Lagoon. Without a word, Iris and Lou took off their shoes and got on the dusty path leading toward the ocean. As they walked through the reeds, they looked at the white egrets perched on long black stick legs, digging for worms. Then they sat on the sand between the lifeguard's post and the surf school near the pier.

Lou took out her camera and snapped pictures of the surfers in the golden light.

Iris closed her eyes, drinking in the murmur of the sea.

"You okay, Mom?"

"Sort of, it's just hard taking all this in. I'm quite lost."

"You mean that he died without saying goodbye to you? Would that have changed anything?"

Iris turned her head to stare at Lou. "Why do you say that?"

Lou shrugged.

"I would have loved for you two to meet, baby. I wish I had done more to make it happen. It's so unfair to you. I am so sorry, Lou. I never thought he would die."

"Whatever, Mom, I don't want to talk about that now. But his pictures are sick, I had no idea. They're killer good. I'm feeling kind of proud now."

"Proud to be Gus's daughter?"

"Yeah! Big-time. You're not going to turn over the estate to his family, are you? They'll sell it. You're going to Paris to get the rest back, right, Mom?"

Iris said nothing. She turned her head back toward the ocean, her eyes full of tears. Clasping her knees with her arms, she said, "I don't know if I can."

Lou snorted with contempt, got up, and wandered down the beach to take pictures, clearly wanting to lose herself in her surroundings instead of trying to understand the complicated mechanisms of her mother's motives.

Later that evening, over Mexican food on Rose Avenue in Venice Beach, with Iris's friend, Eva Loom, they toasted to Gus's life and to their fashion memories of many years before.

Iris had not wanted to go out, let alone see anyone, but feeling that Lou needed some distraction and frivolity she had called her old friend, now a renowned celebrity stylist in Hollywood.

From the moment Eva Loom walked into the restaurant, Iris was flooded with memories as she watched her friend approach. Eva's vivid face was still full of mischief, the naughty glint in her eyes, her loud and infectious laugh, the Cockney inflections, the dark blond hair that twisted in thick, sexy locks down her back, and the baby-soft pale skin that was so British and made Iris think of clotted cream and scones with raspberry jam. Overflowing with enthusiasm and a genuine love of fashion, Eva had always declared an unabashed prefer-ence for the front row of a fashion show over the galleries of the Louvre. *"Darling, a Galliano show IS art! It is opera, theater, the movies all rolled up in one."*

Eva's amazon figure was poured into a beautifully cut shift dress so narrow at the bottom that she tottered over to them, taking tiny geisha steps in her seven-inch heels. Sweeping Iris into her arms, she enveloped her in a heartfelt embrace and held her tight for a few seconds.

"I'm gobsmacked, Iris. I only just heard the ghastly news. I am so sorry."

"Yes, it's brutal."

Eva ordered a mezcal and kissed Lou on the cheeks. "Hey, gorgeous, I follow you on Instagram. You grew boobs!" Lou shuffled uncomfortably under Eva's teasing stare. To Iris, she said, "She's your clone! What a stunner, she should model . . ."

Eva downed her mezcal in one shot and ordered another. Her face went grave. She asked, "And you? How are you doing?"

"It's so difficult, Eva, I'm devastated. Even though we'd lost touch, I see his spirit in many things. What he taught me, the way I look at the world, I still think of him every day. Let's drink to that," Iris said, lifting her beer at Eva.

"Why did we wait so long? And why do I feel as if we just saw each other?"

"Brain waves?" Iris chuckled. "And don't yell at me, because I know that it's all my fault. But here I am finally, after years of emails. And you, Eva?"

"We were lucky, Iris; things have changed so much, it's all so corporate now. Remember when we did the Genius Factory job without showing any clothes? That was fucking brilliant of Gus! Oops! Sorry, sweetie," she said, looking at Lou and not sounding sorry at all.

"I could never get away with that now. Clients have too much power, they control everything, their image is micro-managed to the last detail, nothing is left to chance, there's no improvisation, *and* the photographer must obey. When I style celebrities, I have the ridiculous publicists and handlers choosing the clothes and standing right behind the photographer, in the celebrity's line of vision, telling their client what to do, how to pose, or mainly what not to do. There is no more creative intimacy, it's pure intrusion. Then they run to check digitech between each pose, breaking the photographer and subject's flow."

"Digitech?" Lou cut in.

Eva turned her gaze toward her. "Yeah, the digital-capture monitor, where the digital technician sits."

Lou nodded, making a mental note.

Eva sipped her mezcal and stared at the little glass, shaking her head. "Publicists who have never opened a fashion magazine in their lives are choosing clothes and imagery for their stars. It's so frustrating. *We* never created images just for their Instagram value, as backdrops to a *selfie* . . . clients now choose the edgiest photographers from the fashion mags, only to be terrified of their angle and then have to control the results. What's the point? I hate it now, clients make everything so safe, so sanitized, so much about product and brand identity . . . celebrities have *themselves* become products and brands. Our fashion days with Gus? Unfathomable now."

Eva turned toward Lou. "Your mom was a *real* model, unlike the dilettantes I have to deal with these days." She flicked her gaze back at Iris, shaking her head. "Model agencies have rushed to open offices in LA and are signing up the 'spawn of,' kids that have entertainment ties and what they call 'built-in name recognition.' The industry has changed dramatically because of social media . . . it's depressing. I crave a supermodel, a proper great model, not just someone that poses."

Lou stared at Eva, mesmerized, taking it all in. "What was that shoot with no clothes?" she asked.

"Bloody hilarious! Gus won a bunch of prizes for that job. Best Fashion Campaign 1998 for *Ad World* and whatnots. But we had no idea what we were doing! I had prepared all these looks and a tight casting for Gus, and when the clothes did not arrive, he said, '*Sod it! Naked, everyone naked.*' Most of the models ran away, like '*I have to call my agent,*' but your mum over there—she didn't, she stayed put."

Lou turned to Iris and looked at her. "Wow, *Mom*, gnarly!"

Iris blushed.

"And that's how your mum and Gus met. Gus was brilliant in that way, he always wanted to defy the expectation

of what was *thought* to be fashion photography. He challenged
what people wanted to see, it was a dare. If he believed in it, he
would do it. He had a fuck-you attitude that paid off creatively.
Sorry, pumpkin, must have been hard for your mum in the
long run. Maybe it had to do with his . . . health issues?"

"Health issues? You mean the cancer?" Lou asked.

Iris shot a look at Eva, who lowered her gaze and went back
to sipping her mezcal *veladora*. "Shall we order? I'm starved."

It's cold that November day in Paris, raining very hard. Winter is
finally here. It's my eighteenth birthday. I am homesick and sad.

I walk into the massive studio at Chrome Bastille searching for Gus de Santos. An improvised production office has
been set up at the far end of Stage One, where a gangly and
beautiful boy who must be de Santos stands with his stylist,
a woman with Jane Birkin hair, both going through piles of
model books, turning the pages at a frenetic pace. A bolero is
playing on the studio system: *Me cansé de rogarle, me cansé de
decirle, que yo sin ella de pena muero . . .* I look at the cassette on
the table. The cover is a vintage sepia portrait of a mustachioed
man in a big sombrero. Pedro Infante, "Me Cansé de Rogarle."

Their faces are dead serious.

"Can you call your agency?" asks the stylist when she sees me.

"Is there a problem?" I ask.

"Well, maybe. The campaign has changed. We don't have
the collection, we can't find the owner, he's sailing around the
world on a catamaran. Yes, I know it sounds crazy. It's too late
to cancel, and the photographer wants to go ahead and shoot
without the clothes, lots of naked bodies. Gus?"

Gus looks up from his pile of model books. "*¡Hola!* What's
your name?"

He has a gap-toothed smile. My knees go weak and my
stomach fills with butterflies. I try not to stare at him, but I

have never seen a face with so much presence, a body with so much bearing; Gustavo de Santos looks manly and delicate at the same time. His hair is long and shiny, his skin dark; he has soft brown eyes and a long, angular face. His full lips and beautiful mouth are the only things I can focus on.

As a teenager, I had an old sepia poster of Apache chief Cochise in my room. I also had one of Captain Blood, the pirate. Gus looks like both my childhood heroes, but he is standing in front of me, waiting patiently for me to talk.

"Iris de Valadé. My agency showed me your work. I like it a lot."

I give them my book and wait while they go over it in their corner.

Gus looks up from my portfolio. "You know it's nudes, right?"

"I already warned Iris." The stylist interrupted.

I gather my courage. "I'll do nudes."

"Really?" Gus asks. "I don't want problems with your booker. I'm about to call some friends at the Crazy Horse, you know, the art cabaret on George V; that's where I go when I need naked girls. They have no problems with nudity," he chuckles. His eyes study my face. Mine do not leave his. *Crazy Horse girls? Dare me, I'll show you.*

"Can I take some Polaroids now? With no clothes."

"Sure." I shrug.

I look straight at him as I take everything off, stripping slowly, waiting for a cue.

I kick off my wet sneakers, then peel away my sweater. My white T-shirt comes off with it, followed by my leather belt and heavy cargo pants.

I stand in my panties. "These too, right?"

Gus stares back at me and his gaze runs over my body, appraising, measuring, framing. Cocking his head sideways, he squints. "Yes."

Standing naked in front of Eva and Gus, I ask, "Where do you want me to go?"

CHAPTER 11

I am confirmed that evening for a shoot in two days. We are eight models, girls and boys both.

My call time is 8:00 a.m., and when I get there, I see that I am the first model to arrive. I wander about discreetly, seeking a familiar face among those swarming around the studio, all focused on their tasks. Maria Callas sings full blast, the same aria Papa used to play. The infinite white background of the seamless studio creates the effect of being inside a giant egg.

Not knowing where else to go, I sit alone in the makeup room and stare at my reflection in the bright mirror.

A few minutes later, two shy Japanese boys introduce themselves and start unloading suitcases full of hair extensions, wigs, makeup, and beauty products. They are Toshi and Satoshi, hair and makeup team.

Eva Loom click-clacks into the room on a pair of dangerous red mules and gives us bosomy hugs.

"Do you know what we're doing today?" they ask her.

"Not an effin clue, duckies," she replies cheerfully.

A few scraggly models trickle in, yawning, herded by Gus and the guy I'm told is his first camera assistant, Cyril.

"Toshi, Satoshi, can you start getting everyone ready and send them to wardrobe? Start with Iris, please, then I want Victoria and Walter. I'll do singles today," Gus instructs in a calm and self-assured voice. "I want bare skin, no shine, no gloss, matte, please, no mouths, natural nails, short. And when you're done, we'll try the hair in wardrobe and take it from there. ¿Órale?"

I sit on a tall chair facing the mirror and catch side-glances of an up-and-coming model named Victoria, who I sort of know. Victoria sits on the chair next to mine. She smokes and chats to Satoshi. "My agency did *not* want me to do this job because of the nudity, but for Gus I'll do anything. His shit's tight. He's so fucking talented, he's going to be a star, mark my words. And I can smell a star a mile away, right?"

Satoshi nods and dabs at her forehead with the moisturizing base, waiting for her to finish her cigarette.

"I mean, we all know what this job means, right? We all want to do it desperately."

Still nodding, Satoshi massages Victoria's face, preparing her skin for the foundation.

Toshi stands in front of me and gently pulls away my bangs, studying my face closely. "You have beautiful skin. You're gorgeous, we don't need to do much here."

I smile at him. "Thank you."

"Have you ever worked with Gus before?"

"No, why?"

"You're shaking. Are you cold?"

"Kinda."

Toshi massages my shoulders and speaks to my reflection in the mirror. "Don't be scared. He's demanding, he's impatient, they say he's difficult, but we love working with him. Satoshi, Eva, myself, we jump at every opportunity. Gus always knows what he wants. If he's pushing you, it means he's interested in what you've got; otherwise he gets bored fast and will move on from you."

Now I'm panicked. I turn around to look at Toshi. "What does he expect from a model, what do I have to do?"

Gus leans into the makeup room. "Toshi, can you come to wardrobe with Iris?"

In a white bathrobe, I follow Gus and Toshi to the fluorescent-lit wardrobe room, where Eva has folding tables lined up, piled high with accessories and fabrics.

"Can you try this on?" She hands me a leather chest plate with side buckles that sit on my hips, barely covering my breasts and panties.

"Thong please, Iris, need to see all the skin."

I take off my white cotton underwear and put on Eva's tiny nude-colored stringlike thing.

"Okay, everything off, please, except the thong. Can you try on these boots?" Eva says, grimacing.

The high-heeled boots come halfway up my thighs. They are charcoal colored and shiny. I like the way they hug my legs and make them look longer.

"Put this on, Iris." Eva hands me a black mullet wig.

Gus looks at me, squinting, his head tilted to one side.

Eva seems annoyed, her face contorted.

"Okay, off please. Just keep the boots."

I stand in the middle of the room, covering my nipples with one arm.

Gus scrapes his hair back with an impatient gesture.

"What if we did nothing, Eva? I mean, I have such a feeling of déjà vu—the big Patti Smith hair, the leather stuff, the kinky rock thing. Boring, *hermana*; another theme, another 'story.' I don't know what the fuck we're doing today, but whatever it is, it's not this. I don't want a *pinche* story, I want a vibe.

"Iris, you come with me. Toshi, Eva, on set, please. Where's Cyril? I need him *now.*"

I follow Gus as he paces toward the seamless set, tucking his hair behind his ears. His jeans are low on his hips; he hitches up his belt. He cradles a heavy camera in his arm. I can see his bicep bulging. A row of white polystyrene boards closes the set to everyone except his immediate team.

I stand and face his camera. Eva ties a piece of heavy dark jersey around my breasts and lets it drape to the floor. She looks at Gus, who nods. With my knee, I part the slit in the cloth and make sure that all of my thigh shows.

Toshi runs his fingers through my hair, crunching the ends and fluffing out my roots to give it a Mohawk shape. He winks at me. *I am not intimidated,* I want to tell him.

Cyril stands nearby and measures the light, then moves a reflecting board slightly to the side of my bust.

Gus comes up to me and, standing very close, says, "I just want you to look at me, don't pose, be who you were the day before yesterday."

I shudder. That girl does not exist anymore.

I look at him sitting sideways on a stool, his folded legs so long. His Rolleiflex is on a tripod under his face. He stands up to look into the viewfinder and adjusts the lens. I gaze at the crown of his head and then his lifted face. He sits on his stool again. Cyril measures the light and moves the reflector boards.

As they work endlessly on the lights and scrims, my mind drifts.

On the studio sound system, Maria Callas sings "Flower Duet" from Delibes's *Lakme.*

Cyril props a full-length mirror in front of me. I use it to check my poses and study the light.

"Lift up your chin. Turn slightly to your right, a bit more. Stop. Look at me. Look away. Tilt your head to the right. Don't move, Iris. Cyril, Polaroid, please."

Gus presses the shutter release on its long cable. He gets up and comes near me, staring with a quiet intensity that makes me feel strange. He hunches his shoulders as his head bends over the viewfinder. He takes close-ups, his lens in my face.

It's at that very moment, looking at myself in the mirror, moving to Gus's voice, that I sense it is not all about me, it is about knowing how to fill the page.

I close my eyes and imagine the music enveloping me like a silken robe. The sweetness of the melody penetrates my pores, giving me goose bumps, and I hum to it. I can feel the heat of his body near my skin.

"Beautiful, Iris, open your lips please. Move sideways and bend your head down a little bit. Don't open your eyes."

For a few frames, I give him the girl that he wanted, the girl of two days ago. But now, right now I want to give him someone else.

I am in an Avedon photograph. I stretch my arms out, one over my head and the other in front of me, fluid, not theatrical, and I become Dovima with the elephants. I no longer need to act. Irving Penn comes to mind and I am now Veruschka. In Penn's picture, I pose with a leopard, looking docile but ready to pounce. I make my body taut for Gus, my muscles ripple.

Images of Charlotte Rampling looking straight at Helmut Newton and then beyond his camera. What goes through her mind? She is feral, mysterious. She is a femme fatale with hooded eyelids, that is who I want to be today.

I remember when I did the *danse musette* for the first time. My French cousins had taken me to the dance hall, a rustic *guingette* on the Seine where old couples shuffled in unison, surprisingly light on their feet, never breaking a step as if glued to one another.

"I teach you, is easy, juss let me lead you. Is like ballroom dancing but European style, popular, not stiff and snob, and much more funnier." My cousin Eric grabbed my right hand and lifted my arm higher than my face, then he wrapped his left arm tight around my waist and drew me close to him. "Juss follow me. Don't fight me. Close your eyes until you start reading my steps. Truss me, you won't fall."

My body had followed his, at the slightest pressure from his fingers on my waist, I had turned or stopped. My hips became one with Eric's as we glided around and around, challenging each other, changing pace. And then I led him, to see who was the nimblest of foot and lightest of touch.

Now I look at Gus behind his camera. He cocks his head when I do, he parts his lips when my mouth opens, his chin lifts when I turn mine to catch the light. We are dancing now, dancing the *ballo liscio*. I am leading him and he trusts me.

He understands the art of the model, the art of the pose. He understands my passion. I give him what he wants, the vision of me that he thinks is his, that belongs to no one, only to that moment in the seamless studio. Then it will be gone, captured on film and on to the next *ballo liscio*, the next photographer, the next fashion moment. I become a model on this shoot.

The breeze from the fan parts the draped cloth, and I feel Gus's gaze on me, caressing my skin.

"Open your eyes."

I am shocked by the intensity of his stare. Confused, I turn my head. Then Gus walks away, flapping the Polaroids in the air to make them dry faster.

Eva and Gus study them. They say nothing. Gus walks toward me and shows me one.

"This is it, this is the campaign, I think we have it," he says with a smile. His eyes glow.

Satoshi takes the Polaroid from Gus's hand, and together we inspect it.

"Wow!" says Satoshi, grinning at me.

I study the shot. I like the way my limbs look distorted on the Polaroid. The cinematic light that Gus uses makes deep shadows that pull my body in every direction.

My eyes are closed, and my eyelashes and cheekbones catch the glare. I had twisted my shoulder in the opposite direction, so my breasts had popped out and over the black cloth, a sensual mound of white flesh against the grainy backdrop. I wonder what Delfine would think of these? Her name is a heavy burden that I am proud to carry today.

I look up from the Polaroid and catch Gus observing me.

"Come with me, Iris," Satoshi says.

Satoshi holds my elbow and I walk across the studio in the high boots, dragging the long cloth behind me.

"Leave those on," Satoshi says, pointing to the boots. "You'll look better if you pose in heels. Your ass will stick out, you'll curve your back, and your breasts will look amazing."

I smile at him, thankful for the tip.

Gus has Cyril close the set, sealing it off with white polystyrene boards.

Cristina Fanna, the Genius Factory PR, stops by the studio a couple of times to shout at Gus and Eva. "You are going to have me fired, *capito? Fi-Red! Madonna, ma perché io?* What did I do to deserve this shit? Naked, everyone naked, are you fockin crazy? Out of your fockin mind? This is a fashion shoot, not an art project. How can you shoot my client's campaign without his clothes?"

She sits fuming in a corner, excluded from the closed set, making long-distance calls to Italy while Eva and Cyril try to calm her down with endless coffee and cigarettes. There is nothing Cristina can do; Gus has been given creative carte blanche, and he is calling the shots.

We shoot for three long days. Single shots, doubles, triples, until the grand finale on the last afternoon, where all eight models are in the same shot, a pyramid of soft, white skin and big hair, sharp angles and delicate curls, sooty shadows and little light. The shoot has the bravery that comes with youth, freedom, and inexperience and from having nothing to lose. Gus photographs a mood, and the faces and forms that embody that mood—girls and boys that convey his idea that fashion is not cerebral, fashion is pure emotion, it is tactile, it is not quantifiable.

The moment Gus captures is extreme and raw. We see the beauty in something that is stripped back, brutal and bare. Purity. There are no client clothes in the end, just fabrics and some neutral pieces belonging to the models: a white T-shirt, a black hat, a tank top, heels.

Something sacred, something unique, is taking place in the studio. It does not matter that my eyes are dry and burnt from the lights. I do not care that I cannot feel my aching limbs when I leave the set in the evenings. We are part of something that will never be repeated, no matter how hard a client or magazine tries. It's a *moment*, it's magic, and then that moment, that magic, is gone.

Waiting for my turn in the empty makeup room, I lie down on the couch in a corner.

Cristina Fanna sits at the makeup table and speaks on the phone.

"*Ma* . . . but what can I do? Gus de Santos is untouchable. He's the new darling at *Revue*. He's Ada's protégé slash boy toy slash whatever. She loves them young and delicious. They must be having lots of sex. *Torrrrrrrido.*"

And with this she laughs; it is loud, it is lewd, I feel dirty. Cristina Fanna sullies the mood.

The Mexican restaurant on Rose Avenue had become noisy. Eva shook Iris's arm, interrupting her thoughts. "Do you want another beer?"

Startled, Iris shook her head.

"And that was it, right, duckie? Love at first sight. Lou, what I'm going to say might be inappropriate, but what the hell." Eva turned to look at Iris, who shrugged.

Eva continued. "So there was your mum standing in front of us without a stitch of clothing; she was stunning. She had this trusting attitude, she had this burning look in her eyes, she cast her spell. Do you follow me, Lou? Gus melted, who would not? We should have called that campaign the Iris de Valadé Butt Naked Show because all Gus wanted to do was shoot your cute mama."

Iris asked the waitress for the ladies' room and excused herself.

CHAPTER 12

Iris and Lou unlocked the self-storage unit under the pale glare of LED lights.

"It's a bit creepy, Mom," Lou whispered.

"I know, but I need time to process this before his family comes."

"Have you ever met them in person?"

"No. Gus spoke a lot about them. He loved them, they were very close, but his father didn't talk to him for a year after he told them he was going to art school. It was heartbreaking for him.

"Ramón, Gus's father, is very proud and has a temper. Gus tried to put his brother, Nico, through university, but Ramón pulled him out after one year and put him to work."

When describing his family to Iris, Gus had said, "We are Chicanos, we're Mexicans that live in America. My parents are originally from Guadalajara. My father is a groom, he works in a stable in Thousand Oaks. My mother cleans people's houses in Calabasas. My mother's name is Guadalupe, like the Virgin of Guadalupe, the national icon of Mexico; whether we want it or not, we Mexicans are all Guadalupanos. She is our Reina, our Queen, our Mother. My parents work very hard. They're good people."

"Did Gus have more siblings?"

"No, just his brother, Nico. They were both born in Los Angeles. His uncle, Tío Damián, helped him get a scholarship into Parsons School of Design in New York. His parents wanted him to work, to make money for the household, but Uncle Damián pushed him to get an education and to study art and photography. There was little space for beauty and art in his home. What can be more important and urgent than feeding the family?

"His father was always angry at him and showed no interest in what he accomplished at Parsons. In Ramón's mind, Gus had betrayed him. Nico never forgave Gus for abandoning him. He had to work double because Gus wasn't there. Nico sold churros in the stands at the Lakers' arena. It was very hard work, his throat was so sore from shouting 'Churrrrrrros' that he couldn't talk for days after a game."

"And Gus's mom?" Lou asked.

"His mother was the only one there for him; she sent many letters, which his cousin wrote for her because Guadalupe couldn't write very well.

"With the first money he made, he bought her a Chanel belt. She used the beautiful glossy shopping bag it came in until it fell apart but never wore the belt; she was too scared she would get robbed on the way to church. But she loved that Chanel paper bag to death."

The ceiling light in the storage unit made an unpleasant buzzing sound.

Gus's assistant in Berlin had done a good job of dismantling his home and studio. Gus's possessions sat in front of them, ensconced in bubble wrap. Detailed labels were stuck to the packages. There were also three large crates of books.

Reading from the list of furniture that Andy Marshall and Matthew Cook had given her, Iris recognized many names: Arroyo, Villegas, Barragán, Mallet-Stevens, Jansen, Parisi, Dumond, Adnet, Prouvé, Paulin, Eames, George Nelson . . . Gus's pieces were an eclectic and unique mix of styles from the 1940s to the 1970s. All modern collectibles. Per his will, Iris and Lou would get to choose first, and the remaining pieces would go to his family, except for his desk. His desk would go to Lou.

At the back of the unit was a small pile of cartons and five metal trunks. Thick leather luggage tags dangled from the handles. Gus had written "PERSONAL" in bold black letters across them.

"Lou, can you open those three trunks for me? I'll start on these two."

Iris carried the smaller trunk to the front of the unit and sat on the floor with her back against the wall.

Tears welled up in her eyes. She leaned her head against the cold metal. Her hands shook.

The first steel trunk was sealed. She opened it with care and breathed in deeply, searching for Gus's scent, the scent of sandalwood, not wanting it to escape the trunk.

The first thing she found was a clamshell box marked "POLIS." Scattered inside were the casting Polaroids that Gus had taken the day they met: small, faded, black-and-white studies of Iris's nude body, close-ups of her face, eyes, lips, hair, skin. Iris sitting, looking over her shoulder shyly, her bent back bony and muscled, her rib cage outlined. Iris hugging her knees, her lithe body folded in half, looking off-camera, pensive and moody. So many emotions conveyed in the small Polaroids, a surprisingly large range of expressions laid bare. Youth and attitude. In her eyes, always, the smoldering look that would make her famous. The Polaroids revealed an innocent sexuality, an intimacy, that now shocked her. On the backs, Eva had marked *Genius Factory casting, Iris de Valadé, 1997.*

Iris shut the clamshell. Gasping for air, she stood and walked to the entrance of the unit. She closed her eyes, leaned her head against the metal wall, and sobbed.

"Mom?" She felt Lou's hand take hers. "I'll help you."

She walked back to the trunk with Lou. Sitting on the floor with Iris, Lou was silent as she pulled the photos from the clamshell, studying each shot of her mother. When she finished, she turned, searching for Iris's gaze.

One by one Iris pulled out of the trunk Gus's most precious objects: a heavy black fountain pen, three work notebooks, the penknife that never left him, his favorite belt, a soft leather backpack, a navy-blue cashmere scarf, a worn-out wallet, his beloved vintage Rolex, a black felt hat, and, finally, the thick silver chain with the medal of Nuestra Señora de Zapopan that he never took off his neck. At the bottom of the trunk was a rare first edition of Guillaume Apollinaire's *Letters to Lou*. Lou pulled it out and opened to the first page. She ran her finger over the inscription and read out loud: *"I will write you 365 love letters a year every year of our lives."* Iris finished reciting the inscription that she knew by heart: *"I worship you forever, my Iris. Your Gustavo."*

Lou looked up from the book and gazed at her mother. "Is that how I got my name?"

"Yes."

"His cameras are in the other metal trunk, and an acoustic guitar. Can I keep them?" said Lou.

"Yes, of course, they're for you. What's in those boxes?"

"Photos of him and you." Lou's voice broke. She turned her head away from Iris.

Iris reached out for her hand. Lou turned her gaze toward her, eyes full of tears. She continued. "Dad was so handsome— you looked so happy . . ."

Iris pressed a folded Kleenex into her daughter's hand. "And what else did you find?"

"Letters from his family, two photography books, his notebooks, an envelope addressed to me . . ."

"Did you open it?"

"Not yet. Mom, is Gus really my father?"

"Yes, why?"

"I don't know." Lou shrugged. "It's not important."

Yes, it is, Iris thought, *and why you ask is also important.*

Together they loaded the trunks and boxes into the Chevy. The crates of books would be sent to Dos Casas. Iris left all the furniture to his family, except for a Barragán lamp made of thick rope and parchment paper, and the desk for Lou. The desk was by Mallet-Stevens and made out of dark rosewood.

The wood was stained and scratched, full of soul, imbued with his spirit.

The sale of the furniture could bring the de Santos family enough to tide them over for a few years.

Running her index finger over the smooth wooden surfaces, Iris remembered how Gus had taught her to feel emotion with her fingers, with her palms, through the skin on the back of her hands. A twig, a branch, a root, a piece of driftwood . . . like skin, wood was tactile, alive. Had Gus surrounded himself with objects that felt like Iris's skin?

"Are you sure you want to give all his furniture away?" Lou said.

"I don't need things to remind me of a person," Iris murmured.

CHAPTER 13

"Iris?"

Iris nodded, and Ramón de Santos engulfed her in an emotional hug. Looking over the tall man's shoulder, she could see Lou's shaken face.

"I am so happy to meet my son's girlfriend, *por fín*. You are more beautiful than the pictures. *¡Que guapa! Mírala, Lupe!* Look at her!"

Ramón's tone was jovial, but his shoulders were stooped and his eyes somber. He dragged his left leg, holding on to his thigh through the fabric of his trousers.

Poor man is wearing his Sunday suit. It's too small and hot for a day like today, Iris thought as she turned toward the woman who must be Gus's mother, Guadalupe, a diminutive woman with a beautiful, lined face.

Iris hugged her, holding her for a long time.

Guadalupe said nothing. Tears streamed down her cheeks. Pressing a hankie to her mouth, she turned expectantly toward Lou and touched her arm gently.

Lou smiled and kissed them each somewhat formally after they ignored her outstretched hand.

"*Yo soy Lou,*" she said haltingly.

Ramón turned toward a man who must be Gus's younger brother, Nico, and pushed him in the back.

"Say hello to your American family, *¡pendejo!*"

Everyone stood around uncomfortably while they waited for Andy Marshall and Matthew Cook to arrive.

"Shall we get some coffee?" said Iris, pointing across the street at a diner.

Guadalupe held Iris's hand while they walked. Through her clasp she felt all the desperation and sadness of the universe.

Lou walked between Ramón and Nico, looking at them kindly and trying to speak in Spanish. She was as tall as the two men.

Sitting across the table from Lou, Guadalupe said to her, "You look so much like my son. I miss him very much. Will you come back to Los Angeles and visit us? You will meet your Mexican cousins; you will like very much."

Without a moment's hesitation, Lou glanced sideways at Iris and said, "*Gracias*. I would love to do that, Señora de Santos."

Nico scowled at Iris from across the table. "So now you own my brother's name and his work?"

"I don't own it. His daughter owns it. I will only run the estate until she's older," Iris replied slowly.

"That's stupid. It won't make money for you or for us. You have to sell it." Nico's voice was hostile.

Iris tried to remain calm. "I looked at the entire collection yesterday on paper. It's a beautiful body of work. If things are done properly and slowly, it can bring the world a lot of pleasure and make us significant money. It will be worth much, much more down the road. Aren't you proud of your brother's legacy? Why should anyone that is not related to Gus own it?"

"My brother's legacy means little to me if our roof leaks and I have no car to go to work in every morning. Look at *mi madre, mi padre*. They are tired, they are sick. We are poor, *desesperados*. My brother's monthly allowance solved many problems. Now we have nothing, just a legacy. We cannot eat that legacy of yours.

"My father had to retire last year because a horse kicked him and broke his leg, and he has no medical insurance to fix it and no pension. Now we live with my small salary and what my mother makes."

"Nico, *¡callate, pendejo, basta!*" Ramón's voice cut through the air, leaving them all staring in embarrassed silence at their coffee mugs.

"I loved my son very much, but I did not tell him that and now he is dead." Ramón gazed at Iris, a lost look in his eyes. He cupped his mug in his scarred, leathery hands, his frayed cuffs brushing the table.

"I have many admirations for him, he was a good son; he always send us presents and money, he call us, write many letters. He ask us to come to visit him in Europe, but Lupe and I, how can we travel? We have to work. Lupe show me magazines with his name on the pages, I am very proud of him. Nico say he is also in some museums? People pay to see his work, my little Gustavo, and now he's gone." Ramón's voice cracked with emotion, and he looked out of the window to hide his sorrow. "I am happy to know his other family," he said quietly.

Tears shone in Lou's eyes. She brushed them away with her shoulder and looked in Ramón's direction.

Guadalupe caressed Lou's hair. "Next time I see you I will make you a pretty dress. What is your favorite color? Pink? Red?" she whispered.

The table was silent until Matthew Cook and Andy Marshall arrived and sat down. After ordering black tea, they proceeded to conduct business in a clipped and formal way.

A look of relief passed over the de Santos family's faces upon hearing Iris's wish to leave them the furniture except for the lamp and desk. Matthew Cook had a former client at Sotheby's who could help evaluate and sell the furniture very quickly.

Guadalupe and Ramón's faces became shadowed when they entered the container. Moved by their suffering, Iris gave Gus's scarf to his mother. Guadalupe buried her face in it. She sobbed, searching frantically for her son's scent.

Iris contained her tears and handed Ramón the Rolex watch, knowing that he would never sell it.

To Nico she gave Gus's old wallet, penknife, and hat. Nico looked at the floor.

The belt, backpack, and the medal of Nuestra Señora de Zapopan she kept.

No one spoke.

Many things needed to be left unsaid.

CHAPTER 14

The hotel room on Wilshire was bland and convenient.

Iris lay on the bed with Lou.

"It sucks," said Lou, looking at the ceiling fan.

Their bodies were limp, exhausted from the day's tension.

Iris moved her foot toward Lou's and touched it with her big toe.

"You were a champ, thank you, I'm proud of you."

"Whatever." Lou continued to stare at the rotating blades.

Iris's head was about to explode. She got up from the bed and closed the shutters, killing the bright light that poured into their room.

"Why did you tell Matthew Cook that you don't want to run the estate? Does this mean you want to sell it? Why did you then tell the de Santos family that you were going to build the name? So you don't want to sell it, then?" Lou asked.

Iris let out a long sigh and went to the bathroom to get an aspirin.

"Lou, back off a little, will you? I need to think. I don't know what I want, but I do know that I don't want to go to Paris. It's too hard."

"You're scared. I know it. It's Gus's agent."

Iris studied Lou's face, her daughter's head cocked to one side, looking back.

"What happened in Paris, Mom?"

Iris turned her eyes away. Lou picked up the laptop as her Skype started to ring. "It's Chuck. We should take this."

Iris took a big breath and clicked to accept, thankful for the dim room.

"Bones? Hey! Can't see you," said Chuck in a cheerful voice.

"Better. You don't wanna see me."

Lou grabbed the laptop from Iris and put her face near the screen.

"Helloooooooooo there, Chuck! Howzit?"

Taco's face took over the screen, his nose leaving a slobbery smudge across the lens.

"Taco! Hello, Taco! Have you ever been to LA, you hick?"

Iris lay on the bed, smiling, happy for the diversion.

Lou plopped the computer back on Iris's lap. "Hey." She waved weakly.

"When are you back?"

"Tomorrow. I think." Iris sighed.

"I'll get you food in case you arrive late."

Iris grinned at his blue eyes. Taco's muzzle was still in the foreground, sniffing around the keyboard and blocking the rest of Chuck's face.

"Lou? Hey, Lou!" he called.

Lou turned the computer.

"Be nice to your mom."

"'K. Maybe." Laughing, she waved goodbye, then it was Iris's turn.

"Thank you for the laugh. Adios, Dos Casas. Adios, Taco. Adios, Marlboro Man. Can't wait to see you! Mean it!" And she hung up.

"Mom, I really want you to keep the estate and run it. If you don't want to do this for Gus, then do it for me and his family. They are *our* family if you think about it. They'll be grateful to you one day. I'm sure that Nico will also be happy even if he hates us now."

"How do you know that?"

"I walk in their shoes like Chuck taught me to do. It helps me understand people better like that."

"You're not angry at Gus anymore?"

"Don't know, Mom, I just don't get him. I *want* to understand."

"Understand what? We broke up. He hurt me a lot. We never saw each other again. That's all there is to it."

Lou stared into Iris's eyes. "Why don't I believe you?"

"Stop this, Lou."

Lou huffed loudly.

"Did you read his letter?" Iris said.

"Yes."

"Want to talk about it?"

"No."

"Let's go home."

"When, now?"

"Yeah, right this minute. If we leave now, we can get there just after midnight."

"Wicked! I'll tell Chuck."

CHAPTER 15

Iris drove four hours until the sun set behind the coastline mountains.

At San Luis Obispo, they stopped for a slice of fluorescent pink cake at the Madonna Inn, a favorite of theirs from past road trips.

Iris gulped some coffee and kept on driving. Lou curled up on the back seat and went to sleep.

Duty. That's the word I was looking for. Motherfucking duty. Lou was right. But then—why? Iris's sadness was giving way to resentment and anger.

Alone in the truck with her thoughts, her mind wandered.

Iris had never imagined how hard it would be to raise Lou alone. The first years of living with Delfine and Ludo in their New York apartment had been hell.

Night after night, Iris woke up crying from a nightmare. It was always the same one. In it she would run and run down interminable corridors, escaping from a black beast, a dark, shapeless mass. But her legs would not take her far, her feet would get stuck to the floor, and she would have to crawl, with every ounce of strength, drag her body away, watching over her shoulder for the beast to appear. Every night she would find herself running away from that black beast down never-ending tunnels and in the same murky rooms. Fear, pursuit, chase. Trapped. To Delfine and Ludo she explained little. All they knew was that she had come back from Paris in a terrible emotional state and that she was pregnant.

Nobody questioned anything. At times Ludo would ask her about the boyfriend she had left behind, and Iris would cut the conversation short when, unfailingly, it became about his ailing wife. As expected, all she got from Delfine was an appointment with a shrink.

Aunt Julie and Aunt Nicole had been there for her, and she visited them every week, sometimes every other day.

Ludo spent ever more hours on his terrace garden, hiding from his wife and young pregnant daughter.

Delfine sat night after night on the sofa and stared at the TV, saying little and never anything nice. One evening she turned toward Iris and said, "We ruined our careers, didn't we?"

"I'm only pregnant, Mum."

"The de Valadés always had brilliant and long careers."

"I am sorry I failed the de Valadé name. You must be so ashamed of me."

Delfine turned back toward the TV, ignoring the biting sarcasm in Iris's voice.

Iris continued. "Speaking of careers, you never told me what you thought of mine before I *ruined* it. I sent you my first big job, the Genius Factory one, I was so proud of that. I kept thinking about you while we shot. I thought to myself, *'Mummy would love this, Mummy would approve,'* but you never said anything. It was the highlight of *my* career." Tears welled up and she turned away to wipe them with her sleeve.

Iris stood up and walked into Delfine's line of vision, searching for her eyes.

Without taking her gaze off the TV, Delfine replied, "Iris, dear God, child! We must take you to the hairdresser's, we look so dowdy! And are we getting too fat?"

Iris went to her room and burst out crying on the bed.

After Lou was born, Iris snapped out of it and her survival instinct kicked in. Thanks to her aunts and her oldest cousin, Chloe, she learned how to take care of her beautiful baby, and the nightmares were soon gone. The mental exhaustion from bringing up her child in her parents' environment made her collapse in a heap every night and sleep deeply for a couple of hours before Lou woke up whimpering for milk.

Ludo had immediately fallen in love with his grandchild and liked to cradle her every evening, cooing and singing to her. Delfine only held the baby when she was asleep and her diaper was clean.

"Have patience with your mother, for my sake," Ludo would plead.

"Papa, I'm trying real hard. But why is she so mean?"

"She misses Paris, pumpkin, she misses her old job. You represented everything that she no longer was. She, your mother, had trouble with that . . . she must have felt that you were rubbing it in her face . . ."

Shocked, Iris did not reply.

A short time after her baby was born, Iris had the visceral need to make things with her hands. The feel of her baby's velvety skin made her sensitive to touch, and the scent of her hair drew her to things that were alive. It also made her want to keep away from Delfine's gloom and toxicity.

"When are we going to get a proper job? Making a living is so hard. Isn't it time that we looked for something serious? Stop messing around. You know, neither your modeling money nor your looks will last forever," Delfine would preach. *Thanks, Mum, I love you too.*

Iris had made good money during her short modeling career, and Ludo had invested it for her. With what was left, she bought a derelict loft in Chelsea near her parents' brownstone, where she moved when Lou was two.

When the weather was good, Iris would take Lou for walks around the art galleries in the neighborhood, her little girl bundled in her tiny stroller. With a diaper in one pocket of her cargo pants and a sippy cup in the other, Iris would wander for hours at a time, feeling free and at peace. She had never imagined being able to make a living as an artist, but the prospect now kept her alive and helped heal her broken self. *"It's you and me against the world,"* she would tell her baby every morning as they walked out of the house.

Having to provide for their well-being became Iris's daily battle. After Lou's birth, she never thought again about those last days in Paris, her last Gus days. She had buried those memories in a deep and dark place.

On a couple of occasions, a booker from Blitz New York had visited her, trying to convince Iris to return to work. Iris was one of the hot girls, a supermodel in the making. Paris wanted her, as did Milan and New York. When she'd run away, Iris's bookings chart had been full for the next six months. *"Burnout,"* the agency told her clients as they canceled all her jobs. Nobody questioned it; hot girls often had breakdowns and had to stop for a few months. Clients would feel important since they'd had the vision to book a girl so hot that she had collapsed from overwork, making the girl even more desirable.

"In an ashram in India. She's in a kibbutz in Israel. Gone back to Poland, father sick. Visa problems."

Iris knew girls that had ended up in mental institutions or in "mental detox," as it was called, so broken and dispirited that they'd never recover. There was a lot of collateral damage in the industry, but thousands of new girls tried their luck every year anyway.

Iris shuddered suddenly, the memories all too vivid. She looked in the rearview mirror. Lou was asleep, curled under her jacket—placid, docile, for once. *I needed to be there with her. I wanted to bring up a good person.* Her heart filled with love.

Iris focused back on the road and turned on the radio.

CHAPTER 16

The first rays of sunlight woke her. Dazed from lack of sleep, she lay in her bed, listening to Rancho Dos Casas rising. The rooster crowed, and the mustangs stirred in their corral, snorting at each other. Taco barked at the squirrels and rabbits.

She heard the front door open and close with the arrival of her cleaning lady, Sonia. *Fuck! It's Saturday already?* Iris dragged herself out of bed and went to check on Lou, finding her fast asleep.

"Lou, baby, wake up. You have to go to class."

Lou opened one eye and grumbled loudly. She covered her face with her comforter.

Iris pulled back the bedsheets. "Lou! NOW!"

Lou rolled onto the floor and crawled out of her room on all fours, her hair over her face. "Mom, *please!* I only slept four hours. Gimme a break, yo! Please, I beg you."

"I give you exactly ten minutes! Sonia's already here to drive you."

As soon as Sonia's car pulled out of the driveway, Iris lifted Gus's boxes and metal trunks out of the truck and stacked them in her hallway, not sure what to do with them. There was a knock on the front door.

"Bones?"

"Chuck! Hey! Come on in. Just made coffee."

Chuck looked her up and down and smiled.

"Yeah, sorry, superhot, right? It was a battle to get her out the door."

"I don't have lots of time, just wanted to drop in and make sure everything was okay." Chuck made his way toward the kitchen.

"Thanks for filling the fridge, deeply appreciated."

Chuck smiled his twinkly-eyed smile. "So?"

"What? You mean LA? Two words: sad and confusing. I need to think about what just happened, but one thing is sure: our lives will never be the same again."

"In a good way? Or bad?"

Iris shrugged. "Depends on the choices I make and who I'm making them for. Lou was very warm toward her LA *abuelos*, and in truth they did feel strangely like family even though I had never met them before. Anyway, it's all a mess and it brings a lot of scary new responsibilities, important decisions, and I need time to think everything through."

"Is Lou happy she went to LA? Did you two talk?"

"I think so and not enough. Whenever we disagree, she gets angry and clams up."

Chuck paced the kitchen with a coffee cup in his hands, frowning. "Do you want to discuss it later? I'm a good listener."

"Are you sure?"

"I'm happy you're back," he said.

Tell him—what are you waiting for, dingbat—tell him you're happy too.

Chuck's phone rang and he took the call in the vestibule. When he hung up, he kissed Iris on the cheek and ran to his pickup.

"Later then." He waved from his window as he drove away in a cloud of dust.

At eight thirty the house was silent. Mug in hand, Iris went into the airy studio, feeling the need to be with her sculptures.

As she sat by the carved wooden pieces, a sense of calm washed over her. A long time ago she had looked at vintage photographs of Brancusi's atelier in Paris, and the images had haunted and inspired her. Iris had tried to imagine what it would have been like to live in the midst of that beautifully arranged clutter, his forest of supernatural objects organized with care and purpose into a sacred order. What was it like to sleep in the small bunk bed by the metal chimney, or to cook on the open fire? To create with your bare hands those essential and abstract shapes of plaster, marble, and wood?

One day she had simply started. Working first on soft woods that were easy to carve and then moving on to reclaimed wood from old train tracks she had found in a lumberyard. The timber was dark brown, veiny, with a small grain and was a bitch to sculpt. From the small pieces, she had moved on to bigger ones: totems and streamlined birds made from beams recovered in industrial sites. She called that production *Brancusi Mon Amour*. She never was more at peace than in her studio, holding a piece of wood in a gloved hand, her chip-carving knife in the other, and Lou sleeping in a small bed by the tall windows.

The phone rang, startling her. Iris looked at the +44 number and did not recognize it. "Hello?"

A woman's raspy voice with a heavy British accent replied. "Good morning, my name is Amanda Greenwood, I am an editor at the *Daily Stand*, may I speak to Iris de Valadé, please?"

Iris's heart skipped a beat. *The Daily Stand?* Her skin crawled as the image of the tabloid's graphic logo and shrill vulgar headlines came to mind.

"Who is this?"

"I already said. Amanda Greenwood. I am looking for Iris de Valadé."

"This is she."

"Wonderful to speak to you, Miss de Valadé. I am sorry, is this a good time?"

A good time for what? "What do you mean?"

"A good moment to talk? I am writing a piece on the late photographer Gustavo de Santos, and I wanted to ask you some questions."

Iris heard Amanda puffing on a cigarette. "Ask *me?*"

"Well, yes, you seem to be the person closest to him at the beginning of his career. You were his muse and girlfriend, correct? I understand that he was a bit of a wild child, somewhat decadent, what? I just need to ask you a few questions about your life with him in Paris; must have been quite the 'drugs, sex, and rock 'n' roll,' what?" Amanda cackled.

"Miss Greenwood, would you please excuse me? I don't feel comfortable with this conversation. I'd rather pass on the interview. I'm sure that you can find other volunteers who will be glad to help you."

"Oh no, *no*, it is *you* we want for the interview. Our readers *adore* a good fashion story with models and photographers and whatnot. I looked at your daughter's Instagram: she *is* a beauty. Is she going to follow in your footsteps? Can I interview her too? Why did you quit modeling at such an early age?" Amanda blew smoke into the receiver.

"Miss Greenwood," Iris snapped. "Miss Greenwood, do you have children?"

"Miss de Valadé, I am *so* sorry, but I am just doing my job!" Amanda whined. "I cannot publish a detailed piece on photography's bad *bad* boy if I don't have access to all the fun saucy bits. I found paparazzi shots of the two of you out on the town through The Box online archives, but I need juicy details, you know what I mean." Another cackle.

Iris's voice was calm: "I cannot stop you from publishing those, but I have nothing to add."

"Nothing to add? Why, de Santos's agent has very *nicely* given me access to some of the early archives, and *you* are in most of those shots. I just need you to give me details about them. Anecdotes, names, you know, anything that will make for a good read."

"De Santos's agent?"

"Yes, Mr. Campisi, Clemente Campisi, in Paris."

"Miss Greenwood, Campisi is *not* Gustavo de Santos's agent, and he definitely does *not* have the permission to handle any publication of any photograph."

"Well, you sort it out with him, Miss de Valadé, because that's not what he told me! Furthermore, if you cannot help me, I will use his material. I mean, some of those photographs can be found on the internet. Therefore, I do *not* need anybody's permission to run them, but it would be brilliant to have some personal stories to go with them. Lovely chap Campisi, he has been so charming and helpful. I interviewed him already. He had a lot of interesting things to say about Gus de Santos . . . and you, of course, what?"

Stunned, Iris scrambled to think.

"How did you get my phone number?"

"Well, Campisi obviously!"

Iris was silent.

"Iris? Are you there?"

"Yes, I'm here. Miss Greenwood, this is a bad time for me to speak; can we reschedule the call?"

"Oh, so sorry again. Very good, love, this is my number. Please call me back as soon as you can. I have a *deadline*, you know? At the most I can give you five days." Amanda's tone of voice had changed to curt and annoyed. She blew smoke into the receiver for the last time and clicked off.

Iris's heart thumped. "Oh shit. Oh shit!"

She ran to her computer and logged onto the *Daily Stand*. Finding a tab called "Sunday at the Stand," she read the head-line: "Coming soon—the depraved life of photography darling Gustavo de Santos. Dead at forty-four. Did his toxic love for supermodel Iris de Valadé kill him in the end? Read it soon on the *Daily Stand Sunday*: the drugs, the parties, and the sexy pictures that made him a millionaire. By Amanda Greenwood."

She punched *"Iris de Valadé Gus de Santos"* into Google. Several grainy pictures of Gus and her coming out of a night-club popped up. She zoomed in. Her hair was knotty, her makeup smudged. Her blouse was unbuttoned, showing a breast. Gus was giving the finger to the photographer, an ugly snarl on his face. She traced the pictures to a website called Party Dirty Diaries.

"No, no, no," she said out loud, her heart racing.

Her phone rang. She took a moment to compose herself before answering; it was Matthew Cook.

"Iris, good morning. I have been trying you, but your line has been busy. It's rather urgent, I'm afraid."

"Morning, Matthew. You mean the *Daily Stand?*"

"Indeed. An editor called Amanda Greenwood rang me earlier, inquiring as to your whereabouts."

"Thank you, I just got off the phone with her. One question, Matthew: Did you contact Clemente Campisi to tell him I was in charge of the estate?"

"Good heavens, no! Why do you ask?"

"Because he's collaborating with the *Daily Stand.* Can we sue him? What about my right to privacy?"

"Iris, as much as I sympathize with the sentiment, I don't think we have grounds to bring legal proceedings at this stage. Let's see if there is any value in approaching the *Daily Stand* about not going ahead. Failing that, let's assess if we have any realistic prospect of obtaining injunctive relief. I am by no means sanguine about our chances on that score either. Above all, to have the option of suing him, we would need to be able to prove that he is the one distributing the photos on the internet. I should say that a matter like this would be messy, involve multiple jurisdictions, and would, of course, potentially be expensive. And if they have already published, the damage will largely be done. Sorry to say this."

"It will break my daughter's heart. They're going to drag our names through the mud. Amanda Greenwood made me feel so debased . . ."

Matthew was silent for a moment. "Please forgive me for being blunt, Iris. I should best warn you: if you have skeletons in the closet, you can be sure that they will find them."

"I'll go."

"I'm sorry?"

"To Paris, Matthew, I'll go."

"Splendid. How fast can you get there?"

"Give me two days."

CHAPTER 17

'Wanna go for a ride NOW?' Chuck had texted.

'YOU BETCHA!' Iris had replied.

The days before her departure had been tense and not very happy. Lou had refused to stay at Maca's and a shouting match had ensued. Lou had remained locked up in her room for the entire day.

As she rode Bandida up the woody trail toward the top of Cerro Negro, a sense of calm finally washed over her body, and she closed her eyes to take in the smells and sounds of her surroundings. Chuck cantered ahead on Fang. The air around them was scented when the horses brushed the bushes of wild thyme and rosemary on the narrow path. The horses' hooves clattered on the rocky ground. Taco panted as he trotted under her stirrup as close as he could to her, his face covered in saffron dust from digging up gopher nests.

Iris watched how loosely Chuck rode, his body swinging to his horse's gait, relaxed but aware.

Riding is like dancing, I bet he is good at that too. Chuck held a long skinny branch in one hand, and with it he caressed Fang's neck and sides, clicking his tongue as he rode. Fang's ears twitched back and forth, listening.

"Makes him less jittery. He's scared of the boulders," he had explained.

Near the top of Cerro Negro, they stopped at an abandoned farmhouse and tied the horses in the shade by the well. The afternoon was hot, and Chuck loosened the horses' girths, then emptied cold well water into their trough. They drank, making loud slurping noises that made Iris smile.

A grassy meadow full of orange poppies surrounded the sturdy stone house. On the edge where the thick oak forest started was a low wall made of black rocks. At the end of the field beyond the house was a small wooden barn and a grove with overgrown fruit trees.

"Oh my God," Iris said softly.

"You said it, Bones. I dream of moving up here for a few months every year so I can write. Soon I will."

"Won't you get lonely?"

Chuck's gaze turned away from her. "What did you decide? Does going to Paris mean you're handling the estate?" he said.

"Don't know yet, there're some issues with the will I have to resolve and . . . complicated stuff."

"You can leave Lou with me if you need to."

"Thank you, Chuck, she's being a royal pain. Her exams are coming up and I need her to be with Maca so she's close to school and to Amy. I'll be back in a few days, before her summer break."

"And if you're not? She'll get even angrier."

Iris shook her head slowly. "What's new? She's mad at me for everything these days. I told her to make her Instagram private, and she slammed her bedroom door on me. I told her I had to go to Paris, and she stopped talking to me. I told her she would stay at Maca's, and she went ballistic. I told her I was doing this for the estate, for her future, and she said, 'Whatever.' I don't know what to do. I thought this would make her happy."

"Maybe she wants to be with you in Paris?"

"I didn't think of that. Why doesn't she tell me these things?"

"I'll speak with her."

"Thanks. She listens to you."

Chuck stroked Fang's neck. Iris studied his hand on the horse's dark coat and forced herself to look away.

"We never had our talk after you came back from LA. I had to stay in the city. I'm sorry I wasn't there to help you sort things out," he said.

"It's fine, you've already done so much."

"Can I call you every now and then, just to say hi?"

"Chuck, I'm only going to Paris! It will be a week, at the most." Iris laughed.

He turned toward his horse.

"Being here these years . . . Dos Casas," Iris said, "has been a new experience. Where I come from, no one really knew what I did, where I was . . ."

"It's the Jewish mother in me, makes me want to take care of everyone."

"I'll miss you," she said quietly.

Chuck looked up as she turned away from his gaze.

Tightening Bandida's girth, she said, "I need to get home."

That evening in Maca's kitchen, Maca tied a red string around Iris's wrist.

"I'm putting a spell on this, Iris. Each knot represents a wish that will come true."

"Your wish or mine?"

"Does it matter?"

Iris shook her head wearily.

"May you travel safely," Maca said.

Knot.

"May your trip bring you success."

Knot.

"May your daughter speak to you again."

Two knots.

"May you meet a nice French lover boy and finally have an affair."

Knot.

"May you and Chuck start dating soon, for fuck's sake. Amen."

Three knots.

Iris was propped against the kitchen wall, arm outstretched in Maca's direction while she busied herself with the knots. "Anything else you haven't told me?" Maca asked.

"Apart from the fact that I am being blackmailed *and* threatened *and* about to be tabloid fodder? Heck! What else could there be? Oh yes, and I inherited my ex's estate, which everyone wants except for me. Nope, nothing else, just that."

Frowning, Iris let her body slide down the wall and sat on the floor cross-legged.

"Are you sure you want to go to Paris alone?"

"I *am* alone. I'm so frightened—"

"You frightened? You alone? That's the first time I heard you say that. Ever."

Iris choked back tears. "Gus didn't even leave me a letter. I have the feeling that he's using me to get his art back. *My art. My art. My art.* That's all that mattered to him. He obviously wanted his legacy to make him immortal at my expense. I don't even know why the fuck I'm bothering, if not for Lou. She insists I complete the archive and handle the estate. I'm so furious with Gus. I don't want this. I don't know how to do this. I don't know where to start . . ."

Her shoulders slumped, and all the air went out of her.

Maca sat by Iris on the floor and held her in her arms. "It's okay, baby, just let it all out."

Iris sobbed over her friend's shoulder. She closed her eyes. *If only I could spend the rest of my life leaning against this neck. It smells soothing, sweet. It smells of lily of the valley and bluebell.*

Iris lost the concept of time and drifted off. Then she heard the kitchen clock ticking and the sound of Maca's breathing.

"Hey, Iris? You all right there? You've been out for a while."

Iris came about, feeling drained as if awakening from a deep sleep. "Sorry. Do you have a Kleenex?" She rubbed her hand across her nose, her eyes were red and swollen. "It's all bullshit. Son of a bitch—"

"He's still under your skin *and* in your heart. You should do something about that."

"What the hell are you talking about, Maca?"

"Hey wait, let me tie another three knots on the Chuck wish, because honey pie, seriously? You need to move on from the ghost of Gus *and* you need a proper man," Maca said.

Iris snorted, trying to laugh. "You're exhausting."

"Girl! I mean it. You better get your act together with Chuck because I know a lot of the ladies out there are crazy for him, and you know men. They can't be alone for too long, specially a handsome and successful one like him; oh, and did I say nice?"

"Great, thanks for the nonpressure, Maca. But honestly, that's the last thing on my mind right now."

"You're still messed up that bad?"

"Yeah."

"It haunts you?"

"Yep."

"Well, whatever. Let it all out of your system. It's time to move on and get a life, honey buns. Do whatever you have to do in Paris, or try at least, will you? And then come back and get a nice fellow by your side who will protect you, keep you company, and help you take care of Lou. I think she needs a dad figure and all the rest."

"Men? Look who's talking!"

"Well, I have big news for you! You missed out on all the fun while you were in LA: Toby and I are dating again. Perfect arrangement. We live in separate houses but see each other every evening, could not be better. The kids are thrilled to have their dad back, but I don't have to put up with him twenty-four-seven. Oh, and the sex? Terrific. We're at it like rabbits. It's an ex-husband with benefits."

Iris winced.

Maca continued. "Can't wait to get you back here after Paris. We're gonna put you in a skirt, heels, lingerie, loads of bling to make you shine, and makeup, lots of makeup. Turn you into a boudoir goddess and we're gonna find you a good man.

"I wanna see you swiping left and right on Hinge, Match, Tinder, JDate, Latin American Cupid, Black Cupid, Asian Date . . . all of them, you're joining every single effin dating site we can find. There's a book club in La Arboleda. That too, you're going to join. No, wait, the dads are at soccer, baseball, basketball . . . Lou will have to get on the teams . . . get her out of the science lab and onto the grass and we follow with the coolers, food, and folding chairs. There're a couple of nice divorced dads hanging out on the fields. *Those* are the ones you're targeting. Even the one with the ponytail who drives a Hummer, Paul whatshisname?"

Iris cringed and rolled her eyes. "Suddenly, spinsterhood isn't looking so bad."

Maca chuckled. "Lou will help me set up your profile, and we'll write the text. She'll take pretty pictures of you looking docile, nothing weird or scary. No pictures with dogs, and cats are even worse. Hobbies? Dunno . . . baking? Gardening? Charity? Art? Men love food and women that paint. And no more Gus excuses. Girl, your life is about to begin."

"Yeah, right, dismally," Iris replied. "Like in my worst kind of nightmare."

CHAPTER 18

Iris woke up, startled by the flight attendant nudging her shoulder. "Seat belts, please."

"Are we nearly there?" she asked.

The flight attendant shook her head. "Three hours to go and it's going to get bumpy."

Iris moaned. *Three more hours of this torture? And with the seat belt sign on?*

The plane bobbed up and down and lurched from side to side. Iris was sick to her stomach, not sure if it was fear or motion sickness.

The plane stopped rattling, and after watching an episode of *Veep*, she began to feel drowsy.

She stood up, needing to relieve her cramped legs. She stretched her arms and folded her body over to touch her toes. *Who do they make these coach seats for? Children? They should have a warning: tall people, keep the fuck away. How can anyone over five foot five sit for eleven hours without going insane and dying?*

Iris looked out of the window into the inky blackness. Yawning, she returned to her seat.

It was six in the morning when her taxi stopped at the corner of the place du Marché Sainte-Catherine and rue d'Ormesson.

Iris unloaded her bags and, finding a bench by the square, sat down to kill time.

In a sleepy daze, she observed a street sweeper with his bright overalls and green plastic broom laying an old piece of carpet on the water outlet and starting the process of cleaning the street into the gutter drain.

"*Bonjour, monsieur,*" she said with a smile.

"*B'jour, mamzelle.*" He nodded at her, focusing on his bits of wet carpet.

The day dawned cloudless. A nightingale began to sing in one of the mulberry trees on the square. Iris's eyes were closing, and she pinched herself to stay awake. The square smelled of wet leaves, damp cobbles, and coffee. *I am going to faint right now. Please, someone give me a coffee IV, please?* Iris crossed the small square and sat on the bench facing the entrance to Joan's flat.

CHAPTER 19

I sat on that bench the first time. The first time that Gus kissed me. I had let him walk me home that night. We hadn't spoken for a week after the Genius Factory shoot.

Eva had left me a message: "Oi! You! It's me with Gus and the team. We're working on the dummy for a new mag. It's gonna be groovy. We're thinking that you'd be perfect for the beauty story. You'll have some clothes on this time. You in, luv?"

A couple of days later we're shooting in a small place near République. Eva, Toshi, and Satoshi are in the makeup room. Toshi pulls my hair into a tight chignon, and Satoshi paints scarlet lips on me so thick and glossy that they drip. I have heavy, smoky-blue eyeshadow, fake eyelashes, and long red talons. A fur coat draped on my shoulders partly covers my naked body, a pearl choker adorns my neck.

"You're done, luv. Gorgeous sexy beast, off you go! Work it like an expensive Monaco hooker in the Casino de Paris," Eva instructs me.

"I thought you said I would have clothes on this time."

"Here, put these on." Smiling wickedly, Eva hands me a pair of black silk panties trimmed with pearly lace. They're the size of a matchbox. "Sabbia Rosa, darling, made to measure."

"Why do I need couture knickers if no one can see them under this thing?" I ask, pointing to the black coat.

"You're an upscale harlot, remember? An expensive woman few men can afford. We'll guess you are naked underneath, but how can you even think sexy in a pair of grotty cotton Marks and Sparks?" Eva says laughing, while she swings my nunlike undies around her index finger.

Gus walks into the room with his assistant, Cyril.

I feel beautiful and seductive. Swinging my hips with my hands on my waist, I stride toward Gus in impossibly high fuck-me pumps, while the team waits for his approval.

I cannot look him in the eye. My heart beats so loudly I know he can hear it thump. His fingers touch my collarbone as they adjust my necklace, lingering, but just for a second. *You look beautiful,* his eyes say. I close mine, pretending the glare is hurting them, and feel myself blush. Gus turns away.

That night after the shoot, we sit on the bench facing Joan's door. I know she's still up, and I don't want her to see me come in, my face is so easy to read. Gus's thigh presses against mine and I shiver.

"Are you cold?" he asks.

"Yes, very."

He puts his arm around my shoulders and turns me softly. With the tip of his index finger he touches my lips and draws a line around my eyebrows. The air smells of rain and dead leaves. The last customers leave Chez Josephine and hurry across the square, eager to get away from the cold. Their footsteps get fainter and we are alone on that bench.

"Can I kiss you?" he asks.

I look at his mouth so close to mine and, parting my lips, I cover his. I shut my eyes and he holds my face, his fingers entangled in my hair. He presses my back, and my breasts crush against his chest. We do not move. I feel his breath heavy in my ear, and the pounding of my heart.

"Mi niñita Iris," he whispers.

Joan's flat goes dark. "I have to leave," I say, tearing myself from his embrace.

He takes me to the door and holds my chin in his hand. I look at his eyes; they are very somber. I turn away from his gaze and open the door.

"When can I see you again?" he says as the door closes.

I think of Cristina Fanna's words and do not answer.

CHAPTER 20

Beautiful, chic models come in and out of the offices of Sonia Rykiel. I go through with the casting even though I don't think I'm what they're looking for. To kill time, I wander through the store and take in the playful Frenchness of the brand. When it's my turn, I put on a colorful tricot jumpsuit and walk out in my bare feet to face the designer and a room full of people.

An army of atelier assistants descends on me, and they deck me out in a pair of eight-inch Mary Janes, a floppy beret, a clutch bag, and a pile of custom jewelry. I stare at myself in the long mirror and feel their eyes on me. The jumpsuit makes a long graphic line. *I need to break this up.*

Tucking the clutch under my arm, I shove my hands deep into the pockets and spin slowly on my toes, my eyes never leaving those of Madame Rykiel. I walk away from her and hold the pose.

Thinking of Helmut Newton's models, I cave my chest into my shoulders to give my body shape, to disrupt that line. Madame walks toward me and says, *"Enlevez-moi tout ça."*

The swarm of assistants descends on me again, and they remove the beret, clutch bag, jewelry, and shoes.

"Iris, put your own boots on," Madame says.

I lace up my black riding boots and cuff the jumpsuit to just below my knees. I unbutton the tight sleeves and roll them above my elbows. Madame lights a cigarette and gives it to me.

Posing in front of the mirror, I scrunch up my hair and make it messy, tucking one side behind my ear while the other covers my eye. I lift my chin. I hold the cigarette in the corner of my lips.

"Don't move, Iris. Polaroid, please?"

An assistant takes several Polaroids, and Madame points at me.

"Voilà. This is what I want; *La Nouvelle Parisienne* need not be festooned like a Christmas tree with all that frippery. Call her agency. Iris, send my *bonjour* to your lovely mother, Delfine. *Elle va bien?*"

I leave happy. I call my booker, Magali. "Am I done for today?"

Magali is excited. "The Rykiel office just called. Madame loves you. She said you brought a new air to their *Parisienne*, an air of . . . ?"

"Orgies, pills, and rock 'n' roll? Louche Saint-Germain? Existential Slut?" I say, and we both laugh, feeling silly.

"Magali, that was wack. I thought I was at the wrong bloody casting, man. Did they option me for the job?"

"Oh *oui*! You're optioned! Hopefully they confirm? *On verra.* That's it for today. No more go-sees, enjoy the rest of your Friday. I'll fax you next week's schedule. *À lundi!*"

It starts to drizzle, and the sky is gray and low. I cross boulevard Saint-Germain and go into the Café de Flore, eager for a hot chocolate out of the cold. I ignore the outdoor *terrasse* full of tourists and showy types and head straight to the main room. At the door, the maître d' greets me warmly. "Oh, Miss Iris, what a pleasure to see you. You never come to visit me anymore. You break my heart."

I hug Francis and say, "But Monsieur Boussard, I live in le Marais now, le Flore is far for me and too expensive. When my father picked up the bill . . . *helás*! Now I have to work hard to pay for your *chocolat chaud*. The most expensive *and* delicious in Paris."

Francis guffaws and takes me to Marie Laure sitting in the cashier's booth by the stairs. "*Regardez qui est lá!* Look who is here!" he tells Marie Laure.

"*Ça va, ma petite Iris? Ça caille, quel horreur.* It's *freezing.*"

I kiss her warmly on both cheeks, happy to be in the company of the nice people that my father loved.

"*La banquette au fond comme d'habitude?* Bench at the back as usual?" Francis asks.

"*Oui, merci, Francis.*"

I follow Francis through the crowded room, and he seats me at my father's favorite table in the corner. From here I can study the place, away from the clanging of the cramped kitchen.

"That is Simone de Beauvoir's seat," Papa would tell me unfailingly on each visit, "and that was Jean-Paul Sartre's, and over there was Picasso's. A lady could leave her husband reading the newspaper at les Deux Magots and cross the street to meet her lover at Café de Flore, and the husband would never find out."

I loved listening to my father talking about our neighborhood, of the revolutionary thinkers and artists who were the bad boys and girls of Saint-Germain. Postwar stories of Miss Vice and Miss Dumpster in the cellars full of bebop, the feeling of freedom was pure joy and life. Pale girls dressed in black carried white mice on their shoulders and spent their nights in those *caves* of jazz. I imagine myself as Juliette Gréco meeting Miles Davis when I was twenty-two. I love Miles and he loves me. I sing poems about love and kissing. I fantasize of le Tabou club and the muses of the Left Bank. I read Françoise Sagan and dream of being an existentialist.

I see Gus looking at me from across the room, and my heart stops. He smiles. The man he's talking to turns around to look in my direction. He's wearing purple Ray-Bans in the dimly lit room.

I drink my *chocolat chaud* and feel a longing for those moments with my father. It has stopped raining and I want to go walk in a garden. As I pay, I stop to say goodbye to Francis and Marie Laure.

"We miss your father, he is a *real* gentleman, always a kind word. When is Monsieur Ludo coming back? And your mother? Send your parents our regards and come back soon. *Tu me le promets*, Iris?"

I am moved by their sincerity and warmth.

"Iris! Iris?" I turn to see Gus walking toward me. My heart is thumping and I cannot breathe. He slings a leather backpack over his shoulder. His black boots are muddy and wet and so is his tan raincoat. A paperback sticks out of the knapsack pocket.

"Where you going, *chiquita?*"

"To the Luxembourg gardens."

"I live near there, it's on my way. I'll walk with you."

"Sure," I say with a shrug.

We walk through the maze of tiny streets that lead to the square of the Saint-Sulpice church. We do not talk.

The afternoon is damp, there are few people on the streets. Gus stops by the massive fountain in the middle of the square. We watch four dogs play ball and chase gray pigeons. A Labrador jumps into the water and we laugh. The square is less formal, more beaten up than other tourist haunts in Paris. The imposing church seems out of proportion.

"I'm going in," he says, pointing at the church with his chin.

Saint-Sulpice is dark, sepulchral. Gus lights a candle in front of the statue of Mary. He opens his shirt and pulls out the silver medal that hangs around his neck. He kisses it and tucks it back. His eyes are closed.

I look at his long hair against his strong chin, and the way his lips move when he prays. He gazes at me, his eyes full of longing and sadness.

We head down rue Ferou and stop in front of Man Ray's studio at number two. Opposite is a tiny street, rue du Canivet. "That's where I live," he says.

We continue on rue Ferou and pass number six. Gus points to the apartment of Ernest Hemingway in a building that has a colossal door framed by two sculptures of crouching sphinxes, their long tails wrapped around their haunches like ropes. Farther down, Gus points out the home of Athos, one of the Three Musketeers. We stand in the middle of the narrow cobbled street. He grabs the camera from around his neck and shoots the sphinx silhouetted against the stormy sky. A single ray of sunshine pierces the soupy clouds, a slab of liquid yellow shimmer.

I gasp. Gus turns to me and takes my picture. I laugh self-consciously. "My mouth was open!"

"You're so expressive, *niñita*, and complex. One minute you're cool and detached, and then you're a kid, an innocent little thing, a grown-up child who talks like an adult. You're a girl that looks like a boy that looks like a girl. My buddy with breasts. I can see you thinking all the time. I can't stop looking at you. I'm fascinated by the nuance."

I blush and turn away.

I walk slowly ahead of him and hear his camera clicking every now and then. His footsteps stop echoing against the walls of the narrow street, and I turn to see that he's standing in front of the windows of a printer's shop.

"Iris, quick! Look at this poster. She kind of looks like you!"

I see a young Patti Smith in a leather bomber jacket with army cargos falling off her hips. Her face is beautiful under the brutal light. "It's by a photographer called Lynn Goldsmith. My mother did a fashion story called 'Muses' around the New York art scene in the seventies, and she used that as a style reference. I have stared at that picture for years," I say.

Gus looks at me, his eyes full of admiration. "You are so right, *chiquita*! Is the poster for sale?"

We peer through the windows looking for someone, but the shop is empty and locked up. We continue to walk aimlessly toward the gardens, and I am aware of Gus's body near mine. "Eva just told me your mom is Delfine de Valadé, *the* Delfine de Valadé. It hadn't clicked until now."

"You know her?"

"Who doesn't? I mean, not personally, but she turned *Revue* into the coolest magazine in the industry. That's the reason I came to Paris. When I was a student at Parsons, all I did was dream about shooting stories for *Revue* in Paris. All these guys, the big photographers, owe their careers to her. She was the first to book David King, Antonio Sanchez, Lucas Walker . . . and the supermodels? She *made* Lily, Cassia, Yaya, Celia, and Ann-Margret, to name but a few. It's a pity she left Paris."

"She didn't leave, they removed her to New York against her wishes. Her boss didn't have the balls to fire her because it would have looked bad for the magazine. They hoped she'd quit. It's all over for her now."

Gus stops and gazes into my eyes. His are troubled.

I feel proud of my mother, and I want to call her and speak to her. But I know that I won't be able to make that call, and I'm not sure why.

We walk in silence and cross rue de Vaugirard into the Luxembourg gardens. I take a deep breath and exhale slowly. I need to release sad memories.

We walk by the foreign men playing chess; their eyes are intense, and they smoke strong cigarettes with no filters. We take a left toward the *orangerie* greenhouses and peer through the glass doors at the soaring potted palm and lemon trees that are stored for the winter.

"Why did you become a fashion photographer?" I say.

"I'm not just a fashion photographer, *chiquita*. Fashion magazines are a pretext to do images with lots of freedom and get them published, put them in your portfolio, and eventually make the bucks doing advertising jobs," Gus says.

"I didn't know you shot other things."

Gus stops again. "Fashion is a language. With magazines I can express my point of view, make statements about women and what I believe in. Fashion photography is my creative path. A great fashion picture is a feeling with a fantastic girl.

It's about creating dreams. But it's important to know what you stand for. Otherwise you're just shooting girls in dresses."

After a long silence I turn to him and ask, "And what do *you* stand for? What is your point of view?"

"And why do *you* model?" he replies. "You don't model like other girls, there's art and passion in what you do, and a respect for everyone's job. You're obviously not doing it because you want to wear expensive clothes and get all dolled up in high heels."

I look down at my scruffy leather pants and nylon flight jacket and laugh with him.

"But I love fashion!" I reply. "I mean, I don't go all mental over a pair of shoes, but fashion and clothing are immediate, they're about self-identity, about who you want to be. Fashion is a reflection of the way we live. I'm not a fashion freak like my mother was. She played up the dream element and the aspirational side, the exclusivity of it. I'm not interested in that."

I stop walking and turn to face Gus. "For me, being a fashion model is about *being* different characters and understanding the clothes and the mind of the designer or photographer. It's my way of participating in the creation of something, whether it's at a shoot or a fashion show."

I start to walk again as I speak. "To make it even simpler: I styled my plain and very single cousin and took her shopping for pretty clothes. That evening she scored and got laid."

Gus smiles.

"You can dress like what you are, or you can dress like who you want to be. That's why I think fashion is important. Your turn now." I glance at him.

"I don't want to turn women into sex-crazed vamps panting over a perfume bottle. I despise that. I don't want to work on the lightweight, the forgettable. I want to make beautiful images of strong and powerful women who don't need to reveal skin to feel sexy. Women should not need to show off and flaunt their femininity. That's what I believe in, what I want to prove through my images, ¿entiendes?"

I nod, reflecting on his words, as we continue down the unpaved lane. I face him as he speaks.

"My mother is a beautiful, strong woman who made herself look sensual and feminine for my father with what little she could afford. She made him happy that way, she even taught me how to make my own clothes. I can sew, you know?" Gus glances at me. "My mother always had flowers in her hair, in our house. Her grace, her modesty, her posture, her mystery . . . it's the attitude that counts. My mother is my favorite subject. I never tire of shooting her, or my aunts. I love shooting withered faces that have *duende*: passion, emotion, soul . . . those are the women I shoot for and the women I want to show in my images. You're either sexy or you're not. It doesn't matter how much skin you show. You can walk around with half your ass hanging out of your dress, but that doesn't make you sexy."

I chuckle.

"I also want to make images that kids will want to stick on their fridges. Images that will stay on after I'm gone."

He looks at me with burning eyes. I understand legacy, I get his obsession.

"I want to earn enough money to help my family. But I'm never going to stop doing my art photography, my portraits, my still lifes, the reportage—I have to work hard, improve my printing, shoot and shoot and never stop shooting. And one day I'll get a good gallery and I'll sell my prints, that's my dream. All this could take a long time. I'm not in a hurry, but I have to support myself here and help support my family in LA, *chiquita*."

We walk across the esplanade, and the yellow sandy earth is compact under our feet. The wind has risen. We pass a group of ponies being led to their stables. Their coats are long and shaggy, and the wind blows their manes. Gus takes pictures of their hooves as they approach. The groom has big, veiny hands, and Gus shoots close-ups of them holding the thick ropes.

I watch his tall silhouette crouching near the ground. His black hair whips around like the ponies' manes, and he squints to protect his eyes. We walk past baroque vases made of gray stone, filled with trailing chrysanthemums that look like auburn beards flying in the gusts of cold air. I stand beneath the mantle of flowers, laughing.

"Don't move," Gus says.

He points his camera at me. I catch his eye and stop laughing, turning my head as the blooms cascade down like an extension of my hair. I hear his camera clicking furiously while he hovers around me, shooting from every angle. I unbutton my white shirt and bare my neck and chest; my fingers brush my exposed skin. Gus comes so close to me that I can hear him breathe. He never stops shooting.

"Cover up, *chiquita*, the *gendarmes* are coming."

We laugh and I button up as a couple of policemen stroll past, looking stern. Or maybe they are just chilled to the bone.

We go sit on the green metal chairs arranged in a circle around the pond. The metal is cold, and I shiver. I point to the man with the toy sailing boats for rent. "My father used to bring me here every Saturday after brunch at le Flore. It was our routine. My mother would be at the Carita salon, having a facial and her hair and nails done while I got to hang out with my father. *Mille feuilles* and *chocolat chaud* at le Flore, and then the jardin du Luxembourg to run around the pond playing with the sailboats while he read *Le Monde*."

Gus laughs. "Seems you had a great childhood, and I'm not being sarcastic."

"I lacked nothing material, but . . ." My body tenses up, and I wrap my arms around my legs to hide my clenched fists from Gus.

Gus draws his metal chair closer to mine and looks at me. "Call them, tell them you love them. Tell them to come visit you. I wish mine would come, but they can't."

I shrug and pretend not to care, but I do. It's been so long that I'm kind of used to it. I don't feel sorry for myself, but I am lonely.

Gus sees my dark mood and wraps his arms around me. "I know who you are," he whispers in my ear.

I am enveloped in his arms, and I don't feel alone anymore. My eyes are closed. I lean my head on his neck, and his hand caresses my cheek so gently I think it's the breeze. This is where I want to be, in his neck, on his shoulder. I can smell his shirt. It smells of sandalwood and his leather backpack.

It starts to rain.

Gus pulls me up from the chair and holds my hand while we run across the garden. The sky has turned black, and a blast of thunder crashes above us. The rain is now a curtain of water, and I can hardly see my way through the puddles.

We run down rue Ferou, and Gus pulls me toward rue du Canivet. We go through a massive wooden door and enter a small courtyard. I follow him into a doorway on the ground floor, and a pool forms at our feet while he fumbles with the key. We laugh and shake our wet hair, and drops fly everywhere as we step in.

I stand shivering by his door. Gus takes off my jacket and hands me a thick robe. I look for a place to change, but I am in a big open room with a bed in a corner. Gus closes the shutters and turns a radiator on.

He goes to the tiny kitchen and puts a kettle on the gas burner. He busies himself making a tray with two mugs, spoons, and a jar of honey. I undress under his robe, then spread my soaking clothes out on the radiator.

Thunder and lightning rip the skies apart, and I see the flashes through the wooden shutters of the small studio. The robe is soft and thick and smells of clean skin. I pad around the room in my socks and notice the height of the brick ceilings and the dark wooden beams above my head. The stone floor is partly covered by exotic patterned rugs that are bright and cheerful. I touch one with my toe.

"Those are from Mexico, from Zapotec," he says.

Stacks of illustrated photography books are used as low tables, and they occupy every inch of the small space. There are hundreds of them, some look very old.

An entire wall of the studio is covered with pages torn from magazines. Black felt hats, silk scarves, long satin ribbons, drawings, and four large black-and-white prints cover the other wall. Long hairpieces hang from hooks. In a corner is a metal table stand containing cameras, lights, and leads. Next to it, a wooden desk neatly arranged with white drawing paper, loose pieces of black charcoal in a box, and ink calligraphy pens jammed into an elegant ceramic vase. A sense of rigor permeates the space. A worn-down guitar with a broken string is propped against a wall.

"What a special place . . . and the ceilings!"

"It was d'Artagnan's stable, remember I showed you Athos's house on rue Ferou? It's funky, a bit dark, it's small, but it's home. On Saturday afternoons I have to close the shutters because guided tours from Japan stop here, and the history freaks peer through the window taking pictures."

I laugh.

"And those?" I say, pointing at his walls.

"Props and stuff I use on shoots. Tear sheets that inspire me, my mood board, my last proofs . . ."

I get closer to the unframed prints on the wall. A scruffy dog in a fake fur coat sits on a bench in a square. A couple walk by the Seine embankment, their heads down and their stride wide, wind-blown leaves fluttering around them. A black cat, burning candles, plastic blooms, and a boom box on Jim Morrison's tombstone in the Père-Lachaise cemetery. A nude, her back turned to the camera, sits on the barren floor of a seamless studio. I recognize myself.

Gus comes next to me and hands me a mug of tea. "Can I shoot you? Just as you are, in the robe and socks."

I say nothing and nod. I feel desired and no longer shy. I sit cross-legged on the bed, holding his gaze. Mine is brazen and defying. I am enveloped in the soft robe.

Gus takes his camera and shoots me looking up at him through my wet bangs and steam from the mug. I smile conspiratorially. I put the mug down and lean my hands on the bed, squaring my shoulders and raising my chin. *I know you want me.* I tilt my head, my hair cascades down my shoulder. Gus bends over to push it behind my neck, and his hand grazes my cheek. My robe falls open and he catches his breath.

"You must go now, please," he says.

I look at his eyes and they are very dark again. He fixes me with his gaze. "If you stay, I will hurt you, *chiquita*; we'll make love and then we'll suffer."

"I want to stay," I say.

"I am bad for you."

"I don't care."

He groans and turns away from me. He gathers my clothes and hands them to me. "Go. Please go."

"No."

He kneels on the floor and kisses me on the rumpled bed. My body goes limp, and his lips crush my mouth. He licks the lobe of my ear and buries his nose in my hair. His hand is inside the robe and finds my breast. With his other hand, he presses my back against his chest.

His hands are strong yet nervous, he caresses my skin gently. His lips travel down my neck to my nipple. His palm pushes my breast to his mouth and he gently cradles its roundness while licking the tip.

He pushes me away and jumps to his feet.

"Stop! I'm going crazy," he moans under his breath. "I'll call you a taxi. Do you need money? Here, take this," he says hoarsely, shoving a crumpled bill in my hand.

I am dazed. I put my damp clothes on and walk out of the door without turning back. I go home to Joan's empty flat and lock myself in my room.

CHAPTER 21

For days on end I think of nothing else except seeing Gus. I do a frantic succession of go-sees and shoots. I accept every job that Magali throws at me. Fall will soon turn to winter, and the days are short, the nights long.

One rainy Sunday afternoon, I aimlessly pad around Joan's kitchen. I call my parents and ask them to come visit me. I tell Delfine that I miss her, but she changes the subject and gets Ludo on the phone. I hear opera music in the background. Joan leaves the room, pretending not to listen to my phone conversation.

"I am so homesick, Papa, it's been since the summer. Are you coming to visit?"

"Your mother is not well, pumpkin. I don't think I can leave."

"Thanksgiving's coming up, I can take a few days off. What's wrong with Mum? Can you talk?"

"Not really. Did you call Aunt Clotilde?"

"Yeah, a week ago . . . not very helpful as usual. Want to call me from the office tomorrow?"

"Yes, munchkin. I love you. Send all my best to Joan, will you?"

"I love you too, Papa. I love you more than cake."

Ludo chuckles and hangs up.

Joan comes back into the kitchen and looks at my face. "Bad?" she asks.

I tell her about my call, and she embraces me. Sacrificing family life in order to further her career, at thirty-six she has become the fashion director of *Revue* and a force to be reckoned with. Dedicated, hardworking, and a fervent supporter of fashion and its people, Joan is my mentor and inspiration and the sanest person I know in the business. She is everything to me that Delfine is not.

"You look so thin. Have you lost weight, *bébé*?"

I shrug. "I run around all day, don't have time to eat."

"You must eat properly, Iris. You look sick. Your parents will accuse me of child neglect."

"I'll eat, I promise."

Joan scrutinizes me. "This is kind of inappropriate, but even if I got your skinny, I'd be tits on ribs. What can I do about this pair? I'll never be able to wear Margiela!"

I laugh and look at her. She looks feminine and womanly in her tight Alexander McQueen pantsuit, all curves and tight buttons and plunging neckline. Her chestnut hair is slicked back and parted in the middle, gathered at the nape of her neck in a tight bun. She is impeccably made up.

"No, seriously, Iris, you're working so hard; I never see you these days. Anything fun, *oui*?"

"Yeah, I shot for *Guru* with Thomas Bailey. He was so difficult to work with, Joan. He chain-smokes, grumbles, snarls at his assistants, he doesn't give directions either, so you don't know if he hates you or loves you."

"With Thomas Bailey? Iris, that's huge! I'm so proud of you! You're a star, *bébé*!"

"The clothes were amazing: oversized men's suits with no shirts, tailored, sexy, at least my kind of sexy. Simple gray backdrop, a brutal light, no wind machine . . . it inspired me because it was down to the basics, lo-fi, not overproduced like a lot of others. I studied the book you have on his album covers and copied some poses. Did my homework."

I open the fridge and scan the near-empty shelves. I take out a yogurt. I put three spoons of raspberry jam in it. "Oh, and I did a casting for a Guerlain perfume and a go-see at Balenciaga for a campaign that will only run in airports in Asia, but it's a start. I also did a shoot for a magazine dummy with Gus de Santos and Eva Loom. Those were the good ones; the rest were pretty middle-of-the-road, lots of catalog work, mainly. The Genius Factory campaign doesn't come out until the new campaign season in January, but it might be the one that lands me major bookings, and hopefully some good shows."

"Can't wait to see it, Gus is so talented. He's on his way to becoming very big. If only we could book him more! He's never available, it drives Ada mad."

I wince at the mention of Ada's name. "Maybe she should back off," I blurt out.

"What do you mean? Did Gus say anything about Ada?"

"No, it's just a thought," I say vaguely. "I saw his personal work, his artwork. Maybe he's concentrating on that?"

Joan puts a spoon of Lapsang souchong tea in a pot and pours hot water over it. She sits at the kitchen table across from me. I breathe in the fragrance. "It's a careful balance for a photographer, to combine the personal work with the fashion commissions and bread-and-butter advertising shoots. They are taught at art school that photography is an art, not something you do to sell anything. If you shoot for advertising and fashion, the art world doesn't take you seriously, and yet you need the money and the outlets. It drives a lot of them to stop, or they become unhinged, or they do crazy things." Joan picks up her teaspoon and looks at me with a serious expression on her face. "Until Gus gets a sponsor, or a gallery, he's going to need the fashion and advertising industry, so he better wise up and shoot for us as much as he can. *Revue* allows him to do pretty much what he wants. No other magazine gives him that much freedom. It's all about building industry relationships. And using your fear."

Joan's phone starts ringing, and she leaves the room.

Using your fear? What exactly did she mean by that? I make a mental note to ask her. It sounds troubling.

Outside, the rain has started again, and I focus on a dead leaf stuck to the windowpane. There's a smudge of red lipstick on Joan's teacup.

She comes back to the kitchen. "Coincidentally we've just booked Gus on a big shoot with Eva. It should be up his alley. I want to do a fashion story on minimalism and Gothic romance. I want this story to be about new fashion: fresh and white and feminine with lots of unstructured clothes from the Antwerp lot, clothes that swathe and swaddle the body. Adios, recession and *No Future*. I see it in black and white, stark and severe but sensual. Maybe we find a barren field. Nature and urban clothes for strong modern women who want to feel sexy without having to show their breasts. Women dressing for other women, not for men. Textures, many textures, plowed earth, rocks, old stone walls, leafless trees, thick linens, shiny cottons, parachute silks." Joan takes a sip of her tea. "They wear heavy black boots, like the Australian ones you wear. Girls with dresses and blouses that flow in the wind and disheveled hair, beautiful pale skin, simple but strong, extreme beauty."

Joan's hands flutter as she talks. I notice her scarlet nails and the gold bangles that tinkle on her wrists.

"Joan, you sounded like Delfine! She was the best at creating an atmosphere, like a living, talking mood board. *'It's about red,'* or *'It's about Jimi Hendrix,'* or *'It's about brutalism,'* and off she would go . . . Delfine could create a whole world from that one word. I totally see what you mean. I love the feel of it."

"Your mother taught me everything, Iris. She is unique *dans son genre*, one of a kind, an icon. I wish she was still at *Revue*. People respected her vision, the way she smashed boundaries. I have to fight so hard to get my ideas through and not have them watered down just to please the advertisers: *'Show the clothes better,' 'Needs prettier girls,' 'We want total looks,' 'Do not mix our runway looks with the other designer's,' 'This looks too extreme, dial it back.'* Advertisers are beginning to have so much say, especially after the recession. They need to feel safe and reassured. It wasn't this bad before, and I think it's going to get even worse.

"I told Gus that I wanted to book you on this job, and he agreed. It will be you and Saskia Jensen. You both look heroic, cerebral, assertive, ferocious. If I see another piercing or flannel shirt, I'll scream."

That night I cannot sleep.

CHAPTER 22

Ludo calls me as promised and says, "Your mother, she's not doing good, princess, she's very depressed. She doesn't want to see anybody. I can't remember the last time she visited her family. I called Uncle Emile in Lectoure and asked him to invite her over for a few days, told her she should visit Paris and see you. But she'll hear nothing of it. Any mention of France is a rotund *NON*."

"Is she seeing a doctor?"

"No. She refuses."

"I'm so sad, Papa."

"I'm heartbroken for us. For you and for me. I cannot leave her alone, though, not for now. But I do want to see you, princess."

"I'll come for Christmas. I'll tell the agency to clear those days for me."

I call Aunt Clotilde in Lectoure.

"Daaaaaaarling Iris, how *are* you in Paris? We must be getting dreadfully cold, *noooon?*"

Aunt Clotilde has the annoying habit of going all posh when she speaks to me, dragging her vowels and speaking in the third person just like Delfine now did. *We? She's there alone with her fucking cats, for fuck's sake.*

I ignore her question. "Tante Clotilde, I need to speak to you about my mother. Papa just called me, and she's not well."

"Oh dear, oh dear. And what is her problem *now?* We love our dear sister, but lately she has become *sooooo* needy."

Needy?! I am seething but contain myself. "Tante Clotilde, I really think you should go visit her in New York. You could go with Oncle Emile. She's too sick to come to you in France."

"Oh, Iris, this is *suuuuch* an inconvenient time. We are so busy, and you know, Oncle Emile runs a business. And what will we do with the cats? I cannot leave them alone. When you say 'too sick,' you mean her nerves again, *n'est ce pas?*"

You horrible, wretched witch, I think to myself. *You're always busy, and Uncle Emile is always busy. Your kids are in boarding school, Uncle has a hundred employees, you have a dame de compagnie—a paid companion, and neither of you can leave Lectoure for one week to visit your ailing sister?*

"Iriiiiiiis? Helloooooooooo? We will give Delfine a little tinkle on the phone. That will cheer her up. And what are we doing for Thanksgiving? Are we eating the turkey in Paris?"

She obviously does *not* want me to come down for *la Toussaint* holiday, and I ignore her question.

"Lovely speaking to you," I tell her, knowing that she will not get the sarcasm, "and please send my best to Cousin Eric."

I put down the phone feeling lonelier than ever.

CHAPTER 23

I stomp up and down the dirt road arm in arm with the diaphanous and striking Saskia Jensen, a tall Dutch model with transparent freckled skin, pink lips, slanted gray-green eyes, and platinum hair. Saskia and I had bonded at the Guerlain casting, and we have become inseparable.

The white Ann Demeulemeester dress I wear has long skinny ribbons that tie loosely and catch the wind as I walk. Saskia wears the same dress in black, and the draped neckline falls off one shoulder, revealing a lot of pale skin. Eva calls us "Black & White" like the terriers in the Scotch whisky ads, and if it wasn't so cold, I would think it was funny.

We move quickly in spite of the slippery frosted ground that crunches under our boots. Every time we stop and turn around to face Gus's camera, Eva, Toshi, and Satoshi immediately descend on us to adjust the dresses and retouch our hair and makeup.

Gus shouts at them impatiently, "Quick! You're in the frame. I'm losing light fast. Get out, looks fine."

Saskia and I walk toward him a hundred times until he finally says, "Next!"

Satoshi runs to us with blankets to shield us from the bone-chilling wind as we walk to the motor home for a change of clothes. I am so cold that I can no longer feel my hands or feet. I look at Saskia and we laugh because our noses have turned red.

"*Stront,*" Saskia says.

"Yeah, that's right, Saskia, *merde*. And soon we'll look like frozen *merdes*."

We are in the fields that belong to a grand castle twenty miles outside Paris. The grounds are enclosed within an ancient stone wall that runs the length of the vast property. There are many barns, and a network of animal paths and unpaved roads crisscrosses the property. We are lucky with the weather, and the sky is blue and clear. It could always be worse: it could also rain.

Saskia drinks vodka out of a metal flask and offers me a swig. Her eyebrows and lashes are white, and she has an unhinged look in her hooded eyes that makes me grin. The alcohol burns my throat and feels warm in my gut.

In the motor home, I step into my next outfit.

I study my reflection in a mirrored wall and play with the pockets and sleeves, making the outfit mine. The clothes are not tailored but draped; they wrap around our bodies, warped and crooked. I turn to look for the best angle and try to understand the soft fall of the garment. Toshi puts more products in my hair and makes it sticky as if wet, while Satoshi dabs concealer on my eyebrows, making them invisible to match Saskia's.

The walkie-talkie in the motor home crackles with Gus's voice. "I need Iris out here *now*. I don't care if she's not ready. Just send her out."

We find Gus, Cyril, and Gus's second camera assistant, Babar, setting up by an abandoned harvester. The machine is rusty, the blades menacing. Gus is distant. He focuses on his camera. I ignore him and lean against one of the big rubber tires. "Can you sit on it?" Gus asks me. He does not look me in the eyes.

Eva's assistant, Leila, covers part of the dirty tire with my blanket, and she and Babar help me up.

I dangle my bare feet in the air, perched as I am, high up on the wheel, and look at Gus. He has set up a tall tripod, and he stands next to it looking at me. He lifts a hand, and with his finger points to the left. I turn my head and I hear the shutter go. I continue to move my head slowly, I change the angle of my shoulders and sit up straight, bringing tension to the pose. The clothes are coarse, but I feel their romance. I look at the bottom of my pants and see that the hems are frayed and undone. I imagine myself making those clothes, leaving them unfinished. Understated clothes, essential, complex. I want to get to their core, read the story they tell. I have to bring less romance and more strength to the pose, I have to make myself strong for these clothes.

I shoot an insolent side-glance at the camera. *I got it.* Still glaring at the lens, I push a strand of hair away from my face. A breeze blows wisps of hair into my eyes, and I shield them with my hand, careful not to make a shadow over my brow. Cyril points the reflector toward my face, and I can feel the warmth of the rays beating on my skin.

"Thank you, Iris. We're done."

Babar and Leila help me off the tire, and I cover up with the blanket.

I sit shivering in the motor home while Gus takes pictures of Saskia. Sadness covers me like the blanket. Gus feels far away in spirit. His dark mood envelops me in uncertainty and doubt. *I don't inspire him anymore. I suck as a model, am I too fat? I just gave him so much, what else does he want? Is he already bored? Did he move on, as Toshi had warned me?*

I want to put on my clothes and go home. The walkie-talkie goes off again, and I hear Cyril say, "Send Iris out, please."

My heart jumps in my chest, and I barely stop myself from running. I stomp out in my rubber boots and find them setting up near the stables, moving bales of hay.

Gus takes me apart. His eyes are very dark, and his beautiful mouth does not smile. "I want to do a nude of you on the hay. Is that okay?"

A lock of hair is in his face, and I long to flick it away. Instead, I shove my fists into my pockets.

I nod. He takes me to a pile of golden chaff on the floor. "Can you lie on this, stomach down? I'll go as fast as I can. I know you're freezing."

I take off my clothes behind the blanket, and I lie on the straw. Closing my eyes, I think of a warm chimney while Toshi arranges my hair into loose ringlets. Gus and Cyril set up a ladder, and Gus climbs directly over me. Babar grabs his legs and hands him a loaded camera. Cyril holds the reflector board over my torso. "Polaroid, please. Cyril, what the fuck are you waiting for? What's the matter with you today? You're so slow, *hermano.*"

I feel bad for Cyril, who is covering for Babar's mistakes. Cyril takes the three heavy cameras and stores them in the bag around his neck. He holds up the board. From where I am lying I can see the sweat trickling down his forehead.

I stop shivering while Gus shoots with his Rolleiflex. He gets off the ladder and kneels right by my side, pointing the camera at my face. "Beautiful, Iris. Open your eyes. Now look at me." But I only see the crown of his head.

Eva covers me with the blanket while Gus and Cyril inspect the Polaroids.

"Can I see?" I ask.

Eva kneels by me and shows me the Polaroid. I am surprised by my look. In the Polaroid I scowl full of anger. "You look fierce," Eva says. "It's the bloody chill."

Yes, must be the chill.

Gus shoots me belly down on the hay, and I start to turn. I am naked but I don't care.

"Cyril, Babar, can you go?" Gus waves at them without lifting his eye off the viewfinder.

Eva and Toshi stand back too, and I am alone with Gus. I turn over completely and bring up my legs to cover my groin. I hear him breathing as he shoots fast.

I hate you, I want to say. *Why do you ignore me?* my eyes ask. *I'm not pretty enough for you? You don't desire me anymore?*

My muscles taut, I turn toward him as he stands over me, focusing on my face. I part my mouth slightly, wetting my lips, and relax my tense jaw. He touches my cheek to remove a piece of straw. *"Chiquita,"* he rasps. I look at his full lips and I want to caress them.

He pulls away from my face and climbs up the ladder again. Babar rushes over and grabs the wobbling structure as Gus shoots my body lying on the ground. I uncoil my dancer's muscles as I tense my belly and arch my feet, pointing my toes. I am the solo dancer in Pina Bausch's *Vollmond*, and I writhe slowly, performing my emotions. My long hair nearly covers my face, my lips are parted, and my eyes are closed.

"Beautiful, Iris. Yes, that's it, perfect. Look at me. Now close your lips. Relax the jaw. Don't move. Don't breathe. I said don't breathe . . . *¡Órale!* We're done!"

Eva runs to me and covers me with the blanket. "You were amazing, luv. Thank you! What a trooper. You must be bloody freezing. You free after this? Let's go for a drink."

Night has fallen and I sit at le Rouquet with Gus, Eva, Toshi, Satoshi, Saskia, and Cyril. It's late Friday, and I have nowhere else I would rather be. We are still chilled to the bone, and we huddle on a leather banquette, drinking red wine. "To Saskia and Iris." Eva lifts her glass to us, and Saskia whoops loudly. I catch Gus looking at me from across the table, but I cannot read his eyes.

I want you to want me. I want you to hold me, I want you to make me feel loved like I know you can do.

I shiver. The cold is under my skin.

We stumble out into the night and look for taxis to take us home. Gus hugs Cyril. *"Perdón, hermano, te pido perdón.* I am sorry I shouted at you. *Gracias por tu trabajo, campeón."*

Cyril nods and smiles his timid smile. *"C'est cool, pas de problème."*

I find myself on the sidewalk alone with Gus.

"I'll walk you to the *métro*," he says.

I am emboldened by the red wine and the afternoon's shoot. I feel brazen. "I don't want to go home," I tell him.

Without replying, he looks at me for a long time, then holding my hand, he walks me toward the place Saint-Sulpice.

His palm is warm, our fingers entwine, his grasp is tight. We stop at a light, and, fixing his gaze on me, he turns my hand over and kisses my wrist on the tiny beat of my pulse.

"What are you thinking of?" I ask.

"Making love to you."

CHAPTER 24

I had fallen asleep in his arms. I wake up in the middle of the night and feel his breath on my hair. Turning gently, I untangle myself from his embrace and observe his sleeping face. He has a small scar on his left shoulder, and I trace it with the tip of my finger. He wakes, his eyes grave and full of wonder, as if surprised to find me in his bed. He trails his index finger, designing the curve of my mouth, neck, and breast with slow, delicate strokes. I shiver, faint with desire and the need to make love again. I lie down next to him and his mouth is on mine, parting my lips with his tongue. His hips push against mine. I feel his sex hard against my belly, thrusting, hot, impatient. His hands grasp my face and he swallows my tongue, sucking and drinking my spit. He covers my body with his and thrusts his sex into me. Deep, rough, urgent. I dig my fingernails into his back, panting, and scream into his shoulder. "More," I say. "Fuck me hard."

Gus stops moving inside me and leans on his elbows, looking at my face. He gazes at me tenderly, puts his finger on my lips and forces it into my mouth. I suck on it and bite it furiously. I lick his lips. "More," I shout.

We are soaked in sweat, and my hair sticks to my cheeks. He moves in me slowly, and I groan with sublime pleasure and want.

"More?" he asks, smiling with his eyes.

"Yes, again and again."

I heave myself on top of him and he holds my hips, lifting me up and down slowly, grinding into him. I kiss his parted lips as I stop moving on his sex. I put my hand on my belly, wanting to touch him inside of me.

His hands clench my buttocks and slowly he rocks me back and forth, back and forth. His eyes close and I know he is about to come. "Please go slow," he begs. I lean into him.

"Stop!" he cries.

He comes in me and shudders as if in pain. I let my body fold into his and we lie side by side, drenched and spent.

We don't leave the bed for two days, and Gus's flat becomes our den. We go to the Café de la Mairie across the place Saint-Sulpice and drink bowls of milky coffee, then hurry back home to caress each other, to offer up the most vulnerable parts of ourselves. We listen to Radio Nova and dance around his room, our bodies entwined. Gus takes his small Nikon and shoots me without pause. I lie naked in the tangle of sheets, and he photographs me laughing, my skin tingling with sensations and need. I come out of the shower and he is still shooting me.

"My turn," I say.

I point the lens at him and focus on his sinewy back. I photograph his buttocks and legs as he gets dressed. I admire his body from behind the lens. A wiry body, lean and long, the body of a boy not yet a man. At noon we buy food and wine at the Marché Saint-Germain and feast. We make love again.

We lie on the bright rugs, my head on his lap. Gus is strumming his guitar and we are singing along to Isaac Hayes's "A Few More Kisses to Go" . . .

We got one more
No two more
We got a few more . . . kisses to go . . .

Gus's phone rings.

"Hi, Clemente. *Sí*, all good, *hermano*, you?"

He faces me as he talks and holds my hand, kissing my knuckles. "I'm sorry, my phone was off all day. Tonight?"

He gives me a questioning look and I mouth, *What?*

"Okay, tonight, sure it's worth it? Oh, all right, then, *órale.* I'll be with my girlfriend." And he flips his phone shut.

"Sorry, *mamacita.* That was Clemente Campisi. He's an agent. He's been after me for a while. He wants me to go to a party at les Bains for Helmut Lang's perfume launch. He says it's part of the job description, I have to be seen. We don't need to stay long, I promise."

I smile at him. He called me *his girlfriend.*

"Can you lend me some heels and lipstick?" I say.

"What for?"

I roll my eyes in reply. I need to change into clean clothes. Joan is in London, so I take Gus to the empty flat. He goes straight to Joan's library and browses through the books. "*¡Híjole!* My dream place."

I leave him sitting in the living room with a book on Brian Duffy, and I go take a shower. Gus comes upstairs to the mezzanine and lies on my bed. He observes me through the open bathroom door. "I'll never tire of looking at you," he says.

I won't either, I want to look at you all my life, I think.

I put on a pair of tight black jeans, a fitted black T-shirt, a skinny YSL tuxedo jacket that belonged to Delfine, and flat Chelsea boots. My hair is clean and loose, my skin glows from our lovemaking, and my lips are bruised from our kissing. I smudge black kohl around my eyes. Gus grabs my hand as I pass near the bed.

"You! You're lovely." He pulls me down next to him. "You'll have to get ready again, I still have . . . *a few more kisses to go.*"

I coo, "You're so bad."

Gus's body is hard and tender.

CHAPTER 25

A crowd presses against the doors, trying to get in. On the stairs leading up to the main entrance, a snarl of revelers pushes and calls the hostess's name. "Vanessa! Vanessa, it's me!" "Vanessa! *Ici!* Here!" Tiny Vanessa is perched on a tall stool. She points a finger at someone and the crowd parts to let him in. Two colossal bouncers in black suits and shiny black shirts clear the path with their outstretched arms, making way for the lucky one.

I make a face at Gus and say, "Let's go. This is not my scene *at all.*"

Vanessa notices Gus and points him out to the bouncers, who push against the crowd so that we can come in. The crowd parts again, staring at us as we walk up the stairs hand in hand, pressed against other bodies. I feel the power of the moment, and some fear.

A short man with a pointed face stands by Vanessa, talking in her ear. I recognize him. He wears the same Ray-Bans that he wore at le Flore. Vanessa kisses Gus on the cheek. "Daaaaarling Gus! So 'appy to see you here. Enjoy the party. Who is zee pretty girl? Your *petite amie?* Your girlfriend?" Vanessa wears towering scarlet wedges, fuschia Bakelite hoops, and a nouvelle vague gamine haircut. Gus smiles at her as we are pushed in by the group of carousers behind us. I recognize Linda with her model boyfriend "Hans the Hunk" and the Irish designer Leon Keating. We are crushed against them; they don't smile.

The short man with the purple Ray-Bans and tightly gelled curly hair hugs Gus and kisses him twice, while he stares me up and down. Without removing his sunglasses, he takes my hand in his and kisses it pompously. "Clemente Campisi, and you are?"

"Iris."

"You are very *divina*, Iris," Clemente says. "Why have we not met before?" I am uneasy under his suave gaze. I do not bother to reply.

Gus steps in. "Iris is in the Genius Factory job I did. Remember? I showed you the Polaroids."

"Ah! Yes, *bellissima!*" His stare never leaves my face. His face stretches as he smiles, and I think of a mongoose.

We are standing near the entrance, and the hallway is a crush of people trying to go upstairs to the restaurant and downstairs to the dance floor. The mob moves like a tight, sweaty shoal of fish in a strong current. We have no control over where we are going. Gus asks, "Up? Down?"

A flustered man carrying a heavy camera with a threatening flash asks us for a pose. Clemente stands between us and wraps his arm around my waist. The flash goes off. The photographer comes up to Clemente and they fist-bump. The man brings out a tiny notepad and writes down my name. While Clemente and Gus talk in a corner sheltered from the excited mass, the photographer introduces himself to me. *"Merci,"* he says. "My name is Jean Marc Firmin, or JM to friends."

I shake his hand and smile. "You're a photographer?"

"Not a photographer. I am the paparazzo of the Paris night. I'm here to bother everyone into posterity. Thank you, Miss Iris, for making my work so pleasant. I'm sure to see you soon again. You are by far the most pretty girl here. My compliments."

Jean Marc walks away to prowl the room, looking for faces to photograph. He knows everyone; his flash never stops.

I look around and recognize a tipsy fashion editor from a magazine I just worked with. The couple smoking and deep in conversation over in that corner are a famous hatmaker and his boy muse I've seen many times in the party pages of

Vogue. A pretty, young PR from an important fashion house holds a glass of champagne in each hand, downs them in one gulp, then waves at me with a smile. I wave back even though I cannot remember who she works for. The supermodel Terry pushes through the crowd, and someone in her entourage shoves us aside as if we were cardboard cutouts. Terry wears a tiara and a long black dress full of slits that reveal most of her enhanced breasts. I smell sweat in her wake, and I look away, disgusted. Trailing behind her, panting like a puppy, is Spain's star flamenco dancer and Terry's new lay. I recognize the performance artist Lola as he walks by, dressed as a Red Cross nurse in a tight white latex dress and huge fake breasts that are rubber balloons full of real milk.

Saskia arrives, already loaded. She introduces me to the handsome black man dangling from her arm. "Meet my gay walker, Raymond, he's my booker. He escorts me to parties so I don't get drunk and sloppy and pawed by the *dawgs*." Saskia's pale beauty is otherworldly, and her gray-green slanted eyes flash mischievously as she scans the room looking for trouble.

She downs a shot of something yellow. "*Klote!* That's strong."

In another corner, I recognize Cecile, the stylist from *Revue*, swigging champagne deep in conversation with Eva. Eva turns around and looks surprised at seeing me with Gus. People talk loudly, they're so happy to bump into one another, to be in each other's company. Guests embrace, kiss, gush, hug— what a wonderful time they're having. I grab a glass of champagne from one of the waiters and look for Gus. Clemente is close to him, talking into his ear, a hand firmly gripping Gus's arm. A stunning woman with smoky eyes in a leather pencil skirt passes by on sky-high stilettos, and Clemente reaches out for her, steering her toward Gus, blocking me out of their conversation.

I ignore him and make my way to Gus's side. He puts his arm around my waist, and the woman walks away. I cannot keep away from Gus. I need to touch him and feel he is mine. I clutch his hand. "Let's dance."

I pull him out of Clemente's clasp and look for Eva. Saskia bounces up to our group. With her is a striking girl with corkscrew curls and burnished skin named Audrey Hai. Saskia yells in my ear, "Downstairs, darling, that's where the paaaaaaaarty is."

I am giddy.

Holding on to Gus's hand, I follow Saskia and Audrey down the narrow stairs to a big room with glistening white tiles. There are hordes of people everywhere. Young, fresh-faced girls on very high heels and in tight dresses that show too much skin. Men look at the girls and drink with other men. Everyone smokes. Another photographer comes up to us and takes our picture with a ring flash. Saskia drapes herself around me and vamps to the camera, flirting with the photographer, drink in hand. From the corner of my eye I see Clemente watching us. He leans against a pillar and smokes slowly. I feel his gaze on me, studying me from behind the tinted lenses on his face. *Leave us alone. Stop slinking around, you're creeping me out.*

Endless trays of champagne are carried by waiters over the guests' heads. I down another glass. We get to the dance floor, and around us couples grind and sweat. Fake snow falls from the ceiling. "Always There" by Incognito is playing, and Eva, Saskia, Audrey, and I jump up and down with joy, the happiness of being alive in that moment distilled into a song. From the corner of the cramped dance floor, Gus looks at us and laughs.

We belt out the chorus at the top of our lungs. I never want to stop dancing.

The throbbing techno beats of "Radio" by Wishmountain drive us blissfully crazy, and Saskia and I wrap ourselves around the massive speakers. The rhythm of our hearts falters against the heavy bass that rattles our rib cages.

Gus peels me off the wall of speakers so that we can dance together, locked against each other's bodies in the steamy room. My lips are parched and my throat dry.

"I'm starving," Gus shouts in my ear over the throbbing acid house music. "We go?"

I look for Saskia and we find her in the upstairs bar deep in conversation with Clemente. "We're outta here," I tell her. "Wanna come?"

Saskia is sitting on Clemente's lap, and this makes me uneasy. Clemente is sweating, and he fiddles with his black curls, patting them down to make sure that the gel is holding. *"Ciao, bellissima. Ciao, carissimo."* He smiles to us through a clenched jaw and gives Gus a thumbs-up.

We meet Eva at the coat check. "Let's go."

"Anahi?"

"Too broke, *hermana*. How about *choucroute* at Pied de Cochon? That's my budget."

We jump into a taxi and make the ride in silence, the music still thumping in our ears. I am uncomfortable holding Gus's hand in front of Eva, so I squeeze my thigh against his instead. "That was fun," I say.

"Fun? Fun my ass," Eva says. "Not one person in there was having *fun*, except maybe you kids."

"But everyone was having a good time, Eva!"

"To start with, everyone's working too hard at these events to have a blast. You're hustling, you're networking, *and* you're focusing on not losing it in front of industry people."

"Losing it?"

"With booze and tons of blow, didn't you notice how many people were off their heads?"

"Oh." I suddenly worry for Saskia, whose behavior was out of control, high and impulsive.

Eva leans over me. "Hey, Gus, what did that sleazeball Clemente want? You were very in cahoots with him."

"He wants to rep me. What do you think?"

"I would keep away from him."

"*Hermana*, he's very powerful, I'm told. Ada seems to like him a lot. Clemente is her agent. They must have a convenient deal because most of the people Clemente reps work for *Revue*. Clemente also told me he would give anything to have you in his roster, he would make sure that we were always booked together as a team."

Eva snorts loudly and laughs. "Yeah, I'm sure he would *love* to have me too, but he scares the shit out of me. A little birdie told me the reason he's so powerful is because he has all these sleazy Polaroids of the big cheeses in the industry. You know, blackmail. Clemente started a decade ago as a messenger for M.M.T. Models, lugging model books around town on a moped. Very quickly he became an enabler, finding drugs and 'baby prostitutes'—young girl and boy models—for some hotshots in the business. One thing led to another and he created a 'file' on each client, photo-reportage included. I'd steer well away from him."

"Oh come on, Eva, can you prove it? That sounds like a lot of unfounded industry gossip."

"You know the photographer Jared Temple, right? Two years ago, he was partying with a group of friends in his flat, and a makeup artist from London OD'd, as in died. Guess who Jared called to 'fix' it? Jared cannot leave Clemente for that reason. And this is a true story," Eva says.

"That's bad." Gus looks out the taxi window. I see his jaw clenching. He rolls down the window to let in a blast of winter air. We drive on boulevard Sébastopol and reach the Gothic façade of the Saint-Eustache church.

Gus runs his hand through his hair. "I'm done, Eva, I need an agent desperately. I can't continue dealing with clients, production, editing, invoicing, negotiations, filing negs. It's doing my head in, I lose my mojo, I can't focus on taking good pictures. There's too much other bullshit stuff involved, taking up too much time. I'm sick of being a one-man show."

"True. I know, doll, it's fucked up. I'm in the same boat. It's great, means we're going places, but at this stage I would give my tits for a good agent. You know what Clemente's Italian nickname is? *Clemente Mente.*"

Gus bursts out laughing. "Clemente Lies?"

"Watch out, will you, darling?" Eva says.

I'm desperate for Gus's touch but careful not to interrupt their shocking conversation. *OD'd? Blackmail? Fixer? Baby prostitutes?* I bury my hand under his thigh on the cold leather car seat. I inhale, searching for his scent, my fingers reaching for his.

"Yeah, but who else is there, Eva? Catherine Laval is having a nervous breakdown and losing it in every sense of the word. She repped André in New York when I was assisting him. She was amazing, but now she's burned out and loves the bottle. Xavier Renaud is good, has offices in New York, Paris, *and* London but is a total cokehead. Then there's Ruby Simmons, who I love and I met with, but she can't rep me because David LaChapelle has her on a worldwide exclusive. So, you see? Not that many choices at this stage. Or you can go with Foto Partners and you're one of a hundred people they rep. But they don't like their photographers spending too much time on their art projects. For them it's just *'Show me the dollar.'*"

Eva sighs and looks out the car window. "I don't know, Gus, but I'm not going with Campisi."

Gus's hand is burrowing under my seat, touching my buttocks. I close my eyes, thinking of his caresses on my skin just a few hours before.

We arrive at the lively Au Pied de Cochon brasserie, which is open all night, by the bleak les Halles shopping mall. As we cross the dining room I hear a voice call out, "Gustavo!" Gus spots a woman sitting on a bench at a crowded table, surrounded by men and a beautiful African girl. "Shit, it's Ada Shaffer," he whispers under his breath.

I balk and move in the opposite direction, but Gus's hand is on the small of my back and he steers me toward the group.

Ada's hard eyes observe me as I walk toward her, her teeth clenched into a fake smile. Her face is perfectly made up. She wears a man's white cotton shirt, unbuttoned to reveal a plunging décolleté and a black lacy bra. Big gold chains sit on her freckled, tanned skin. Her brown hair is shoulder length and looks as if she just stepped out of the hairdresser's. I am hypnotized by her hands, which look like dry and bony claws covered in sunspots and heavy gold rings.

"*Bonsoir*, Gustavo. *Bonsoir*, Eva. *Pardon*, everybody, this is my new discovery, Gustavo de Santos, and I am *not* sharing him. And the wonderful stylist Eva Loom that most of you must know by now, especially as she works mostly for me, *n'est ce pas*, darling Eva?" Ada holds Gus's hand tightly and pulls him toward the table.

The other six people look us over and raise their wineglasses to Gus and Eva. Ada ignores me, and I glance around the table, recognizing some of my mother's former best friends. The legendary designer Yves de Sarcelles in a white silk jacket with black lapels smokes a cigarette out of an ivory holder. A young pretty boy sits next to him. The up-and-coming fashion star Pierre Delhomme—all leather, knuckle rings, piercings, and a butch cap on his shaved head—is hunched over the table, munching peanuts and sipping straight whisky with his muse, the Sudanese top model Yaya. Pierre Delhomme's eyes never leave Gus's face, and he whispers in Yaya's ear. Next to him is Antoine Carrio, the bon vivant fashion editor of *Le Monde*, disheveled with long, stringy hair and dirty eyeglasses, and the fashion PR queen Sylvie Tomei, composed, guarded, and observant like a sphinx. At the end of the table is the head of France's most important fashion school, the dapper and mysterious Horace de Montesquieu, in a three-piece suit with long cuffs falling unbuttoned out of the sleeves, the ensemble worn with incomparable panache.

Gus gently pushes me toward the group and says, "Ada, this is my girlfriend, Iris de Valadé. I shot her on Friday for *Revue*."

Ada's smile freezes on her lips. She shakes my hand with a limp clutch. "De Valadé? Are you related to Delfine?"

I feel everyone's eyes on me, and the back row at the table sits up and leans forward, straining to catch the conversation.

"Yes, Delfine is my mother."

"Oh!"

Yves de Sarcelles turns to face me and takes my hands. "Delfine! I love Delfine so much! When is she coming to Paris? She is too *cruelle* to leave us without her company. Will you tell her? And you, Iris, look how beautiful you've become, *n'est ce pas?*" Still clutching my hands, he turns to the others at the table, who nod and murmur their approval. *"Chéri,"* he says, speaking to his boy toy. *"Chéri,* can you take Iris's number and the name of her agency and call them on Monday, *sans faute?* I want to do a fitting with her. She would be *divine* for my interview in *Vogue* America: 'Le Chic Made in France, the Parisian vagabond.' Iris reminds me of Zouzou, *n'est ce pas?* Instead of some silly American socialite I will have the French American daughter of Delfine de Valadé. Wonderful!" He claps his hands, fluttering like an excited child.

"Yes, Iris is divine. How funny, who would have thought . . ." Ignoring me, Ada turns her attention to Gus.

"And you, *mon petit*, when am I seeing the shoot? Can you show me something by Wednesday? I now desperately need the story for our January issue, not the February one."

"Wednesday? In four days? I thought I had three weeks . . ."

"Yes, *mon petit* Gustavo, in four days. I wait for you at noon on Wednesday. *Bonsoir.*" And she turns her back to us.

We pile into a table at the end of the long dining room, and Eva checks to make sure that we are safe.

"Whoa! What just happened?" she asks, looking straight at me.

"Ada was NOT happy to meet Iris, is what happened," Gus replies.

"Not happy? If looks could kill, she would have nuked Iris. Hilarious fashion drama moment. And when Yves de Sarcelles was holding Iris's hands, I was peeing my pants looking at Ada's apoplectic face."

Gus picks up a menu. "I'm starving, *hermana*. It's two in the morning, can we please order or I'll kill someone right now. I'm about to go all *Chucky* on you. I'll have the *choucroute*. Iris?"

"I'm fine, I'm not hungry."

Eva leans toward me across the table and says, "Don't let Ada's nonsense bother you, silly goose; she's a horrible person, she hates most people, especially women. She's a total fag hag."

Gus turns toward me looking concerned and holds my hand sweetly. "Eva's right. It's just a girl thing, it'll pass."

"It's not Ada, I don't give a shit about her. It's those people, my mother's *supposed* best friends. I have known all of them ever since I was a baby, they were always at our house having drinks, dinners . . . when Delfine was kicked out of Paris, not a single one of them called her, except for Yaya. Yaya was discovered by my mother when she had just arrived from Sudan as a refugee. My mum launched her career and booked her as much as she could. Yaya kept in touch and still writes to her."

I am happy for the feel of Gus's hand on mine. I need to be soothed, and my anger is not appeased. "The others? Miserable lot, and to see Ada hosting all of them at the same table makes my stomach churn. That should have been my mum and instead it's Ada. My father told me that he suspected Ada was behind my mother's firing. Now I believe him. Ada destroyed my mother's legacy in one month, with one issue. She crushed her."

Eva shakes her head. "That's the business, Iris. It's a ruthless industry. People's love lasts but one season. Take advantage of Yves's interest in you, it will protect you against Ada blacklisting you *and* Gus. She does that, they all do. Even if

Joan personally options you two, Ada would make sure that the bookers at *Revue* take you off their lists."

"Even if Gus is their favorite photographer?"

"Yes. Ada is sick with jealousy, and you brought the specter of Delfine back to Paris. If you're in an American *Vogue* story with Yves de Sarcelles, every top designer and photographer here will want to work with you. Ada can't get rid of you because Yves's fashion group is her main advertiser. It would also make her look daft not to have you when everyone else wants you. She'll tolerate you for as long as she absolutely has to, not one day more."

Gus feels my misery and puts his arm around my shoulders, holding me tight. "It's okay, baby, there are lots of other great magazines we can work with. Don't think about this now. Let's just eat lots of pig's trotters and drink buckets of wine and fuck the world. *¿Órale?*"

That night Gus draws a young naked girl with long black hair and little wings. She is flying toward the moon with a smile on her face. Birds, mice, and squirrels fly with her. I find the drawing on my pillow. Scrawled across the bottom of the page it says, *I come with you to the end of the world.*

CHAPTER 26

Gus lies asleep on his stomach. It is still dark outside. I am sad and unsettled by this world that I might never learn to navigate. I want to call my father, but I must wait till I get home to Joan's. I worry for Saskia, who I left at the club, high and drunk and in the hands of Clemente. I have texted her but she doesn't reply. I am lonely and cold, and I cradle my body as close as I can to Gus, who does not wake up.

Light begins to filter through the shutters, and I see the leaden sky heavy with rain. I nibble on Gus's neck. He rolls on top of me, pinning me down with his legs. We make love gently. It is slow, his sex deep inside of me.

Gus falls asleep again.

I run out for croissants and bread at the bakery on the corner of the place Saint-Sulpice as the church bells toll. There is something comforting about the many families running up the stairs into the church. I follow them into the cavernous sanctuary and sit in the back row for a few minutes, finding peace. Delfine did not believe in religion, and catechism lessons were done more out of duty than creed. I cannot remember when I stopped going to Mass. Here in this church, now, I feel protected and sheltered, so why am I still scared?

I call Saskia. Her voicemail is full. I text her again. Joan calls me, checking in.

When I get back to Gus's flat, he is sitting in his boxer shorts at the desk, looking over a contact sheet with an eye loupe. Jorge Negrete is singing "Amor con Amor Se Paga." Gus croons along, *Despacito entraste en mi alma, como entra en la carne una daga . . .*

He does not acknowledge my presence, so I make coffee and sit on the bed with a wooden tray covered in bread and croissants, butter, honey, and jam.

"Hey! Morning to you too!" I say.

Gus does not reply. I drink my coffee.

"*Chiquita*, come here, take a look."

I go to the desk and bend over the contact sheets with his eye loupe. I move fast, zipping from one frame to another. I squint, a reflex I learned from Delfine when she reedited stills. *"First thing is to look at the movement. If that works and your eye moves around as it should, from top to bottom, right to left, one corner to another, then you focus on the clothes. If they look good, then, and only then, you look at the girl,"* she had taught me.

The black-and-white shots are bold, elegant, stark. We had made the clothes swing in the wind with our bodies. Nature was woven into the narrative. The trees, fields, and walls framed the poses and enhanced the fashion. "This one, and this one, oh, this one too." I go through rows and rows of shots and quickly edit as I look.

"Good ones, Iris! *Pura raza!* Purebred of Valadé pedigree."

I stop at the last contacts and the naked shots of me, the ones on the floor covered with hay. *They're beautiful. I'm proud of those shots. I put my trust in you then, I still trust you now.*

Gus gets up and pulls me to the rug with the breakfast tray. "Food! *Por Dios!*"

CHAPTER 27

A rainy November turns into a dark and cold December where the low clouds never lift and the sun never shines.

I do not get invited to Lectoure for Thanksgiving, and my cousin, Eric, calls me to say, "My fucking mother, I'm sorry, *ma petite cousine* Iris. I'll come to Paris soon to visit you, *d'accord?*"

I speak to Ludo every week and give him a report on my work. I hear Delfine breathing down the bedroom receiver, but she never comments except to say, "Paris is dead, Paris is over. Come to New York."

I tell her about her friends at Au Pied de Cochon. I tell her that Yves de Sarcelles wanted news of her and he has booked me for *Vogue*. She snorts and says, "*Ce connard.* That asshole." I am shocked by my mother's language. I've never heard her swear. She is placid when I mention Yaya, though.

Days are a blur of castings, go-sees, fittings, and a few shoots. Gus lives on a constant deadline, forever editing or printing late into the night.

I don't see Saskia anymore. She doesn't have time to see me, she says. I prefer to be angry at her, so I have a pretext not to get involved in her messy life.

Joan accepts my relationship with Gus in a resigned way, but I am not allowed to sleep over.

"You're way too young. Your father would have a heart attack. And how old is Gus?"

"Gus is twenty-four. Mum wouldn't care!"

"Well, yes, that IS the problem. You said it, she wouldn't care because she's not herself, but I do and you are in my house so you live by my rules. And by the way, an artist? Really? Why couldn't you choose a banker? Or a lawyer? Someone who'll take care of *you*, not a needy artist."

"But Joan, *please*! All the girls are shacking up with their boyfriends! I'm already eighteen!"

"Over my dead body, understand? I'll get you a cat, that way you'll have to come back every day to feed it."

I shrug and give up because I really don't care. Joan is away so much that most of the time I do what I want anyway. From the virgin beaches of El Nido in the Philippines to the Atacama Desert in Chile, to Saint Bart's in the Caribbean or Asilah in Morocco, Joan jets twice a month to the hottest new destinations with sophisticated names in remote places. She's in constant demand by the top photographers in the *Revue* roster, while a junior Eva works with Gus and stays local for lack of budgets. *"Fashion hierarchy, darling."*

Joan's path and mine cross every so often in the corridors of her flat.

During Fashion Month, it's survival mode. Sometimes we cook for each other, but mostly we are in our own worlds, too tired to communicate or share. Joan is disciplined when I am sloppy, orderly when I am messy, measured when I cannot contain myself, prudent when I want to be reckless. I seek her approval. Just knowing that she is there makes me want to try harder to get noticed and land good bookings. Joan is encouraging and motivating in a world where each person is on their own. I find it odd that she never expands about her family, even though I try to engage her in the conversation when I miss mine. But whenever I get home and see black Tumi bags open in her dressing room, I feel guilty pangs of happiness knowing that she will travel again and I will sleep at Gus's.

I am learning how to be with Gus. I am slowly understanding the way he becomes strange and focused when he edits an urgent job, capable of not uttering a word for two days until he has finished. His storyboards are works of art, and he fills pad after pad with ideas he wants to shoot, stories he needs to tell.

We are comfortable in our silence. Gus is not a talker, he does not fill the spaces with meaningless blather, and I am serene with this knowledge.

I browse through his photography books. I read on the floor his out-of-print editions of Manuel and Lola Álvarez Bravo and Flor Garduño, content to simply be near him. Though sometimes I am lonely in his company because I know that his art is his real love.

I buy photography manuals in English at the WHSmith bookstore and learn about f-stops, diaphragms, and tungsten, HMI, and Fresnel lights. We store the film in our fridge to stop its degradation, and I learn about its fragile emulsions. Gus explains to me the delivery process for his clients, the distinction between an original or repro print and a master print, the difference between a vintage print and a later edition one. I buy a drawing pad and doodle imaginary layouts of magazine spreads I would like to be in. When Gus has finished editing, I reedit the stack of contacts with a greasy red pencil, and I am over the moon for those short moments: deciding, involved, an accomplice in his art.

I spend evenings alone while he's in the lab, and I laugh as I picture him looking over the shoulder of the old printer, watchful and untrusting.

Sometimes in his bed I turn and find he is not there. He is hunched over his desk, going through his receipts, his forehead furrowed as he chews on his pen. He looks up and I smile and go back to sleep. We have very little money but a lot of work. Editorials do not pay the rent, and Gus spends everything he has on shooting for *Revue* when their budgets do not cover the costs of his ambitious ideas. I know that he is good, very good, but will people get his work? We live on hope, fervor, inspiration, and drive. We support each other emotionally, and we forage for food and hustle for jobs at fashion cocktails, where Gus downs tray after tray of hors d'oeuvres.

I ask my booker at Blitz to get me every far-flung catalog she can, and I demand cash. I accept Asian campaigns for
sodas, cookies, tampons, and cat food. I'm on a bus shelter in
South Korea, so who cares? After one of these jobs, the bills
bulge in my breast pocket, and I shop for groceries and pay for
our taxis. We have each other and that is all we need. That is
a lot.

We hole up in our little world at Gus's studio. Gus accepts
my charity with a frustrated and angry look on his face. He
has no choice. Gus never asks for anything. At times he goes
without food and his flat is cold, the radiators turned off, and
I see my breath in the chilly room. Other times he disappears
for a few days. I ask no questions when he comes back and fills
the fridge with new rolls of film. Life is hard, but that is life.

Clemente calls Gus and offers him a cash job for a Japanese
catalog. He accepts, worn out from worry and near despair.
That weekend he returns with a triumphant look on his face
and puts a thick stack of bills on the kitchen counter. "*Mi niñita,*
this should hold us for a while."

On the weekends, we walk around Paris, and Gus shoots
me for his art. We climb over the wall at the Père-Lachaise cemetery one sunset and catch the die-hard fans of Jim Morrison
partying on his grave. I lie naked on an icy gray tombstone, my
skin a flash of white. My body shakes from the cold and Gus
cannot focus his camera, and we know that the shots will be
blurred. We laugh and run away when the guards come.

In the Buttes-Chaumont park, I pose for him in the Temple
de la Sibylle all the way at the top of the cliff. White stone,
vines, columns, the views of Paris, and my face in the wind.
On the south side of the park we take shelter from the rain in
the grotto, and we embrace passionately. We fuse into each
other's flesh, leaning against the sharp mossy rocks that dig
into my back.

Like a thousand students before us, we walk on the wind-
swept riverbank of the Seine with a bottle of plonk, a loaf of

bread, and a slab of cheese and sit at the end of the Île Saint-Louis, looking at the gray waves the Bateaux Mouches make as they chug by. We dive into the soot-black cathedral of Notre-Dame to get out of the rain, and Gus lights red candles at every chapel where he prays. We eat cheap couscous on boulevard de Belleville and drink house wine by the jug in the bars of the Bastille. We go to small art-movie houses in the middle of the afternoon and watch the French black-and-white classics of eras gone by. In the vast public library of the Centre Pompidou, we browse through books on Paris, its people, and its art. I find the model and singer Zouzou in a Richard Avedon book and photocopy faces and looks for Gus.

"Let's do a beauty story, Iris. You'll be a sixties Paris muse . . . you'll be Tina Aumont, Anna Karina, Dani, Jane Birkin, and Barbara Dixon. Let's talk to Eva and Joan." So many stories are born this way with us. Our imagination is never still, our curiosity never satisfied.

We read, we draw. I practice shooting Gus's angular face and lithe naked body, and he doesn't make fun of my fumbles. We are high on each other. We feed off our shared passions, intellect, culture, and curiosity. I am proud to support my man, and he takes care of me as best he can. I am his muse and this troubles me. A muse is a silent person. Don't muses have sad lives with bad endings?

Every week Gus sends a postcard of our explorations to his mother in LA. We choose them and sign them together. *"Mi querida Mamá. Acá una postal de la catedral del Sacré-Coeur en lo alto de un monte en Paris que se llama Montmartre. Es muy bella, lisa, muy blanca y muy, muy grande. A ti te gustaría mucho. Te quiero. Tu hijo, Gustavo, y mi novia, Iris."* He translates to me: "My dearest mother. Here is a postcard of the Sacred Heart cathedral, which is on top of a hill in Paris called Montmartre. It is very beautiful, smooth, very white, and very, very big. You would like it a lot. I love you. Your son, Gustavo, and my girl-friend, Iris."

Guru magazine invites me to an exhibition for Thomas Bailey. Gus and I jump at the opportunity to see the master's black-and-white portraits. I bump into Saskia on the arm of Clemente; her eyes are hollow, hard. Through her sheer black T-shirt, I can see her nipples. They are pierced. She towers over Clemente in tiny leather shorts and very high heels, her coat dragging on the floor behind her. I do not recognize my beautiful friend. Where did her dewy complexion go? The sparkle in her gaze? The magic that drew you to her like a magnet? All I see now is another fashionable clothes hanger, thin and bony with a dry smile and bleached-white hair with no shine.

"Saskia! Finally! Where have you been? Let's hang!"

"Been busy, Iris. I don't stop working."

Working where? I don't see you at any castings, and you look like hell.

Saskia grabs a glass of champagne from a waiter and drinks it in one gulp. *"Proost!"*

I am hungry, so I drink one too.

Jean Marc, the photographer, appears out of nowhere. "Oh! My favorite people. Ever so beautiful. Can I have one with the men? Thank you, and now one of my lovely girls?" Jean Marc's flash blinds us, but we smile for him, knowing the unspoken rules of the fashion society pages. One party picture in *WDD* and your career advanced one step. Jean Marc holds my hand gently and bows. "Thank you, Mademoiselle Iris, always a pleasure. You're so gracious to me."

I smile at him and give him a hug.

"Gimme a fag, let's smoke." Saskia nudges me as she untangles herself from Clemente's arm. We go outside for a cigarette break. Clemente's eyes follow Saskia from afar, and I see him checking on her from the other side of the glass door.

"Are you okay?" I ask.

"Oh yes, Iris, very okay. We're dating, we have much, much fun. We party and party, and he's introducing me to many nice people that are good for my career." Saskia giggles. "I am making mountains of money." As if to make her point, Saskia shows me her tiny pale wrist from which dangles a large men's Cartier watch. On one of her fingers is a garish diamond ring.

"And that?" I say, pointing at the ring.

"I'm working, Iris, never worked more. I don't stop, thanks to Clem. In my culture when you make money, you buy jewelry that you can run away with if the world gets attacked by zombies."

In my culture when you make money, you save it, I think. "Saskia, excuse me for telling you this, but you look like hell. Are you sure you're all right?"

"What you mean 'hell'? I just lost some weight coz Angelo at the agency told me I was too fat for haute couture in January."

"Some weight? You look fucking anorexic. Your head is way larger than your body. And what's up with that makeup, man? You look like Courtney Love on a shitty day."

Saskia giggles. "But I lost my huge hips, now I can do haute couture! Well, I did get a little help from these friends, maybe I overdid them?" She puts her hand in her pocket and brings out five blue-and-white capsules. "The best! Really, Iris. You feel hungry or tired? You swallow a couple and BOOM! You're again great. You should try them."

"Where did you get those?"

"Everyone goes to this doctor to lose weight. I mean *everyone* in Paris . . . models, designers, the old socialites. They're amazing. Clem sent me. The doctor is his friend."

"You mean Clemente is okay with this?"

"Hell yes! He knows how pissed off I get when I'm feeling fat and hungry. You know what I mean, right? They keep me awake, but what does it matter? We go out a lot anyway," Saskia blabs, her words coming out so fast I can hardly follow her.

We finish our cigarettes. "Saskia, I'll call you this week, all right? Let's go for coffee. Are you doing the Clarins casting on Wednesday? We can hang afterward."

"I don't know, Iris, I'm too busy. We'll see."

Too busy for what?

The gallery fills up quickly, and I join Gus as he stares at the stark portraits on the walls. I'm galvanized by their bluntness and the way his subjects glare at the camera, uncluttered by the fuss and frills of fashionable clothes. Sixties tomboys with whip-thin hips and no breasts: Leslie Caron, Celia Hammond, Tina Aumont, Judy Dent, Talitha Getty, Anita Pallenberg, Patti Smith, Jane Birkin—iconic faces made beautiful and timeless by his sharp, unrelenting lens and nothing else.

Thomas Bailey is barricaded in a corner with an army of withered muses and friends who protect him against vacuous chat. He looks feisty. On his arm is a petite woman of a certain age showing a lot of bouncy cleavage. Her laugh is loud and contagious, and Bailey stares at her adoringly through his glasses. Will that be Gus and me when we are old?

I excuse myself and go to the ladies' room, where I wait in a long line.

Bailey's petite companion appears by my side at the end of the queue. "I am peeing myself. My back teeth are swimming, I'll burst if I don't tinkle."

I smile at her and say, "I'll deal with it."

I go to the front of the line and say to a girl about to enter the stall, "I beg your pardon. Can Madame Bailey go ahead of you?"

The sassy petite lady smiles like a Cheshire cat and slides into the bathroom, dragging me with her. "Excuse us, we're together. Pardon, *mesdemoiselles. Merci.*"

I busy myself at the sink in front of the stall and look at my reflection in the mirror, pretending to fix my makeup.

"Hello, sexy girl. My name is Kitti Vice, with an *i*. And yours? Are you with the pretty boy that looks like an Apache?" Kitti is sitting on the toilet, the door open. "Ohhhhhh, that feels sooooooo good."

I wave to her from the sink and laugh. "I'm Iris. Yes, the dark boy with the long hair is my boyfriend, Gus."

She flushes the toilet and totters out on shiny high-heeled boots, struggling to zip up her latex catsuit. "This fucking thing. It's so tight I have to pee every hour . . . and the heat! My titties are melting in here, and it's getting kind of swampy down under. Thomas likes me to dress like a whore. He's my dear old friend. I like your outfit."

I am wearing an oversized denim jacket with a large, embroidered Union Jack on the back. I tuck my scraggly *God Save the Queen* Sex Pistols T-shirt into my tartan skirt and look at my scuffed Mary Janes. I smile at Kitti. "Thank you, Kitti. Homage to Mr. Bailey and London and all the Cool Britannia lot."

Kitti stands in front of the mirror and applies her lipstick. "I miss London. That's where I'm from. But I've been a Paris girl for years now."

Kitti holds on to my arm, tottering on her metallic stilettos, and we walk back to Bailey's corner. "That's me here, and here, nice tits, yes? And this is my ass in my bed at home. I was very young there, it must have been the early sixties? Who knows, we were all kind of out of it all the time anyway. I fried my brain."

I walk slowly across the gallery and grab another glass of champagne to silence my growling stomach. I spot Gus and nod. He joins us.

"What does your pretty boyfriend do?" Kitti asks.

"I'm a photographer."

"What kind of photographer? Fashion? You look like a model."

"Well, sort of fashion photographer. I'm shooting fashion now, but what I want to do is art photography. I'm a big fan of Mr. Bailey's. He has the career that I dream of."

"I'll tell him; he likes passionate young things. And what do you like the most about Thomas's work, Indian Boy?"

"Its power, the gravity, the tension. His portraits tell me who the people are. I can't stop looking at the people."

"That's the point of photography, isn't it? Well, you better work hard, pretty boy. Thomas does, that's all he cares about, drinking good wine and taking pictures." She turns toward me. "And you," she says, pointing at us with her champagne glass, "you two are so divine together. If I were young, we would have a threesome." She cackles loudly, her joie de vivre contagious.

I am now tipsy. I titter. Kitti takes out a tiny gold pen and a dainty pad and writes her telephone number. "You'll call me, yes, Iris? Come to my house, I give many dinners. I *adore* people like you, poor little starved ones. You are the chosen ones, but your road to success is paved with sacrifice, hardship, danger, and strife. Tread carefully. I *know* this, listen to me, I'm a witch. Just don't bring cheap wine."

We leave Kitti back on the arm of Thomas Bailey, and an eager crowd engulfs them again.

Her words will resonate in the back of my mind for years to come.

CHAPTER 28

Yves de Sarcelles: Le Chic Made in France. Vogue *introduces us to the quiet refinement of Yves de Sarcelles's atelier while he fits his couture collection on his muse, Iris de Valadé, daughter of the legendary fashion editor Delfine de Valadé.*

Delfine sits at her narrow desk in a sparse office at the end of a long corridor. She sharpens her Caran d'Ache pencils and rearranges them by height. She moves her Filofax to the left, her Moleskine notebook to the right. She places her glass of water at the far corner of her desk. She closes *Vogue* magazine and sets it aside.

She opens the latest copy of *Revue,* fresh out of the Paris office pouch. She flicks through the pages and then stops. She looks at the opening page of the Genius Factory *groupage.* It's a close-up of Iris's face. She turns page by page and studies each image with attention. At the end of the *groupage* she starts all over again.

She reaches for the phone on her table.

CHAPTER 29

I remember the place Saint-Sulpice studio, the days we had gone hungry and my first Christmas in New York away from Gus. At home, I had been subjected to Delfine's bitterness and her lack of interest in anything that I had done. "She's ill," Ludo would tell me. "Let her be, she's not herself."

Gus had stayed in Paris, unable to afford a ticket to be with his family in LA. He delivers on his promise, sending me a letter every day.

The month the Genius Factory *groupage* was published, we never looked back. For a while we start to doubt less. My face and Gus's photographs seem to be everywhere now. We have become choosy and less strung out about money. Gus signs with Clemente, and advertising jobs trickle in.

The months go by at lightning speed when you work so hard, when your focus is so clear, driven by fashion's never-ending cycles: prêt-à-porter, haute couture, cruise, men's, women's, runway season, advertising season, summer downtime.

I travel to Milan, London, and New York, walking in sixty shows a season.

Gus shoots his first *I-D* magazine in London.

I jet off to the Maldives with Joan and shoot three bathing-suit stories back to back.

Gus and I meet in Paris for two days and I leave again, this time to Tokyo on a big job.

I come back to the couture shows and shoot in Rome for Valentino.

Gus shoots me for *Revue* and we have our first serious fight. Gus shoots his first cover for *Guru* and we reconcile.

Do we fight and make up because he needs me more than I need him? We can't live apart, but I suffocate in his studio, because at times he leaves me no space. I drown in his intensity, his unpredictable moods, his moments of despair, the distance he imposes when we are together. "I have to be selfish to create," he says.

"But you create so much . . . you're always creating . . ."

"Iris, you can't understand. I have to look for new ideas because I always need to be in a state of artistic anxiety and insecurity. If I feel sure of myself, I cannot be creative."

Is that the fear that Joan had mentioned? "Talk to me . . . ," I plead, but he shuts me out.

Our frantic months turn into three years. Spring in Paris has long nights that never seem to end. We live in the streets when we can, escaping the cramped flat on rue du Canivet. Flower shops burst with lush peonies, and we gorge on *gariguette* strawberries and *griotte* cherries that announce the beginning of summer; we stand under the fragrant linden trees and breathe in their exquisite perfume. August finds the city deserted, and we use it like an open-air studio.

I stay with Gus when Joan goes on summer holidays. We have a month to ourselves. Gus shoots for his art, and we read books to each other. And then September comes and I am on the road again.

In Joan's flat, I park my open Tumi bag next to hers, always at the ready to depart.

"We never see each other anymore. Why don't we take a break after Paris Fashion Week, just you and me," she says. "We could go to a thalasso in Brittany, do a cure."

"Yes, let's." I am so tired that I am despondent.

"It takes its toll, you know?" she tells me.

I think of my mother and say, "I know."

Saskia's little blue pills help me get through the constant jet lag and exhaustion when willpower fails. Days are early and long, nights are sleepless and short. The partying takes the edge off the fear. The pounding music makes me reckless, and at times this turns into bad things. The pressure is always on to play my "Iris de Valadé Model" role: beautiful, successful, strong. I have learned how to pretend to myself, how to pretend to others, that everything is great, that I am never afraid, that my life with Gus flows sweetly, that all at home is smooth. I have learned how to twist the truth. Sometimes I lose my shit.

The only other people I feel close to are Joan, Eva, and Kitti. In the chaos of my new life I seek the company of the grounded ones: Joan is stable and predictable, Eva is sober and sedate. Like them, Kitti is a rock, an adopted mum, the sister I never had, the shoulder I can cry on but never do. Kitti is a witch. She can read my eyes, interpret my moods, knows when I am strung out, coming down from a day of pills and a night of booze, or worried by Gus's disappearing acts. Kitti knows all that and also when I miss home and Papa.

"Be careful, little girl," she tells me, never judging but always aware. "Those pills are shit. Two decades ago I took diet pills to party and stay thin, and I ground my teeth all night. It's always the same: alcohol, pills, blow . . . people never learn, do they? You can't party forever; you'll end up dead or crazy.

"I'm too old and fat to fuck, but my dogs love me, and so does Thomas. It's all I need—but you? Who do you have? Go home. Be near your family, go to university. This is no place for a child on her own. You're playing with fire."

Kitti should know; she once was a famous model, a muse, a London party girl, a beautiful appendage to rock stars and bad lads. I have seen the collection of fading Polaroids on her toilet walls. "Why do you and Thomas live apart? Why aren't you married?"

"Live with a man? Heavens no!"

Kitti makes me laugh. She has that effect on people, the effect of changing your life. I seek her down-to-earth company when I am sad, her savvy views on life and love and sex. I seek her sweeping statements of unedited truths, her blistering tongue, her unchecked spontaneity. Kitti doesn't give a damn; unfiltered, she doesn't cushion the facts. I can't even imagine living in her head.

I live surrounded by people whose job it is to make me feel important and useful for one day at a time, not more. The shallowness of purpose and lack of moral fulfillment defeat me. Kitti is generous with her time and likes to smoke joints on her sofa while doling out advice and her oracle facts. "Men are shit," she says. "They're babies, they fuck like rabbits with no brains, and they're shit, but we love them so we try a little bit harder. Your Gus, Iris, your Gus is fragile, take care of him. He's a nice boy and he adores you, he's very talented. But don't let him get lost. He needs to take care of you, not the other way around. That will be good for his head. He needs to feel needed, but you are stronger than him. *That's* not good. You scare him, because you're too independent. Why don't you pretend a bit?"

"I don't know how to play those games."

"Just tone it down every now and then, be needy and girly. He's so beautiful . . . Oh! To be young and fuckable again. I would put him in my bed in a second. You wouldn't mind, would you?" Kitti laughs loudly and takes a drag from her joint. Her eyes shine. "Stay away from Ada Shaffer and her clique. Nothing good will come out of being around them, not even for work. They're not good people."

"How do you know Ada?"

"Paris is small."

"And?"

"The fashion world is a village where everyone knows."

"I don't see Ada. I don't like her," I say.

"But your pretty boy Gus does. You didn't know?"

No, I did not know. Kitti's words kick me in the stomach. *It must be for work,* I assure myself.

Kitti goes back to cuddling one of her yapping dogs.

"This is my baby. This one here, *he* is the love of my life, right, Bubu? I love you too." Bubu licks her face.

I like the perks of my newfound fame. The black cars that rush me to castings are part of the bubble in which I now live for weeks at a time. A designer rents the Opera for a black-tie ball, so the others rent the Rodin museum and the Grand Palais for their shows. You get used to the excesses quickly. You have to keep feeding the dream. Elaborate artifice and gold tinsel, fashion's escapism suits me fine. I do not question my life.

I love the runway. I have learned how to walk it and limit my hips' sway, crossing one foot in front of the other at an impossible angle. As I stride expressionless toward the wall of photographers, I look for the silver telephoto lens of my friend Piero Biasion at his usual place high up in the pit, dead center of the rapid-fire shuttering block. When the guys in the pit bellow instructions or meow in unison like horny tomcats, I use Piero's affable face as my focal point. I now open or close most shows and am given the best dresses to walk in. I have fewer of those "Show me your tits and I'll get you into *Vogue*" moments. Predators roam, but I have become too famous for them to risk it. Every season, a certain fat and ugly Hollywood producer walks backstage among the clothes racks while we dive for cover in our thongs. Magali shrugs when I complain. "He's too powerful, Iris, you can't do anything about it." No one ever cares. We do, us models care when we catch him leering at our bare breasts.

I am learning fast about the art of exploiting myself, which jobs to reject and which to accept, the low moral standards that are part of the fashion world. I get used to being stared at like a piece of meat. I cruise through the glamour, the shine and the grime of the business, professionally beautiful and immune to its sick love of the surface, of the appearance. The blindingly bright, venal lights of fashion. I am an articulate object. I know how to bring with me what fashion looks for next. I succumb

to the punishing pace. Photographers project their own fanta-
sies onto me, and I play their games.

Have fun while it lasts, I think, *for it doesn't last long.* I am
twenty years old and my shelf life is limited.

Gus's creative requirements have changed. He is only
excited by artistic choices that feel dangerous. He needs the
extreme just to get by. To gamble, to take risks. *You are unafraid
because what you do is not what people do, what they want to see, but
you know it is good, or maybe you are just drunk and it is all shit.*

His art imitates his life, and I worry and watch.

A journalist writes about our carefree years saying, *"It's the
most talented and the most beautiful that everyone wants to make
love to. They are doomed by their talent, their beauty, their joie
de vivre; they are damned for the wrong reasons."* The article is
accompanied by a picture of the two of us leaning against a
wall, smoking in a club. We look insolently at the camera. We
are *damned.* We are *doomed.* I shiver, but it is not cold.

Saskia leaves Paris and never comes back, and I am too
busy to ask Clemente for her whereabouts.

I despise Clemente. He has wormed himself into our lives,
clinging on like a tick to a dog's fur. Clemente is everywhere
that Gus is, he lives off Gus's glow. I am repelled by his languid
body language, his expensive flashy suits, his histrionics on
the phone, the way he stares at me behind his Ray-Bans, the
gelled curls, and the baby models on his arm.

The day Gus signs with Clemente, I am at the meeting. I
look over Gus's contract and I say, "Separate invoices."

"*Come?* What?"

"I said separate invoices for you and Gus. You invoice the
client your twenty-five percent, and Gus will invoice the client
his seventy-five percent. Why should he wait for you to pay
him? Why shouldn't he know what he really makes on that
job? Fast and clear, right, Gus?"

Clemente's voice oozes repressed anger and contempt.
"*Bambina,* this is not how it works. *I* am the agent. I have been

an agent for years. I am number one at my job, and this is how *I* do it. Ask anyone, they all know Clemente Campisi, *capito?*"

"Tough, Clemente. This is how it will be done with Gus. No like? We sign with Marion de Beauford."

Gus shoots me an amused glance and kicks me under the table. I look at Clemente's rabid face and think he is about to have an attack. I am enjoying this.

Clemente gets up from his shiny glass desk and comes around to my chair, putting his crotch at my eye level. *"Allora,* since when are you the expert? You're a model."

"Since I've been around photographers longer than you have, listening to them complain about being stiffed by their agents."

"Stiffed? *Cosa é* 'stiffed'? You mean cheat? After all I do for their careers? They would be nothing, nowhere, without agents' work. We work like dogs for you. *Madonna!* The bull-shit I have to hear."

"Clemente, it's a deal breaker for us and it makes no difference to you except that you will not get to hold on to Gus's money."

"Don't you trust me?"

"No. I don't even trust my mother."

"Karla, *Karlaaaaaaaaaaa, vieni qui subito!"* he shouts across the hallway to his assistant. He goes to his desk, sits down, and throws her the contract. "Type this, point nine, change the invoicing to separate seventy-five/twenty-five invoices. Now."

"Soddisffatta?" he asks, turning again to me, his voice dripping with sarcasm.

"Yes. Better. But we also want you to get back from *Revue* all of Gus's original prints after they are published. Back from *Revue* and straight to Gus, not to you."

"Iris, are you on drugs, *bambina cara?* I can't get those back! It's an understanding in the industry that a magazine like *Revue* keeps those for their archives. *Ma siete pazzi?* Are you crazy?"

"Bollocks, Clemente. I know for a fact that Newton gets his back even though he's on contract. Those belong to the artist if he pays for them. Imagine that Gus wants to show those one day, why should we beg *Revue* for them? The repro prints are expensive to make, and *we* end up paying that cost. We always have to waive our fees to add money to the production budget.

"I don't want Gus's work prints floating around. I want you to add to Gus's contract that we get the materials back after the job. And also get back all the stuff of his that they already have."

Clemente swears under his breath.

"Why, Clemente, use your leverage on Ada. She's also your client, so what's the fuss?"

Clemente jumps up from his desk, his chair scraping the floor with a loud noise.

"Are you scared of her? I haven't seen that subservient side of yours."

His face goes red again, and he stomps out of his office. "Karla! Karlaaaaaaaa, *vaffanculo*, Karla! Where are you?" He bangs on the toilet door.

Gus shoots me a shocked look.

Karla comes out flustered, zipping her jeans. *"Arrivo subito! Scusatemi."*

What an asshole. I smile up at Karla. *You should not have to be treated like this.*

"Anything else while we are at it?" he says, looking directly at me. He clenches his jaw.

We walk home that night, and when we pass the entrance to the Saint-Sulpice church, Gus does not go in.

CHAPTER 30

Joan Jett in *The Runaways*, Jane Fonda in *Klute*, that's who I look like. With my shag haircut, I now have bangs of all lengths and thicknesses, and frayed loose strands frame my face. I try to tidy the wisps of hair around my forehead but give up. Magali at Blitz says it will start a trend, unfazed by the bookings I might lose. "Beyond that, baby, you are beyond that," she declares.

The shag celebrates my coming-of-age. The day I turn twenty-one, I move with Gus into an apartment on boulevard Voltaire, near the place de la République.

We carry our small worlds in a friend's minivan, and we ask ourselves how we got by with so little space before.

High ceilings with old-fashioned baroque moldings, worn-out flooring of dark oak boards, and eight floor-to-ceiling windows with shutters that wrap around the last story of a once-grand building.

The walls are covered in strips of peeling wallpaper, gold patterns of leaves on pale greens, which we decide to distress even further for texture. From our top floor, perched up above the gray Paris roofs, we can see the Sacré-Coeur on one side and Notre-Dame on the other. The Eiffel Tower is a tiny speck in the distance by the gunmetal Seine.

I open a prosecco and drink from the bottle, unable to find any glasses. *Happy birthday to me!* The views make me breathless and I call out for Gus, needing to share in this moment. I sit with him, holding hands in the narrow wraparound terrace on two rickety metal garden chairs left by former tenants. Gus winks at me, his face pure happiness and pride. "Iris! Look at this, *mi amorcito,* can you believe it? Our first grown-up flat together. Are you scared?"

Yes, I am scared, I think.

Gus's birthday present is a silver Navajo pendant in the shape of an abstract cross and a hand-sewn leather book of printed photographs of us. Our initials are embossed on the spine. We turn the pages together. *How could I have been so open, so willing? So unafraid to show myself to Gus's camera?* I am stunned by the purity and innocence of the pictures, by the trust I don't think I possess anymore.

"I remember this one . . . we had just met. It was in the jardin du Luxembourg, that day it rained. And this one? I had forgotten this one! When did you take it?" I blush at the many images of me, tangled in his sheets. I am disarmed by a close-up of my ear and the nape of my neck, that spot where Gus kisses me and nibbles on my hair. "This day we made love for the first time," I say, and I look into his dark eyes.

Gus clasps the pendant around my neck and, lifting my hair, kisses my clavicle. We walk through the sunny flat hand in hand and make light conversation about the furniture we must buy. "Lots of bookshelves," Gus says. "The big office we can share. Your bathroom, my bathroom, your closet, and mine. Not that it matters, you steal all my clothes. The bougie dining room can become a guest room. When my parents come, they can stay there," says Gus as he smiles.

It's lightness and happiness, a repeat of the conversations we have had twenty times in the past month. We're in a good place; we have committed to sharing each other's lives. Gus feels safe in this space where we can talk about our future.

Moulié delivers an exuberant vase of my favorite Pierre de Ronsard roses. "Must be from Papa!" I shout with joy and grab the fax stapled to the pretty silk wrapping paper. *"On the most important of birthdays. I am so proud of my little girl. Your Halloween visit was too short, please come back soon, my beautiful rosebud. We love you. Delfine and Ludo."* The fax is covered with my father's funny little squiggles of bunnies and hearts. I touch the soft pink blooms and I want to cry with joy, and pain too. Gus comes behind me and folds his arms around my waist. I feel the warmth of his chest against my back. He turns me around and kisses the tip of my nose.

We sit on the floor and sift through our boxes. Every meaningful trace of our Paris lives has been carefully recorded and filed. I am moved by his nostalgia. Gus builds a life of tangible memories that he can grab on to. I am not interested in looking backward. I like people who know they are going to have a better day tomorrow.

The boxes are filled to the brim with tear sheets, drawings of each other, doodles on paper napkins, writing pads full of notes, Gus's sketches. A mass of snapshots and Polaroids of us, invitations to parties, letters from our families, old menus, postcards from our trips, and used plane tickets. "Jeeeeez, what on earth is all this? Are you hoarding?" I tease him, pulling his hair, and he wrestles me to the floor, forcing my lips open with his tongue. I cry out, "Stop! We have to finish! Cyril's coming, remember?"

We open more boxes and Gus pulls out a copy of the Genius Factory campaign, and we cheer loudly and toast, swigging from the prosecco bottle. I snatch the copy away from him, and we look at it together. "We were so young. I look so different now, not older, just different," I say.

"Happy birthday, my old lady," he teases.

"If you could go back to those Genius Factory days, what would you change?"

"I'd run away from you," Gus jokes. "No, seriously, Clemente. He's wack. And you, *princesa*?"

"Same here, I despise Clemente, I don't want him anywhere near me. Also, I miss my father and want to see my mum. Why don't we move to New York? We're getting so much work from America, it would make sense. We can be closer to our families." *And I could keep Clemente away from us,* I think to myself.

Gus hugs me tenderly and whispers in my ear, "Why not? I'll go anywhere with you." Gus kisses me and I get aroused by his tongue in my mouth. I slowly unbutton his shirt. "Does the birthday girl get anything she wants today?"

We make love tenderly on the floor, and afterward I lie on his shoulder, staring at the ceiling.

From the boxes we bring out stacks of magazines with our editorials. Publication after publication of Gus's fashion work, and some advertising too, the three Genius Factory campaigns that launched our careers, the American *Vogue* with Yves de Sarcelles's story on a six-page double spread, which catapulted my career into the stratosphere.

"What did Delfine say about those? Did she love them? Was she proud of you?" Gus gazes at me and smiles.

"She didn't say anything, about that or any other shoot. I FedExed copies to her, I asked her many times. I thought that she would have mentioned your photographs at least. But she does not care, Gus, never said a word. Papa loved the Genius Factory campaigns. He gave those copies to everyone he knew, and he also showed the *Vogue* to all the cousins in New Jersey."

Gus holds my gaze. I can see my pain reflected in his eyes.

I go back to digging in the boxes and find Gus's many *Revue* spreads, as well as those in *Stern*, *I-D* magazine, and *The Face*. Publication after publication in the edgiest magazines in Europe. Gus handles each magazine with care. He finds a copy of *Vogue Australia* with my picture on the cover. It's a dramatic black-and-white close-up of my face with an orchid in my hair. Opening it to an earmarked page, he reads to me in a bad imitation of an Australian accent. *"Meet Iris de Valadé, our March cover girl ...* blah blah *... nuanced, responsive, unique, versatile, chameleonic ...* blah blah *... a photographer's dream and a strong mysterious personality also known as 'The Gaze.'* Do I know this girl? Is this you?" Gus turns to me, laughing.

"Oh God, stop! That interview was so embarrassing! I said way too much. Never again. I've learned my lesson." I punch him on the arm and we tussle on the floor, giggling. *Where did the years go? They went so fast.*

Gus goes to the lab. Cyril arrives and helps me unpack the office boxes.

To celebrate my birthday, Gus books our favorite table at Anahi. I am wearing the Givenchy dress that he loves and my highest suede pumps. The restaurant is full of people I know, and I wave at a table of close friends. I drink a kir royale and wait for him to arrive from the lab. His phone goes to voicemail.

Anahi is now empty. I ask for the bill and get up to leave.

"The drinks are on the house," say the owners, Carmina and Pilar. "Are you going to be all right?"

I walk home under a cold November rain and find Gus curled up asleep on our floor.

Where were you? What are you hiding from me? Don't retreat into your dark place. Please talk to me.

CHAPTER 31

The couturier's black car drops us off at an opulent baroque villa on the outskirts of Rome.

I hold on to Gus's arm as I tiptoe on the gravel to keep my spiked satin heels from sinking in. Hundreds of candles line the winding pathway to the stairs.

It is Couture Week in Rome. The red velvet dress I am wearing is the same one I walked in down the Spanish Steps only a few hours ago.

Servants in starched uniforms and white gloves pass silver trays laden with champagne glasses and petits fours. A baroque ensemble plays in a courtyard, and Gus and I wander around ornate rooms filled with silver candelabra and low-hanging chandeliers.

I need to find the powder room and fix my lipstick. We get lost in a maze of corridors and endless doors. We hear laughter coming from the back of the villa, and we open a metal door that takes us to a winter garden with potted palm trees, orchids, and ferns.

A crowd is gathered around a small fountain. Gus and I approach. A boy not older than eight stands naked on a marble pedestal in a shallow alabaster basin. The little gypsy boy poses like a plump, pink, spouting cherub, but he is dark skinned and a bag of bones. The male guests take turns urinating on him. The women cackle and clap.

I grab Gus's hand, and we flee.

CHAPTER 32

I am so happy for our move. *Boulevard Voltaire will fix things*, I think.

Gus will spend more time working from our home. I want to have a real home, a home of love and dreams, the kind of home my friends talk about when they say, *"Come to our home."* A home that waits for you after a difficult shoot, a long night, a raucous party, a bad decision, the wrong move. Like the homes that Gus and I left behind were at times. Like Joan's home, whose heartbeat I will miss.

Gus is booked in Paris for a South Korean beauty catalog, and I wait for him night after night. I open a drawer in the new office and take out the prints of our latest shoot. The painful beauty of the pictures comes as a near shock. The shots are brutal, with a grit to them that I have not seen yet in his work. The starkness and quality of the tones, my naked body on the sofa, my hair in a snarl, makeup smudged under my eyes, the look on my face. I look haunted.

I remember that day way too well, I'd just found a small sachet of blow in a tangle of his clothes. I have done nothing about it. I don't know what to do. The prints remind me of that day.

I call Eva and we meet in the Marais in the most anonymous brasserie I can think of.

"Iris, hello, luvie! Everything good? Love that shag! Brilliant! Must shoot you immediately, before anyone else does. Let's see . . . we can do a story for *I-D* mag. There was this seventies musician in London, Gaye Advert . . . gorgeous. She had your shag. She wore a black leather jacket and panda-eye makeup. She was the first to define that female punk-rock look and . . ." Eva's voice trails off. I am not listening to her. I reach for my pack of cigarettes, and my hands shake as I light one.

I look at Eva in her bright-pink faux-fur cocoon jacket and the floppy dark-blue beret perched sideways on her head, amused by how the clothes she wears define her. Eva looks like a sexy French art student. Torn black stocking and tall Dr. Martens stompers add to the look. A sexy French *poupée*, a doll.

"Eva, has Gus been acting weird?"

Eva leans over the table and her mood changes. "I don't know where to start. This conversation is overdue, but I didn't want to distress you until after you'd moved into the new place. And by the way, you're wasting away. You really are too thin, luv. You just finished Fashion Week and then you move into a new flat with Gus? You must take time off and rest for the rest of the month, promise? You can't look haggard, you'll lose jobs. People will say you're on drugs."

I am on drugs. Those blue pills keep me going, moving, running, racing, smiling, posing, traveling, catwalking. I'll stop, but not now. I am too tired. If I stop those blue bombs, everything else stops. I fear I will collapse into a blubbering heap of insecurity and exhaustion.

Eva is the only one to tell me this, to warn me, apart from Kitti. Kitti feeds me like a heifer when I am too skinny, reprimands me when my skin looks dull, my eyes hollow. Magali at Blitz? She doesn't give a shit, aren't models meant to be lank and stringy? Magali faxes me schedules that get longer and longer and are now updated every few hours. She does tell me not to drink champagne before a cosmetics job: *"Bubbles, ma chérie, bubbles are the enemy of the face; they make the face puffy."* She also tells me not to take up yoga or my arms will bulk up. She's not my guardian, that's for sure; she's just a well-paid secretary to me.

"Eva, is anything off with Gus lately? You spend more time with him than me."

"We're all off, innit? A bit mental." Eva guffaws. "It's hard to keep up. I mean, this pace. Like, what other industry do you know starts from scratch every six months? Or whose product is created from zero every new season? It gets to the point during Fashion Week that I am so used to sleeping on the floor at Marc's showroom, of pulling off four all-nighters in a row, that I don't even find it insane anymore."

Eva drinks her black coffee and takes a deep breath. "Gus? He's worse than ever, now that you ask. He's always shooting, printing, editing, retouching, drawing, prepping—obsessively. I ask him to hang out after jobs, to call you for a drink, but he comes off those shoots and totally slumps. One minute he's jumping up and down behind the camera, manic, and the minute after, he's collapsed in a corner, alone and depressed, not talking to anyone. Is he taking meds? Antidepressants?"

"I found some cocaine in his jeans."

"Oh shit."

"Yes, oh shit. And he's acting so strange. Sometimes he's Gus. He's sweet and attentive and caring and present. We have a good time. Sometimes we party but nothing major, just booze and some E or joints. He never misses an appointment and he's very professional, always working. But then . . . other times . . . he'll just disappear. He'll go off to the lab to print, and he'll spend the night there. Or he'll be on a trip and won't pick up his phone for days. Is that normal? When I ask him he says nothing, he just retreats into himself. I can't get through to him on those days. He never opens up about his feelings, not anymore."

"Do you still have sex?"

"Hardly." I look away, avoiding Eva's gaze.

"When did all this start?"

"This year, the past few months, maybe longer. I don't . . . I don't know if I can go on like this . . ."

Eva grabs a cigarette from my pack and orders another coffee. "Who are his friends? Who does he hang out with?" she says.

"He's a lone wolf, Eva. He's *always* working, it seems like he's only happy *when* he's working. And then fucking Clemente calls him all the time and is constantly dropping in on his shoots and asking if he can come with us to parties and stuff. He says it's for networking, to introduce us to people. Bullshit. He has a crush on Gus is what I think. Just the thought makes me ill."

"Clemente does a lot of coke, you know?"

"I imagined." I shrug. "But who doesn't in Clemente's gang—they're too successful too soon, they make too much money, they're too hot . . . they're high on themselves."

"I wouldn't feel comfortable if my agent did coke," replies Eva. "I think you should watch Gus closely. Maybe he's having a nervous breakdown from stress. In any case, I really think he needs help. It's spooking me out. He looks so . . . vulnerable." Eva shudders lightly as she says this and zips up her pink furry thing.

"Now that you mention it, he's been miserable about his work. I think it's because he loathes the advertising industry. He's crushed by the lack of freedom, but he has to accept the jobs in order to pay for his artwork and his family in LA. He hates working with people that lack a sense of context and culture. He asks himself why they insist on working with him if they just send him mood boards. He hates their fucking mood boards and their fucking laziness. How is he when he is with you?" I ask.

Eva looks away. Then she fixes her gaze on my face. "It's bad. The other day we went to a prepro at Trimedia. They were casting the Beach Beauté bathing-suit campaign, and the client made him confirm two dirty-looking girls that were obviously hookers. At the prepro, the clients and creatives sniggered. They played with the words *Bitch* Beauté . . . he was disgusted.

The agency pretended nothing was happening. Now he's freaking out because we have to spend a week in Saint Bart's shooting with the client and his whores. All these things that we take as normal because we're used to them, they're *not* normal, Iris, they're hideous. Gus has always been very sensitive to the fuckery in the industry. He had a very strict upbringing, catholic, he's easily perturbed."

Tears roll down my cheeks, and I wipe them with my sleeve.

Eva continues. "Normally he doesn't let it affect him because we're surrounded by brilliant and creative professionals doing amazing things, and that alone is uplifting, but when he's down, he questions everything. Now he's saying that his *Revue* editorials are becoming pedestrian, middle-of-the-road. He's less motivated because he's trying to please too many people; Ada, Joan, the art department, the advertisers, they all have their say, and he tells me that they're slowly strangling him, killing him."

I take a paper napkin from the table and wipe the tears. They don't stop coming.

"Eva, he wants to quit, he wants to give up his dreams."

Eva looks at me for what seems an eternity and holds my hand. "I didn't know it was so hard for Gus. He should just think of the money, like a mantra: *Just think of the fucking money.* Repeat: *Just think of the fucking money.*" Eva shrugs. "For now, it's the only job I love and I have. Doing anything else is out of the question. I *still* adore my profession when I get to create; I *still* get excited when I meet the people that are in it for the good reasons. You know, the weird ones, the mad ones, the freaks, the ones that choose fashion as an art and a passion. But it's a hard and scary world to live in and thrive, especially if you have a conscience. Right now, I confess that I'm trying not to overthink things because I really don't have a choice."

"Eva, do you ever think about raising a family? I think Gus wants to have kids."

"Raising a family? I can't even raise myself! I'm desperate to have kids. It's very difficult, Iris; the business goes so fast that if you stop, you're over in one season. This job is not an ideal place for family. Where would a poor kid and husband fit in all this? I just can't afford to have kids right now."

Eva pauses, puffs on her cigarette, and blows smoke through her pursed lips. "Listen, why don't you two go away for a week? Rest a bit, take a break from all this pressure, talk to each other. You could drive to Normandy and stay in a little bed-and-breakfast, walk on the beach . . ."

I nod.

"I'll book it for you. I know just the place. I'll organize everything. You just have to clear up those dates and go."

"Thank you, it feels good to talk."

"Promise me that you'll take care of yourself," Eva says.

"I will."

"I'll try to keep an eye on Gus, see who's giving him drugs . . . but this is serious. If you think that he is using a lot, please call me immediately, okay?"

I walk home in a daze, more anxious and afraid than before my meeting with Eva. As I turn into rue de Turenne, I see Saskia's face on the side of a bus shelter advertising raincoats. I stop and stare at her portrait. She is laughing, her white hair chopped in a funny bad bob that is partly tucked into the collar of her coat. Her green-gray eyes glint mischievously like the Saskia of before. Someone has graffitied *Fuck Fashion* over her face.

I touch the poster thinking of the last time I had seen her. It hadn't been too long ago, a month, tops. We had walked the Marc Jacobs show in New York and shared some cigarettes afterward, making plans for the weeks ahead. That evening at the after-show party I had found her doing shots by the bar. She was alone. I took in her unkempt appearance and smudged makeup, the red-wine stains on her coat, her expensive handbag on the dirty floor. "Saskia, I think you better go home."

"No, no, not home. He is there. Home. I cannot go home." Saskia clutches my arm and shakes her head, her eyes wide open.

"Who is home, Saskia? What do you mean?"

"He. He is. He's coming to get me. They are. I have to be careful. I cannot go home."

"Saskia, what's wrong, for fuck's sake? Stop drinking. *Now.* Come to my hotel, spend the night with me."

Saskia rolls her eyes around the room and starts laughing maniacally. "It's okay. I'm very good. I'm a big girl. I go now. See you tomorrow. *Vaarwel*, my friend."

"Your bag! Saskia, you forgot your bag. Where's your ring?"

"My ring? What ring?"

I pick up Saskia's purse from the floor, and I button up her coat. I slide off her Cartier watch and tuck it into the front pocket of her jeans. Holding her arm, I take her to the door of the club and put her, still raving, inside a taxi.

That was the last time I saw Saskia. I want to call her now. "Hey, dog face! I'm looking at your ugly-ass Dutch mug on a bus shelter. Where are you? Let's go dancing and bouncing."

I suddenly remember that Saskia is gone. Where, I do not know. Her agency was vague. I feel terribly guilty.

Gus is at home bent over a stack of contact sheets, his loupe glued to his eye. He looks up as I come in and rushes to me. He holds me tightly. "I love you so much that you cannot even imagine, *mamacita*. When I'm away from you, I love you in my pictures. I love you here . . ." He kisses the spot where my ear joins the nape of my neck. "And here . . ." He kisses the tip of my nose. "And here . . ." He holds my face in both his hands and kisses my forehead. "I love your mind . . ." He kisses my eyelid. "Your beauty . . ." He kisses the palm of my hand. "Your kindness. You are my best friend, the only person I trust. My beautiful girlfriend. You are good for my soul," he murmurs in my hair.

He pulls away from me and stares past me. I see he has been crying.

"Did you speak to your father? Is he coming?"

Gus shakes his head. "No, he told me to get a proper job and stop the fashion *mariconadas*, the queer stuff."

"Did you speak to your mother?"

"He wouldn't put her on the phone."

I hold his hand and pull him toward the bedroom. We sit on the bed, and I put his head to my bosom and rock him gently like a child.

That night we make the most tender love.

I wake up before dawn and he is gone. He has left a drawing by my pillow, of a naked girl with short, spiky black hair, bangs, and pink lips. She holds a bleeding heart in her hand. Tears stream down her face and make big blue puddles on the floor. *I don't know how to love you,* it says.

I sit on the bed and sob in the darkness of our room. *Loving you is hell. I don't love loving you anymore.*

CHAPTER 33

"I never invited Clemente to the party, he creeps me out. Why didn't you tell me he was coming?" I turn away from the chopping board to face Gus.

"Baby, there're gonna be so many people here that you won't even notice him. Please?" Gus holds my chin between his thumb and index finger and moves it up and down. "Come on, my little angel. Make an effort. See? Your head is saying yes."

I don't laugh as I slice a baguette into a basket of assorted breads. "Why? Why does he have to come here? Our home is a Clemente-free zone. Of the few Clemente-free areas left in this city. I don't want that toxic piece of shit in our home. He's going to pollute it."

"Iris, seriously, just burn some sage after he leaves."

I glare at Gus.

"I don't want to offend him. Not now that I have to tell him about moving to New York next year. He's going to bite my head off when I break that one."

I shrug. "Tough, Gus. It's inevitable, it's what happens in this business. And then, once we're there and your contract expires, we don't renew it. Three years, done our duty. Bugger off, Clemente. Ciao, *bello*. Sayonara, asshole."

"Gangsta Bitch" is playing loudly in the kitchen. Gus goes to the pantry, brings out a bottle of mezcal, and pours two shots. "Whoa! You look sexy as hell, *niñita*. Especially in that dress when you're angry and holding a knife."

I down the shot of mezcal and change my mood. I smooth out my short Azzedine Alaïa knit dress and smile at him. "Just wait till I put on my heels. Ooooooh, baby!"

I crank up the booming bass, then wriggle my ass in the tight black dress as I dance around the kitchen, singing to the loud music.

Always in trouble and definitely fuckable . . .

Gus takes the compact Canon from his pocket and starts shooting me. I turn around with the knife in my hand and blow him a sexy kiss. I stare him in the eyes as we toast and see a look I've never seen before. "How many have you had?" I ask.

"How many mezcals? Don't know, lost count. Who cares. We're gonna have us a great party. It's important, baby, it's our first party in our first house. Does it really matter how much I drink?"

It's not the drink, I want to tell him, but I bite my tongue. *Now is not the time.* I shake my head. "Don't get shit-faced, 'k?"

The food is gone. The music is pounding. Friends, and friends of friends, drop by and then leave, only to come back again in an interminable flow all night long. An endless stream of party-loving people with bottles in their hands. Most of them I don't know.

Our apartment becomes hot and sweaty with the heat of the packed bodies. Someone has dimmed the lights. I'm in Gus's study with the door locked and the windows open as a wave of nausea surges over me. Lying on the couch, I unhook the front of my dress; my skin is clammy and I swallow gulps of cold winter air. There's a knock on the door, and reluctantly I get up to open it.

"Are you okay?" Gus comes in and closes the door behind him. "You disappeared, I was looking for you."

I lie back down on the couch and Gus sits next to me, holding my hand. I notice that his shirt is damp and sticks to his body, his hair is wet with perspiration, and his hand shakes. I close my eyes. The smell of whisky on his breath makes me even more nauseous. "So-so, I think I drank too much and didn't eat. You?"

"Just dancing, having fun," Gus says.

I turn my head toward him. His body is rocking back and forth and one leg twitches. "Gus, look at me. How much coke did you do? What else did you take?"

"A little bit of this, a little bit of that . . . don't spoil my fun, *mamacita*. Don't do the lecturing, baby. It's a special evening. We're celebrating."

"Gus, this must stop. We have to talk. What are you doing to yourself?"

He stares at me through bloodshot eyes, his mind a thousand miles away. "Everyone's asking for you. Eva just left with Kitti, and we've run out of cigarettes." He caresses my hair, tucking a strand behind my ear. "Are you coming back?"

I nod and get up slowly from the couch. I wish I could go to bed. Unlike everyone else here tonight, I don't feel like losing my mind. I walk through the apartment with Gus and don't recognize any of the people that are still here. It's the night crawlers, those who spend their evenings going from party to party until dawn, the zombies. In the kitchen, Cyril hands me a glass of cold water and says goodbye. The living room empties, but the music is still playing loudly. My head is bursting. My headache is getting worse.

Gus is in our bedroom lying on the bed, laughing with Clemente. A small tray sits on the bedspread between them.

"*Carissima!* I have not seen you all night. Were you hiding from me? You're breaking my heart." Clemente jumps up from the bed and kisses my hand. I snatch it away from his wet lips, and he mocks me with a petulant toss of the head. "Oooooooh! The supermodel does not want to be touched? I am too ugly for you? I am not famous enough? You always hate me, *bambina*, you mock me, you laugh at me. Why you make me suffer? I work very hard for your *fidanzato*, your boyfriend, I deserve a little love too, no?" Clemente holds me by the arms as his body gets closer. He cracks a side smile and licks his lips slowly. Reptilian. His eyes bore into me. My stomach turns looking at his mouth. Drops of sweat form under his nose. I turn toward

Gus, who is lying on the bed, staring into space, sucking on a joint.

I back away from Clemente and hiss, "Enough. Stop this."

Clemente shrugs nonchalantly while continuing to leer at me. He takes a small camera out of his pocket, shoves it in my face, and snaps a picture. "Say cheese, *carissima*."

I am livid. I want to punch his smarmy mouth. "Did I interrupt something?" I say, pointing at the white lines on the tray. "Don't mind me. Going to the bathroom, I need something for my headache."

I take two tablets from my medicine drawer and gag. Grudgingly, I grab the bottle of Perrier that Clemente offers me, and I swallow the tablets. *I hate your face.* I wander around the flat, turning the lights on, chasing out the last revelers. I turn the music off. My head stops throbbing but I feel dizzy, drunk. I want to lie down in bed and I need to close my eyes. I go back to our bedroom and sit on the armchair, resting my head on the soft velvet cushion. Clemente. He's still here, motherfucker. *Go away, leave Gus alone.*

My eyelids feel heavy, and I fight the urge to sleep. Clemente's shrill laugh jars me. I look up from the armchair with contempt as he snorts two lines of blow and hands the tray to Gus.

CHAPTER 34

For a moment I blink and stare at the ceiling, not quite knowing where I am. I try to push my hair away from my face, but my arms and hips are pinned under a weight lying across my body. It's Clemente.

I struggle to think clearly. I have lost all my strength. I turn my head to the other side and I see Gus's naked back a few inches from me. I have no concept of time; the shutters are drawn and the room is dark. I am slowly beginning to grasp the situation, but I am confused. Am I in a dream? Or is it a nightmare?

I look at Clemente lying naked across me, and waves of fear and revulsion hit me. *Oh God, oh God, please no.* I try to twist my loins out from under his, but I am too weak. I stare at the back of his head and the long stiff curls in disarray. He snores loudly.

I inch myself out by pushing on the bed with my feet and hollowing out my body from under his. *Oh God, oh God, please God, please, this cannot be.*

Careful not to make any noise, I shuffle toward the bathroom. Clemente's snores drown out my steps while Gus fitfully tosses and turns.

Holding on to the sink, I stare at my blurred reflection in the mirror. I want to throw up. I sit on the edge of the toilet, holding my head. I notice that my thighs are bruised and chafed and my dress is hitched up around my waist. I have no underwear on and a sticky mess clings to my pubic hair and stomach. I look up from the toilet and see Gus standing naked in the bathroom doorway. Tears pour down my face. I am choking. "Gus?" I sob. "What did you do to me?"

"I don't know. We were having fun and then . . . ?"

"And then?"

"I can't remember . . ."

"Having fun with me?"

"*Dios mío* . . . I, I don't know."

"You raped me? Or was it Clemente? Or did you both take turns?" I wheeze through swollen lips. I stare at Gus's blurry face through the tears.

"It wasn't me. I promise, *mi niña*. I did not do it."

"That's even worse," I say.

A wave of vomit hits the roof of my mouth and I throw up in the bidet. The vomit splashes the floor. I wipe my mouth with an embroidered towel and see a smear of blood coming from my split lip. I hold my face in my hands.

Gus kneels on the floor by the toilet. "*Dios mío.* What have I done to you?"

I look at the bruises on my thighs. I touch the scratches on my wrists. "You have no idea."

Drops of blood stain the tiles.

he wanted Othilia to be with me. His ex-wife is in a bad relationship, and he needed his daughter to be away from all that."

"A real boyfriend? Like a serious one? I didn't know, you didn't tell me!"

"How would you know? You're the one not returning my calls. His name is Gaston and he's pure Parisian, born and raised here. He's a scientist. We have been together for six years."

"A scientist? I thought you would end up with a rock star . . . or a film director . . . but a nerd?"

Joan laughed. "Scientists *are* the new rock stars! You'll love Gaston. He has a company called MoonWave that generates electricity from wave and tidal energy. He created the technology that is used to harness this energy."

"Holy shit. I love him already. Lou's also a nerd, an artistic nerd. She's taking an online course on the perils of AI."

"Artificial intelligence?"

"Yeah. And I don't mean Siri. She became obsessed by this book called *Superintelligence* by a Swedish professor. She knows his TED Talk by heart."

"I think it's wonderful that you two are so connected," Joan said.

"Connected? Wishful thinking. All this I know from my neighbor, Chuck. He's the one that my daughter speaks to. She tells *me* nothing. Do you and Gaston live together?"

"Not yet, but soon. I'm getting used to Othilia living here and she with me. I'm trying to make myself more available for life. I am looking at other options too."

"Other options? Are you leaving *Revue*?"

"It's fortuitous that you came to Paris at this time in my life. I desperately need your opinion and advice."

Iris smiled. "Happy to help you, Joan."

"The way the magazine is going now, I might soon be fired and replaced by a millennial *influencer* who costs a fraction of my salary. Or even by one of Lou's robots, if magazines still exist at all in a few years."

"That's a depressing thought."

"It's sad, Iris, but it's what is happening now. Magazines have gone crazy trying to jump on the digital train. Fashion used to be scared of the internet, they kept it locked out because they couldn't micromanage their image on it. But now the monologue has become an 'unconditional surrender' and a dialogue where everyone wants in. People, the normal people, not just the fashionistas, share *likes* and looks. They have virtual shopping carts, they trend their favorite pieces and make them go viral in seconds. How that translates into sales we still don't know, but the front row is populated by It girls with millions of followers, bloggers, influencers, and YouTube stars. They're the new celebrities."

Iris nodded. "I saw Eva in LA a week ago. She's also having problems."

Joan continued. "Magazines are kicking out their best writers. Shooting budgets have been slashed, any kid with an iPhone can now take a good picture. Photographers and models are being booked based on their digital imprint and not their portfolios and experience. Exceptional designers who used to 'transport you to heavenly worlds,' now have to produce six to eight collections a year. That means a collection every six weeks with no margin for trial and error. What can I say? Time for me to move on? It's the sad dumbing down of an unparalleled industry, but also time for it to adapt to the new era, like the music industry had to do a few years ago. I just heard that Colette is closing down. Colette, of all places! What does that tell you about the future of retail distribution?"

"Do you have to let go just like that? Can't *you* adapt?"

"Yes, I have no choice but to embrace these changes, *ma chérie*, or else I too become obsolete. It's going to be tough for many of us. I'm not a techie, I have no idea how all this works, but I can't afford not to care anymore. It's the end of an era.

Advertisers are now giving a substantial part of their yearly budgets to digital advertising, and *Revue* opened its own digital department to produce content. On any given shoot, there are four camera teams filming, each one of us has our own crew. It's as if the print is there only to provide content for the digital version of the magazine . . . where do people like me fit in the new status quo?"

"But it's your entire life!"

"Well, yes, it was. But I have Gaston and Othilia. It might seem funny to you, but now I just want to be the woman of a man doing important things. I'm getting older and wiser and I am seeing beauty elsewhere. I need creative and business challenges. I need to do things that are meaningful, and sadly my position at *Revue* is not giving me *that* anymore. Othilia and Gaston give me that. I have tried to have conversations with Ada about the directions to take together, but she'd rather sit in the conference room listening to the suits talking about numbers. These suits have never seen the hundreds of howling fashion groupies that now wait outside the *défilé* tents in the jardin des Tuileries. The shows used to be mobbed by fashion students; now it's very young kids and fans. These fashion-obsessed kids are the ones we have to target, not the people that receive our magazine monthly through the mail. The kids, they follow the models, the celebrities, that's how they connect with fashion. There's so much we have to do to get it right. But I am alone, Ada is not there with me, and *she is* the editor in chief after all, she is my boss. I am looking into the abyss and not quite sure if I am ready to jump. And the abyss does not look like *Revue*."

"This sounds pretty scary, Joan, challenging, because it's new and happening so fast. But I'm not at all surprised. Give me time to think about it. There might be something in here for you, new tools, new platforms . . . if you know how to use them."

Iris was pensive. It was so familiar. It made her think of Delfine. She felt afraid and defeated for Joan. She sipped her coffee.

Joan put the chopped vegetables into an iron pot. "And you? Do you have a boyfriend?"

Iris blushed and looked at her ragged cuticles. "I need a manicure. I just came off the ranch. I feel so uncouth next to you," she replied.

"Iris, do you have someone? Who takes care of you and Lou?"

"We manage. We take care of each other. We don't need anyone." Iris shrugged. "I'm content in my mum role, I get to determine it."

"You mean?"

"Delfine was a terrible mother. I want to be a good mother, the best I can. In a way, I became a model because of Delfine, because I was so porous to her world. Lou will have her own life, she'll be able to choose without being influenced by me or my past. She lives in the instant like all her generation. I have to keep up to date with her world, not the other way around. It's not like me as a kid looking to fit into Delfine's world."

"And money? Do you have money?"

"Financially we're okay. My father's company had amassed debts, they had overextended during the last years before his death, but he left just enough for us to get by, and I sold my New York loft. I sell my sculptures . . . we're very lucky, we have a privileged life where we don't need much and we live quite simply because that is how I choose to live. I never surrounded myself with things that became necessary. But my worry is Lou's university. Without a scholarship, I won't be able to afford one of the top ones."

"Your sculptures are very powerful, Iris. Do you mind if I show them to my friend Florence Dubac? Her gallery is one of the best in Paris."

"My sculptures? How have you seen them?"

"I Googled you, darling. There are a few images from your last exhibition floating around the internet. Bravo, *chérie*."

Joan started heating water in the iron pot. She made herself a cup of tea and sat at the table, facing Iris. They remained in silence for a few minutes. "Anything else you wanted to tell me?"

"Joan . . . as I told you on Skype, it's about Gus's body of work, I need to—"

"I know you're anxious to look at everything, so I asked our interns to photocopy files of every story that Gus did for *Revue*. Everything is on your desk, it's three years' worth of work."

Iris picked a dried petal off the table and gazed up at Joan. "That's great, Joan, thank you. I left Paris in November 2000. I have no idea how many more stories he did for you after that. When I lived with Gus, I filed everything. I knew the archive by heart: negs, Polaroids, prints, personal tests . . . Clemente has all that now."

Joan took both Iris's hands in hers. "Gus never shot a fashion story again after you left. Not for us, not for anyone. Those fashion shoots are unique."

Iris sat in stunned silence. She felt the tears welling up again.

"Gus was the only photographer that we gave prints back to after publication. That was smart of you. I don't know how you got away with that."

Iris lowered her eyes. "*Revue* never put Gus under contract. Why?"

"I don't know, that was Ada's call. I often told her that we needed to put him under contract, that he could leave us at any moment, and he did. On the other hand, you got away with murder, *chérie*. You'll do a splendid job of running his estate. I meant to tell you: some *Revue* prints have turned up here and there during the last two editions of the Paris Photo fair. Some were not stamped, but I recognized them—they were Gus's. The merchants are selling them as his, but unsigned."

Iris's face went dark. "Clemente could be selling those. Gus's gallery only sells signed limited editions with certificates and vintage prints. The vintage prints are by far the most valuable, the ones printed around the time that the picture was taken. The prints you are talking about must be the original prints from shoots. They were working tools, not art prints. They should not be in circulation."

Joan said, "This was normal in the predigital era. Photographic archives got lost, burnt in a backyard bonfire in a fit of anger, artists high and crazy, negatives exchanged for drugs, or even thrown away by mistake. It was messy. Artists die, or they stop paying for their storage units. Entire archives are tossed into a dumpster. So many unique photo archives were lost this way, forever. You've got a lot of work to do, my dear . . . it was a long time ago."

"I'm meeting Cyril tomorrow. Remember him? Gus's first camera assistant—" Iris never finished her sentence. The front door closed with a loud thud, and something crashed on the floor by the entrance.

"*Bonsoir, tout le monde.*" A teen in a gauzy white dress and opaque black stockings with high-tops bounded toward Iris and kissed her warmly on both cheeks. The girl's cool skin smelled of violets. "*Salut*, Iris, *je suis* Othilia. Joan told me a lot about you. You're a supermodel, *n'est ce pas*? Welcome to Paris."

"How was your day, *chérie*?" Joan asked.

"*Bof*, meh; science lab all morning and coding all afternoon. Finals in a week. Can I finish my pizza then go to my room? I have much, much homework for tomorrow."

Without waiting for a reply, Othilia plopped an overflowing plate in front of Iris and Joan and started munching on a slice of pizza.

"Othilia is studying computer science, and in her spare time she works on her own biotech project in our basement.

She feeds trash to bacteria in order to produce electricity, or something like that."

"Sounds wicked!" Iris said.

Othilia stopped chewing her pizza and lifted the slice. "The idea is that as long as you feed your battery with organic stuff, it will not run out. So the potential energy of the organic trash—pizza, cardboard, anything that rots—will be transformed into an electrical current."

Iris turned to Joan and said, "Sick . . . wait till I tell Lou."

"Othilia, you know that Iris has a daughter your age?"

"Ah *oui?* Cool."

"Yes, she likes art, she likes music, she likes tech. She makes things with her hands, she also plays the guitar and takes pictures," Iris said.

"*Génial!* I wish I could play the guitar, that's *fantastique.* Joan told me that you live near Silicon Valley, *non?* And Stanford, my father says the best labs in America are in Stanford. You're lucky to live in California, *non?*" Othilia folded her pizza slice in half and stuffed it into her mouth, scrolling through her phone with her greasy index finger. Joan looked at Iris and smiled.

Taking her plate to the sink, Othilia turned toward them. "*A toute à l'heure.* Have to study. Happy to meet you, Iris. Now I can say at school that I know a supermodel. Joan has never taken me to a fashion show."

"Othilia, *chérie,* I'll remind you that you're the one who says that fashion is so stupid. Voilà, so I don't take you. Last time you said you preferred to go to the Salon de l'Agriculture to look at the farm animals. And tractors."

"I don't blame her. Joan, do you know that photography book with the beautiful farm animals and their dignified owners that Yann Arthus-Bertrand took? It's my favorite, I gave it to Lou," Iris said.

Othilia high-fived Iris as she walked past. "*Bestiaux.* Masterpiece, I have it too."

Iris looked at Othilia as she picked up her bulging back-pack. Her nonchalance was so Parisian. Unlike Lou's school friends, who aspired to look like cheerleaders or beauty pag-eant contestants in a reality show, Othilia had a modesty and a look that said, *I don't try very hard.* The more she observed her, the prettier she found her, with her creamy pale skin, large, soft brown eyes with long lashes, thick silky hair gathered into a sort of chignon, and a normal figure for a teen who probably did not have the time nor desire to work out.

Iris's WhatsApp started ringing. It was Lou.

Speak of the devil, Iris thought. "Hey!"

"Yo, mom! Wait, lemme pass you on to Maca."

Maca came on. "Hey, gorgeous, just wanted to make sure it's all's good. We miss you heaps. *Bonsoir, Paris!*" Iris heard the phone rustling, and then Lou came on again.

"Chuck checked in with me and sends you his love. We played chess. We just wanted to know that you were okay."

"Hey, wait there just a minute, miss," Iris called out. "Everything good at school? Are you making progress on your bats?"

"They're not bats, I told you two million times," Lou said, sighing into the receiver, and then she hung up. Iris stared at her phone and turned to Joan, who rolled her eyes.

"Don't be mad at her," Joan said.

"I try not to, but they're so different, you know?"

"And you mean?"

"Othilia, Lou . . . they're not afraid of the future because they don't have a past. They have no idea how the world will be in ten years because it's all changing so fast, at lightning speed compared to ours, yet they have less fear because they adapt so quickly. They are more flexible than we ever were . . ." Iris said.

"I never thought of that, you're right. I have hope in this generation. They seem more serious than I was at their age. I used to think that they were all self-absorbed narcissists living through their virtual lives, but Othilia and her friends have proven me wrong. *I* am the one feeling selfish and useless now, I'm part of the old establishment, the old set of values . . ."

Iris's phone rang. Seeing a private number on the screen, she let it go to voicemail. With a sense of dread she listened to the message.

"Iris de Valadé? This is Amanda Greenwood from the *Daily Stand*. We need to talk ASAP. Please get back to me." Amanda's annoyed voice clicked off.

Iris stared at her phone, frowning. "Joan, I need your help. The *Daily Stand* wants to interview me and publish a story on Gus and me next Sunday. I'm running out of time, I have to give them something. I need you to speak to them. Would you do that for me? They're looking for corpses."

"You have to be kidding me, the *Daily Stand*? Oh, *merde.*"

CHAPTER 36

Like a mantra, Iris repeated, *Strong, strong, be strong, negotiate, negotiate, negotiate, more time, a little more time* . . . then took a big breath.

Sitting on the bench in the square facing Joan's apartment, she called Amanda.

"Amanda's phone."

"Ms. Greenwood, good morning, this is Iris de Valadé. I'm sorry I could not call you before but I was traveling. Is it too early for you?"

"Call me Amanda, would you please? Oh, splendid, Iris, about time you called," Amanda whined.

It took effort for Iris to remain silent.

"I was getting an earful from my editor in chief. With or without your interview, I need to finish the piece this week, not one day more, sorry, love. Where are you?"

"Amanda, I don't have anything juicy for you. I have not seen Gustavo de Santos in sixteen years, and my memory is shot."

"Well, that's a shame. Are you sure? Because I found a couple of people ready to be interviewed, what?"

"Good for you. But there's little on me. I'm not on social media, and I stopped modeling many years ago. Since then I have been conducting a very mundane life. I live on a farm with chickens and coyotes. Do you really want to bother?" Iris noticed that her voice was becoming shrill. *Tone it down. Tone It Way Down.*

"It's up to me to decide whether or not I have enough good bits for my piece. Seeing that I'm going to publish it anyway, why don't you just reply to my questions. What?"

"And they are?" Iris rasped. She cleared her throat and listened as Amanda rustled some papers.

"Hang on, dear," then the sound of a lighter and Amanda blowing smoke into the receiver. "Well, first of all, how did you meet de Santos? Was it love at first sight? Did you take many drugs with him? I've seen paparazzi shots of you two falling out of nightclubs. You were very young then, would you let your daughter become a model too? How was the relationship between de Santos and your daughter? Can you tell me more about your celebrity friends? Why did you stop modeling at the height of your career? Why did you break up? Your mother, Delfine de Valadé, was once a very respected figure in the fashion world. Is that how you became a model? Can you give me some tidbits about your mother and what it was like to be raised by a famous fashion editor?"

Iris's heart sank and she scrambled to find a way out, someplace to maneuver. "I'll answer some of these if you put in writing that I can approve the photos you'll run. Also, you can call Joan Hutley at *Revue* magazine, she's the fashion director. Joan knows me well and was close to Gustavo professionally. She has agreed to be interviewed."

"I won't guarantee anything, of course. I need to review your demands with my editor."

Iris's voice was becoming thinner and thinner. *Man up, for fuck's sake. What's the matter with you?* "How many pictures are you planning to run?" Iris said, detecting a pleading tone to her voice.

"Ten? Fifteen? Some artistic portraits of you, unpublished party shots of the two of you, some photographs you took of de Santos . . ."

On the verge of bursting into tears, Iris replied, "I'll get back to you," and hung up.

Iris sat on the bench staring straight ahead, her heart thumping. *Things have a way of coming back to bite you in the ass, no matter how hard you try to run away from them.*

Rubbing her bleary eyes, she looked at her phone. There was a WhatsApp from Chuck: *'Bones we miss you come back soon is everything ok? how does paris feel? taco and chuck.'*

Iris replied. *'Thank u taco and chuck everything k well no actually things started quite shit but i'll survive will be in touch very soon and post you on progress, miss u too sorry i'm such a loser and i don't call.'*

Iris started to walk down rue d'Ormesson, checking out her old neighborhood with a mix of curiosity and dread. An absinthe shop had replaced her favorite cheese shop, whose pungent smell she had been able to pick up from a block away. A gluten-free cupcake shop stood in lieu of Chez Josette, a bakery that had opened at six in the morning and sold buttery croissants and grayish *baguettes classiques* with chewy dough. A couple of trendy chain clothing shops had taken over from the orthopedic underwear shop specializing in mature women's lingerie.

At the corner of Rivoli and Saint-Antoine she found her café. It was busy. She sat at a wobbly table on the sidewalk.

The sun was just beginning to appear through a thick pile of Chantilly cream clouds, warming the chilly spring air. Drowsy clients at nearby tables read the newspapers and smoked.

On her right, a couple of students recited lines to each other from an old book. The girl's pale thighs grazed those of her handsome companion. *He's into her, but she's taking it too seriously.* Intense, with the intensity of a teenager who thinks that the whole world revolves around her. Iris observed them, happy to watch the little things that did not matter.

Across the way was the bustling intersection of the place Saint-Paul, framed by the baroque façade of the

Saint-Paul-Saint-Louis church and next to it the *métro* station, a children's carousel, and a newspaper kiosk.

Watching from her table on the sidewalk, Iris felt her heart catch in her mouth. Nothing had changed very much, or at least not right there, where she had waited for Gus so many times. With her eyes closed she could have made her way across the street, navigating between the busy food shops and the crowds of passersby and students that waited at the top of the *métro* escalator.

The past was too close.

As she made her way up rue de Turenne, Iris noticed the neighborhood had been cleaned up for the tourists that flocked to the Picasso museum and the place des Vosges. Gleaming white art galleries, American-type juice bars with crafty logos, and expensive independent boutiques lined the sidewalks once occupied by a cobbler, family-run food shops, and a laundry where Iris used to sit talking to the owner, Madame Delvaux, about how the neighborhood was changing so fast.

At rue Jarente, Iris made a left and strolled away from the narrow street and into the tiny Impasse de la Poissonnerie. Standing in front of the Jarente fountain, she reached down and ran her fingers over the head and mouth of the bronze satyr from which the water spouted. Making sure that no one was watching her, Iris stuck her index finger into its open mouth and pulled out a coin that was tucked into the crevasse. Smiling, she put the coin in her pocket. As she turned to leave, she walked past the minute Hôtel Jeanne d'Arc. The once-decrepit hotel was being refurbished.

Iris walked and walked, needing to numb her feelings, peel them off her skin like she would her sweatshirt. Deep sadness permeated every step she took, and a sense of foreboding marred the day. *I didn't want to come back, ever. What am I doing here?*

She continued up rue de Turenne, past a family of Roma going through a garbage container, pulling out used clothes and piling them onto a wheelchair. A little boy with sad, runny eyes stared at her from the gutter, where he was playing with a plastic bottle. A withered man wearing a cocky hat slapped him, reprimanding him in a guttural language that she could not recognize. On the quaint rue Charlot, a homeless man slept sprawled across a bench inside a laundromat. Plastic buckets full of lilies of the valley lined the sidewalk by the supermarket next to her beloved couscous joint, Chez Omar. An old lady walked three lapdogs, leaving behind a pile of shit in their wake. *This is more like it,* Iris thought.

At the Café Charlot she went inside and waited for Cyril.

CHAPTER 37

She recognized him as soon as she saw him hovering on the side of the covered terrace, clutching his beret in his hands, too shy to approach the harried waiters. He spotted her, and a smile lit up his pinched face as he walked to the table.

Iris felt odd. When Gus shot, it had always been Gus and Cyril, Cyril and Gus, never one without the other. Cyril assumed the role as Gus's first camera assistant with the utmost pride and solemnity, as if blessed to have the job. Cyril was loyal and faithful, devoted to Gus and a reassuring presence, filling in for Gus's technical black holes and bad organizational skills. Cyril had never aspired to be a professional photographer himself, he just wanted to be the best photo assistant in Paris.

Cyril kissed Iris on both cheeks and sat at the table, still holding tightly to the beret on his lap.

Iris found herself unable to speak, and her eyes started to tear up.

"You have not changed," said Cyril gently. "You look as beautiful as . . ." His voice trailed off and Iris studied his face while she waited for the wave of emotion to pass.

Cyril had the French-looking face of a character actor in a Jean Renoir film: an angular face with pale skin, watery eyes, crooked teeth that had never been fixed, red ears, and a long nose. "It's the French face you get when you eat all that Camembert," Gus would say jokingly. Gus and Cyril had shared a special bond. One look from Gus, and Cyril was there with the right lens, a loaded camera, or ready to move the scrim just that one inch away. When things got noisy and confused on a shoot, Gus would retreat to Cyril's camera table with the piles of marked film rolls and huddle there, searching for a safe haven, a respite.

Cyril's dirty blond hair had grown long and wispy. His chin was covered with pale fuzz. The kind look in his eyes was the same.

"I am sorry for Gus," Cyril finally said after a long silence. Iris noted that his heavy accent had not improved. "You know there is a Gus de Santos fan page on Facebook?" he asked.

"No! I didn't know," Iris said. *Why did Lou not tell me?*

"It's *incroyable* how many people have posted things. People from all over the world. A lot of them are photography students talking about how inspired they are by his work."

"When did you stop working for Gus, Cyril?"

"Two years after you left, more or less. I was going to follow him to LA, he always say to me that he wanted to be near his family, but—"

"Why? Why did you stop?"

"Gus had a mental collapse, you know? He could not work for many months after you leave Paris. He did not answer his phone. I had no more jobs from him, so I went to work for Rakim. A few months later Clemente Campisi called and asked me to come back to work with Gus because he was going to be very busy."

Cyril took his *citron pressé* and stirred four lumps of sugar into it.

"So, you went back. Was Gus working?"

"Gus was taking many drugs. He was using every day and he was working from the apartment. It was very disorganized and there were many people coming in and out all the time. He did his productions from there, castings . . . it was a mess."

"Was Clemente around?"

"Yes, he arrive when I leave every evening."

"What kind of work was Gus doing then?"

"He did many portraits, stuff for record labels, some big *cosmétiques . . .*"

"Fashion?"

Cyril shook his head. "No, no fashion, no editorials either. Just advertising and his artwork."

"Where were the negatives? And the prints?"

"They were always in the office, like before you left, in the same clamshell boxes, the ones you made for Gus."

"The black shiny ones with the metal corners?"

Cyril sipped his *citron pressé* and, grimacing, added another lump of sugar. "Yes, those ones. Gus told me one day to prepare the archive for transport because a specialized company was going to put it in storage. I did a list of contents, I file everything with photocopies of the contact sheets. I digitalize also and put this in the office computer. There was not much to store because Gus only shoot one or two rolls of film per shot, but all his vintage prints were there. And then everything was gone. I remember I see the empty office and I am surprised. Everything gone, except for the computer. *Pouff!*"

Iris leaned over the table, getting closer to Cyril. "Do you have a copy of that list? A CD-ROM? Can you tell me what happened afterward?"

"Afterward I stop working with Gus because I was not getting paid. Gus would tell me to call Clemente because he was in charge of the money, but Clemente was always finding excuses to pay me late. Gus was very bad at that time. He was sick very often. He was difficult with clients, he was late on shoots, late on postproductions. Sometimes he did not even bother to show up, and I had a hard time working with him, it was *impossible.* Many times, I had to shoot for him because he could not focus. I spoke to Clemente about this because he was the agent, but I think Clemente encourage this behavior."

"What do you mean 'encouraged'? You mean enabled?"

Cyril looked away, focusing on a faraway corner of his memories.

"Yes. Clemente take care of all the business and money. Clemente handle the clients and take the meetings and never let Gus out of his sight. Gus was like a prisoner in boulevard Voltaire. He did not have any friends that I know of, because I always see him alone. I was worried that he do something crazy and I told Clemente this, I told him Gus was using too much drugs and was not well. I was Gus's only friend, but then Clemente fired me because he say that Gus did not want to work with me anymore. I was very unhappy. All of a sudden Gus left Paris and went to live in Los Angeles, I think it was two years after you left. I never hear from Gus again until a month before he die."

Cyril took the ashtray from the table next to theirs. He took out a cigarette and offered it to Iris, who shook her head. Inhaling deeply, he gathered his emotions and continued. "He call me a month before he die to say thank you for my work all those years. He say I was like a brother to him and that he owe his success to you and me, to *our* work for him, for believing in him and making his dream possible, and he ask me to pardon him for being such a . . . *pinche pendejo*, an asshole, that was the name he use. I ask him why he had fire me and he say he had not fire me, Clemente had told him that I had left to work with Rakim. He had no idea that this was not true, it was a Clemente lie. Very *triste*. Very sad."

Cyril looked down and stirred his glass. When he looked up, his pale eyes were red. "A few days after he die, I receive a FedEx. He had send me a check, it's for a lot of money. I did not expect this money from him. What I did, I did because it was my duty, it was my job. He was my boss, he was a good boss, I was proud to work for him."

Cyril turned his gaze away from Iris. "I don't know if I still have a copy of the list, but I will search for you."

CHAPTER 38

"Cut? All? Short?"

"Yes, cut everything, please."

"But your hair make you look so young and pretty, shoulder length like this, and with the bangs in your eyes."

"I don't want young and pretty. I want groomed. How do you say *groomed* in French? Can I have a manicure too?"

Iris looked at her reflection in the hairdresser's mirror, dismayed at how the Californian lifestyle had transformed her image. Her black T-shirt looked shapeless and beachy in the city, and her shoulders needed structure, power. Crossing her legs, she sighed in dismay at her grubby Converse and faded black jeans with ripped knees. *How can I show power if I look like shit?*

Rudy the hair stylist fussed over her. "You look like a model. Are you an actress? I think I know your face. Your French is very good. Are you sure you want to look so hard? All my clients want your California bobo look and you want to look like a bourgeoise businesswoman from Neuilly. *Mais pourquoi?* Why?"

Because that woman is who I want to be. I want to be somebody else. Iris got her phone and, after a search, handed it over to Rudy. "I want a chunky bob. Do me an updated version of Valentina, you know, Valentina from Crepax. Look here on my phone, *W* magazine says the blunt bob is the hot haircut of the next season."

"Oh *oui! J'adore Valentina. Sado-maso, érotique, trés forte.* Sublime. You remind me of her. This will be so much fun!" Rudy clapped his hands like a child before getting started.

Iris closed her eyes while a sweet Croatian manicurist called Irina worked on her hands. Her phone rang.

"Iris, it's Joan. I spoke to Amanda Greenwood."

"How bad?" asked Iris, holding the phone against her ear with one shoulder.

"Vile, *chérie*. They're running the piece in a few days no matter what, and they want to make it as lewd as possible. The questions she asked were terribly inappropriate. I tried to steer her in another more professional direction, but all she's looking for is scandal. I told her they could use a couple of photos from our archives, from the stories that Gus shot with you modeling."

"And?"

"And she was not pacified. She wants more. I told her she should interview Mick, Iggy, Johnny, Angelina, Serena; is there anyone Gus did not shoot? But no, *chérie*, she's obsessed with you and only you. In my opinion, even if you negotiate with her and give her an interview, she is still going to look for never-before-published intimate shots. Who has those? Campisi?"

Rudy took out his hair dryer.

"Joan, thank you, thank you, for your precious help. Gotta go now. Later."

Iris walked out of l'Atelier de Rudy on rue Saint-Honoré and stopped in front of the shop windows at Colette. Ten mannequins dressed in black suits sat on a white wooden bench as if at the front row of a fashion show. Iris went inside, walking through the bottom-floor setup and the sneakerheads fondling the myriad of expensive exclusives. At the art-book stand she browsed through a display where a massive tome called *Model* was propped. Iris leafed through the glossy pages distractedly until she came to a black-and-white portrait of her by Thomas Bailey. Her hair was loosely tied with a black velvet ribbon, and the collar of her white shirt was wrinkled and undone. Around her neck was a leather cord with the Navajo pendant

alphabetically by agency. At the front of the file rack was a box with a few composites labeled "HOT. I LOVE."

The only two other computers in the room were turned off.

Down the corridor was Clemente's office. A wave of nausea washed over Iris. Gagging, she went to the bathroom and locked herself in.

Afraid of vomiting in front of Clemente, she held on to the sink and jammed her index finger down her throat, but only a small trickle of bile came up. She splashed her face and wrists with cold water and fixed her makeup. Then she went back to her chair and forced herself to breathe deeply.

She closed her eyes.

A loud clanging of keys at the door made her jump out of her skin. The girl scurried past her. Iris heard Clemente's voice as he turned the corridor, then stopped in his tracks. "Well, well, well, look who's here, it's my little *cara* Iris. What a surprise, what a surprise indeed."

Iris stood up, towering over him, and stared into a pair of purple shades while searching for his eyes. "Hello, Clemente."

"Let's go to my office. Ilaria, bring us some prosecco, will you? It's time for prosecco, no, *cara*?"

Iris said nothing and followed Clemente down the corridor. Squeezed into skinny black jeans that made his calves look like sausages and a snug shirt in a shiny navy-blue fabric, Clemente looked shorter than she remembered. His pants tapered off, bunching at the ankles over a pair of boots with Cuban heels that clicked on the wooden floor ahead of her. Iris perceived a flash of silver from the rings on the stubby fingers swinging in front of her as he swaggered on.

Clemente opened the door of his office for Iris. As she walked past, he whistled under his breath. "You are more beautiful than before. How is this possible?"

Clemente's leering eyes ran over her body. His gaze fell on her drawn, unsmiling mouth.

"Take a seat, *bella.*"

Iris sat on a black leather chair. The crunching and creaking of the leather was the only sound in the vast office.

Ilaria knocked gently on the door. *"Permesso?"*

She walked in carrying two ornate glasses and a chilled bottle in a silver ice bucket, a pretentious and well-rehearsed ceremony that must have been reenacted hundreds of times.

Clemente smacked his lips. "Ahhhhhhh, *buono.* Nothing like prosecco in the spring. Enough of that bullshit French rosé. I'm a prosecco man, and you, dear Iris?"

Pouring two flutes, Clemente leaned his body against the desk in front of Iris. She clutched her shaking hands so tightly that her nails dug into her knuckles, and shoved her fists between her thighs to keep them still.

Her silence made him talk.

"It's been a long time, no, *cara?* The last time—"

"Clemente, cut the fucking crap, will you? You know very well why I'm here. Move away from me or I'll kick you in the balls."

Laughing, he walked around his desk and sat down, pinning her with a frozen smile. "Me? No! I don't know. Why *are* you here?" He shook his curls dramatically and raised his clasped hands to heaven as if imploring the skies. "Because you missed me?"

"Forget the bullshit. I'll give you a hint: Amanda Greenwood from the *Daily Stand.* Ring a bell?"

Clemente downed his glass in one gulp. "Oh *sì*, Amanda. What about her? She's a client of mine."

"I now run Gus's estate, and you're not authorized to grant usage of any of his pictures. In fact, I'm here to recover all his negatives and prints. Everything he, or rather we, had when we lived on boulevard Voltaire and everything that Gus shot in Paris after I left."

Iris took out an envelope from her breast pocket and pushed it across the table.

"It's all here. A letter from Gus's lawyer, for you."

Clemente pushed the letter back toward Iris. "*Cara* Iris, what are you thinking? I don't need to read anything. I own all of that. Gus gave the rights of his Paris work to me. After all, I am responsible for all of his success, for his career. I MADE him, *capito?* He needed money to move to Los Angeles, so I lent him money, lots of money, and he pledged his rights as collateral. *Come si dice, una garanzia?* A guarantee? He never paid back the money, and now? Now he's dead." Clemente crossed himself. "So, I own the rights of that work, including the intellectual rights. Those six years, they are all mine. I have a contract."

Iris's right eye began to twitch. A spasm shook her body. "I'm taking you to court. Abuse, theft, embezzlement, extortion, you name it. You're a disgrace to the trade, Clemente. You knew that Gus needed help and yet you facilitated the drugs. Gus would have never sold the rights to his artwork, to our personal pictures, ever. Gus was not reckless with his legacy like that, he knew the value of his art."

"But *cara*, desperate people do desperate things. Go ahead, do as you please, you cannot prove it, and it will take you years to mount a case. I would not open that can of worms. The expense, the *scandali* you would expose yourself and your family to, not very simpatico. And how is your pretty little daughter, Lou? I saw her on Instagram. Does she know that her father might be Italian? Oh! The fun we had that night. For once you were so sweet to me, you were even obedient. I was happy to have my camera, did anyone tell you how photogenic you are when you are getting fucked?" At this Clemente guffawed. "Gus was very generous in sharing you with me. He knew that I always wanted a piece of that tight little ass—"

Iris leaped up, shattering her untouched glass on his desk and spilling the contents over a stack of papers.

Raising his crystal flute and his eyebrows above the frames of his sunglasses, he toasted in her direction and cocked his head, smiling.

Iris's legs started to shake as she walked backward toward the door, the taste of bile in her mouth again. Glaring at Clemente, a strange calm came over her. "You'll see me again. I'm not finished here. And don't ever, ever say my daughter's name again or I swear I will kill you. *Capito?*"

Surprised by her tone, Clemente shouted, "Ilaria! *Vieni subito.*"

Ilaria's expressionless face appeared in the doorway. Clemente said through clenched teeth, "Take Miss de Valadé out and clean up this shit. The meeting is over."

Iris brushed past Ilaria, then, standing at the door of Clemente's office, she turned.

"I will never, ever forgive you."

CHAPTER 40

Iris ran out of the building and right into rue de Rivoli. Crossing the bike lane, she found herself in oncoming traffic. A massive mototaxi swerved around her, barely missing her. The rider gave her the finger, shouting obscenities as she sprinted across the asphalt. Gasping for air, she ran up the stairs to the gated entrance of the Jeu de Paume museum and then changed her mind and walked down again, slowly this time, heading toward the soothing green trees of the Tuileries gardens. Digging into her pocket, she pulled out her phone and turned it on. Three messages popped up on her hub: Joan, Lou, and Chuck.

Iris's chest heaved, and she tried to control her breathing. Through the dark leaves of the chestnut trees she spotted the cheerful red awnings of le Medicis café and made a beeline for it. Sitting down at one of the wooden tables, she grabbed some paper napkins from the metal dispenser.

Her WhatsApp pinged.

'Mam? U there? Helllooooooo anyone home? I c ur online'

Iris wiped at her tears and blew her nose before dialing. Lou answered on the first ring.

"Mom?"

"Baby! How's everything? Where are you?"

"At Maca's, studying. And you?"

"Sitting in the middle of a beautiful public garden called les Tuileries about to have a coffee before heading back to Joan's place."

"How did your meetings go? Did you resolve everything?"

"Nope."

"Is it better than before?"

"Nope." Iris's voice caught and she stifled a sob.

"Mom, are you okay? Mom? What's the matter?"

Despite her efforts, Iris's voice broke. "Yes, baby. Just had a hard afternoon. It's the jet lag, it's making me very emotional. And I miss you."

Lou remained silent for a few seconds and then replied slowly, clearly weighing her thoughts carefully. "Mom, remember when I was younger and you talked to me about bullying, about standing up to the rotten people at school? It really helped me. I haven't been bullied since. You told me that fear was our own worst enemy, remember, Mom? And you told me not to react but to act."

"And . . . ?"

"You told me that bullies were weak people who envied your courage, you told me to ignore them and walk away. If you are stronger than them and they need to bully you because they're in the wrong, perhaps you should find out more about *them*, because information is power. That way you can stand up to them. I also punched Ronnie in the face and he stopped torturing me."

Iris sniffed again and smiled. "Lou, thank you for reminding me. Yes, and you also semibroke his nose and his mom filed a complaint with the headmaster, *and* I had to pay the doctor's bill, *and* I could have done without that, but hey . . . whatever works, right?"

"So, practice what you preach, duh." Lou chortled. "Not the punching maybe, but all the rest . . . yo, by the way, love your new haircut. Tight."

"New haircut? We're not on video chat. How do you know?"

"Aww, Mom, come on! You're like Wilma Flintstone! Never met anyone so challenged on social media. You're tagged on Instagram! Some French dude posted a selfie with you in a shop #Irisdevalade #topmodel #fashionfierce #colette."

God, news travels fast, Iris mused.

"Mom, when are you back?"

"Baby, I only got here yesterday. Will be as fast as I can."

"If you're delayed, you'll miss my last day of school."

Iris sighed. "I'm really trying, Lou, believe me. I want to get out of Paris as soon as possible, but I have a drop-dead date to rectify the situation, and I can't leave until it's done."

"Mom?"

"Yes, Lou."

"Mom, what about if I came to help you in Paris after my exams? I can hang out with Ophelia if you're busy, or I can be with you if you need me."

"You mean Othilia?"

"Yeah, whatever, the French girl. I won't disturb you. It's my birthday soon, maybe Chuck could come too?"

"Chuck? Why Chuck?"

"Dunno, just a thought."

There is never such a thing in Lou's brain as "just a thought." Even in the middle of a stream-of-consciousness-type rant, Iris knew that Lou's thinking process was always quite purposeful.

A waiter appeared at Iris's table. *"Un café crème, s'il vous plait."*

"Lou, it's not the right time for a Paris visit. And your birthday is not for another three months."

"Whatever. Battery's dying. Please hurry back."

"I love you too," said Iris as Lou hung up.

The ache and fear in her heart had a dulling effect on her thoughts, but Lou's words and urgent tone resonated somewhere deep, going around and around on a loop inside her brain. *My daughter* needs *me.*

Bracing herself, Iris dialed a number that she still knew by heart.

"Hello?" A wall of raucous barks almost drowned out the voice on the phone.

"It's me, Iris."

"Who?" The dogs barked even louder this time.

"Iris de Valadé, Iris Newman!" she shouted into the phone. People at the tables around her turned and glared.

"Iris? My Iris?" the voice said, followed by an incredulous silence and then a torrent of words that came out so fast Iris had to hold the phone away from her ear, flinching as the attack went on, relentless and bruising.

The waiter came by with the check but turned on his heels and left.

"How could you do this to me I was worried to death you never said goodbye you just left Paris and did not even leave an address or a message for me I thought we were friends I was sick with worry and sadness that you did not think of me and how much you hurt me disappearing like that I did not know any of your friends I did not know who to contact I asked your boyfriend and he did not call me back and I saw him at a party and he said you were okay but I did not believe him because I read in my oracles that you were not well and something bad had happened to you I have thought of you every day since you disappeared but you never even remembered me I am so mad at you and so hurt . . ."

Iris remained calm while listening to the onslaught. Then it stopped.

"Kitti, can I come see you? I've missed you so, so much."

CHAPTER 41

Kitti sat across from her on a midnight-blue velvet sofa, smoking a joint and stroking a fat shih tzu with cataract eyes and a long, drooping tongue.

"That's it, Kitti, that's my story. I've never told it before. I wanted to see you in person, I wanted you to know, but I couldn't bring myself to call you because you would have been angry at me, you warned me so many times . . . I didn't have the balls." Iris was slumped on the sofa facing her.

"But this is awful, Iris," Kitti said as she rubbed tears off her cheeks, making her mascara run. "I never imagined all this. I knew something bad might happen to you. But this? My poor little friend . . . why didn't you tell me?"

It was right before dusk, the blue hour. The floor-to-ceiling doors shone, stained in a cobalt-and-pink light, bathed in specks of gold.

Kitti's apartment was a cozy, modern two-bedroom cube in a '60s high-rise near boulevard Raspail. Small nervous dogs and a slow cat had the run of the place. The silky dark-plum walls of the living room were covered in framed oil paintings of erotica signed *Kitti Kat*. Every other available surface overflowed with memorabilia: photographs of Kitti and Thomas throughout the decades, phallic table sculptures in marble or wood, quirky trophies on a glass shelf, a collection of hash and marijuana pipes, ashtrays in every size and color, an old Polaroid camera, a chewed-up teddy bear, and many pairs of reading glasses.

"What are you going to do?" said Kitti.

Iris wiped her eyes with her sleeve. "I haven't a clue, but I feel better now that you know. For the first time in sixteen years, I feel relief. I knew you would understand. I can't share this with Joan."

"Joan?" rasped Kitti as she took a long drag from the joint.

"Yeah, you know, my sort-of guardian since I was a child. Remember I lived with her when I moved to Paris? Joan's world is too fluffy and insulated, disconnected, she hasn't lived what you have. She could never cope with a rape story, in the fashion industry, involving her protégée and people *Revue* has worked with. She would flip out, I don't want to put her in that situation."

Kitti nodded slowly and they sat in silence. Iris noticed the little things that she had missed so much about her friend. The soft arms and ample bosom that had enveloped her as she walked in through the door. The ash falling from her joint onto her cleavage. Kitti's petite figure clad in stretchy, black faux-vinyl leggings that enhanced her slim legs, a sheer, long-sleeved tunic with a deep décolleté over a black push-up brassiere. Bare feet, shiny black hair, square bangs, deep-red lipstick, and a dash of Diorissimo.

"You should have told me before. I would have listened. It's not good to live with that eating away at your insides," Kitti said.

"I was too ashamed."

"You were ashamed all these years? How have you coped with that? Have you asked for professional help?"

"No. I don't want my daughter to suspect anything."

"You're a fool, little girl. You need to deal with this or it will ruin your life."

"I am effin dealing with it, Kitti. I am here in Paris now, staring at its ugly face, figuring out what to do."

Kitti shook her head and gazed at her. "That's not what I meant."

The landline rang and Kitti picked it up.

"Yes, my darling. No, my beloved. Yes, my big pussycat, of course I miss you. How much? Well, just hearing your voice makes me horny." She took a deep drag. "Now?" and she giggled so hard that another piece of ash fell down the front of her tunic. "Ummmm, sounds delicious. But later, my piglet, I'm with a friend now. I'll see you later, *mon petit cochon*. Maybe." Kitti's face lit up with a naughty expression, and her eyes twinkled mischievously.

"Thomas?"

"Yes, still with the randy old bugger. He moved into a flat five floors below because his heart gives him problems and he didn't want to be catching taxis to come see me every day, which reminds me that I should get a defibrillator just in case."

Iris laughed. "Why don't you live together?"

"Live together? I live with four senior rescue dogs and a suicidal cat called Roar, what do I need Thomas in here for? By the way, it's a shame your ex is gone. He was a nice boy, fucked up but nice. Did he tell you that he was doing sex work before you met?"

"Sex what?"

"I didn't say anything, because what was the point of giving you more heartache? But my friend Pierre Delhomme, the designer, told me right before you left for good. He said that your boyfriend was an escort. He also had a couple of sugar daddies that he whipped around a bit and let them feel his muscles. That's what Pierre told me. He met Gus that way. Pierre introduced Gus to Clemente, and Clemente fixed Gus up with Ada. Gus couldn't pay his rent, he was sending his money to his family, and—"

"Pierre is still a good friend of Ada's?"

"Yes, that's why he and I are no longer friends. I hated the Ada mafia. Gus was part of it before you met, probably because he was her *boy* for a while. Ada is talentless and ugly, but having her court around her kissing ass in exchange for favors, it makes her feel powerful and fuckable."

Sex work? Escort? Iris was too stunned to comment. She stared at the zebra pattern of Kitti's rug.

"I'm sorry I had to tell you this, but if you're going to go digging into that Italian agent's past, he'll bring this up as blackmail, so it's better you hear it from me first. He's friends with that lot. He's their fixer, and Ada has a silent deal with him to hire all the talent he represents. It's all shit, Iris."

"Who says I'm going to go after Clemente? I'm not going to deal with him anymore, Gus's lawyers will."

"Well, you're not going to sit around and mope all day and let that asshole walk all over you, are you, little girl? And what about your boyfriend's archives? Don't you want your pictures back? And your daughter? What's she going to go through when all the sex stuff is brought out in the open?"

"What are you saying, Kitti?"

"That agent will make sure that the *Daily Stand* finds it all out. He'll plant the information so that even an idiot could find it. Except that it would not be called rape, it would be called consensual group sex. That's how it works. Can you see the headline? *THE ESCORT AND THE TOP MODEL.* He'll break you if you don't have the will and the energy to fight him. So get your shit together and go after him. Now! You're smarter than that oik, you can do it. Grow a pair, little girl. I don't expect any less from you."

"I don't have a choice. I'm so fucked."

CHAPTER 42

Joan and Othilia were sitting at the kitchen table when Iris came in. She bent over and kissed them on the cheeks.

"The haircut, Iris!" said Othilia. "Love it! *Trés* cool."

"Dressed for business, I take it?" said Joan. "Colette sent your old clothes here. The *concierge* brought the bag up for you."

"Madame Perrot?"

"No, she retired, thank God. Now we have a sweet Spanish lady called Blanca. I was worried for you after your text. Have some food, you must be starving."

"I was at Kitti's. Yeah, I could eat a whole cow. Your fridge is full of food now, I like that. Your fridge used to always be empty . . ."

Joan smiled and placed a heaping plate of chicken and roast potatoes in front of Iris as Othilia got up and waved on her way to her room.

As soon as Joan heard Othilia climbing up the mezzanine stairs, she said, "I was scared for you being at Clemente's. Never liked that man, he gives me the chills. He has a wretched reputation, but he *is* powerful . . . or at least he was."

"Thanks, Joan, I made sure I went during office hours. Business must be bad. There was just one employee."

"And?"

"In sum, he says he owns the Paris archive."

"Doesn't sound good, does it?"

"I also had a long chat with Cyril. It's a mess. Clemente ran Gus's affairs, handled his money, stole from him, separated him from his friends, and fed him masses of drugs. Gus became erratic. Desperate to leave town, he borrowed money from Clemente, and Clemente's story is that Gus pledged his Paris archive as collateral against the loan. I don't believe the last part. I need to see proof of that contract, I want to do some research. And as for the *Daily Stand* interview . . ."

Joan held Iris's gaze and said gently, "If you're sure that you want to stir this muck up, then that's what you must do."

Iris nodded and chewed on a piece of chicken.

"In normal circumstances, I wouldn't give a damn about my reputation, but if I'm going to represent my daughter's estate and I'm the face of Gus's collection, I'll be dealing with heads of museums and other public institutions, and this is *not* the kind of story they want to read about."

"Bingo! That is exactly what I meant. And by the way, you definitely look better than yesterday. You looked like a little sparrow yesterday, on the edge, about to break. You scared me."

"I was full of fear yesterday, but right now I'm full of anger, and I do well when I'm angry. Today I touched the bottom of my misery, it can't get worse than this. The only way out of it is up: *Take arms, rise up, fight, and get tougher,* to quote one of my favorite songs."

As she listened, Joan made herself a cup of herbal tea. Outside, the clouds drifted apart and an orange moon burned through the wisps. Joan stood by the kitchen window and looked out at the courtyard.

"How's it going with you, Joan?"

"It was one of those days I want to forget. *Revue* laid off three colleagues this afternoon. More than ever I feel the sword of Damocles hanging over my head. Recently they hired a new art director just out of art school. This new kid is every-thing that I dislike: arrogant, rude, full of hot air. He wants to get rid of our roster and bring in new teams. I can understand, it's his new approach. But when something's not broke, why fix it? *Revue* was doing okay, but obviously not well enough if they're desperate to make such radical changes. This kid wants

"He's a retoucher at Studio Imagine for five years now. And on the side, he's helping me digitalize the analog from my first years. Which reminds me: What are you looking for?"

"I need to look at your early archive. I want to recall the people we hung out with, the places we went . . . I also need to see the photos that you didn't use."

"Everything? But there are thousands of pictures, *ma petite*."

"I won't bother you, Jean Marc, I'll be very fast. I *have* to be fast. Just put me in a little corner with a laptop and I'll go through your hard drives and boxes. I really appreciate this."

"We don't know each other very well, and I know you're a good person with good intentions, but you have to tell me the truth. A lot of these are client assignments, they wouldn't appreciate me letting you see this material."

"I'm looking for anything on Clemente Campisi, Campisi with Gus, Campisi with his other clients . . . I need to understand who he is . . ." *And maybe I'll also figure out who Gus was.*

"Ah! Campisi . . . ," Jean Marc said, studying Iris's face closely.

"I'm having problems with him. He was Gus's agent," she said.

"Tell me one person who hasn't had problems with Campisi. I'm happy he's in trouble now. He burnt all his contacts. You don't do that in Paris, Paris is small. It's the bad karma coming back to get him. Anyway, he has no money and he's being audited, again. Apparently, he lost most of his clients. He owes me a lot of cash too. He hired me on assignments but never paid me, not even my expenses."

"What do you mean on assignments?"

"I am not just a paparazzo. I go to parties and events where I have been invited and I take portraits on commission. I do that for magazines, newspapers, and PR companies. Everyone knows me, so I get people to loosen up and pose for me, including famous people who never desire to be photographed.

Everyone knows that I don't give magazines shots that make my subjects look unattractive. Clemente wanted me to boost his career and those of some of the talent in his agency, so he would tell me when he would be at a given party and I would have to take pictures of him, either with someone famous or with one of his clients *or* with his little model girlfriend of the moment. He kills to be in the press, that one. I suppose that his plan did not bring him enough jobs, or maybe he caught the eye of the tax people; someone denounced him. He's desperate for money. Last week he called me because the *Daily Stand* is running a story on Gustavo and you. They interviewed him and he needed shots to support his fantastical tales. He's a bullshit artist, a con man. A scandalous life sells tabloids, no one cares about the tame ones, do they? He asked me to send him everything unedited that I had on you two. I said I would send nothing until the *Daily Stand* called me directly, and then I would only send to them."

"Did they? Did they call you?"

"Yes, this morning."

"What do you have on me, Jean Marc?"

Jean Marc got up from his stool and opened the kitchen window wide. "Breathe, breathe this air, you don't feel like you're in Paris, do you?"

Iris humored him and took a deep breath. "I smell fries and mustard. Best smell in the world."

Jean Marc burst out laughing. "Are you hungry? I'll ask my friends at the couscous next door to deliver some *frites*." Jean Marc placed the order on the phone, then turned back to Iris.

"So, what do you have that the *Daily Stand* might want?" Iris asked.

Jean Marc shrugged. "I don't know, *ma petite* Iris. I have not looked at everything yet, but depending on how you illustrate an article, you can make someone look pretty bad, or not. I have many pictures of famous people using drugs, stoned, looking like roadkill. Beautiful people doing ugly things. I

The studio began to get dark, and Jean Marc walked over to turn on a lamp.

Iris jumped out of her seat.

"Didn't know you were still alive; it's so silent. Did you find something?"

"Thank you, yes, I'll go now. Sorry I outstayed my welcome," said Iris, standing and stretching her arms over her head. She closed her eyes. "Would you have an aspirin, by any chance?"

Jean Marc puttered around the kitchen and then walked back to Iris with a glass of fizzing water.

"Can I please come back tomorrow? I have to finish, no matter what."

"Finish what?"

"Finish ten more years."

"Ten more years of Clemente?"

"Yes. Please. I need another day."

Iris walked out of Jean Marc's alley and into rue du Faubourg Saint-Antoine. At the place de la Bastille she turned into boulevard Richard Lenoir and found a brasserie with a terrace where she could sit.

It was early evening, and crowds of kids roamed the streets in search of innocent fun. Around her all the tables were full, a dozen youths to each table, sharing Oranginas and Cokes. Iris watched their mating games, their unworried faces and untroubled indifference. Kids with T-shirts that read *F**K U* and *S.L.U.T.*, kids who believed that wearing a rude tee was a sign of transgression. *I was never that naive.*

Her phone rang. "Bones?"

"Chuck! So happy to hear your voice. I was beginning to feel homesick."

"We miss you, Bones. The mustangs are asking where you are. I'm calling, first of all to get news because you don't reply to my messages, and second because Conrado wants to know if you plan on fixing the dirt bike for Lou's birthday. He can start working on it if you want."

"Oh God, I forgot, my brain . . ."

"It's okay, I understand . . ."

"I am not myself, Chuck, my head is far away in the past, stuck in a photo archive, not Gus's, another archive."

"How's it going?"

"Not well. I had a very bad meeting with Gus's ex-agent. My back is against the wall and I might have to go to court. I'm digging up stuff—it makes me feel ill . . ."

"Are you going to be all right?"

Iris's heart missed a beat. "Yes, I am, I have a good support group, so to speak."

"What can I do to help?"

"Can you call Lou? Take her riding on the weekend, play chess with her, please? She loves being with you. And not a word about the bike, it's a surprise."

"Nothing else?"

"Well, it kind of helps to know that you're there."

There was silence on the line. Then a group of kids started hitting each other and shouting.

"Where are you now? What's the noise?"

"Just spent six hours looking at contact sheets, and now I'm sitting at a café at the Bastille, about to order a big glass of wine and get smashed before I go home. I have to rinse my eyes and brain. Alcohol might do the trick." Iris chuckled. "This place is full of students and they remind me of Lou. I miss her and I also feel homesick. I wish she was here."

"I miss you, Iris." Chuck's voice was quiet.

The waitress dropped a menu on the table, interrupting the conversation, and looked at her impatiently.

"Sorry, I have to go. I'll call you in a bit."

Looking at Jean Marc's archive had saddened her. Sitting at the café, a wave of memories hit her. She remembered Delfine's absences and her empty room in rue de Varenne. A into a mix where *what* you are is more important than *who* you are. *The beautiful and the damned.* It girls, rent boys, trust-fund babies. Poets, producers, directors, composers, designers, art directors, models. Backers, spenders, number crunchers, sponsors. The men and women that sat in the fluorescent-lit offices of the new towers in the suburbs and made it all happen, invited to the parties and then ignored. The nameless, fameless suits in the background of many shots. The CEOs, the COOs, the VCs, the MBAs. Providers, enablers, fixers. The ones in the shadows, cropped out of the frame by Jean Marc's merciless black Sharpie. Good and bad people having fun, and also not. Working, networking, selling, buying, exploiting, guiding, ignoring, destroying. The hunters and the hunted. The glitter ball of success and power always at arm's reach, at the next party, at the next deal. A promise, a word, an *entente*, a shake of hands, a wink, contacts exchanged, and some temporary relief.

Iris closed her strained eyes, stood up, and stretched her limbs, massaging her tired shoulders. She yawned loudly and walked to the kitchen to get water. Bertil's head bobbed to the music in his headphones, his eyes trained on the computer screen. Discreetly she stood behind him, watching as he retouched a young model's skin.

Bertil emerged from under his hood and slid the headphones off his ears. Glancing at Iris, he said, "Pores."

"What do you mean?"

"The photographer wants to show pores, but the client wants them all erased. It's the eternal fight."

"It's fucked up, man, looks like it's sandblasted. How old is the model? Eighteen? Her skin is perfect."

Bertil turned his swivel chair to face her. "*Je ne me prends pas trop la tête* with this. How do you say? I try not to think about it too much? Otherwise it does your head in. I just think of the money; I have mouths to feed. *Tu comprends?* My only worry now is my little girl. I just hope that she never believes in the magic and she sees things for what they are. Young girls are even retouching their social media feeds. It makes me angry."

"I have a sixteen-year-old daughter."

"Yeah, my father showed me yesterday on Instagram. I love her collages. She's beautiful and quite the artist."

"That's the problem," said Iris with a sigh. "She wants to be a model."

Bertil looked away, frowning. He shook his head. "Iris, there's something you should see. There're photographs that my father wants destroyed when he dies."

Iris froze in her tracks and perched on his desk. "Yes, I know. He told me."

"You want to see those."

"I can't, Bertil, they're in sealed boxes."

"I know which hard drive they're on."

"Your father wouldn't be happy."

"He won't know. The day he sells his archive, those pictures will be gone, or even before. But I want those bastards to feel threatened. I think of my baby girl, of your young daughter, of all the little ones that fell into their hands. It makes my blood boil. I can't do anything, nor can my father, we need these brutes as they need us. Who else can they trust? But you—you should . . ."

"I should what?"

"You should know," he said.

"About the Red Room?"

"Yes," he said.

"What good will it do?" Iris said.

"I don't know. I just feel it's important that I show this to you."

"Bertil, did you tag Gustavo de Santos often when you digitalized the archive?"

"Yes, a few times."

"What do you have?"

Bertil took a small SSD drive from the bottom drawer of his desk and connected it to a second computer. He entered a password and clicked on a nameless file. "Gustavo de Santos: twenty-seven matches. Let me see: at Helmut Lang's perfume launch, at Maxim's for Elektra, at the Petit Palais for YSL, at the Hôtel Salomon de Rothschild for AMK . . ."

Bertil opened another folder, and a series of thumbnails of Gus appeared on his screen. Iris looked quickly at all of them. Four were blacked out.

"What are those? The blacked-out ones. Did you file those?"

"No, my father did. I don't want to look at those."

"Shit. Can you pull my name up?"

Bertil punched in "Iris de Valadé," and thirty-nine matches turned up. He selected them and clicked on the second folder. The thumbnails appeared on the screen. Six thumbnails were blacked out.

Iris scanned the thumbnails and pointed to the censored ones: "Same thing?"

Bertil nodded without even looking at the screen.

"Can you please look for Clemente Campisi?"

Bertil swung around to face Iris. His eyes were somber. "Campisi is blackmailing you," he said.

"How do you know?"

"Because that's what he does. He puts people in situations at seemingly innocent gatherings and they do things that they regret. *Tu comprends?* The Red Room was not public, it was a sort of members' club, cordoned off by a bouncer. What went on in there was kept private. It was before my time, but my father told me everything. I'm happy it closed. The same things still happen, but now they take place in people's apartments. Phones are confiscated and nondisclosure agreements are signed. I know because I listen to the photographers and clients chatting while I retouch. They get bored and they talk amongst themselves while I work."

"So, nothing has changed, then."

Bertil nodded and turned to his screen. He punched in Clemente Campisi's name, and a few hundred thumbnails came up. One-fifth of those were blacked out.

Iris felt sick, as a wave of apprehension washed over her. She walked to her desk and grabbed her chair. Bertil's eyes followed her every move. Taking the chair, she placed it in front of him.

Bertil continued. "I feel that I can talk to you. I'm worried. Some of the pictures in the black boxes belong to Clemente. He brought his rolls of film to my father; my father used to develop for him. My father made copies of the contacts and put the negatives in his art storage in Montrouge. Clemente has been pressuring my father to give him his pictures. There's a lot of paper trace on him and he might want to get rid of it, get his negs back, digitalize them, and destroy that paper trace . . . Clemente is threatening my father. I see my father getting very upset."

"Why would Jean Marc keep all that?"

"My father keeps everything. His pictures are his diary. But now it has become a problem, and it goes against his conscience."

"Clemente informed the tabloid that he had 'revealing' shots of Gus and me, so he's telling the truth?"

Bertil nodded. "I can't bring myself to look at those contacts, so who knows what's in there. Clemente is desperate for money. His grand scheme is to buy my father's archive with a silent partner because he has no money himself. He would then bring attention to my father's work, four decades of images of Paris nights, by releasing some books, syndicating some pictures, involving my father in exhibitions."

"Including the Red Room ones?"

"Yes. My father would have to retire, who would hire him anymore? Debauchery and scandal sell, we all know that. My father did a lot of other photographic subjects. He shot still lifes for years: animals, street photography, lifestyle. I don't want to think what would happen with all of my father's work if Clemente was to own it. I'm sure he'd flip it eventually, making a big profit, playing up its scandalous nature. Or maybe he would sell it off in bits. Or he would sell unlimited editions of signed or unsigned prints until the market is saturated and no one wants them anymore."

"But does Jean Marc have proper release forms? He couldn't use the explicit ones unless he has those forms. It's against the law."

"Of course he doesn't have signed forms! Those are candid pictures, reportage style. Most of the people are unrecognizable. My father will never show those to anyone, he will never use them, but those are the ones that Clemente wants to use, to show, and to publish. Publish and be damned."

"Why don't you destroy them?"

"My father's Red Room images?"

"Yes, and Clemente's stuff."

"You're playing with fire. Clemente is an unpredictable and dangerous animal."

"I'm not frightened of him anymore, Bertil. I'm sick of his fucked-up games."

"You should be scared, Iris. Keep as far away from him as you can."

Iris looked the other way.

"There's one more thing. My father needs to sell soon. He's getting old, and won't be able to work much longer. He teaches photography three times a week at the Beaux Arts, but that's not enough to cover costs. My grandmother has dementia. She needs twenty-four-hour care, and my father pays for that too. When he was forced into the digital era he had to buy expensive machines, lots of equipment, a professional high-res scanner. And this place is ancient, a ruin. The glass roof leaks in the winter, it needs to be completely redone. Work is getting scarce because there're so many new guys ready to do the job for cheap. They work in teams, they zip around the city on their Vespas and cover four events a night. My father can only do one, maybe two, and only if they don't overlap. Granted, you have a legend shooting at your party, but as the crowd gets younger, fewer people know who he is."

"But couldn't he find another buyer?" Iris said.

"I agree with you. I wouldn't sell to Clemente either. And why my father hangs on to all those Red Room pictures, I don't know. They're good pictures, maybe that's why. He's an artist, and it's his art."

Iris took a deep breath and exhaled slowly.

"I am ready now. I want to look through the hard drive."

CHAPTER 46

Images flew past on her screen: beautiful girls in small dresses, mirrored tables covered in white lines of blow, buckets of Grey Goose on ice, glistening magnums of Cristal. Figures slumped on red velvet sofas. Iris looked at a shot of Audrey flashing her breasts, her head tilted backward while Clemente cheered her on. A young girl with an angelic face grinding on the lap of a fat advertising mogul that Iris recognized, her underwear around her thighs, not a day over sixteen. A birthday cake, more underage models, some of them boys. Pierre Delhomme grabbing the crotch of a beautiful child who looks like he just lost his soul. Saskia, Audrey, Billie, Nastasia, and Clara, one after the other, in dozens of shots. Iris in a picture with Gus, bending over a mirrored table, the glow on their laughing faces making them look like ghosts. Razor-blade lines of coke, rolled-up bills, a credit card. Gus smiling while Iris looked away. Saskia, with glazed eyes, askew on the red cushions, fondled by many hands. A man in a suit and a woman in a short dress having sex in a dark corner against a wall while a small crowd egged them on. Clemente groping Billie, his hand between her legs, as he chatted to a man with an eagle tattoo on his neck. The photographer Jared Temple taking a swig from a bottle of vodka, his fly undone, rings of sweat drenching the armpits of his unbuttoned shirt.

Iris scrolled through more thumbnails until she found a folder called *CC*. Clicking on it, she opened a series of subfolders: *Birthday S, Daddy Day, Sweet Sixteen, Studio Studs, G&I*. There were fourteen Clemente Campisi subfolders in all, dated and in chronological order. Iris fast-clicked through the first few folders. Leaning back on her chair, she paused for breath. Her hand shook as she clicked on *G&I*.

Iris immediately recognized herself, eyes downturned, Clemente's hand holding her by the hair while she gave him head. In another shot Gus sat naked on the edge of the bed, his eyes glazed and vacant. Reluctantly she clicked to the next picture, her stomach turning. In it, Campisi stood over her limp body sprawled at the foot of the bed, face up, blindfolded. Her legs were spread open, feet nearly touching the floor. Campisi had one hand on the camera, focused on Gus blowing lines of coke off her right breast. Out of focus, Campisi's other hand held a flesh-colored object that penetrated her. As Iris stared at the picture, she was thrust back to the exact moment she lost all ownership of her body.

A shooting pain traveled from between her legs up to her stomach. The pain turned to nausea. Halfway through the folder, she stood up. As she rushed toward the bathroom, she vomited by the door. Bertil jumped from his chair, knocking it over. Taking her by the shoulders, he steered her toward the outside gate. He grabbed a towel from the kitchen and handed it to her as they walked. "You need air."

"I'm so sorry . . . I—"

Bertil shook his head with a pained expression on his young face. He went back inside, and Iris heard the clang of a metal bucket and the swoosh of a mop.

Later they sat on the cobbles, backs against the wall.

She pounded her fist on the street over and over. "That animal, he's a fucking animal . . . a fucking beast . . . fucking beast . . ."

Iris leaned her head on her crossed arms and sobbed, the convulsions racking her ribs. She wept for Audrey and Saskia; she wept for the girls and boys in those pictures, all the age of Lou. She wept for Gus and for the desperation in his eyes when the camera caught him high. She wept for that night and the crude and grainy pictures of their sex and the jizz on her face.

Iris burst into laughter as she recognized her friend's husky snarl. "Same to you, dipshit Dutch-assed peasant, you fuckwad."

"Great. You still remember me. Okay, so I'm in Paris, I need to see you."

"Where are you?"

"Walking down Raspail toward Saints-Pères. I'm free, now?" Saskia replied.

"I'm sitting under our lamppost. Can you jump in a taxi? It's chilly here, hope you're warmly dressed," Iris said as she retreated farther into her jacket.

Saskia snorted. "You're saying that to a Dutch? You really are an idiot."

"I love you too."

"*Tot ziens.* See you soon, my old friend."

Iris leaned her head on her crossed arms and wept.

CHAPTER 48

A tall woman in a flowing black dress walked down the riverbank. She had long blond hair, endless legs, and an unmistakable stride. Iris sprang up and ran toward her.

Saskia and Iris embraced, laughing with joy.

"Look at you!" Saskia said, holding Iris at arm's length. "You look the same, you bitch. Have you had something done? Botox? Minilift? You look insane good. Say no and I throw you into the fucking river. I hate you."

Iris smiled and looked into Saskia's gray-green eyes. "*You* look amazing, baby, what the hell are you talking about? You look beautiful and healthy."

"Fat. I'm fat-assed, a Dutch cow. Fashion-speak *healthy* is plain *fat*, you don't need to sugarcoat it. But it's either the arse or the face, right? I've put on twenty pounds at least, thinking it would make my face look younger, but it all went to my stupid tush," she said, slapping her rump. Saskia rummaged in her large black backpack. "Here, I brought us this for the old times' sake." She pulled out a corkscrew, two bottles of Haut-Médoc, and a baguette broken in half.

"That, for appearances' sake," she said, pointing to the bread.

They walked to the wall bordering the embankment and sat on the cobblestones.

Saskia uncorked one of the bottles and took a swig. *"Proost,"* she toasted. "To the future."

She passed the bottle to Iris, who said, "Yeah, fuck the old times. Don't wanna toast to those. Good bottle, eh? We never drank plonk, did we?

"How did you find me?" She asked, after knocking back some wine.

"Your daughter gave me your number. I found you on Instagram a while back. Yesterday, for some weird telepathic reason I DM'd the account. Your daughter replied. She told me you were here."

"What took you so long?" Iris asked.

"I wasn't ready for the world."

Iris looked at the river, then turned to meet Saskia's eyes. "What happened to you?"

"I lost it." Saskia shrugged. "*Kut.* I locked myself in my hotel room during New York Fashion Week. Management called the police. I was blabbing, I heard voices, all that loony stuff. My parents had to borrow the money to fly to New York to get me. They put me on board in a straitjacket, granted it was under my Margiela coat, but still . . . Have you ever tried peeing on a plane in a straitjacket?" Saskia chuckled. "I was taken away, put in a funny farm for years."

"Shit."

Iris looked at Saskia's beautiful face. There was a hardness in her eyes and lines around her mouth that had not been there before. Her skin was smooth, pale, and freckled. Her blond locks were wild. Wisps of hair framed her face like a platinum halo. Turning her gaze away from Iris, Saskia twisted her hair into two braids that looked like ropes.

"I'm sorry I never looked for you after you left so suddenly. I'll never forgive myself. It still haunts me," Iris said. "What happened to us?"

"Fashion has no compassion. We were part of all that," replied Saskia, her eyes focused on the other side of the river. "They wouldn't let me have any contact with the outside world . . . they would have never informed me had you tried. So I preferred to believe that you attempted to find me."

"I Googled you many times these past years."

"I changed my surname."

"Did you hear about Audrey?" Iris asked, turning her head toward her friend.

Saskia took a swig of wine and passed the bottle to Iris. She stared into Iris's eyes. "I was trying to help her but I couldn't. Same pattern as me: speed, booze, overwork, loneliness, abuse, depression—but she never recovered. Too far gone, too late."

Saskia pulled out her phone. She swiped a couple of times and handed it to Iris. It was a small piece in the *Daily Stand* with a picture of Audrey as a teenage beauty queen and another one of Audrey closing the Valentino show in the bride's dress. The article was by Amanda Greenwood.

Saskia wiped at her eyes. She broke off a small piece of bread and put it down on the cobbled ground. "I'm working on a platform for models where they can find advice and guidance, everything we lacked. A kind of union. A safe space. I want to protect them from the industry that treats them like goods. I want them to know that they do not have to accept sexual harassment as part of the job. I want someone to watch over them. Do you remember how everyone survived on Adderall and Red Bull for months at a time? And . . . did your booker *care*? Nowadays it's IV drips instead of food. And speed. Any kid can be 'discovered' through social media, so the modeling industry churns them out . . . they're children when they start, and when they reach puberty, they're disposed of. That's why I'm in Paris, Iris, looking for funding and interviewing the younger ones."

Iris leaned back against the stone wall and, gazing into the distance, said, "I see. That's admirable."

"Admirable? Is that all you have to say?" said Saskia, staring at her.

"You were always strong," Iris said, avoiding Saskia's eyes.

They sat in silence, no need for words. As models, Iris and Saskia would sip wine together for hours without uttering a sound. Just being there, knowing. This felt like one of those bygone days.

"Saskia, you mentioned abuse . . ."

"Yeah, I was sexually abused, many times, by Clem's friends. I was out of it more often than not. There was his photographer too, Jared. He took advantage of me, promised me work. Same with Audrey, she was abused by the same lot, in the same way. As long as they promised work or kept you high, you didn't say anything because you needed the money, because you needed your drugs. You didn't dare accuse anyone . . . it would have killed your career . . ."

Iris's stomach began to cramp.

"Disgusting stuff. Clem ruined my life. Audrey took hers. But I'm from Viking blood, I'm going to barrel through so this doesn't happen again, to anyone. I know you tried to keep me away from Clemente, but I was hooked by then: opium pills. Clem was the only way I could get them."

The Seine became more turbulent, the water darker. Three ducks defied the strong current and bobbed by the girls' feet, hoping to get bread. Turning her back to the water, Saskia hitched up her silky black dress and crossed her legs, facing Iris. *She is more beautiful than ever,* Iris thought.

"Did Gus take them too?" Iris asked.

"Does it matter?" Saskia shrugged. "I'm really, really sorry for your loss, Iris. Is that why you're here?" Her tone of voice became gentle. She held Iris's hand. "He was a good guy, your Gus. He was respectful toward the models, unlike others, those pieces of shit. I remember he always wanted to know who you were, and he talked to you forever before a shoot. He knew what he was doing, and when he didn't, he had no problem letting you know. He made you participate in the magic. You always wanted to give him more of you, that one last shot. *Just one more,'* he would say. You could put your trust in him because he was that kind of person. When you're a model, you're desperate for people you can trust, you need validation . . . it's a fine line."

Iris nodded and picked at a feather poking out of her jacket.

"Why did you two break up? You were like the perfect couple."

"I am good at pretending. It was very hard in the end."

"And?"

"And then he did something despicable."

Saskia was silent. Iris's eyes were downcast.

Iris swallowed and cleared her throat. "Saskia, I've been looking at pictures, don't ask me where or why. Nastasia, Audrey, and Billie, how old were they when we worked together?"

Saskia shrugged. "Fifteen? Sixteen? Nastasia was Clem's girlfriend before me. She supported her family with her pay. They were farmers in some small village somewhere. She disappeared off the Russian radar, I pray she went back home. Her agency refuses to take my calls, are you surprised? Clem is a partner."

"A partner of Elektra Models?"

"Yeah. That's how he preys on little girls and turns them into baby prostitutes with drug problems."

"And Billie?" asked Iris, taking a swig of wine.

"She's okay. She's back in Oregon, growing organic chard or whatever. She has a bunch of kids now. It could have ended badly for her too, though. She was passed around by Clem and his lot. There were *roofies*, you know, Rohypnol . . . she fled to Shanghai and enrolled in a god-awful agency that scammed her—she never got her money. After a year, went to an ashram in India, became a Buddhist, all that. She's going to work on my platform."

"Give me some bread. I'm feeling sick."

Saskia handed the bread over to Iris and threw a little piece at the ducks. "I was the pretty one in the family. My older sister, she's not pretty. She's worked all her life in a sardine cannery. I was blessed, but I fucked it up. Where did all the money go in the end? Remember my jewels? My mink coat? The Cartier? I got so wasted that I couldn't even remember where I left them, who I gave them to." Saskia shrugged. "Forgot them in some nightclub most likely. But this is my future, right this minute. I am not going to fuck up again. My parents are proud of me now. I love my life."

Saskia shook the empty bottle of wine and swore under her breath. "That was fucking good wine." She took a swig from the second bottle and passed it to Iris.

"Oh, and I got married two years ago. I have two boys. Twins. You must come visit us in Amsterdam. My husband gave me the idea about the platform. He got it out of me, my whole story. I told him everything, I didn't hold back. He is so supportive."

Iris looked away, avoiding Saskia's gaze. She was beginning to feel drunk and weepy. "I don't know how you do it. I'm fighting that bastard for Gus's archives and a ton of other shit just surfaced. I'm on the verge of giving up."

"Why?" Saskia said.

"It's too much for me. He's blackmailing me and is going to get my daughter involved," Iris said.

"So? What else is new? Join the club. What did he do this time?"

"I don't want to talk about it."

"For real? Seriously?" Saskia asked, raising her voice.

"I don't have the strength." Iris's shoulders slumped against the cold stone wall.

"Oh, for fuck's sake, Iris! Get over it. Stop eating tofu and eat some red meat instead. Whatever. Forget your California basicness for just one moment, will you? No one else is going to fix this for you. You're ashamed of something you did? You ashamed of what people will think?"

"I feel . . ." Iris's voice trailed off. She took another swig of wine.

"Fuck feelings, you're not at Burning Man popping med-ical-marijuana gummy bears, for fuck's sake. No one cares about your stupid feelings. This is the real world here. Shit happened to us, we deal with it."

"I can't. I can't do anything. I saw things . . . I'm scared . . . Lou . . ."

"Iris, you have to tell me everything. Otherwise I can't help you. I need to know what's going on. And I also need *you* to help *me*," Saskia said.

Iris looked into Saskia's piercing eyes. Shaking her head, she turned her gaze toward the cobbles and pulled at a blade of grass.

"No," Iris whispered.

"Motherfucking idiot," Saskia said. Picking up the empty bottle of wine, she jumped up from the ground and walked away, hurling the bottle into the Seine as far as she could.

CHAPTER 49

The next morning, Iris stumbled into the kitchen and sat on the bench, looking absently at her plate.

Standing at the counter, Joan held a delicate teacup and saucer in one hand and a leather notepad in the other. Cheerfully she said, "*Bonjour!* There's food in the fridge for the weekend. I just need you to make sure that Othilia eats proper meals and gets some fresh air, *d'accord*? Please get her mind off her studies. Take her to the movies, something, anything, poor kid."

"'K," Iris mumbled, her voice croaking as if she had not spoken for a year.

"*Bébé*, what happened to you yesterday? I came home and your door was locked. Are you sick?"

"No."

"Want some eggs?"

"No. Thank you. Do you have an aspirin?" She groaned.

"An aspirin for breakfast?"

"I drank too much."

"Hangover."

"Yes. I feel like puking."

Joan stopped puttering, put down her cup and saucer, and slid daintily to sit in front of Iris on the bench.

"Do you want to talk?"

"Not now."

Joan studied Iris's rumpled face and the smudges under her eyes. "Do you want me to cancel my trip? You look sick."

"I feel like crap. But it's all my fault."

"Who did you see yesterday?"

"Saskia Jensen."

"How is she? Dear old Saskia. *Revue* loved Saskia. Then she disappeared . . ."

"Yeah, she disappeared, so many do . . ." Iris murmured.

"What?"

"Nothing. We had lost touch," Iris said, sinking into her roomy T-shirt.

"Thank you for the chat we had the other day. Got me thinking, *chérie*, to be continued, okay?" Joan said.

"I'm happy I could be of help to someone," said Iris, propping her head sideways on her open palm.

Joan glanced at her phone and slid out from the bench. "Iris, have to run. Call me later. I want to know that you're okay." She reached into a cabinet, then placed a box of aspirin and a glass of water in front of Iris. "Knock yourself out."

Iris looked at Joan as she squeezed into her jacket and grabbed a black suede Hermès weekend bag, envying her composure.

"Thanks again for watching over Othilia. You're a trooper, *chérie*," said Joan, bending to kiss the top of her head. Then she hurried out of the kitchen, leaving behind a trail of Penhaligon's Bluebell and the receding sounds of tinkling bracelets and clicking heels.

Iris swallowed two aspirin and sat in the silent kitchen. She touched Othilia's empty mug, still warm, thinking how many times she had repeated this same gesture in her own kitchen, secure in the knowledge that she and Lou were in a place where no one could touch them, where the darkness could not reach them, the filth could not splash them. This was before. Everything had changed now. The memory of the afternoon with Saskia came back to her. Saskia pleading for her to open up, to get involved, shaking her head with a mix of pity and anger. Iris had walked home and locked herself in the bedroom, unable to face anyone. She had lain on her bed and closed her eyes as the walls spun around her. She ran to the toilet and, holding her hair away from her face, vomited the red wine and bread.

Lying on the bed again, she had heard Othilia as she came in and dropped her backpack on the floor, and Joan's muffled voice. She looked at the ceiling and the flickering shadows of the magnolia leaves fading as sunset turned to dusk.

Her eyes closed and she drifted into sleep. In her dream, she held Lou's hand tightly as they ran. She tried to run as fast as she could, yet her legs took her nowhere. She forced herself with all her might, but Lou was too heavy and slow and pulled her back. She continued to pull on Lou, but her legs would not move. *"Motherfucking idiot. Motherfucking idiot. Motherfucking idiot,"* Saskia shouted at her.

Iris woke up. Her phone was beeping. The light on the screen gave the room a ghostly feel. There was a text message from Cyril.

'Can we meet today?'

She groaned. Another today had come. She dragged herself into the shower and leaned her head against its glass door.

CHAPTER 50

"You always drank those *citron pressés*. Never met anyone else that drank the stuff."

Cyril smiled. "It's a habit. When you feel sick because you eat too much butter, foie gras, all that heavy stuff . . . it helps against the *crise de foie*, the bile attack, you know? Even though I don't eat like that anymore, I now have the lemon juice habit. I like it with hot water in winter."

"Is it good for hangovers?" Iris said, smiling at his quirkiness.

They were at Cyril's favorite *bistrot* in the Marais, le Loir dans la Théière. They avoided the deep and cozy flea-market armchairs, even though sinking into them was tempting. Instead, they sat on stiff chairs at a small wooden table.

The place was empty; too early for the dinner crowd and too late for the lunch one. Two waiters hovered, fussing over them.

Cyril averted Iris's gaze and rummaged through his messenger bag. He pulled out some papers and a CD-ROM.

"I printed Gus's lists for you. The low-res pictures are on the CD."

"Wow, Cyril. Brilliant. Best news of the week, thank you. Can I?"

"*Bien sûr*, they're yours."

Iris scrolled down the lists with her index finger, her lips moving as she read.

Cyril continued. "When I worked with Gus, I kept on top of his archive. I update it the whole time. I listed the work by year in chronological order and by format. I also separated the editorial, the advertising, and the personal work. On the left is the titles of the work, the names of the stories he shoot for the magazines or for his own personal series. I also separated the film formats and the deliveries so you know if it was a Polaroid, a Polapan thirty-five-millimeter roll, a paper print, a transparency, or a slide. Some scans were done later, but I have specified their dates."

Iris looked up from the list and met Cyril's troubled eyes. "All this work in seven years? It's huge, Cyril."

"That was all he did," Cyril replied. "That was his life after you leave. He just work and work. He take beautiful pictures. At first he only want to shoot flowers, botanical things, and also architectural details of Paris. He did not want to shoot people, no portraits. He was very disturbed then. I think I told you that also. He only want to shoot things that did not scare him, that were beautiful in another way."

"And all this is what Gus, or Clemente, moved from the apartment on boulevard Voltaire into special art storage?" she asked.

"Yes. Including your work, Iris, the big brown box you had labeled with a Sharpie: *This is Iris's box. If you touch I cut your hands.*"

Iris cracked a pained smile. "Oh God, that box. I remember that box so well. I threw in the tests I took, most of them of Gus. He was so patient with me. He used to sit for me for hours while I fumbled around with my camera."

"That went away at the same time. Also, a flat black canvas bag labeled *Iris*," he said, fidgeting with a pack of cigarettes.

"A flat black canvas bag?" she asked. Her phone pinged. It was a text from Amanda.

"Sorry, Cyril, I have to read this."

Cyril nodded. "I'm going for a smoke."

Iris dear, editor-in-chief does not give you photo approval. where are we at? he wants me to finish. with or without ur interview we are going to press. I'm available this weekend too. best amanda'

Iris shuddered. She looked through the windows at Cyril smoking outside, his thin body a contorted mass of nerves. He saw Iris peering in his direction and waved at her, smiling shyly. Gratitude washed over her and brought her some comfort.

She closed her eyes and imagined the boulevard Voltaire apartment and tried to picture a black canvas bag in it, but her mind was blank.

Cyril sat back down. Iris smelled the cigarette smoke on his clothes.

"Cyril, what was in the black canvas bag? I don't know that bag."

Cyril shrugged. "Gus always have it on his desk. He use it like a briefcase when he went to meetings. He told me to send it to the storage with the rest. Is there anything else I can do to help you?"

"Help? You have been so much help already."

"I hope you get Gus's work back. It's very important. It makes me sad because I was on those shoots and I know how much of himself he put into making them."

CHAPTER 51

Joan's flat was quiet. Iris sat at the kitchen table and read Amanda's text again. *Oh God,* she thought.

'Amanda I'll answer some questions on Monday morning.'

She sent a WhatsApp to Lou. *'Hey, you! Call you later after your tests. Toes crossed.'*

To Maca she sent, *'Sup? All good in MacaLand? how's the monster behaving? don't wanna disturb her on her first day of exams, but still, worried.'*

Maca replied immediately. *'Amazing! She's already forgotten you exist, she's been studying hard. She's so ready for her exams Chuck is a dreamboat he calls her twice a day and has taken her out to El Molino.'*

'Crap! she sold her soul for a couple of tacos? wheres the loyalty?' Iris replied, smiling as she typed.

'Well what ya expect? You've been away for ages she needs to replace you'

'Ages???? comeon gimme a break been only three days four if you count today'

'Howzit going? Resolved your stuff?'

'No not at all'

'Crap'

'Yeah crap'

'When u coming back?'

'Dunno'

'Monster really wants to go to Paris. you should consider it'

'No way . . . not gonna happen bye now, will call monster later'

'Call Chuck too will ya? Hes driving me crazy asks about u everyday'

'But I write to him we also spoke two days ago'

'Be nice to him! Two days ago? Call him again, youre such a loser old spinster'

'Thanks babe. love ya, mean it.'

'later'

Iris scrolled quickly through her emails. She heard the nightingale sing in the magnolia tree. Outside, the afternoon light was turning a dark gold.

She opened the fridge and brought out a bag of mâche and a vegetable lasagna.

Iris hummed as she prepared dinner for Othilia. From the cupboards and drawers she took the prettiest china plates, heavy silverware, and thick linen napkins, smiling as she set the table. Looking around the house, she found an obscenely large bouquet of roses with an engraved card: *Thank you, my dearest Joan, for the divine pages. You are my queen.* Recognizing the name of a pompous geriatric designer she disliked, she pulled out a few roses from the arrangement and put them in a silver vase on the kitchen table.

The landline rang. Iris let it ring until the answering machine picked up. Immediately it began to ring again. Iris answered. There was silence on the other end of the line. "Hello?" she said. *"Allô?"*

Iris heard breathing and the line clicked off. The living room was dark. She went to the window and looked outside. The square was empty.

The front door opened with a thud, and Iris heard Othilia's backpack hit the floor. Relieved, she returned to the kitchen.

"*Salut*, Iris! *Ça va?*" Othilia walked in, grinning, and kissed Iris.

"Hungry?"

"Oh yes. Starving. Beautiful table, *merci beaucoup.*"

"What time is it? They working you to death at the *lycée?*" Iris asked as she turned on the oven.

Iris's phone buzzed, and Othilia picked it up and handed it to Iris. "It's Joan."

"Checking in on the hungover party girl. All's well?" Joan asked.

"Very funny. Othilia just walked in. We're about to have dinner. All good your end?"

"Yes, *chérie*. Busy, busy, and running out again. Can you pass her the phone? And also, Iris? Try to take it easy, will you? You're looking strung out, you worry me."

"'K."

Othilia spoke rapidly in French to Joan. Laughing, she blew kisses into the receiver and clicked off.

"Do you miss your dad?" Iris asked Othilia, her back turned.

"So, but so much. He's coming back soon, in twenty days and seventeen hours, to be precise. We Skype every night before I go to bed. I love Joan too. Does your daughter have a dad now?"

Surprised by her bluntness, Iris turned to face her and replied, "Now? No. Her father just passed away, but he didn't live with us."

"I'm sorry, Joan told me a bit about your ex-boyfriend. Did Lou love him? It must be hard."

Iris looked into Othilia's pretty face and was overcome by the frank innocence in her eyes. She turned away and busied herself with the oven thermostat. *Did Lou love him? I don't know,* she thought. *I never asked her how, or if, or why she would have loved Gus.*

"My dad has a surprise for us," Othilia blurted out.

"A surprise?"

"Yes, don't tell Joan. Promise you won't tell her anything? You cross your heart and hope to die?"

"I swear to God I won't say anything. Why are you telling me?"

"Because I have to tell someone or my heart will explode into a million pieces. And I know how much Joan loves you," Othilia said, smiling.

Iris put the lasagna in the oven and turned on the timer. She tossed the mâche in the salad bowl and placed it on the table. Then she sat facing Othilia. "I promise, I swear. I'm very touched that you chose to tell me your surprise."

"My dad is proposing to Joan. He wants to marry her."

Iris opened her mouth, but no sound came out. A feeling of great joy overcame her, and like Othilia, her own heart felt about to burst.

"I . . . this . . . I have no words! Othilia, this is the best news! I haven't met your father yet, but I know that you'll be a happy family. Joan is crazy for your dad. I've never seen her happier."

Othilia beamed and whooped, then high-fived Iris. "My father wants to marry Joan, and we'll all live together in Paris or America or wherever. Joan is like my mother for years now."

Looking at Othilia's thrilled face, Iris was sad for Lou.

It was late evening by the time they finished dinner and had cleaned up. Othilia excused herself and went to her room to study.

Iris sat at her desk and opened Cyril's CD on her computer. As promised, he had set up the inventory with thumbnail images and detailed descriptions of the sizes and deliveries. Iris could not bring herself to open the pictures. On her desk was the stack of photocopies that Joan's office had put together. The photocopies corresponded to Cyril's list, and for each *Revue* run there were additional pictures that hadn't been used, in many cases Gus's first selections.

She got up from the desk and stared in dismay at the clock; it was past midnight. Then she padded to the living room and looked outside.

Iris returned to her desk and scrolled down through Amanda's email containing her interview questions.

CHAPTER 52

Iris had set out early with Othilia.

There was a spring in their step as they walked north up rue de Turenne toward Belleville.

Othilia had needed little persuasion to get out of the house and away from her school books for a few hours. Iris found that walking cleared the noise in her head and helped put things into perspective. *What am I going to gain right now by worrying about Amanda's interview, by looking at Cyril's lists?* She texted Bertil, thanking him for his help and asking how Jean Marc's opening had gone.

'Speak later?' Bertil had replied.

She texted Cyril to ask technical questions about the drum scans and repro prints on his list. Cyril had not replied.

More than anything in the world, Iris wanted to go on a ride with Chuck and Conrado up Mount Cerro Negro, serene and mindful, enjoying the hollow clip-clop of the horses' hooves clattering on the rocky ground. Walking around Paris would have to do.

"When the streets are empty, you can see up to the top of the buildings. When the streets are crowded, one is too busy dodging people. Up top there are things that will make you dream: a terrace full of flowers, a pergola, ateliers with huge windows, places you would give anything to live in," Iris said as they walked past the open doors of the buildings that housed old garages, button factories, trendy art galleries, and artisan workshops.

Othilia nodded and stopped in front of Weber Métaux. "Do you know this place?"

"Yes, but I've never been inside."

"Come, I show you." Laughing, she took Iris's arm and led her behind an art gallery made of glass and into a dark passageway that took them to a car repair shop and a parking lot.

"Hurry, come," Othilia begged.

Iris stopped to take pictures of the narrow walls with their peeling retro letterings and logos. Layer upon layer of text and images covered the cement bricks, creating a mad pattern of random shapes and colors, scraped in some places. Metal flakes from car bumpers were ground into the passage walls.

Othilia beckoned from behind a fig tree at the corner of the twisted alley. "Hurry, you must, *must* see this place. This is where I came to have my special trash boxes cut, you know, for my biotech project."

"Your trash-eating bacteria that produce energy and that live in the cellar?" Iris flashed a big smile.

"Yes! Look."

Othilia dragged Iris by the hand to the back of the courtyard, where a large industrial work space stacked to the roof with metals and plastics of all sorts hummed with activity. She hopped and bounded ahead, and Iris's heart skipped a beat. She would have given anything to share this moment with Lou.

Othilia's thick, long hair had come undone, and her skin glowed, flushed with the exercise. She wore a short flowery sundress over a long-sleeved T-shirt with bold lettering on the sleeves. Chunky black eyeglasses, an old jean jacket covered in embroidered patches, thick black stockings, and black Vans added to her look.

"Look, Iris, this is the steel, that's brass, this is copper, aluminum, that's lead, here's the tin, some bronze, zinc, nickel . . ."

She went deeper into the dark shed and straight to the racks with the plastic sheets and Plexiglas tubes. "Plexiglas, Lucite, acrylate, Perspex, PolyCast," she said, pointing. Next to it an entire wall displayed mosaic mirrors and adhesives.

A selection of tools covered another wall. "Bricolage heaven," Othilia said.

Iris smiled. "I don't know any other girl who would call a DIY shop 'heaven,' but I get it. Lou would go mental taking pictures here."

They continued walking up boulevard du Temple, past the vast square of place de la République, where Othilia insisted they stop in front of the improvised monument to the victims of the November 2015 terrorist attacks. Overwhelmed, Iris sought Othilia's hand.

They then headed northeast on rue du Faubourg du Temple, avoiding boulevard Voltaire as they passed near it.

Unlike the sleepy bohemian and hipster Marais, the Faubourg du Temple neighborhood was teeming with life and sounds. Othilia walked ahead of Iris, and Iris appreciated the silent companionship.

They passed Afro-Antillean shops selling bright plastic toys, perfumes, spices, and cosmetics, and a shop called Bollywood Design that sold faux georgette saris, dusty boxes of incense piled high, and gold *bindis*. Past a shop that rented garish party costumes, past the nightclub le Gibus, the Théâtre le Temple, and past the Palais des Glaces. Chinese noodle bars and dim-sum joints shared sidewalk space with old-fashioned French bakeries showcasing rows of creamy pastries. A shop selling esoteric arts was nestled between an Asian African Caribbean supermarket displaying buckets full of giant tree snails, dark-brown plantains, massive breadfruits, jackfruits, and stacks of banana leaves cut into squares, and a telephone-and-internet parlor. They passed halal butcher shops, a Kurdish sandwich shop, kebabs, tandoori restaurants selling fried fish, takeaway couscous joints, a Sri Lankan DVD shop, and a fat-lady shop with African boubous in the brightest colors. Asia, Europe, Africa, the Caribbean, and the Middle East colliding and yet sharing a long and crowded street where no two persons spoke the same dialect.

Iris beckoned Othilia into a Chinese fishmonger shop, at the back of which was a hidden alleyway lined with tubs of water containing bullfrogs, turtles, crayfish, and catfish that splashed as they walked by. Othilia squealed and ran out giggling.

"I used to come here a lot," said Iris. "I would focus on identifying the languages, see how many I could recognize. I should have recorded it, done a sort of soundscape archive."

They continued their walk through the cacophony of the bustling street.

Feeling the pleasure of living and connecting with the world and each other, they walked and walked until they passed the art-deco façade of la Java music hall, where Othilia stopped to take a picture in homage to Edith Piaf and Django Reinhardt. The midday sun baked the asphalt.

"Follow me! I'll take you on a perfumed experience." Iris sought out a narrow side street lined with linden trees in bloom. The creamy-yellow star-shaped flowers were nothing exceptional, but they exhaled the sweetest, most powerful fragrance. Iris and Othilia stood under one that buzzed with bees and life.

"*Tilia,*" Iris said, closing her eyes. "Heaven. When the sun came out in the late spring and there was no breeze, like today, I used to look for the linden trees to walk underneath. I miss them in California. What does their perfume make you think of?"

"Honey and lemon peel," Othilia replied, her nose in the air.

They continued east on rue de Belleville, and then headed north until they reached the park of the Buttes-Chaumont.

"Hungry?" Iris asked.

Othilia had tied her jean jacket low around her hips. Her sundress was open at the neck. "Fainting. I'm starving from being around all those food places . . . I know a spot here in the park, a *guinguette*, where we can buy something."

Following the eastern border, they walked up a shaded path under the beech trees until they came to a small turn-of-the-century pavilion that had housed a dance hall in the early 1900s.

They bought food and then lay on the grassy slope under a willow tree to eat.

A crowd was gathering by the wooden benches and tables on a terrace outside. Young couples drank beer and rosé while children ran around their legs.

"Nice one, Othilia. Lou would love it here."

"My best friend lives in an apartment overlooking the park. Her parents bring us here for brunch sometimes. In the afternoons, it's like a beer garden."

Iris unwrapped their containers of rice and lentil salad, *tarama* and artichoke dips, serrano ham and cheese. She broke the baguette in half and gave it to Othilia.

"Do you miss living in Paris?" Othilia said.

"I don't miss it when I am in California, but now that I'm here I do. A lot. But things change and you adapt to anything, eventually," Iris said.

"What do you like most about Paris?"

Iris smiled. "That we're not scared of people who have loud opinions, we are not easily offended, we like things that stink and some that taste of poop, we like sensations that are strong, oh and men that stare at us, I like that."

"Poop?"

"Cow manure fertilizer, the real deal, the taste of *le terroir*."

Othilia laughed. "Why don't you get your daughter to come? You're always mentioning her, *non*?" she said, taking a paper napkin and wiping a dab of pink *tarama* off her lips. "She can share my room. My dad doesn't come for another nineteen days and twenty-three hours. If Lou comes after my exams, I can hang out with her if you're not available."

"What a good idea," said Iris, busying herself with the ham.

"You had already thought of that, *n'est ce pas?*" Othilia asked.

Iris looked up and met her gaze. "I think of her all the time. I wish she was here. She would love Paris. I long for her every hour of the day."

"I mean it. Bring her. We had so much fun today. I learned many things from you. We could do more walks, and Lou could take pictures, do her thing," Othilia insisted. "Why don't we set a date? When are Lou's exams?"

"This week. I'm worried because I'm not there and I'll probably miss her last day of school."

"So why don't you say that she comes in seven days. That way if you don't get home in time, she won't mind because she's coming to you." Othilia held her gaze.

"It's complicated. I need to think about it."

"You promise?"

"I promise," Iris said.

"You commit?"

"I commit to giving it some thought," Iris said.

Iris lay down on the grass, resting her head on one arm. "I am quite tired now," she said, facing the sky.

Othilia lay next to her. Iris felt a lot of love for this child who was like hers.

Later that evening, Iris sat in Joan's kitchen with her photo lists and dialed Bertil's number.

"Iris! Good to hear you. Are you okay?"

"I feel better now. I wanted to thank you and your dad for your help. How did the opening go?"

"Iris, I just found out that Ada terminated my father's contract with the magazine."

"What? You have to be joking, Bertil . . . when?"

"Two days ago."

CHAPTER 53

"Mom! When. Are. You. Coming. Home?"

"Are you studying? Are you being nice to Maca?"

"Mom! Mom, listen. When are you back?"

"When I finish what I came here for."

Lou sighed loudly. "Did you do as I said?"

"Meaning?"

"Did you stand up to the bullies? Show them how strong you can be?"

Iris smiled. "Not yet."

"What are you waiting for?" Lou sounded exasperated.

"It's too long to explain."

"You have to do things with all your might, you know? Not half-assed."

"Like you with your exams?"

"Aww, Moooooom!" Lou said, annoyed.

"And since when did you start using *half-assed*?"

Lou blew into the receiver. Iris could feel her daughter's temper brewing and changed the subject. "What else have you been doing?"

"Nothing much, just studying."

"Did you take any pictures?"

"Chuck's coming to pick me up later. We're going riding."

"Terrific. And how's Maca?"

"Good."

"Listen to her, okay? She's also worried about your exams. I'll light a candle tonight and say a little prayer every day next week."

"You're such a drama queen. My exams are lame. I'll sail through them. Dead easy, dude."

"Stop saying *dude*. Use proper vocabulary. Be ladylike."

Lou snorted. "'K, dude. But I'm not a lady like you."

Iris sighed. "It's just an expression, Lou."

"Mom, are you okay? Can I come see you in Paris? When will I meet my French cousins?"

"No, you can't come, Lou, it's not a good time. Why do you ask me every single day if I'm okay? Of course I'm okay."

"I need to come to Paris."

"You need to study *and* finish school *and* wait for me to come back *and* stop sassing me."

"Whatever. And you stop treating me like a baby. I'm not a baby. Gotta go. Bye."

Othilia was up in her room studying. Iris looked out the living room window. A soft, sad spring rain wet the cobbles of the courtyard.

Iris paced the apartment like a caged animal, incapable of shaking the dread that permeated her. She tried to read, but her brain was unresponsive and her stomach cramped from fear. It was Sunday.

Joan had left a DVD on the kitchen table with a sticky note: *Iris, darling. Look at this, will you? Need ur opinion XOXOX JOAN*

Iris lay on the sofa in the library room and started watching the DVD.

It was a time-coded copy of a television documentary called *Magazine World*. A voice-over explained that the purpose of the documentary was to show the intimate world of a magazine in the six months leading up to publication of issue number five hundred.

Iris recognized the façade of *Revue* as the camera crew followed the director and interviewer into the building. Othilia joined her on the sofa, and they watched as the camera followed Ada and Joan sitting in the office, debating various images for the cover, looking at layouts for stories. Then following them as they went from fashion show to fashion event in New York, London, Milan, and Paris. It showed a couple of fashion shoots and some backstage action.

Every time Joan came on camera, Othilia nudged Iris. The camera loved Joan. She was bubbly and warm, clearly passionate about fashion, and proud of her contribution to it. The documentary itself, however, was tedious and repetitive. The highest moment of drama came when a TV celebrity canceled her cover-photo session at the last minute, and they had to scramble to replace her.

Iris recognized a couple of famous photographers she had shot with, looking older, sober, and tamer. A top model gushed on camera a few platitudes about how excited she was to work for *Revue*. To Iris it looked as if working for *Revue* was as dull as dishwater. Many of the big designers interviewed raved about Ada and her influence on the fashion industry. Othilia rubbed her eyes and yawned.

Toward the end, the director gave up trying to make a detached Ada connect with the audience and just followed Joan: Joan preparing the looks for a shoot, Joan at the Musée du Quai Branly looking at ancient oceanic artifacts, Joan reflecting at her desk, Joan sketching and searching her library for visuals. Finally, a close-up of Joan's mood board, which covered an entire wall.

The last shots were taken at her home. Joan was sitting on the same sofa where Iris and Othilia now sat watching her explain where her love for fashion came from. The camera zoomed in on a regal portrait of Delfine de Valadé by Helmut Newton. Othilia jabbed Iris in the ribs.

"Delfine de Valadé, my mentor, teacher, and inspiration," Joan said, picking up the elaborate silver frame with the black-and-white photograph.

Ada is not going to be happy.

The camera came in for a final close-up of Joan: "She was *The Lady* of fashion. The documentary should have been about her. *Revue* would not exist right now had it not been for Delfine's unique eye, modern point of view, and bold taste. She liked to be provocative, raw at times, merging brutal reality with fantasy, but she spoke in the international language of images. We owe everything to her. She wanted women to think and gave them the tools to do so. She was, and still is, an icon and a muse." The camera went back to Delfine's portrait as the credits rolled.

The documentary ended, and Iris brushed tears from her eyes. She turned slowly to Othilia and asked, "Thoughts?"

Othilia looked into the distance, chewing on her lip.

"You know we're going to get cross-examined by Joan. You know how she expects full explications of everything, right?" Iris said.

Othilia smiled and rolled her eyes. "The only interesting bits are those where Joan appears. Also, I wish they had shown some of your mother's past work. I would be bursting with pride if I were you. Everything else was so stupid. Really, too much talk is spent on too little. It's like, who cares?"

"Your friends don't care about fashion at all? Do you care?" Iris said.

"It's not cool to look fashionable in my gang. I think it's important *not* to be 'fashiony,'" Othilia said.

"Interesting . . ."

"We try to send the message that we're against consumerism, and that's our kind of revolution. We don't throw bricks; we stop buying."

"Aww! But you were looking very fashionable yesterday," said Iris.

Othilia shrugged. "We buy our clothes from thrift shops. We don't look at magazines, they make you feel insecure and they're too authoritarian. *Wear this, wear that, this is in, that's out, this is not how you should look.* It's so silly. They want to rationalize everything, to coerce you."

Othilia propped herself up on the sofa. "Instead, in my group, we create our own thing. Someone will pick up a mood from an old record cover or an old film and we will play with it and interpret it, just for fun." Othilia's brow was furrowed and her face serious. "Fashion just isn't important anymore in the conflicted times that we live in. In a way, I'd rather just wear a uniform every day. One less thing to worry about."

Iris nodded, reflecting on Othilia's words.

"Just don't tell that to Joan, she gets kind of mad at me when I say this. And what did you think of the documentary?" Othilia asked.

Iris paused before answering. "I'll be blunt. It was boring because the subject, *Revue*, is boring. First of all, the magazine lacks purpose, and it's all about teaching women how to seduce, which I think is ridiculous. My mother made a magazine that *'Taught women how to think,'* as Joan rightly said, but I see that *Revue* has become a magazine about sexiness, objectifying women instead of empowering them, and smart modern women don't dig that."

Othilia nodded seriously. "I agree. It's like taking women back a few decades to before they could vote."

Iris laughed. "The second problem is that the traditional fashion-magazine format looks dated. How can you be on the pulse three months ahead anymore? So much can change in that time. What is relevant then is 'over' a month later. Othilia, in my time, magazines were where we got our information, where we found out about new art shows, new fashion, new restaurants, hotels, health, travel . . . can you imagine?"

Othilia smiled and shook her head. "No, I can't imagine."

"Information and visuals go so fast these days. It's like *Revue* has not fully embraced the digital era yet. The documentary should have spent more time on the magazine's digital department; that's what's new and exciting and what viewers want to see. Instead, they just vaguely dealt with it before moving back to the traditional magazine side of things. Opportunity lost, don't you think?"

"*Oui*, you bet. My generation is used to seeing something new every day, and the online platform of a magazine plays as vital a role as the print version. Digital is speed, but some of us still want to touch paper, we appreciate print, we want to linger. For us it's not only about *how* it's delivered but *what* is delivered, so if the content is dumb . . ." Othilia shrugged.

"Did you ever intern at *Revue*? You seem to know a lot about this world." Iris smiled.

"No, but last year my father got me a summer internship at *Loud*, and *that* opened my eyes. Editors there had to learn a new set of skills to monitor analytics across all digital platforms to include social media so the print and digital are perfectly integrated and working together. The people at *Loud* talked endlessly about using digital for the narrative of the brands and their storytelling. It sounds nerdy, but *Loud* was really exciting to me. *Revue* isn't."

The front door opened with a crunching of keys, and Joan called out, "Hellooooo? Anyone here?"

Iris and Othilia jumped off the sofa and went to greet her.

CHAPTER 54

Iris lay on her bed in the early-morning darkness. She looked at her phone. It was 6:00 a.m. As she put the phone back under the pillow, she heard the ping of an incoming WhatsApp. It was Saskia.

'I see ur online can I call you?'

Before Iris could reply, her phone rang. She ducked under the bedcovers.

"Can you talk?" Saskia whispered. "I am so sorry for the other day. I was drunk."

"It's okay. We were both drunk." Iris kept her voice as hushed as she could.

"Well, I meant every word I said to you. Not how I delivered it, though."

"So you're not sorry, then," Iris said.

"I am, you moron. But I'm taking you to face Clem today."

"It's not going to happen."

"Yes, it is."

"What for?" said Iris.

"To tell him what an asshole he is. And to tell him that we're watching him. There's strength in numbers."

"Saskia, I already met with him. You think he cares about what you'll say? You're deluded," Iris replied, still whispering. "I'm not facing him again, period. Gus's lawyers will have to handle it, I don't want anything more to do with him."

Saskia's loud whispers were firm. "Listen to me. I'm going to his office at noon. Been watching his door, I know when the piece of shit comes to work and when he leaves. I'm going alone if you don't want to come with me. And Iris? Fuck you.

Thanks for the help. And Iris? I'm not sorry about the other afternoon."

Saskia hung up, and Iris dialed her back. The call went straight to voicemail.

Iris looked at the dark ceiling and the patterns the shadows made. Her mind raced. She put her hands on her face to blot out the room. She tried to focus her thoughts and not panic as she became more and more agitated, but her chest was so tight that she could not breathe. *Is this what an anxiety attack feels like?*

After an hour, she heard Joan's door open and close, and morning activity in the kitchen. Tinkling bracelets, the scent of coffee, the gentle clanging of pots and pans, the rattling of the cutlery drawer, and the ping of the toaster. Iris covered her head with a pillow and started to sob.

Tinkle, tinkle, tinkle.

A soft ray of sun seeped through the shutters and shone on the bed. Iris tried again to keep out the day and turned to face the wall. Tears dropped sideways on the mattress, and she flipped over to face the other wall. She picked up her phone and dialed Saskia.

"This is Saskia. Leave me a message."

After a while Othilia's steps passed her bedroom. She heard her muffled conversation with Joan in the kitchen and the front door closing. She waited until Joan's heels clicked by, the jingle of her keys and bracelets faded, and the heavy door closed again.

Iris's WhatsApp pinged, and she grabbed the phone.

It was from Bertil. *'Call me asap Iris the daily stand is running the piece this sunday.'*

CHAPTER 55

Iris looked with disgust at the smiley face on the doormat. She opened her phone and sent a message to Saskia. *'Door code 3394 here now. Bye'*

She texted Joan. *'At Campisi's. Later.'*

After adjusting her jacket, she bent over to shine the tips of her boots with a tissue. She took out a comb from Joan's expensive loaner handbag and tidied her bangs. She dabbed matte burgundy lipstick on her dry lips. She reached for the pendant at the base of her throat. Taking three deep breaths, she rang the doorbell.

She heard shuffling, and Ilaria opened the door. Seeing Iris, she tried to close it.

Iris pushed at the door with all her strength and squeezed in.

"Clemente is out. Do you have an appointment?"

"Please tell him I'm here."

Ilaria raised her voice. "But he's not in the office."

Iris heard a door open and close.

"What's going on, Ilaria? *Ma che cazzo*, for fuck's sake; can't a man take a shit in peace around here?"

Iris came face-to-face with Clemente, who was shaking *La Gazzetta dello Sport* at Ilaria as he buttoned up his pants. He stopped in his tracks.

"Oh! *Carissima* Iris. What's the honor of your visit this time? Will you join me for an espresso? Ilaria, *due espressi*."

Without answering, Iris walked to his office at the end of the corridor and waited by the door. She watched as he approached in a snug double-breasted pinstripe suit. His long curly hair was pasted down the back of his neck. As he got nearer, his lips curled into a smile, his eyes hidden behind dark aviators. Iris hated him in a way that she had never hated before.

Clemente opened the door and bowed her in ceremoniously.

Iris stood by the leather chair in silence until Ilaria finished placing the two small cups on his desk. Clemente shut the door behind her.

He stood by his desk. "So?"

"I want Gus's archive back. You have it, I own it. Give it back."

"Anything else?"

"Yes. You have no right to leak or sell any of our pictures to Amanda."

"Too late, *cara*. She is very, very happy with the pictures she *found*."

"You know what, Clemente? Forget Amanda for now. I have enough proof to put you, and some of your buddies, in prison for molesting underage girls."

Clemente took off his glasses and put them on the table. He stared at her with cold eyes and a detached expression. He sat down and sipped his espresso.

"I've seen the pictures you took, and the ones you are in. I took pictures of those pictures. I have everything I need on you," she said.

Downing the rest of the espresso, he then placed the empty cup carefully on the tray.

"I will come out myself and show the world that you drugged and raped me," she said.

Clemente smiled and put his glasses back on. He stared at Iris.

Iris took one step forward, getting closer to his desk. She searched for his eyes. "I know you only too well. Do you think I'm going to give up the fight so you can swoop in?" She pulled a business card from her pocket and put it on his desk. She pushed the card toward him. "Gus's lawyers. Gus was kind enough to put us in touch. Ilaria can do the rest, and you . . . ? You can keep away from me," she said.

"Is this so, *bambina*?" Clemente smiled. "You must miss your pretty Lou. I want to meet her. I sent her a message on Instagram."

Iris leaned over the desk and tore the glasses off his face. Without taking her eyes off him, she threw the glasses to the floor and crushed them with her boot. Clemente did not flinch.

Iris's nostrils flared as she took a deep breath. "I told you before, Clemente: don't you dare say my daughter's name again.

"One click is all it takes. They'll open an investigation; they'll interview all the underage girls that you and your revolting buddies molested. Those little parties of yours—Ada was there too, and Jared Temple, complicit like the rest. *They* won't be happy to know that I've seen the pictures, won't be happy with you either, but it's payback time all around. In fact, I might even send Ada and Jared a couple of those shots myself. And by the way: fuck Amanda and her article, I don't care anymore."

"Oh, Iris, little Iris." Clemente shrugged. "You're just angry because no one cares about *you*. You're an old bitter hag, you need to get fucked, my little *piccola* Iris." Clemente stood up and walked around the table, coming to within a few inches of her. He bent over and picked up the remains of the shattered glasses.

Iris took out her phone. "Let me see. *Select . . . share . . . email*—done. You should be getting them now."

"Getting what?"

"Your repugnant party pictures, Clemente."

Clemente turned on his heels and went to his computer. Swearing under his breath, he punched at his keyboard and then exploded. "*Puttana. Sei una puttana.* Crazy lying bitch. You fabricated these . . ." His face was contorted as he scrolled and clicked, scrolled and clicked.

Click, click, click.

"I'm done here." Iris turned and walked toward the door. Clemente got there first and blocked her exit.

He turned and approached Iris. She could smell the coffee on his breath.

"I did not do anything." Clemente's voice was nearly inaudible.

"What? I can't hear you," Iris said.

"Me, I did nothing of what you accuse me. I promise, I really didn't do . . . I did nothing." Clemente's eyes were unfocused. He ran his fingers through his hair and shook his head.

Iris was taken aback. This was not the reaction she expected.

Straightening up and taking her phone out, she dialed a number. While waiting for an answer, she did not take her eyes off him.

"Hello? Amanda Greenwood? This is Iris. Yes, fine, thank you. Amanda, listen, I have a deal for you. Can we talk now? I have something that will interest your readers much more than your little story on Gus de Santos."

Clemente looked at Iris. A few strands of his long, coiffed hair were stuck to the sides of his face. "I did not have sex with the girls. It was not me."

The sound of a woman's voice came through Iris's receiver. "Hello? Hello? Iris?"

"Amanda, can I call you back in a few minutes? I'm in the *métro*, losing connection. Speak in a bit."

She turned her gaze toward Clemente's face. "What the fuck is wrong with you?"

"It was not me."

"Oh, come on, cut the bullshit."

"I did not . . . I could not . . ." he whimpered as he held back a sob, his head still shaking. He stared at the floor, avoiding her eyes.

"How can you deny? Who's the crazy one now?" she shot at him.

"I did not . . . rape you . . . I did not . . . it was not me . . . I . . . I . . . I was high."

"You what?"

"I . . . could not get hard." He said the last words with a gasp and started sobbing. "I could not rape . . . I swear over the head of my mother."

There was a long, heavy silence, and Iris leaned back against the office wall, her legs too weak to support her.

She closed her eyes and stood there, unable to move. After a long pause, she carefully made her way toward the leather chair and sat down. Clemente took a white handkerchief from his breast pocket and blew his nose.

"Why this circus? Why did you pretend?" she asked.

Clemente whimpered, "How could you understand? You're beautiful, Gus was beautiful. You know what it was like to be around you? To be nothing?" He wiped his nose, avoiding her eyes. "What it feels like to be the ugly wop that couldn't get laid? The little dago with no talents? The one in the shadows, waiting for a look from you, a compliment from Gus, a little pat on the back from one of the guys I represented?" Clemente sniffed. "You always humiliate me in front of Gus, you look over my shoulder when I work for him, you correct me, never happy, always complaining, always criticizing, always telling me what to do, poisoning Gus, undermining my work."

"You made lots of money with Gus, Clemente, you had beautiful girls on your arm all the time . . . what else did you want?" Iris said.

"Why do you think they were with me? You think they cared for me? They just wanted me for access to you. I promised them bookings. They were stupid. I wanted to be with you, to be Gus, to be Pierre, to be Karim, to be anyone but myself. Clemente fucking Campisi from Calabria. Do you know Capo Spartivento? Do you know my village? Have you met my parents?"

"So, you ruined people's lives? My life? You violated our innocence because of your lousy dick problems? There are meds for that, you know? Shrinks, doctors—oh wait, you became impotent because you were high and depressed and you took drugs to help you get by? And of course you did not want to do drugs alone, so you gave them to Gus, to bring him down to your same level of misery. And the little girls, Clemente? The baby models you handed over to your gang? What did you get out of that? Did it make you feel like one of the cool boys? Like you belonged to the club?"

Clemente said nothing.

"What's that, Clemente? I can't hear what you're saying," Iris said.

"You . . . you—"

"What?"

"You can't understand," he said, fixing his eyes on hers.

"Understand? No, you bet I don't. Is that why you wanted Gus's estate? So you could feel relevant and important? Like you were an extension of Gus? Did you have a sick need to look at his pictures of me and think that you possessed me?"

Clemente walked toward his desk. He sat down and put his head between his hands.

"Okay. So hand over the archive. I want the key and address to where it's stored."

Clemente looked up. He pushed a strand of dark hair away from his nose. "I don't have the archive. Everything was in a place in Ivry. In an art storage on rue Ferdinand Roussel. It burned down earlier this year. It's all gone."

CHAPTER 56

Saskia was sitting on the stairway outside Clemente's landing. The light went on when Iris slammed the door and it lit Saskia like a ghost, startling Iris.

"'Sup," Saskia said.

Dazed, they went down the three floors in silence. On rue de Rivoli they walked into the first café they found and ordered Perriers.

"Did you catch all of it? I think you got the whole picture, Miss Amanda Greenwood from the *Daily Stand*," Iris said with a wry smile. She looked at her hand as she reached for her glass. It was shaking. "I cannot believe what just happened."

"Yeah, I heard it all. I am so fucking proud of you, girlfriend. My skin was crawling. I really had to control myself on the phone and not start shouting at the pathetic motherfucker. The whole performance . . . his pitiful crocodile tears . . . what an asshole."

"Saskia, I have to make that call now. Are you ready to talk to the real Amanda afterward?" Iris said.

"Fuck yeah. Super ready."

A waiter hovered next to their table, and Iris asked for the check. "Let's get out of here, too many people."

They crossed into the Tuileries gardens and sat on two iron chairs facing the east pond. Iris dialed Amanda's number. "Amanda? This is Iris de Valadé."

"Iris de Valadé, good thing you called. My editor just put my Gus de Santos story on standby, what? Is this what you're calling me about? Your interview?"

Iris smiled into the receiver and her body went limp with relief. She made a thumbs-up to Saskia. "Yes, I was ready to talk to you finally. The story's on standby? Oh dear, so sorry to hear that, Amanda, after all the work you put into it . . ."

Iris caught Saskia's eye and grinned as Saskia mimed choking herself.

Without missing a beat, Iris continued. "Amanda, you've been in my thoughts because I have an interesting lead for you, a story that is long overdue and nobody dares write about in-depth. It's regarding sex abuse and the modeling industry. I have someone here that you might want to talk to. We modeled together for a few years. She's working on a platform to help young models, to give them support and guidance. I know that you ran a story on a model named Audrey. Audrey Hai."

"The poor girl who threw herself out of a window in New York two weeks ago? I wrote that piece," Amanda said.

"Yes, I know. That Audrey. She was part of our group. Can I pass you on to my friend Saskia?"

"Yes."

Saskia took Iris's phone and walked away with it, talking as she circled the pond slowly, her black skirt billowing in the breeze, outlining her long legs. Iris welcomed the silence and gazed at the reflection of the clouds on the water. She looked at her hands. They were shaking again.

Saskia came back and gave the phone to Iris. She sat down next to her. "Done. She's going to run the idea past her editor in chief and get back to me for a proper interview if her boss is interested."

"Jean Marc has all those pictures. If he lets you use some . . . people will take notice; they speak for themselves," Iris said.

"Okay, and Iris, don't worry, I won't involve you. I won't talk about you," Saskia said.

Iris was silent.

"Thank *you* for this. The *Daily Stand* is massive. They have millions of readers."

Iris nodded. "Use the tabloid people as much as you can. You might even be able to raise funding through them, the exposure . . ."

"And Clem? What do I do about Clemente?" Saskia asked, her eyes narrowing.

"Use him too. Cut a deal with him. Blackmail him. Oops! I mean be very persuasive and get Elektra Models to endorse your platform in a very publicized move. Vile slimy waste of oxygen, that spawn of Satan, he has his image to protect. Ironic, isn't it? Keeping up a reputation as a *tombeur de femmes*, a womanizer, a Casanova . . . and he's a dud? I'm sure he doesn't want *that* piece of information shared, revolting macho jerk. Can't even imagine what went through his head all those years. Everything is so pathetic, that small angry man," Iris said.

"Iris, I know what you're going to ask. Clem and I hardly had sex. Many times he said his *cazzo* did not work because of the partying. When Viagra came out in America, he would beg his friends to get it for him. Petit Zizi, Lil' Dick. That will be his nickname. I didn't care about his *zizi*, I had other stuff to keep me happy, you understand?"

"Thanks, I could have lived the rest of my life not having to know that. Thanks, girlfriend."

Saskia's phone rang. "My alarm, gotta go. Have a meeting with an agency. What are your plans this week?"

"Don't know. I need to be alone in my head. I'm too worked up right now. I could drive a stake through Clemente's heart. I have to cool off and then I can think rationally," Iris said.

"Yeah, mindfuck, right? Scenario one: for sixteen years you think Clem raped you and Lou might be his daughter. Then, you're about to be turned into a junkie by the tabloids and your daughter will think you were a slut, and then Clem tells her she's not Gus's daughter. Then Clem beats the shit out of you using psychological warfare until you are all weak and overwhelmed. Pressured by Gus's family, you sell the estate. But no. Instead, voilà! Scenario two: turns out that The Swine has problems getting it up, Gus is Lou's father, The Swine will never lift a finger to hurt a little girl again, and the Paris archive is gone forever. One less problem if you ask me," Saskia said, shrugging.

"One less problem? But those photographs were beautiful, Saskia, they were important to Gus. I can't get my head around the fact that they're gone forever."

"Important to him? Or important to you?"

"What the hell do I know," Iris said. "I thought I would get closure, but this doesn't feel as liberating as it should."

Saskia turned to face her friend. Holding Iris's forearm, she looked deep into her eyes. Saskia's flashed like lightning bolts, and her pink mouth was curled into a half smile. "Everything happens for a reason, you dingbat. Don't you get it? Turn the page. Live now. Stop reminding yourself of what you had with Gus. The pictures he took of you were an homage to that love. He adored you, he worshipped you, and he also harmed you. You journeyed too far in love, but at least you lived it like you meant it. That's all you need to know. It was nearly two decades ago. Those pictures are now gone, so move on, baby. You've got a new lease on life, enjoy it, for fuck's sake. You're free!"

Iris closed her eyes, feeling strangely numb and light-headed. She held Saskia's hand. "About the rape, well, with your confirmation about his problem, that's now clear, Saskia, and I thank you, but as for the archive . . . that son of a bitch . . . I still don't trust a word he said. I may feel completely free when I have proof that the archive was destroyed."

"Whatever works for you," Saskia said as she hugged Iris. They remained in a tight embrace. "Be careful. Promise me you'll be watchful."

"What do you mean?"

"I know Clem too well to believe for even one nanosecond that he's not going to come after you. You only won a battle; you did not win the war."

"Come after me? And do what?" Iris shivered, her arms covered in goose pimples.

"Finish your business and get the fuck out of Paris as fast as you can. There is nothing Clem hates more than to be humiliated." Saskia's alarm went off again. "*Merde!* Now I really must run."

Iris called out as Saskia started walking toward the place de la Concorde. "Hey, please don't leave me. When do I see you again?"

Saskia turned and shrugged as she made a questioning face. Then she continued walking backward, holding Iris's gaze until she disappeared behind the trees. Iris ran after her.

Turning a bend, she found Saskia. "Saskia! Hey, you!"

Saskia stopped and spun around, a flurry of black silk, platinum tresses, and bright eyes.

"Saskia, you can use my name on your platform. I'd be honored to be one of your founding godmothers," Iris said.

"You mean grandmothers?" said Saskia. Iris laughed and gave her a shove. "Iris, don't be scared. You can count on me. We're in this together, 'K?"

Iris waved and headed down the promenade toward the Louvre, stopping to watch a pair of moat goats mowing the grassy embankments near the Grand Bassin while a gaggle of delighted tourists took pictures. Next to the esplanade was the labyrinth of yew hedges called the Gay Gardens, where sex cruisers would roam at nightfall. At the busy Arc de Triomphe du Carrousel, where the yellowish earth and landscaped gardens joined the pavements of the Carrousel du Louvre, flocks of overequipped Chinese tourists took pictures with selfie sticks. Tall Africans sold counterfeit handbags and souvenir Eiffel Towers painted in gaudy colors. An Asian bride in a frothy wedding dress posed with her beau against one of the Maillol statues. Men with too much jewelry and women in black burkas huddled against a minivan as gusts of wind lifted their heavy robes and coated their sandals and socks in ochre chalk.

The Roma family she had first seen in the Marais was under the arches of the Musée des Arts Décoratifs. The old man was slumped in the wheelchair without his jaunty hat. Nearby, the little kid played with a puppy in a cardboard box that said *We Are Hungry*. A barefoot girl with matted hair and a dirty dress shook a paper cup in her face. Iris gave her some coins.

She continued walking for half an hour on rue de Rivoli, until she reached the Centre Pompidou. The Brancusi Atelier was tucked in a corner of the slanted piazza opposite the museum, a muted and discreet oasis of peace.

Iris sat on a bench facing one of the rooms. After a while she allowed her senses to be lost in the unity of the group of sculptures and their relation to the space. In that room, in that moment, she looked for what was real, not the image, but the idea, the meaning of things. Coming to her senses, calming down, she grasped the depth of her unrelenting anger toward Gus.

CHAPTER 57

My phone pings with a text. Who is texting me?

No one I know texts anymore. The number is masked.

'How are you, Lou de Santos? You are so grownup and pretty. I am looking forward to meeting you soon.'

'Who is this?' I write back.

'An old friend of your father and mother.'

'Sod off I don't text with strangers.'

No one calls me Lou de Santos, that's just my Instagram name. My surname is Newman. I am about to WhatsApp Mom about this message, but I stop myself.

CHAPTER 58

Iris made her way down rue Ferdinand Roussel, where the Finart warehouse had once stood. The red-and-white police tape cordoning off the site was still up in places. A bulldozer tore down a piece of blackened wall by the sidewalk while two men with sledgehammers broke up a cement floor. The noise was deafening. A cloud of dust enveloped the men as they worked. Iris walked around the plastic traffic cones as close as she could. A foreman wearing a protective helmet came out of his office in a metal trailer and shooed her away. Iris picked up a jagged pebble from a pile of rubble.

Back at Joan's flat, she logged on to her computer and browsed the internet, looking for more information.

The fire had raged for two days and had all but leveled the warehouse. *Le Parisien* newspaper had published a full photo spread, including dismal pictures taken from a helicopter to show the extent of the destruction. The fire had ripped through the warehouse and destroyed most of the units. It was believed that the fire had been caused by the explosion of gas canisters that were kept in an adjoining building. As described by *Le Parisien*, Finart was a company that specialized in handling, storing, and transporting art and antiquities. The damage was unquantifiable. Many valuable collections were lost. Everything had burned to ash.

On a specialized art-law website, Iris read that a group legal action had been filed against Finart for negligent conduct. The petitioners asserted that the storage facilities were wholly unsuitable for high-value fine art. Iris found the case involving the insurance claim as well as the complete catalog of the lost pieces by each claimant. Clemente's name was one of three on a list of uninsured clients declaring that they had believed at the time that insurance was included in the storage service. No list detailing the lost art was made available for these three names.

The dispute had been settled through mediation. According to the press, Finart had paid the aggrieved parties.

Iris copied and pasted the relevant information about the Finart case and Clemente's legal proceedings and emailed Matthew Cook and Andy Marshall.

Matthew's call was not long in coming.

"Good afternoon, Iris. I have Andy on the line too."

"Good morning, Matthew, Mr. Marshall."

"First of all, Iris, thank you for this report. It's not the development we expected, of course, but at least now we know. It is a terrible loss. How did you manage to get Mr. Campisi to talk?"

"You don't want to know. Let's just say that I now have some leverage on Campisi." Iris heard Matthew chuckle. "Anyway, it's the version he gave me, but Campisi lies about everything. I'm researching all this for more proof. He could very well have had the storage unit at Finart for the other photographers he represented. Or maybe it was for his private collection. Even though he was not insured, he could have claimed compensation from Finart, alleging negligence, correct?"

"Absent any contrary terms and conditions of the contract he executed with Finart when he took the unit—yes, absolutely correct," Matthew replied.

"So Campisi could have declared that his Gus de Santos archive was in the unit that burned and subsequently get compensation from Finart, correct?"

"Correct," Matthew said.

"And is there any way that we can find out if Gus's work was actually in there when the unit burned down?" Iris said.

"Typically, the French will do an arson investigation. But assuming that the contents were burned to the point of being unrecognizable, then you could not prove that these were not Gus de Santos's archives and were something else entirely."

"I understand," Iris said. "I'm going to look around and see what else I find. I have a list with every single piece that was taken from Gus de Santos's office; apparently, there have been unsigned prints turning up for sale at the Paris Photo fair. I need to find out who sold those prints to the merchants and if they were on the list of what supposedly went to the Finart storage."

"Splendid idea. I admire your tenacity," Matthew said.

"I say, Ms. Newman—may I be so bold as to inquire when you will be returning?" Andy Marshall said. "Mr. de Santos's family want to have a memorial and scatter his ashes. They have put it to me that you should be present with your daughter."

Iris was silent.

"Ms. Newman?"

"I need a few more days to check out some things, Mr. Marshall."

After hanging up, Iris dialed Lou to wish her luck on her exams. Her call went to voicemail.

Joan's flat was silent, and Iris moved to the sofa facing the courtyard. The large windows were open to let in the soft spring breeze. It was late afternoon, and she could hear Blanca sweeping the cobbles downstairs.

Rubbing her temples, Iris closed her eyes as a feeling of lassitude washed over her body. Breathing slowly, she kneaded the tension out of her neck and shoulders. She curled into a fetal position and dozed off.

She woke up to the ringing of her phone. Dazed, she answered, *"Allô?"*

"Iris?"

"It's you! Bonjour."

"Did I wake you up?" Chuck said.

"Yes." Iris turned on her back and stretched.

"Are you okay?"

"Can you make me coffee? Wait, what time is it?" Iris looked at her phone. "Oh God, I slept for two hours. Joan and Othilia will be here soon."

"Just wanted some news. How are things?"

"I was going to call you, but I fell asleep. Had an adrenaline slump . . . it's been quite a day. I made some progress, though. Supposedly, the archive was in a storage facility that burned down a year ago."

Chuck was quiet.

"Chuck?"

"Are you sad?" he said.

"I am, very sad. Maybe not sad enough. Maybe relieved too. Have no idea."

"I see," he said. "So you're coming back?"

"I'm trying to."

"Oh . . ." Chuck paused. "Maybe you should stay and invite Lou to join you."

"Did she mention it?"

"No. She's kind of moody these days, secretive . . ."

"I've spent the last few days thinking about how much I want to share the city with her, but . . ."

"Is everything all right, Iris?"

Iris got up from the sofa and walked to the window overlooking the square. "I've pissed someone off. I want Lou to be away from here until all this dies down."

"I see. Now *I'm* very worried for you," Chuck said. His voice was soothing. "Did you tell Lou about the fire?"

"Not yet. I'll tell her but don't want to ruin her last days at school. I don't know how she'll take it."

"Do you want me to come to Paris?"

Iris was silent.

The front door slammed and Joan's heels clicked in the entrance hallway. "Anyone here?" she called.

"Hold on, Chuck," Iris said. "Joan, I'm here!"

Joan walked past the door and waved discreetly.

"Chuck?"

"There's another thing. A crate arrived from your law firm in LA. I told Lou, and she asked me if Conrado could unpack it and put the pieces in your studio. She wanted you to find them when you arrived. She said they were Gus's. There was a desk and a ceiling lamp. The drawers of the desk had been taped shut for transport. We took off the tape and I opened them, but they were empty. One drawer was locked. I found the key stuck with gaffer tape under the desk. What do you want me to do?"

"Could you open it, please? Thanks, thank you so much . . . Chuck, I need to call you back, Joan just arrived . . ."

"You're welcome," Chuck said.

"Chuck? I wanted to tell you—" But Chuck had hung up.

Iris looked at the ceiling with a heavy heart. A phone call full of unsaid things and unspoken thoughts. Feelings and desires suppressed, replaced by the practical and the utile.

She dialed Chuck back, but the call went to voicemail. She sat up and smoothed her clothes, then went to the bathroom to splash water on her face, scraping back damp strands of hair into a tight ponytail. She needed to think about Chuck.

Joan was preparing Lapsang souchong tea in the kitchen. Iris turned on the coffee machine.

"Hey, what happened to you?" Joan said. "I texted but you didn't reply. I was concerned."

"Oh God, so sorry, Joan. I forgot to text you back. I crashed, fell asleep . . . I was so tired all of a sudden. I met with Clemente; we had an altercation. Don't worry, Saskia was there."

Joan sat at the kitchen bench and looked at Iris. "You had an altercation with Clemente? What happened? Nothing good can come from an altercation with Clemente."

"He finally confessed that the storage unit with Gus's archive burned down. He could be telling the truth, but there's no evidence yet to convince me that Gus's archive was in that unit."

"But this is dreadful . . . I am so sorry . . ."

Iris made herself an espresso and sat down facing Joan.

"There's more: the *Daily Stand* is dropping the piece on us, for now. Another long story, but I'm off the hook for the time being."

"Really? *That* is good news, Iris, what a relief! I was desperately worried about you—this roller coaster—"

"If only you knew . . . by the way, can I have the names of the galleries where you saw Gus's prints?"

"Relentless, *n'est ce pas?*"

Iris smiled unconvincingly. "It's a long shot. And Joan? Don't worry, I'll be out of your hair in a few days. I cannot thank you enough for your help, but I haven't forgotten that your Gaston is coming soon."

"*Mon* Gaston," Joan said with a dreamy look on her face. "The sunshine of my life. I cannot imagine myself without Gaston. I'd give up everything to spend the rest of my life with him."

Iris gave her a side-glance as she walked out of the kitchen.

CHAPTER 59

The coffee was dark and strong. A double espresso with hot milk on the side. The coffee was served in a stubby glass. *"This is how you do it,"* Gus had said time and time again. *"This is how you drink it. Not that pissy, milky, piece-of-shit coffee they drink in Paris."*

Gus had liked to make a big fuss about his *cortados*, cussing at anyone who dared to differ. From him Iris had learned that if the coffee was in a glass you could see how strong it was, and if the milk was on the side you could cut the bitterness, or not. The milk had to be whole, fresh, not pasteurized, not skim, not soy. It had to be warmed, not steamed. The coffee had to froth very little when the milk was added. The texture had to be velvety, smooth, and rich. You filled the glass halfway with coffee and milk, leaving a rim that you could hold with two fingers and not get burned.

Iris smiled and stirred her glass, never taking her eyes off the entrance to the Gallerie Laplace opposite la Palette café.

A church bell clanged. As the last bong rang, a tall, thin young man in a light suit unlocked the gallery door. He carried a bouquet of long branches with red buds. A liver-colored Labrador followed him with a newspaper in its mouth.

After a few minutes, Iris paid for her coffee and knocked on the door of the Gallerie Cristobal Laplace.

The young man was removing a vase of limp tulips from the window display. *"Je peux vous aider?"*

Iris smiled at him. "Thank you, do you mind if I look around? Your window is beautiful."

It was a small, elegant place on rue de Seine in the heart of the antiques district. A wooden library filled the storefront. The shelves contained leather-bound books and singular objects. Abstract marble sculptures, two peculiar metal lamps, a pewter vase filled with orange poppies with curly petals, a glass paperweight in the darkest emerald hue, a collection of small African-animal sculptures in dark matte wood, two graphic white-and-blue earthenware jugs from Andalusia, an abstract monochromatic ink painting by Fernando Zóbel, a Charlotte Perriand chair of ash-tree wood and rush that Iris longed to touch, and a floor lamp made of light-brown cane and faded, stamped parchment. On a low table by the Perriand chair was a pile of brocade curtains in purple silk and matte-gold trimmings. On each side of the library the gallery walls had been painted a dark blue-green teal. Black-and-white photographs in old wooden frames were scattered around in a random way: a rocky landscape by Chris Plytas, two photographs of le Corbusier and Niemeyer buildings by Lucien Hervé, a tryptic of Maria Callas rehearsing by Luc Fournol . . . the window display was an exquisite combination of shapes and textures, hues, shadows and proportions, time and space. Iris browsed in the shop, careful not to touch anything. The man laid the branches on a green granite table whose surface looked like foaming waves, and he clipped the ends off.

The Labrador sniffed at Iris's leg and wagged its round rump.

At the far end of the shop was a wooden print rack. Plastic sleeves containing prints were displayed, and the sheets had large tags with handwritten names in chronological order. Next to the rack was a flat-file cabinet with many drawers, indexed with anthracite cardboard cards written in curly white calligraphy. Iris looked at the names on the tags: Adams Ansel, Avedon Richard, Bailey David, Beaton Cecil, Modotti Tina, Smith Eugene, Stieglitz Alfred, Weston Edward, Winogrand

Garry . . . on top of the cabinet were two pairs of white cotton gloves.

"Are you looking for anything in particular?"

Iris was startled. She swung around to face the gallerist and his dog, now standing but a few inches away from her.

"Thank you, my name is Iris. I'm standing here in total admiration. You have an exquisite collection."

The tall young man smiled and shook Iris's hand. "Cristobal Laplace. And Winnie." The Labrador sat down and wagged her fat tail.

"Do you have any pictures by Gustavo de Santos?"

"*Helás non.* Unfortunately not. I had a couple but sold them last year at Paris Photo. Since he passed away, curators have been desperately looking for them. The only available ones are through his Berlin gallerist, and the prices have gone through the roof. Are *you* a collector?" Cristobal took off his glasses and studied Iris's face. Iris detected an accent that she could not place.

"No, I worked with de Santos when he started in Paris. I'm working with the estate now, in California. Trying to regroup the collection," Iris said.

"How interesting," Cristobal said, tucking his glasses into his breast pocket. "I have not come across any of his vintage prints in a very long time. There are a few in the permanent collection of la Maison de la Photographie. Sometimes they're on show; otherwise there are none in circulation, none for sale. They say that his early work burned in the Finart fire. You know about the fire, *non?*"

Winnie whined and Cristobal bent down to pet her.

"The ones you had, where did you obtain those from?" said Iris.

"I bought them at an estate sale in Drouot, you know Drouot? The public auction house . . . they were part of a lot of twenty-two very old prints. There was nothing of value in the batch; they were prints that I bought to decorate my shop with.

Some funny things turn up in those lots: people's horrifying children, their ugly dogs, their naked mistresses . . . those are the photographs I have in the display there," he said, pointing to the wooden rack. "The valuable ones are in the drawers. The two Gus de Santos prints turned up in the Drouot lot."

"Do you have a picture of them?" Iris said.

Cristobal took an iPad from his desk drawer and scrolled.

Iris looked at Winnie, whose tail was still thumping. Winnie grinned, showing her teeth.

"Here. *Les voilà*, these two." Cristobal handed the iPad to Iris.

They were both in black and white. One was a still life of gutted sardines glistening on a dull metal plate. The other was a wilted bouquet of wildflowers in a glass jug. Both were studies in classic composition. They made her think of death and decay. There was something sad and formal about them, a stiffness she had never seen before in his work. Iris did not recognize them.

"Were they retouched by hand?"

"*Non*, I am sure of that. They were not dated either. They were not signed. There was a sticker on the back with his name. They looked like test prints or maybe the original prints the artist gives to the magazines as reference. I sold them cheap. They were not valuable, but they were *trés, trés belles*," said Cristobal, shrugging. "But all his pictures are beautiful, *dommage* that he died so young, he was one of my favorites. I saw a show he did in Berlin a few years ago. I wanted to buy some of his photographs for my private collection, but now it is too late." Cristobal's bookish face looked mournful.

Iris got on her knees to pat Winnie, who was nudging her shin with a wet nose. Cristobal shooed her away, muttering, "*Ça suffit, Winnie! Coucher! Dodo! Non, mais . . .*" He turned toward Iris and said, "Do you want a coffee? I was at les Puces, the flea market, at five. I need my plasma. I'm sleepwalking like in *The Living Dead*."

Cristobal showed Iris to a pair of Louis XVI bergères upholstered in coarse off-white linen.

"Thank you for your time."

"Oh, it's a pleasure to sit in the company of such a beautiful lady." Cristobal placed their cups on a crowded table and sat down. Winnie came over, looking sheepish, and curled on the floor at his feet.

"It must have been *passionnant* to work with him, *non?*" Cristobal said as he observed Iris. "But what do you mean, working with him? You are too pretty to be an assistant," he said, finally cracking a timid smile.

"I was a model in the nineties. I met and shot with Gus de Santos, he was my boyfriend. I also helped him in the studio with his archive. Now I am to manage his estate. That's why I am looking for his early work."

"Bien sûr!" Cristobal said excitedly. "I know *trés bien* who you are. You were a famous model, *n'est ce pas?* Iris de Valadé? Your mother was the *rédactrice en chef* of *Revue?* I worked at *Revue* when I was young. I worked with the art and culture editor, Arturo Lacloche. I remember your face very well. You worked often for *Revue*, you were on a few covers, *n'est ce pas?*"

Cristobal was smitten. He sat up straight and focused on Iris's face.

"Cristobal, how do you think those prints ended up at Drouot?"

"Drouot is a public auction house. They have six or seven sales a day, six days a week. People die and their estate gets dispersed by inheritors who don't want to deal with the expense of having every single object appraised. Sometimes people's things get seized when they don't pay taxes, or luxury goods are confiscated at customs because they lack the proper paperwork . . . all those things end up in the public auction houses. Maybe the de Santos prints belonged to a lab that was dismantled and sold? Or someone had them in storage and did not pay their bill? Or they were found in a garbage bin? Things like that happen. You remember the archive of Vivian Maier that was found by some amateurs in an auction house? The archive was in cardboard boxes and a couple of old suitcases: undeveloped film, prints, slides. A miracle if you ask me. Imagine finding that!" Cristobal said.

"And what do you know about the Finart fire?" Iris said.

"*Quelle catastrophe.* My friends lost all their stock in that fire. I heard that a collection of de Santos burnt too."

"All his early work," Iris said.

"It is such a *dommage,* a pity. My friends say they met the collector, an Italian. They all testified at the lawsuit for the insurance. Their storage unit was right next to the Italian's."

Iris looked at Cristobal expectantly.

"The firemen could not access the inside of the site for days. I went there with my friends. There was nothing left. Just ashes and *décombres* . . . rubble?" Cristobal continued. "A terrible *dommage.* I have seen other de Santos prints at Paris Photo, but they are not worth the paper they are printed on."

"You mean?"

"They are digital outtakes of low-resolution scans. They looked like advertising work, you know? Perfume, cosmetics . . . nothing of value. Don't waste your time with those," he said.

"So you saw it with your own eyes, then? Everything burned?" Iris said.

"Yes, everything," Cristobal said as he fixed his gaze on her face.

Iris nodded and shook his hand as she stood to leave. Cristobal gave her his business card.

"Wait!"

He came toward her with a book in his hands. "For you," he said.

It was a catalog from the Museum für Fotografie in Berlin.

Iris opened to the first page. At the bottom she recognized Gus's scrawl: *To Cristobal: Thanks for the love, man.*

Overwhelmed, she ran her index finger over the handwriting. Iris clutched the book to her heart and kissed Cristobal on both cheeks. He bent down to pat Winnie's head, then he cleared his throat and put his glasses back on.

CHAPTER 60

Kitti opened the door in a leopard-print caftan. Her tiny feet were bare. Her skin glowed clean, made up with only her signature crimson mouth. Milling around was the pack of fluffy dogs. Roar, the large slow cat, sat on a plastic tablecloth on the dining room table, unconcerned with the din.

"Come in, come in, my darling. So happy you remembered your Kitti. What a surprise!"

Kitti ushered Iris in and herded the pack toward the living room sofa. "I'll get you mint tea. I remember you liked mint tea. I just picked it from the roof."

Strewn all over the sofa were photographs, white cardboard, gold glitter dust, and metallic pens. Iris moved the clutter away and sat down. She picked up a photograph of Kitti in a tight vinyl dress, sparkly stilettos, and sheer black garter stockings. She was crouching, looking at the camera. Her black dress was slit on the side. You could see she wore a garter belt with no panties. Iris picked up another photograph. Kitti again. She was lying on the floor, her legs slightly parted and slanted sideways, black vinyl dress hitched around her waist, with garter belt, black stockings, and metallic stilettos. She was pinching her nipple under the dress. Her expression was pensive. She looked beautiful in the pictures. Her hair was shiny black like the dress and very long. Her almond-shaped eyes were clear.

Kitti came into the living room and put a tray with mugs on the table.

"Kitti! You look incredible in these."

"Oh, those. I had a boyfriend who liked to take naughty pictures of me. I enjoyed it." Kitti giggled. "He had this image of me like some sort of Supervixen with Russ Meyer tits, but I was a skinny bird . . . he had a lot of imagination. They're artistic, don't you think?"

"What are you doing with them? Are you cutting them up?"

Kitti smiled her cheeky smile and cooed, "I'm making a birthday card for my piglet. He loves me playing foxy."

"How old is Thomas?"

"He's going to turn eighty." Kitti's face lit up.

"And you've been together for . . . ?"

"Thirty years. A lifetime. We'll die together. Or maybe I die after him, alone, and get eaten by my dogs."

"That's gross, the dogs won't eat you. And you'll never die." Iris chuckled. "Kitti, I came here to thank you for the kick in the ass."

"You mean you're being nice to that man in California? What's he called? Chet?" Kitti said.

Iris laughed. "No, I meant with all the rest. I'm dealing with issues. And making peace with Paris."

Kitti took a pouch from the coffee table and started rolling a joint. "All that's good and you'll tell me about it later, but when am I going to meet that California man?"

"There's no California man, Kitti. He's just my landlord, and neighbor."

"Sounds good enough to me. You've already mentioned Chet a few times . . . that he's looking after your daughter, that he calls you a lot—"

"His name is Chuck, not Chet. Oh, shit! Speaking of . . . what time is it?"

"I did an oracle for you. You were with that man. And then you weren't," Kitti said.

"Oh, Kitti, please don't go mystic on me."

"I mean it, I saw it. By the way, do you have a picture of him?"

"Nope, no picture. Oh wait! My daughter posted some pictures of him, of my *landlord*."

"*L'amoureux* . . . the lover boy . . ."

"My *landlord*. I'll show you on my phone."

Kitti put the rollie in the ashtray and walked down the corridor toward her bedroom. She came back carrying a small laptop and opened it on the sofa. "I have a computer, you know? I have internet too. Thomas has gone crackers with the internet. We watch American series in bed and he sends me dirty emails all day long. I always said that musicians were the best lovers, until I started fucking photographers, that is."

Iris laughed and covered her ears. "Stop! Too much information." She logged in to Instagram, then turned the screen toward Kitti. "My landlord."

Kitti took a hit of her joint and picked at a piece of grass stuck on her lip. She peered at the screen, squinting. "Ummmmm . . . he looks kind. That's the face I saw in the oracle. He wants you to have a baby with him, but you don't, and he's tired of waiting because he wants kids." Kitti stared into the distance. "I saw another woman in the oracle. She was not beautiful like you, but she giggled a lot at his jokes."

Iris laughed. "I don't know who you're talking about. I don't know anything about his private life."

"Well, you should. He could maybe be the man in your life, if you hurry up," Kitti said, taking a long drag of her joint. "But first you have to let go of your ex."

"I'll never see him again. Kitti, Gus is dead and I have so much anger toward him, even after all these years. Sixteen, in fact."

"That's exactly what the oracle told me. In the oracle I see he's still with you, I see that it fucks with your head."

Roar jumped on the sofa and walked stealthily toward Kitti. He sat on a pile of cardboard and started licking his tail.

"My oracle is never wrong, and you know it." As she said this, Kitti looked deep into Iris's eyes.

Iris held her gaze.

"Is Thomas the most important thing in your life?"

"Yes, my love for him is. And my animals. This is all that matters to me," Kitti said.

"Is Thomas taking care of you?"

"For as long as I'm alive. I'm in his will. He bought me this flat. I'm still young, I'm only seventy. I have so many plans, so many fun things to do. I'm taking an online course on writing, can you imagine? I can learn anything I want on the internet. I'm going to write my memoirs about being a muse in the swinging sixties. London, Paris, New York, Rome, the artists I posed for, the ones I fucked . . . Thomas helps me with my writing course and he's still shooting, you know? He loves his work and I love my life with him. I am the happiest girl in the world."

Iris reached out to pet Roar. He lashed at her hand, scratching it.

"Roar! You shit!" Kitti swatted him away. "Sorry about that, I think he's having a nervous breakdown, traumatized from living with so many dogs."

Iris sucked on her hand and chuckled.

"Little girl, you know how I found happiness?"

Iris shook her head.

"When I realized that what I wanted and what I needed were two different things. Unfortunately, it took me five decades to figure it out."

Iris walked north on rue de Rennes until she reached Saint-Germain. She crossed the busy boulevard and wandered through the narrow streets into rue de Verneuil, stopping in front of the graffitied house that was the shrine to Serge Gainsbourg.

Comment t'oublier? How can we forget you? someone had written next to his stenciled face.

She reached the pedestrian bridge, Pont des Arts, facing the Louvre.

Stopping midway, she looked at the murky river under her feet. A light wind ruffled a flock of gulls perched on the roof of a Bateau Mouche as it glided by. Iris untied the leather cord around her neck and kissed the silver pendant. She waited until the boat was well past the bridge. The pendant sank quickly in the choppy waves.

CHAPTER 61

The apartment was silent. The kitchen light was on.

"Anyone home? Joan? Othilia?"

Joan sat at the kitchen table, the black, gold, and green bone-china cup and saucer from her favorite tea set in front of her. Iris was startled.

"Joan? What are you doing here? Is everything okay?"

Joan looked up. "Have some tea."

Iris took a paper-thin teacup and saucer from the shelf and sat down. She poured her tea. Joan stared at the table. "Ada's been fired, *chérie*."

"What?" Iris said.

"Ada Shaffer. She was fired this morning. She's already gone. I'm in shock. Incredible, no? You work for twenty years at the same place and it takes you only one hour to clear out of that life. Her office is empty. There's no trace of her anymore, even her humidifier is gone."

"Why? Why was she fired?"

"Pay for play, conflict of interest, abuse of power . . . we were aware of it, it wasn't a secret. But Ada blew it, she thought she was untouchable."

"Blimey. I need a drink." Iris went to the fridge and took out a bottle of white wine.

"Yes, blimey. At other magazines, you get a low salary, and to compensate you're allowed to consult for brands. At *Revue*, that's not the case. Ada had a colossal salary with all the fringe benefits, wardrobe included. She believed she was irreplaceable and could get away with murder, bestowing influence like a benevolent queen. I guess she couldn't."

"Holy cow! Good riddance, then. Yeah, I remember how Gus got upset at her because she was always dangling a carrot. Like, *'You shoot for this unknown wack-ass client for editorial rates, and I'll make sure you get the Lancôme campaign.'* Gus refused, and Ada said she would stop booking him for *Revue.*"

"Why didn't you tell me this before?"

Iris sipped her wine. "What difference would it have made? No one seemed to care. Later we discovered that Ada was the art and fashion consultant for both clients, the ugly-assed one and Lancôme. And she would style the shoots too. It was always about pushing her agenda in a transactional way. Her choices were not for the love of fashion."

"That's bad."

"Yes, and she stopped booking Eva at *Revue* because Ada's clients were leaving her to work directly with Eva, who was cheaper, edgier, and more trustworthy."

Joan shook her head. "So she went about her business until heads at *Revue* could no longer quash the rumors. Designers and advertisers were complaining and canceling pages. Officially she has resigned. But we all know the real version."

"Who's going to replace her?"

"The CEO has asked me to become the editor in chief," Joan said, holding Iris's gaze.

"You're kidding?" Iris put her wineglass down.

"Dead serious, *chérie.* I told him I would think about it. I asked for a couple of weeks. On one hand, I am flattered and excited about taking *Revue* to a new level, but on the other hand I am quite sick of the fashion industry."

"*You*, sick of the industry?"

"Yes, disappointed with it and angry. I'm over the immediate gratification, sick of people's inflated self-importance, frustrated with the mental laziness. Sick to death of the irrelevance of the fashion-magazine industry, the advertisers' total control, the emperor's new clothes, the warped fashion press . . ."

"I thought I would never hear you say that."

"I can only tell this to you, Iris. We all think the same, but no one dares say it. We are all too scared of losing our jobs, of being banned from the front row."

"What did Gaston say?"

"Haven't told him yet. I wanted to talk to you first. You've been there before. Your mother . . ."

"You mean you want her career?" Iris said, fixing on Joan's eyes.

"Heavens, no. There is a place for only one Delfine at *Revue*."

Iris smiled briefly. "Hey, thank you for the shout-out to my mother at the end of the documentary."

"It's the least I could do. I owed it to her."

"Was Ada responsible for my mother's downgrade?"

Staring out the window, Joan replied, "Yes."

Iris remained silent.

"I had no choice, Iris. Delfine's days in Paris were numbered. She wanted too much power . . . I was just her assistant . . . I tried to warn her a few times that she was angering the suits at the top, but she refused to listen because she had the unconditional support of the designers . . . but in the end, the designers no longer mattered, only the bottom line. I told your mother repeatedly that Ada was preparing a coup. She paid no attention to me."

"You did? You told her? Why didn't you tell me?"

"But you were too young! Believe me, there was nothing I could have done, short of resigning." Joan turned her gaze toward Iris.

A wave of gratitude for Joan came over Iris. She stood up and embraced her. Joan stroked Iris's back.

Iris went to the fridge and poured herself a second glass of wine. Not lifting her eyes from the bottle, she said, "When are you speaking with Gaston?"

"Very soon, *chérie*, but don't worry, Gaston and Othilia will always come first. I just needed to talk to an insider who's now on the outside. That's you, by the way."

Iris looked up, her face grave. "What are you going to decide, Joan? Your mind is made up already, isn't it? Do you want to discuss? I can help you."

The front door slammed. They heard the thud of Othilia's backpack as it hit the floor. Joan put her index finger to her lips. Iris nodded.

Othilia bounced into the kitchen. "*Bonsoir*, everyone. What are you doing home so early, Joan?"

"I had a headache, wasn't feeling too good."

Othilia kissed Joan and Iris on the cheek, clearly happy to see them. *Just like my monster at home,* thought Iris. *All I get is a snarl and a grunt if she needs to be fed.*

"Are you feeling better? Want me to get you some aspirin?" Othilia said.

"Taken, thank you. How was your day? Those exams?"

Othilia plopped herself on the kitchen bench and peeled a banana.

"Three more days to go and I'm finished. And fifteen days and thirty hours till my father comes home. I'm ready. I'm so fed up with exams, *j'en ai marre*," Othilia said.

Iris and Joan watched Othilia chewing her banana.

"Joan?" Othilia slid closer to them on the bench. "Everyone at school is talking about the TV documentary. It was on last night."

"It was? I totally forgot," said Joan.

"Well, it *is* forgettable, but my friends and their parents raved about you. I was the star of the class, thanks to you."

"People watched it? A documentary about a fashion magazine? That's pretty niche," Joan said.

"You'd be surprised. In my class, everyone loves fashion. Well, you know, not *fashion* fashion, but the models, the celebrities, the parties . . . all that stuff, it's like a dream world. But for the rest, the clothes and stuff, we don't care," Othilia said, shrugging.

"Oh. What else did your class say, *chérie?*"

"They were interested in *you*, because you are so cultured, and it was thought provoking to see how much effort you put into getting ideas . . . all that, and because your enthusiasm was contagious."

Joan smiled at Othilia and, looking at Iris, said, "'Thought provoking.' I guess we better watch it again, right?"

"No one liked your boss, what's her name, Ada. They all said they should have edited her bits down so there was less of her and more of you," Othilia said.

"How ironic," Joan said.

"Ironic?"

Iris cut in. "What are people in your class interested in?"

Othilia poured some of Joan's tea into a mug and took a sip. "Politics, thought, how we use time, ecology, science, finding a cure for deadly diseases, activism, climate change, repairing the *broken* internet . . ."

"And art? Any artists in there?"

"Art is a way of looking at the world differently. Yes, it's a very important tool for us, a tool to help fix the world maybe? The nerds in our class want to learn the process of creative thinking. I read a book on that, they teach it at Stanford. But Europe is so fractured right now that we are all debating what we can do to help it in an immediate way."

"You mean practical?" Joan said.

"Yeah, something we can all participate in. A group of us are going to work on a project, because in my class everyone is very politically involved. We're going to create a website called EuropeIs.org where we can exchange thoughts and ideas with people from all over the EU, from all over the world. We want to unite cities and people, build community, not virtual walls around them. It will be like a safe zone where every-one can express themselves no matter where or who they are, kind of cultural activism. There will be proper mediators and fact-checkers and a theme every month." Othilia got up and opened the fridge.

"That's exciting," Joan said.

"I'll show you the project when it's more developed," Othilia said from inside the fridge.

"How did this start?" Iris said.

"It's a long story, but in my class there are students from all over Europe, and we don't know anything about their countries, or their people. The only thing we know of each other is what we experience in class. We, they, are always telling each other, *'In Italy we do this, in Spain you say that, Germans don't think this way, this just happened in Sweden.'* We figured it would be cool to share the informed thinking, in a positive way, across all countries, so we interpret each other better. We need to be less isolated in our thinking, and we need to shape our own opinions before our opinions are formed by others," Othilia said.

"Sounds like different parts of the USA. We know nothing of each other, and few care," Iris said.

Othilia nodded. She carried a plate of cheeses and put it on the table. "At the same time, I was contacted by an American digital-marketing platform. They asked me to become one of their thought leaders. They said my feed was so interesting and they were looking for English-speaking influencers of my age in Europe. They want to use my digital relationships to help them push their brands. A kind of word of mouth sell via existing networks that they want to penetrate. It's called influencer marketing," Othilia said, munching on a piece of Comté.

Iris looked at Joan and then back at Othilia. "Wow, congratulations."

Othilia turned her gaze toward Joan. "I didn't tell you yet because it was not something I wanted to undertake. You know, using culture to sell more stuff one doesn't need. If my father gives me permission, and if you agree too, I think I should do it because I can use the experience and knowledge to further the EuropeIs.org project."

"That's it, isn't it?" said Joan, looking at Iris. "Witnessing the death, live, of the PR, marketing, and advertising worlds as we know them."

Iris took Joan's hand. "No panic, it will be okay. This is part of the conversation we should be having about your future."

Othilia shrugged. "Don't be dramatic, Joan. It's the way things are done now. It's more direct, you're pushing content straight to the users that are likely to move it around. It cuts out the middlemen. We're studying this in my computer science class along with traditional journalism."

"Influencer marketing. Thought leader. Digital relationship. Pushing content . . . I'm feeling decrepit and depressed now."

Othilia laughed. "Decrepit? You killed it, Joan, you totally rocked that documentary. But you should use your skills in something other than selling shampoos and bags. I'll help you learn about the new media if you want."

Iris said, "Lou's very good at this too. She has thousands of followers on her photo blog. She's created an 'artistic community,' she's totally techie. Othilia and Lou could give us both an intensive course. I think we need a dialogue between generations, an exchange . . . if it was for me, I would lower the voting age to sixteen."

Othilia smiled.

Joan still looked panic-stricken.

"You have to update. It's a new chapter," Iris said, holding her gaze.

"Never better said," Joan said.

Othilia piled slices of bread and cheese on a plate and went to her room to work.

They waited until they heard her steps on the mezzanine. Joan had a glum look on her face. "I'm too old for this. I think this train has passed the station," she said.

"Joan, you're fifty-four, for God's sake. Thomas Bailey and Kitti just learned how to use email. Kitti is taking online courses . . ."

Joan let out a long sigh. "Well then, I suppose I better learn all this digital stuff if I am going to be editor in chief."

Iris sipped her wine. She observed Joan's face.

"How does it feel when you think that you'll be the trailblazer? The face of change? Does it make you feel good? Or are you just going to take the job, leave the state of affairs as is, and make the best of it?" Iris said.

"It would make me feel good if I can implement radical changes. I have ideas on how I can make *Revue* more relevant, and I would start by hiring great writers and featuring amazing people, not just the people that PR offices push on you because they have a new movie or album to sell. I'm thinking about all the other important people who have so much to say but don't get the chance because they are given no voice."

"And you think *Revue* would let you do this?"

"I don't know yet. It will be part of my negotiation. I'll soon find out. *Revue* numbers just went down this quarter. They'll be asking me to perform a miracle," Joan said.

"Are you surprised? *Revue* is looking really bad. Pardon my bluntness and excuse me for expounding, but I browsed the last issue and it was shockingly lame *and* unnecessarily kinky. Page after page: eighties street urchin in fake ghetto looks, baby ho at the Cannes Film Festival, baby prostitute out dancing with very old men, slightly older baby prostitute in hotel room in a thong with very young boy—who wants to identify with these images? It's mostly just sex, sex, sex—women dressing to seduce men. My poor mother, they obliterated her legacy! She must be spinning in her grave. I gather that Ada was targeting a younger readership, but sexualizing teenagers and dressing them like whores in expensive clothes will not sell magazines. This pseudoprovocative imagery sends the wrong message, and the pictures are not even good. It's just visual entertainment; it's meaningless.

"Also, the writing style is prosaic, the subjects are banal because they don't question or challenge, and finally, the layout is clumsy: the new typography is fighting with the images. And in my opinion, Joan, if you are targeting a younger audience, great content will not be enough. How it's delivered is as important now."

"Wow! That was clear! But you're right. I'm in contradiction and conflict with the teams every day. The magazine has become cheap and lowbrow, and I went along with it like everyone else because I'm an idiot *and* I needed my job. I sold out, I admit it. I'm not even excited about the photographers anymore. They're all part of Ada's clique, always the same group. The magazine needs a total overhaul. You should come work with me at *Revue*. We'd make a great team," Joan said, laughing.

"Me? Are you kidding? *Revue* needs people like Othilia and Lou."

Iris's phone started ringing. "It's Chuck."

"Take it." Joan got up to leave, but Iris shook her head.

"Chuck, I'm really sorry I didn't call you back."

"I understand. There must be a lot going on," Chuck said.

"I thought of you today because I saw an ad for the annual horse show in Paris."

Chuck laughed. "Iris, I opened the drawer. I found a large sealed envelope."

"Any name on it?"

"Nothing on it. The envelope is not dusty or faded. Looks like it was put in the drawer recently. There were a few other bits and pieces, but they're not important: old receipts, a couple of phone bills . . ."

Iris was silent.

"Do you want me to courier it to you?"

"Yes, please."

"I spoke to Lou this morning. She sounded good. She says she studied really hard because she wants to go to Paris."

Iris smiled. "When she gets an idea in her head . . ."

"Reminds me of someone else," Chuck said.

"I can't even begin to imagine who you're talking about."

Chuck laughed again. "I'm not around for a few days. Email me if you need something. I'll get it when I return."

"Where are you going?"

He paused. "Canoeing up the Mendocino Coast, on the Albion River."

"Sounds great."

"Will you be okay? Is there anything else I can do?"

"Thank you. Thank you so much. Have a great time . . . canoeing."

She clicked off. *He doesn't call me* Bones *anymore.*

Joan was studying her. "We'll talk about *that* later, shall we?" she said.

"*That* what?"

"Nothing. You know what I'm thinking."

"Joan, Chuck is—"

Iris's phone rang. It was a French number she did not recognize.

"Iris?"

"Yes?"

"It's Ilaria."

"Ilaria?"

"*Sì*, I work with Clemente Campisi. Can I see you tomorrow morning? I need to talk to you. *È urgente.*"

CHAPTER 62

I check my phone alarm; a few more minutes to go. I grab one of my notebooks and a fountain pen.

I put my father's letter to my nose to see if I can smell anything. Maybe a whiff of aftershave?

I study my father's handwriting. It's funny and weird how he mixes capital letters with minuscule, all on the same line. The *T*'s and *A*'s are bold and uppercase, his *E*'s squiggles with twirls. *G*'s have protruding round bellies, and his *I*'s look like sticks. I know the letter by heart. I read it every day, many times a day. It's a long letter.

Look after your mother. Your mother needs your help. What is he trying to tell me with that last phrase?

I fold the letter and tuck it into the soft case of my laptop.

My alarm goes off and at nine thirty sharp I open Skype and call Peggy Rizer in LA.

"Peggy's phone."

"Hello, Peggy. This is Lou. Thank you *so much* for taking the time. Just don't mention this call to my mom, please. I don't think she's ready to speak to you yet. But I am."

"I totally understand," Peggy said. "Okay, so shall we call in Molly?"

I click on Molly Olsen's contact and she replies on the first ring.

"Molly? This is Lou, I have Peggy on the line too."

"Hey, Peggy. Hey, Lou. Greetings from dark and rainy Berlin."

"Molly, I was explaining to Peggy that I would like to keep this conversation secret for now. Mom is still very upset, she's in Paris dealing with some of Dad's things. When everything is sorted out, I told Peggy that I would come to LA to meet her with Mom."

"Hopefully you'll also come to Berlin," Molly says.

"You bet! I'd love that, I'd love to see where my dad lived."

Peggy takes the lead. "Molly, since she'd never met Gus, Lou has asked me to fill her in on who her father was and what his life was like."

Peggy continues. "I started working with your father in Los Angeles fifteen years ago, late 2002. I had approached him in Paris. I had seen some extraordinary pictures he had shot for *Stern* magazine, so I chased him down and we met. I explained how I worked with Molly's galleries in America and Europe and how, as a photographer's agency, we helped manage both the commercial and the artistic careers of our artists. We were the only agents in the world working like that. I asked him if I could rep him in America. He told me he was getting rid of his agent and he needed time because the process had become nasty. Two years later he turned up on my doorstep in LA—"

"Yes, I remember *so well*," Molly says. "We were *so* excited to sign him on worldwide. He'd just shot a series of portraits of runaway LA kids, homeless skater rats. His style was Avedon meets Larry Clark, right, Peggy? Those portraits blew our minds. The *New York Times* published them in their Sunday magazine, and it went *very* fast after that. Even though he was well known in Europe, the US had yet to discover him. The fact that he was American was a big plus."

"Yes, that's correct. After 9/11, advertising agencies and magazines had stopped flying in photographers from Europe. Gustavo living in LA was crucial, he was easier to promote."

"Was my father doing a lot of drugs then?" I say.

Both Peggy and Molly are silent.

"I know he had drug problems. You can talk."

Peggy clears her throat. "Well, hanging out with those street kids definitely did not help, a lot of them were on meth or crack cocaine. But after his first sold-out show in our New York gallery, for a time he cleaned up his act. He went to rehab and joined NA. He became very serious, obsessed actually, about his career."

Molly cuts in again. "After *that* show and as the money started to come, all he wanted to do was commercial work. He said he had mouths to feed."

"Did he mention us?" I ask.

"He was extremely secretive about his personal life . . . Molly?"

"Well, yes, he *did* tell me that he was moving to New York to be near his ex-girlfriend, he wanted to get back together. You should talk to Ilaria Negro, she was his closest friend. Ilaria worked for his former agent, Clemente Campisi. When Gus moved to New York, she was running Campisi's office there. I would often touch base with her because when Gus would go MIA, I could be sure to get news of his whereabouts from Ilaria."

"MIA?"

"Yes, Gus could disappear for long periods of time. He would check out of the world, check himself into rehab . . . or just lock himself up in his studio and shoot and print for days and nights. But Ilaria always found him," Molly says.

"Did you know he had cancer?" I ask.

"No, he informed no one, not even Detlef, his studio manager in Berlin. Gustavo had told us that he had to be careful because he had a diseased liver, hepatitis; he was always drinking artichoke water and nettle extract and stuff like that, took many herbal supplements. Drugs and alcohol were poison for him. We were constantly worried that he would never make it past a binge," Peggy says.

Molly interrupts. "Peggy, I *think* he must have found out in 2011 because suddenly he left New York and moved to Berlin. He said that New York was killing him, he was sick of the pace, the noise, the flimflam . . . he wanted to be in a calmer city where he could focus on his work, *away* from temptations and distractions. Once settled in Berlin, he did not want to travel very much—he said it exhausted him—so clients came to him for shoots. I don't know what kind of treatment he was under, if any."

Flimflam? I write down the word.

Peggy says, "Indeed, and that was also the year that Clemente recalled Ilaria to Paris. You see, even though he no longer represented your father, Clemente was jealous of Ilaria's relationship with him. This must have been his way of punishing him. Gustavo was shattered. He said he had no real friends left in New York that he cared for. He packed up his studio and was gone in a month."

"Did he see his family in LA a lot?"

Molly chimes in. "Gus went to LA a few times to see his parents, and his brother came on a couple of occasions to see *him*. Gus was so *proud* to show him around. He covered all his expenses, of course. Before Gus left America for good, he visited them. He must have known that he was sick by then. With that type of cancer, you don't know if you've got one month or five years left. I was happy, *of course*, because it meant having him in Berlin full-time. I was *mad* for your father . . ."

Peggy titters. "Molly had a crush on Gustavo."

"Well, darling, *you* tell me one person who didn't? I would have gone straight had he asked me."

I smile at the image of the two women fussing over my dad. "What was so special about him, apart from his work?"

"First of all, he was *drop-dead* handsome. He was very masculine with a fragility that made *all* the ladies want to mother him and bed him too."

"Molly, that is totally inappropriate. His daughter does not need to hear this."

"Hell! Why not? I think that explains a lot! And stop interrupting me, Peggy." Molly sounds annoyed.

"Interrupting you? You haven't stopped cutting into me. For Chrissake, just let me finish, will you?" Peggy says.

"*Cutting in? You* have nerve! You talk so *slow*, Peggy. Just get to the point. We don't have all day."

Peggy sighs loudly. "Excuse us, Lou. This is so rude, an old couple bickering . . . how boring for you."

I pretend not to notice. Actually, I think they are super funny. "Molly, you just said, *'That explains a lot.'* What does it explain?"

"To begin with, he liked to be in the company of women. Women trusted him. All his friends and the people he worked with were women, except for Clemente. Gus complained that Clemente was too 'Italian heterosexual' to understand him. Gus thrived on ambiguity; his eyes glinted with curiosity and mischief, you were drawn like a magnet to him. I get why Ilaria was so in love with him in spite of the fact that he could not reciprocate her feelings."

Peggy butts in. "What? Ilaria was in love with him?"

"Oh yeah. At *least* for a decade, until his death," Molly says.

"And how do you know?"

"Gus told me. He was worried because he didn't want to upset her, but he was not in love with her. He loved her like a friend. I personally *never* saw him with a girlfriend, I only saw him with Ilaria."

"What was he like to work with?"

"Very professional," Peggy replies immediately.

"*Very* loyal," says Molly just as fast.

Peggy continues. "We worried for him because at times he had this forlorn look on his face, disconnected from the world. That chap, Campisi, drove him crazy, though. Campisi wanted to rep him worldwide. Gustavo would not hear of it and Campisi would not take no for an answer. Gustavo was making serious money then, correct, Molly?"

"Yes, he was working all the time. Money was pouring in," Molly says.

"Campisi was furious that Gustavo would not renew his contract. He would turn up unannounced in Gustavo's studio, dragging poor Ilaria with him. Campisi seriously believed he would get Gustavo back. I think this was the reason Gustavo kept on relapsing, you know, the tension, that stress . . . there was a lot of shouting and fighting. Also, Campisi had artwork that he would not return . . ."

My heart starts throbbing.

"You see, Lou, we wanted to do a big show in Berlin to present Gus to the city," Molly says. "We asked Gus for the work he had done in Paris in the nineties. Gus was hesitant, he told us he would show some of it, not everything. He said he would ask your mother's permission to exhibit that work."

I close my eyes and imagine him calling Mom.

"Then he contacted Campisi. Campisi said yes of course and we were all excited, but weeks turned into months and then it was two years, and Campisi dragged on and on with all these excuses. One day Gus got impatient and gave him a deadline, and Campisi said he would give it back only if Gus renewed his contract. That kind of traumatized him," Molly says. "I rang up Campisi myself. He called me a thieving dyke and a whore and slammed the phone down."

My eyes spring open. "Sounds like this Campisi dude is trouble."

"Trouble?" Peggy says. "More like dangerous. He was violent. He threatened us a few times, said we had stolen his artist. He said he was going to sue us. After we stopped taking his calls, he had Ilaria pass on his messages. I don't know how that sweet girl continued to work with him—Lou, so that you know, Molly had to call the police once."

"The police?" I shut my eyes. *Look after your mother. Your mother needs your help.*

"Detlef phoned me late one evening. He was worried because Campisi was in the studio, and he said he was shouting at Gus and *smashing* things. Detlef had tried to intervene, but Campisi pulled a knife on him and Gus," Molly says.

"A knife?"

"You heard me right, a *frigging* knife. Campisi was high, he was doing cocaine in the studio and would not leave. Ilaria was trying to calm down Campisi, but he shoved her around and shouted at her, which made Gus crazy, so they went at each other until Campisi pulled the knife. I called the police before something terrible happened."

They go silent. I shiver.

"When did this happen?" I ask.

"A couple of months before he passed away."

"Were you there when my father died?"

Molly does not reply.

"Molly?" Peggy says.

Molly's voice breaks with emotion. "No, Lou. I was in New York the week he was admitted into the hospital. It was Easter in Germany and Detlef was away. You see, *normally* I spoke to Gus every other day, but that week I didn't because it was a sort of holiday . . ." Molly's voice trails off. She blows her nose.

"Are you all right?" I ask.

Peggy takes over. "Lou, we were in the New York office when we got the call from Gustavo's lawyer telling us he had passed away. We were shattered."

"I will *never* forgive myself for not being there," Molly says. "He died alone . . ."

There is a silence. I try to picture my father checking himself into the hospital, to die. My father would have arrived with his overnight bag. In it were his toiletries, a pair of pajamas maybe. Did he sleep in pajamas? In a T-shirt and boxer shorts? He would have removed the chain around his neck, the one with the virgin of Zapopan that my mom took from the steel trunk in the container, then his belt and his jeans and finally his old Rolex. He must have folded everything neatly in a drawer. My father seemed like a neat person. Maybe he thought that he would get out soon and he brought his laptop with him to the hospital? Or a book? What was he reading when he checked himself in? How do you pack not knowing if you will walk out alive? When did he send Virgil the cat away? In the end, he did not say goodbye to anyone and closed the door to his studio forever. My father had sat with his doctor in his hospital room, his doctor that knew him well. His doctor had shaken his head. Maybe he had told him, *"Herr de Santos, this is not looking good"* or whatever it is that doctors tell their patients when they're about to die. My father could have told his doctor, *"This is the number to call when I die. Only inform these persons. They will know what to do."* On the paper were the numbers of Matthew Cook and Andy Marshall. And then what? How do you wait for death to come if your head can think and your heart can feel? They give you lots of shots to dull the pain, to make you sleep, and who do you think of? Did Dad think of Mom and me before he died? Why didn't he tell me anything, why didn't he call me? I would have come, I would have sat by his bed and held his hand until he fell asleep forever.

"And Ilaria? Was she there with him?" I ask.

"Ilaria arrived in Berlin the day he passed away. Detlef told me she arrived too late."

I feel tears welling up. I cannot speak anymore. I am choking on the lump in my throat. Something is crushing my heart.

And fear, I have never felt this kind of fear before.

CHAPTER 63

Iris looked over her shoulder as she walked toward the barstool where Ilaria was sitting.

Ilaria shook her head. "Clemente's never up before ten and he wouldn't come here anyway."

The small café was on a side street a block away from the Opera *métro* stop. It was an old-fashioned workmen's place with a pinball machine, a long zinc bar, and a few tables with rickety Thonet chairs.

Iris ordered a coffee. She smiled at Ilaria and studied her face, which looked very young under the soft lights. Ilaria did not smile back.

"I need to give you this." She pushed an envelope toward Iris.

Iris took out a key and a piece of paper from it.

"Clemente has a self-storage unit. It's on rue Chabrol, near the Gare du Nord train station. That's a copy of the key and the code."

"I don't know what you mean."

"Gus de Santos, Clemente keeps it there. I hear Clemente shouting at you in the office. I could hear all the way down the corridor. I was worried for you because he has anger issues . . . I hear that he took the photo archive and you want it back. I hear him say to you that de Santos's archive had burned in the Finart *entrepôts*. That's bullshit, *stronzate*. De Santos's archive was not there when the fire happened."

Iris opened her mouth. No sound came out.

"This is where it is," Ilaria said, pointing to the key and paper with her chin. "Clemente has been there a few times in the past months, I see him take the key. The archive will fit into a car with a large trunk. You can remove the boxes yourself, they're not heavy. But you should go today."

"Why would you do this for me?" Iris said.

"I have enough reasons."

Iris stared at the key and paper on the zinc counter.

"Are you going to be okay, Ilaria? I don't even know your full name . . . can we stay in contact? How can I thank you?"

"I have your information. I got it from his computer. I'm leaving Paris at noon. I quit my job. I have not informed him," Ilaria said, standing up.

Iris looked at her wan face, the dark circles under her eyes. She wanted to hug her.

"Take care of yourself, be safe," Iris said.

Ilaria shrugged and walked away.

Iris stared at Ilaria's silhouette until she could no longer see her on the street.

She ordered a second coffee.

For a couple of days, it had felt good, the notion that the Paris archive no longer existed, that her memories with Gus were no longer in their physical form.

She had gotten used to the idea that what had been would only exist in her head, would be for no one to see. It was a blow to now think differently.

She searched her handbag and took out the folded list that Cyril had given her. She tried to remember each group of pictures.

The list was thorough, with many lots between 1995 and 1997, before Iris had met Gus: *Cats in cemetery, Old Couples, Wrought Irons, Landscape, Nudes, Ignacio, Santiago, Victoria, Ann-Margret, Ethan*—and then, after, the ones she knew by heart: *Genius Factory, Iris streets & rain, Iris Buttes-Chaumont, Iris nude study, Iris & Saskia Revue White story, Iris Shiny Jewels, Iris bed/ test, Iris balcony Voltaire, Iris boy/test, Iris hands/test, Iris Père-Lachaise, Iris mirror, Iris sex . . .*

Every word said, each crease on a sheet, every goose pimple on flesh, the damp hair, the pulse beating at her wrist, blue veins, Gus's hands on the camera, that look on her face, the hungry eyes. Eyes hungry for ecstasy and passion, eyes of sex and obsession. Love. And then, when there was no more, when that love went astray, and the cruelty came. It was all written down, all those moments of their lives captured by Gus's lens, printed on paper. Prints of their story, theirs.

How could she show those photographs to Lou? How would the lawyers look at them, number them? And the gallery study them, appraise them, catalog them, exhibit them, sell them? What questions would they ask, what would she be expected to tell, to reveal. How will it feel to be deconstructed by the press, to talk about what they had, to let them analyze its meaning and depth. To have them hang over a white sofa in a black loft, to walk into a museum and look at herself smiling and then sobbing. To watch people looking at her love and her pain.

Her bare face and nude body on the internet, in a place with no space for reflection or grief. To be Instagrammed, Facebooked, Pinterested. Reduced to 140 characters in a tweet, cropped to fit a banner in a blog, adjusted to the square screen of a phone. Splintered into a thousand Google results, then two thousand, little digital parts of a story that had no name, another love story, but this story belonged only to them. Gus was dead; now the story was hers.

He was in that room, he had let the enemy in.

Her love became hate. That was the story now.

Iris ordered a third coffee and called Saskia.

CHAPTER 64

Iris showed Ilaria's WhatsApp to Saskia: *'Clemente knows I'm gone.'*

Saskia frowned. "When did you receive that?"

"Five minutes ago."

Iris's heart galloped as she waited for the Avis clerk at the Gare du Nord office to confirm their rental. "There are no cars with a big trunk until tomorrow, *je suis desolé, mademoiselle.*"

Saskia turned to Iris. "Fuck."

"What else do you have? A minivan? Anything big at all? We just need it for one day. Please?"

The clerk with the rodent face looked up from his computer and stared at Iris and Saskia as they leaned over the partition of his desk. He shook his head. *"Non, desolé. Il n'y a rien."*

Saskia pulled the elastic band off her ponytail and let her blond hair cascade over her décolleté. She squared her shoulders, pushed up her breasts, and bent over the partition as far as she could reach, putting her face right in front of the clerk's. His glasses steamed up from the closeness of her breath, as if she were going to swallow him whole. Saskia's eyes narrowed mischievously, and her mouth parted into a wide smile. "Maybe we can pick it up at another office? Anywhere you want, we're easy. But we need it now . . ."

The clerk cleared his throat and got on the phone. He talked fast and nodded a few times, letting the corners of his mouth briefly rise. "There's a minivan at our Gare de Lyon location. Do you want me to book it for you?"

Saskia looked at Iris and nodded. "Yes, please, tell them we'll be right over. I don't know how to thank you. You've been amazing, Jean Yves." She grinned at him, and, blushing, he adjusted his green tie.

As they ran out of the office to jump into a cab, Iris said, "Really, Saskia? You manipulative piece of shit."

"Well, I got the job done, innit? You've been around American folk for too long, you don't know how to deal with Paris folk anymore, do you? *Non* means *maybe* here, get it?"

"Whatever," Iris said.

After picking up the minivan, they maneuvered through lunch-hour traffic, sharing a piece of gum and a small bottle of water. "Come on, come on, come on . . ." Saskia said, hitting impatiently at the steering wheel. Finally, she drove the van straight into the parking lot of the storage facility.

"No, Saskia, out, get out, there are cameras everywhere."

"What?" Saskia snorted. "You think there're no cameras inside?"

"Yes, but I feel corralled here; just leave it outside, will you?"

After parking in a tight space half a block from the storage facility, Iris stood at the gate, paralyzed with fear. Saskia waited for her. Iris took a few deep breaths and punched in the code to the gate. They strode into the building, pretending to know where they were going. Unit #205. The lone guard at the booth took his eyes off his cell phone and waved them in. *"Bon courage."* A football match played loudly on his screen.

The self-storage building was cavernous; the girls roamed the long, fluorescent-lit corridors until they located the small unit past the third bank of elevators on the second floor. Iris fiddled with the lock, then stopped, leaning against the door. Saskia searched her eyes and, brushing Iris's hands away, unlocked the metal door. Iris turned on the light. Metal shelves had been mounted to keep the boxes off the ground. Iris scanned the labels. Every black box was numbered, dated, and named corresponding to Cyril's list. The boxes were shiny and made of a waterproof cardboard covered in fabric, the corners reinforced with metal.

"Get the van and park it in the loading area. I'll put all these in the elevator. Wait by the door," Saskia instructed Iris.

Saskia had the strength and stamina of a horse, humming as she went back and forth, unloading the elevator and loading the boxes into the van while Iris kept an eye on the entrance to the lot.

They moved fast.

As they left the building, they looked at each other.

"I didn't think I would ever find these. Fucker, that fucker, that motherfucker screwed me again, and to think that I almost believed him . . . the crying, that pitiful show he put on . . . motherfucker," Iris said through clenched teeth. "Thank God for Ilaria, whatever her reasons are."

Saskia stared at the road and drove in silence, chewing on her gum.

The afternoon light streamed through the tall windows of Saskia's loft. Sitting on the floor, Iris stared at the pile of boxes, recognizing with a pang their elegant, custom-made design.

"I don't know how you're going to handle this," Saskia said.

Iris gazed deep into her eyes. "This is it, right? This is what I was looking for?"

"Do you want to spend the night here? The sofa's comfortable."

Iris nodded. "Please."

"Don't look so grim, Iris. It's gonna be all right, baby."

"Can you stay by me? I don't want to do this alone," Iris said.

Saskia sat down on the floor. "Are you sure?"

"For Chrissake, Saskia, of course I'm sure."

Saskia scraped her long hair into a ponytail, removed her rings, and started to peel off the black gaffer tape from the clamshell labeled *Iris mirror test.*

Iris took out ten eleven-by-fourteen prints, each in its own protective sleeve. Gus's aura felt tangible, intact. Careful not to touch the paper with her fingers, she examined them, checked the hand retouching and Gus's signature, and passed them to Saskia.

Saskia whistled under her breath. "I'm gonna pretend that I'm not looking at your *punani*, your nether regions. Iris, these are . . . unbelievable."

One by one, they opened the boxes of art prints in a religious silence. *Iris nude study, Iris test bed, Iris balcony Voltaire, Iris boy test, Iris sex*—the pictures were breathtaking. Every one of them was of her; Gus had captured the pure emotion. Pictures that left her staggering, naked, bare, exposed, raw.

Iris gasped for air.

As the afternoon turned to dusk, they stretched their legs at the kitchen counter and drank mugs of coffee.

Saskia whooped when they opened the *Iris & Saskia Revue White story.* She examined an unpublished close-up of their faces mashed together under a linen veil.

"You look the same," Saskia said.

"I'm not the same."

When they had finished going through the flat boxes, Iris leaned back against the wall and closed her eyes, spent. Saskia elbowed her in the ribs. "Don't stop now, Iris."

The small, square clamshells with the negatives were next, and checking each set was laborious. Polapan film and Polaroids came after. At the bottom of the stack were three boxes that contained Gus's most candid work: the small formats, his visual diary, the intimate snapshots of their days and nights.

At dinnertime they opened the last container. Larger than the rest, it contained the brown corrugated box called *Iris* and the black canvas bag. Iris slashed the tape with a pair of heavy scissors and opened the box.

Saskia uncorked a bottle of Bandol and sat on the floor with two glasses, watching Iris.

Her tests were there, the ones she had shot of Gus, as was the hand-sewn leather book with their embossed initials. She turned a few pages, then closed the book gently. Letters from Ludo, good-night cards drawn by Gus were also in there. Iris passed the cards to Saskia, along with a copy of *Belle du Seigneur*. "I hated this book," Iris said. "Doomed love, who wants to read nine hundred and seventy pages of that." She threw it away.

A cassette. Iris smiled as she looked at the cover. "Gus's treasured mixtape. He played it nonstop. I learned the basics of my Spanish from listening to the songs on that tape. He loved music, played the guitar, and sang well . . ." Iris read the track-list: "Caifanes, Bobby Pulido, Guardianes del Amor, Pedro Infante, El Puma, Bronco, Jorge Negrete, Gloria Trevi . . . you have no idea how happy this tape makes me, I thought I would never hear it again." Iris stuck the cassette in her shirt pocket.

She found her favorite camera in its case, a Contax G2. It was not loaded.

Saskia observed Iris and said slowly, "Gus really loved you, Iris. This whole archive is about his love for you."

Iris took a gulp of her wine. "I cannot talk about something I don't understand."

"What is there not to understand?"

"Saskia, for Chrissake, who do you think did it? Who else was there?"

Saskia was silent.

"I don't understand why Gus put in his will that I had to recover the archive as a conditional clause. He wanted his body of work together in one place, I get that, but did he want the world to see these pictures of me?"

"You underestimate him. If he had not written that into the will, you would never have confronted Clemente and you'd be so screwed in the head. Gus forced you to face Clem, and not just for the archive—"

"And then?" Iris said. "What did he expect me to do *if* I got it back from the psycho? Share it? Hide it? Look at it and destroy it? How could he push me to make that decision? I'll have to live with this choice for the rest of my life. Why didn't he write me a letter? It's the least he could have done—"

"From what I see here, Gus wasn't good with words . . . the little drawings he left on your pillow, the leather book, the beautiful pictures by the hundreds, all *of you*. It was his way of saying something *to you*," Saskia said soothingly.

Iris looked away, hiding her eyes.

"He did you a lot of harm and a lot of good as well, but only you can decide what memories you want to keep; you'll always have that," Saskia said.

"I'm scared that if I have to spend the rest of my life talking about these, about the love that was, I'm going to wear it out. It's gone, Saskia, finished. I want to move on. I need closure on Gus. I want to look at the future, past all this, past him. *This* is not who I am. Since I left Paris, I have another life."

"What have you been thinking about for the last sixteen years?" Saskia said gently.

"Raising my daughter, that's all. I'm doing *this* for her, for *her* legacy, because she's alone, not connected to any other family. I blame myself too. I kept her away from Gus, I blocked his attempts to contact us. I lied to her. She thinks he never reached out to her. I hate myself for that. His archive in LA was a way for her to understand who she is, who her father was— but these? Does she really need to have these pictures too?" Iris said, pointing at the boxes. "She just met Gus's parents, they were very warm toward her. She's excited because she now has grandparents nearby. I don't ask for more," Iris said.

"You have cousins in France. You and Lou should visit them," Saskia said.

"Yes." Iris gazed into the distance. "My cousin Eric was a good friend until my aunt and uncle behaved like assholes when my parents died. They took everything from my parents' house in New York, even my mom's clothes. I was too broken to put up a fight. *They* buried my parents in the family plot in Lectoure, near Toulouse. Poor Lou never had a chance, never had any memory of them, not even a cemetery to visit. I never saw my French relatives again."

"*Kut!* That's grim."

"Yeah, our life, Lou's and mine, has been strange."

Saskia reached over and held Iris's hand. "Ada destroyed your mum's legacy, so you *pretend* that you want Gus's legacy just because of Lou. It's not just for Lou, Iris. You should leave it as he created it, leave it intact, whole. *You* were a part of that . . . the Paris archive, it's *you*, with all the good moments and the terrible ones too. You should feel proud, you need to give a sense to those years."

Iris twirled her glass and stared at the pink liquid. Drops of condensation had formed around the stem. She ran her index finger down the side.

"What's that bag?" Saskia said as she pointed her foot at the canvas bag.

Iris picked it up and put it on her lap. She examined the label. The writing was Gus's. "Cyril mentioned it. It says *Iris* but I've never seen it before."

The bag was secured with a thin metal cable lock. Saskia found a pair of pliers in a kitchen drawer and tried to cut the lock open. The pliers were too small.

CHAPTER 65

I hear Maca walking up the stairs and I shut my computer.

"Hey, my lil' Lou!" Maca comes over and kisses the top of my head. "How are you going to celebrate?"

"Dunno. Amy wants me to sleep over, can I? Can I stay with her until Sunday?"

"Yes, of course. Did you speak to your mother?"

"By WhatsApp. I wrote to her."

"Was she happy?"

"Big-time. But she worries over everything. I told her my exams were a piece of cake."

"Let me know if you need anything. I'll be puttering for a couple of hours."

"Maca?"

Maca turns on the steps. "Yes, Lou."

"How did you and Mom become friends?"

Maca sits on the edge of my bed. "Let me see . . . it was a long time ago . . . you and Theo were in kindergarten, so that was eleven or twelve years ago. *Mamma mia*, that makes me ancient."

I look at her: she is barefoot, wearing a sunflower-yellow skirt with flounces and a flimsy blouse that shows a lot of boob. Her face is full of freckles, and her eyes crinkle at the corners. She has deep laugh lines around her mouth. "You def don't look ancient, Maca."

"Thanks, I *def* don't feel it. Anyway, your mother was very different from all the other moms, I connected with her deeply the day we met. We sat together at a parent-teacher meeting.

When I heard that she was a single mom like me, well then, that was it, that sealed the deal."

"Why?"

"Because being a single mom is so hard. You have no idea, Lou. I didn't sign up for single parenting when I got married and had my two angels. Your mom had it even harder because she had just moved from New York and didn't know our little town. I had separated a couple of months before . . . we helped each other through those times. When I was desperate, I could count on my parents to help me out, but your mother had just lost hers, she had no one."

"Mom never talks about it, never talks about why we moved here, nor does she ever mention her American family. I was five when I left New York with Mom, and since moving to California I have only seen my grandfather's family once. We met them in San Francisco, but they never came out west again. They were really nice."

Maca is observing me. She puts a hand to my cheek; it is warm and comforting. Mom doesn't touch me anymore.

"Iris has always been reserved like that. People were put off by her because they said she was haughty, but she's not. She keeps to herself, she has a quiet personality . . . just because she doesn't express things doesn't mean that she doesn't feel them . . . anyway, I loved her then and I love her now; you don't change people. She's not going to start yakking just to please the other parents."

I smile. The idea of Mom yakking is funny.

"I think it's good that she's in Paris, get her out of her comfort zone; maybe after this trip she'll start traveling more with you. You guys should go east to see your grandfather's family. I promise I'll work on it, I'll convince your mom."

Maca leaves my room. I open my computer and Google *flimflam*. It says, *Deception. Fraud.*

I have a bad feeling in my stomach after talking to Peggy and Molly. My mother has gone alone to face that man; it doesn't sound good.

I reach into the side pocket of my suitcase and take out my father's phone. Mom would throttle me if she found out that I had hidden his phone from her. Well, she did tell me to open those boxes. It was the first thing I found: his phone and his cameras. I put the phone in my pocket, but I haven't had the balls to turn it on yet. Who is the scaredy-cat now? Well, it's not that I am scared, it's just that if someone took *my* phone, I would kill them. It had taken me forever to get a phone. My mom had refused, she said kids don't need phones, nor should they watch TV. I finally got a phone after the bullying incidents at school. Mom had told me to call her if anything happened again. But how could I tell her that I was bullied because of her? Ronnie kept on making fun of Mom, said she dressed like an ugly man, that she was a weirdo. I punched him in the face, and his gang of losers turned on me and said that I was adopted, that Mom found me in a basket on her doorstep, that I had no dad. I don't care if they call me Noodle at school, I find it funny actually, because I feel good in my skin, but if you say anything mean about Mom . . .

We still don't have a TV. I complain a lot about the TV just to annoy Mom, but the truth is that I don't care for those reality shows my classmates watch. They're stupid and make my classmates stupid in their brains too. They are pathetic sometimes, my classmates, with the vocal fry and baby voices like the girls on those shows who fake-laugh all the time. The girls at school hunt in packs, go all Barbie on their Finsta and talk about boys most of the time. Boys, breasts, bra sizes, tank tops, fake nails, leggings, curling tongs, drippy lip gloss that tastes of cherry and smells vile. And washing their hair . . . since when did washing one's hair become the event of the day? *Hey Ruby, #pigout at #theYogurtShack? Aww no can't have to #washmyhair.* Wait, *what?* How much time do they spend a day getting ready with all that shit they had to put on their faces and hair? I don't even have breasts. I wear my mom's clothes because she has fly style and no one else dresses like that. This summer I'll get a buzz cut like Amy. Mom said I could.

At school, all I wanted was to be left in peace, until I met Amy. Amy Sachs is my best and only friend. Her dad is an artist like Mom, and her mother is a chef who writes cookbooks and has a brick oven in the backyard. With Amy I can talk about music and photography without getting laughed at. I have tried to get Mom and Amy's parents to hang out, Mom would like them for sure, but it's been three years and they have yet to spend time together. Mom is so strange like that; she has no friends, except for Maca and Chuck. I love Chuck. He wants to date Mom; I like *that* idea. The only times Mom wears lipstick and mascara is when she goes out with him. Chuck makes my mom feel good. She is more relaxed around him, less worried and stressed.

Boys are overrated. I want to be left alone, but I don't want to end up lonely like Mom. The girls at school are always complaining about boys. They are a waste of time, boys are, and so is thinking about them. I want to focus on the things I love, like taking pictures, making music, and horseback riding. I want to be a photographer; it must be my father's DNA. And I want to be a model. This is a new thing, I haven't quite finished unpacking this thought. The idea came to me because I like to direct Amy and Mom when they pose for my camera. I enjoy seeing how versatile they are, how they can become characters and play different roles for me. It's a creative thing to be a good model, Mom told me that. I hadn't mentioned the modeling before the other day on the cliff, and she went batshit on me. What is she so afraid of? She must have done things she regretted in Paris. Dad did drugs, I read that somewhere, so she probably did them too, but what's the big deal? That was decades ago and they were irresponsible times. Nowadays drugs are for losers. But I didn't believe for one minute that she

was telling me the whole story. What else happened there for
them to break up forever like that? For Mom to run away from
Paris . . . ?

So, finally, I got a phone, and now my whole world is in
there . . . if you want to find out who I am, just take my phone.
My phone says more about me than my room. Before I die, I'll
make sure to leave instructions to destroy my laptop and my
phone.

I plug my father's cell phone into my charger and turn it
on. The SIM card is still active, but it's locked. I need the password. I stop rushing and take a big breath. First attempt: I R I
S. *The password is wrong. You have nine more attempts.*

My fingers start to shake.

Second attempt: L O U. *The password is wrong. You have eight
more attempts.*

Screw you.

I breathe in through my nose and close my eyes.

Third attempt: L U P E.

BOOM! It works! I unlocked the SIM card! WHOA! I want
to high-five myself. I connect Dad's phone to Maca's Wi-Fi.
My heart thumps as I open his email. I am spying on Dad!

I scroll through hundreds of emails from Molly, Peggy,
their assistants, Detlef, Andy Marshall, Matthew Cook . . .
then I hear the ping of my dad's WhatsApp.

A ton of messages start to download. The most recent
on his list of chats is Ilaria Negro. When her messages finish
downloading, I open the chat and scroll back to a few months
ago.

I need air. I go to my window and look outside. When my
heart stops going crazy, I come back to the phone and sit on
the bed.

CHAPTER 66

Iris tossed and turned on the sofa, unable to sleep. It was still dark in Saskia's loft when she got up.

She turned on the living room lights and sat on the floor. She began to go through the pictures again.

Looking back at her life and her shattered innocence, she thought of Lou. Iris was her daughter's age when she had started modeling.

She turned on the Nespresso machine and waited at the dining room table for Saskia.

As the early-morning rays shone on the wooden floors, Saskia walked into the open space, talking to her laptop. Iris could hear the voice of a child. Saskia sat at the table and turned the screen toward Iris. "Say hello to my friend Iris. Hello, Iris!"

A little boy waved at her, and Iris waved back.

Saskia kissed the screen and logged out of her Skype.

"He's an angel. He looks like you, well, not the angel part, but the hair and mouth part. Adorable. What's his name?"

"Finn." Saskia smiled as she said it.

"Ready?"

Saskia nodded.

Iris called Amanda Greenwood and put her on speaker-phone.

"Amanda? I've got Saskia here with me. We were quite thrilled to get your go-ahead—"

"Darlings! I have good news. This will be a bigger story than originally planned. I bullied my boss into agreeing to it. I'll be coming to Paris to do the interview in person. How about tomorrow?"

Iris looked at Saskia, who gave her a thumbs-up.

"Sure, let's do it," Iris replied.

"Oh, and can you look into that *paparazzo's* archive? Make sure you can support your story with lots of good pictures, what?"

"You mean Jean Marc Firmin?"

"Yes, the bloke I was in touch with before. Please be a doll, Saskia, and prepare a selection. We'll clear the images at the *Daily Stand*, secure the legal rights to use them, all those formalities. I'll need at least twenty good pictures: some of you modeling, some of the girls you modeled with, a good one of Audrey Hai when she was working—you will be explaining to our readers why you're building a platform to protect young models, so I need pictures of some of the girls that were not properly protected. You understand . . . what?"

"I get it. Iris will help me. We'll give you what you need, after I get approval from some of the girls."

"Will Iris be with you tomorrow?"

"Yes, we'll both be there," Saskia replied, after Iris nodded at her.

"Splendid. Absolutely splendid, what? I'll be emailing you the details."

"Amanda?"

"Yes, dear?"

"Thank you, Amanda."

"It's okay, dear, for a change I'm doing what's right. I want to help you. Should have done it before, written something in-depth, I mean, but I didn't . . . I haven't done enough. Someone has to now. It's a disgrace that it took so long. Toodle-oo!" Amanda clicked off.

Saskia turned to Iris. "Wow!"

Iris nodded.

Saskia grinned, she had a wicked glint in her eye. *"Splendid. What? Splendid. What? Hoorra hoorra hoorra toodle-oo. What?"*

Iris laughed. "I'll call Jean Marc. If he's free, we go. But certain pictures are going to be a problem; you know that, right?"

"Yes." Saskia looked into Iris's eyes.

Iris drank her espresso.

"Hey, my husband and boys are coming to Paris. I miss them too much. I need to be here for more interviews and stuff, maybe some crowdfunding. School's out soon and the loft is available, so we'll all stay here. You'll meet my sweet little family," Saskia said.

"You're lucky . . . I wish . . ." Iris's voice trailed off.

"When will you tell Lou about the archive?"

"I don't know."

"Why? What are you scared of now?"

"Her interpretation of all this . . ."

"You're not going to tell her that you found them?"

"Don't know."

"Oh, for God's sake!" Saskia exploded. "Lou is not a child anymore. You can expose her to some of your shit. She'll handle it. It's life. You can't shelter her forever."

Iris did not say anything.

"I think you should be making the decision together," Saskia said.

"What decision?"

"If you tell Gus's lawyers about the archive, you must include Lou in that decision."

"I don't want to tell them. I'll just make it gone. I've decided to make it disappear forever, and after that I'll get the hell out of Paris before Clemente finds out."

"You're a moron," Saskia said. She got up from the table and walked away.

Iris dialed Jean Marc's phone. He didn't pick up. She texted him.

Iris picked up the breakfast plates and washed them. She could hear Saskia in the shower.

Her phone rang. It was Jean Marc.

"Jean Marc? It's Iris. *Comment ça va?*"

"It's Bertil."

"Bertil? Sorry to disturb you, I was looking for your father."

"Iris, my father's in the hospital."

"What?"

"He's in a coma. He had an accident two nights ago. He fell down the stairs, hit his head." Bertil's voice broke.

"I found him yesterday morning when I came to work."

"Bertil—"

Iris heard him blow his nose.

"Oh, Bertil, this is awful. Can I come to see you now?"

"Would you? I'm back at the atelier."

"I'll be right there."

Iris hung up. Saskia was standing by the doorway, wrapped in a towel. Water dripped from her hair, forming a puddle on the floor.

"Jean Marc's in a coma. He fell. I'm going to see Bertil."

"Fuck. Poor guy."

Iris put on her sneakers and started to gather her things. "I'll call you from there."

"Iris, I don't want to leave this place unguarded."

Iris froze and turned to face Saskia.

"You're right."

"There's an alarm here but still . . . I need to make a call. I have someone in mind."

Iris felt the hairs on the back of her neck stand up. She called a taxi and rushed out of the flat.

CHAPTER 67

Ilaria: *'He's an asshole.'*

Dad: *'I told him a hundred times. No is no.'*

Ilaria: *'He does not listen, Gus.'*

Dad: *'I'm very happy with Peggy and Molly. End of conversation, he'll never rep me again.'*

Ilaria: *'He only wants what he can't get, he's like a child with a huge macho ego. Imbecile.'*

I scan a few messages and continue to scroll down.

'Are you going to be ok Ilaria?'

'Sì, certo, I can deal with it, he harasses me because he wants to get back at you.'

'Hijo de puta. Why don't you leave him?'

'I can't find another job that pays well, I'm overqualified. I'm looking now for months, if I don't find one in Paris . . .'

'I'll ask Peggy and Molly if they need someone.'

'Grazie. Did you get anywhere with your archive? I can't leave CC until you get it back.'

'No. I called him yesterday and he went on about it like a motherfucker again.'

'Sì, I heard him shouting. He's a disgusting human being. He holds on to your archive so you have to go back to him.'

I scroll down some more months.

Ilaria: *'I really have to get out of here. Only use WhatsApp. He reads my emails.'*

Dad: *'Ilaria I can't leave you there with him, please consider my proposal.'*

Ilaria: *'If I go work for Molly, he'll kill me.'*

Dad: 'Something must be done about this guy, pimping out underage models is a serious crime, threatening someone with a knife too. We have the police records. We could get a restraining order.'

Ilaria: 'A restraining order means bullshit to him. I saw a lawyer in Italy, the lawyer said he will not touch the case because CC has ties with . . . his famiglia . . . call me tonight, I'll explain.'

I can't breathe anymore. My father had sent my mother to face a lunatic with a knife? Why would he do this? What did Dad want? I try to remember the date of his will . . . didn't Matthew Cook tell us that Dad had prepared everything well in advance? That's it, then, my father must have written the will thinking that Campisi would turn over the archive as agreed. But Campisi is never going to give the archive back to Mom, ever. Mom has been sent on a dangerous mission, and she is alone. My chest feels tight. I am so frightened now.

I continue to scroll down.

Ilaria: 'Gus, call me it's urgent.'

Two days later: 'Gustavo de Santos where are you? I need to talk to you'

Another forty-eight hours go by: 'Gus, call me. It's about Finart.'

One more day: 'Gus, Detlef is looking for you, and so is Molly.'

'Gus? Where are you?'

'Gus . . . ?'

My father had been unconscious for days, and no one had known it. Then he died.

I put the phone down and start to cry.

CHAPTER 68

I need to go outside; being outside will make me feel better. I need Taco; I need a hug from Mom. I call Chuck, but it goes straight to voicemail. Crap! I remember that he is canoeing.

I miss home, I miss the mustangs, I miss my room, I miss Mom.

I need to speak to Ilaria immediately. Ilaria can help my mother.

Seeing she is online, I send her a WhatsApp message.

'Ilaria hello it's lou I'm gus de santos daughter Can we talk?'

There is no reply.

I get impatient waiting and walk downstairs to grab something from the fridge.

Maca is in the kitchen on her computer.

"Yo."

"Yo."

I help myself to leftover spaghetti and slice some avocado. Maca looks up from her screen. "Lou, since you're going to be at Amy's, I'll drive down to San Jose to visit my parents. I'll be back Saturday."

"Wicked."

"Where's Chuck?"

"Chuck's away. I'll be fine, Maca."

I hear my phone ping. I go upstairs and close the door to my room.

It is a +39 number. The message says, *'Its Ilaria Use this phone'* *'Where are you? can I call you?'*

There is no reply.

I Google *+39*, it is Italy's country code.

I call the number, but no one picks up.

CHAPTER 69

The door to Jean Marc's atelier was open behind the locked gate. Iris rang the bell and Bertil ushered her in, locking the gate again behind her.

Iris was startled by his gaunt face and the dark smudges under his eyes. She hugged him.

"How is he doing?"

"Not good. I just came from the hospital; my aunt is there now. He's still in a coma."

Bertil stepped away and blew his nose on a paper napkin. "I told him a hundred times that the mezzanine was dangerous. It's my stupid fault. I should have gotten rid of it, made him sleep downstairs. My father was always distracted—the stairs, they're steep, too steep for an old man with knee problems."

"It's not your fault, Bertil. Your dad is hardheaded. He would have never obeyed you."

"I don't think I can leave him alone anymore, but I don't know how to keep an eye on him without giving up my job. I got him an intern, but he made that poor kid's life miserable. He's too set in his ways."

Bertil sat down at Jean Marc's desk and pulled up a chair for Iris. "My father had not been himself for the last few days . . ."

"What excuse did *Revue* give for not renewing his contract?" Iris said.

"Ilaria Negro told me Campisi's behind this—Campisi and Ada are close, you know? Of course *Revue* used the usual 'change of visual direction' excuse. After twenty-five years working for them—my father was in shock.

"There's another thing, Iris: the office was broken into Monday night."

"Shit."

"We had gone to visit Mamie at the nursing home. We came back late, the alarm had been disconnected, and the steel roll-up curtain had been forced."

"Did you tell the police?"

"No." Bertil looked away briefly. "Why did you call my father? Anything I can do?"

"I have work for him, but now is not a good time. You need to rest. We can talk another day, when he's feeling better."

"*If* he gets better. But we should talk now, my father needs the money. Without the fixed income from *Revue*, I don't know how he's going to survive . . ."

"We will see about the *Revue* issue. Ada's just been fired." Iris's eyes met his. She held his gaze.

Bertil nodded, some relief showing on his face.

"I hate to burden you with this, but the *Daily Stand* needs pictures again. They're doing a piece on some of the young girls that were modeling in the nineties and went awry. Basically we need to look for photos around the time that I was working in Paris. The focus is on Saskia Jensen. They're doing a big article on her and the dangers that young models often encounter."

Bertil's lip curled into a strained smile as he started taking notes. "We have many of Saskia, as you know."

"Bertil, I need some of the Red Room."

Bertil stopped writing and looked up from his pad. He no longer smiled. "I must think about that."

"I'm familiar with the archive. I know what I'm looking for. Can Saskia and I sift through those years and work on a selection? It will be faster. We are doing the interview tomorrow. We need something by then, if not the final edit, at least something to whet their appetites."

Bertil shook his head slowly. "I didn't say you could use the Red Room ones."

"I'm aware of that. We'll work first and talk about the Red Room later."

Bertil's shoulders were stooped with fatigue. "My father would kill me; he never lets anyone near his archive. Please pretend this never happened."

Iris nodded. "It's a bad time, I know."

"How many did you say you needed?"

"At least twenty. And throw in two full days of research."

Bertil whistled. "That's a lot of money, and good exposure. And sounds like you'll do most of the work . . . when do you want to start? I need to go back to the hospital."

"Now, we need to start right now," Iris said.

She dialed Saskia's number, then turned to Bertil as she waited for her friend to pick up. "We won't move from here until you come back."

CHAPTER 70

I take my father's phone out of my backpack and turn it on. I open his contact list and scroll until I find Clemente Campisi. There are a few old texts from him but no WhatsApps.

I type a text.

'I am watching you'

I press Send.

I look for a hotspot with my phone and log into the public Wi-Fi. I open WhatsApp and call Ilaria.

CHAPTER 71

Iris and Saskia took notes on a large legal pad. They were sitting at Bertil's desk. Two hard drives were connected to Saskia's laptop.

"It's much worse than I thought," Saskia said, squinting at her screen. "I recognize most of them. A lot of the girls are either from Blitz or Elektra. There're a couple of faces I don't know. Jesus, Iris . . ."

"Yeah, I told you it was revolting."

"What the fuck was I thinking? How could I have behaved like that? It's a miracle I'm not dead," Saskia said as she clicked through another Red Room file.

"You were kept high most of the time. It wasn't your fault."

"I only blame myself for this, Iris. Unlike a lot of these poor girls, I had a choice."

Iris chewed on her lower lip. "We were immortal, weren't we? We knew it all . . ."

Saskia clicked on the thumbnails one by one.

"I feel like crying when I see all our friends. I didn't know how sweet we were, how pretty. We were so trusting," Iris said. "We were so young . . ."

Iris's WhatsApp pinged. It was Lou.

'yo mom howzit?'

'All good missing you.'

'MT . . . what u up 2?'

'Working with saskia at a photographic archive preparing an interview she has to do'

'Wicked, which archive?'

'jean marc firmin he's a reportage guy he's like the best in france'

'Sweet, I'll let you get back to it Later mom'
'Later baby I'll call before I go to bed'
'k mom bye'

"Look, it's that asshole photographer again, Jared," Saskia said, nudging Iris.

Iris focused on Saskia's screen. "Yeah, he's in a lot of them. Fetid guy. He's a close friend of Ada's, Clemente still reps him."

"Isn't he like a celebrity photographer now? I think he just did a shoot with your president and first lady for the cover of *Paris Match*. Jared wouldn't be happy if these pictures of him leaked . . . it'd be like the end of his career, right? I'm sure no head of state will want to be associated with him after that."

"That's not what we should be focusing on now."

"I know, just saying. Opportunity lost. Look, here's one of Audrey and me with Billie. God, we look wasted. Gross. I'll use this one too."

Iris took a picture of the selected shot with her phone and wrote down the reference number. "How many do we have now?"

"I dunno? Like fifteen?" Saskia said. "And . . . surprise, surprise, here's *Petit Zizi* with his sad *zizi*. AGAIN. He's in so many pictures. I made a whole folder on him."

"What for? You can't use those."

"Just a reflex."

Saskia hummed as she clicked on the thumbnails. Every now and then she frowned.

Suddenly Saskia went silent. Iris heard the clicking of the laptop. She glanced at Saskia squinting, her face close to the monitor.

"Holy cow, Iris, is this who I think it is? Take a look."

Iris looked at Saskia's index finger on the screen. It was a thumbnail of a middle-aged man in a suit with his face between a girl's breasts. He had a rolled-up bill in his hands. The girl's breasts were covered in blow. Saskia zoomed in.

"Who is that? I can only see half his face," Iris said.

"Jacques de Gardin, CEO of Unika Press."

"WHAT? Are you sure? I can't tell."

Saskia clicked twice on the thumbnail. The image filled the screen. "Yes, look, it's his tie and signet ring. Check these out, the contact sheets with the Arc de Triomphe selects. Here he is posing next to Ada, see the tie and signet ring? You can't mistake those, as well as the pocket square. Then cut to the Red Room and there he is, in the thumbnails no one will see. Or maybe now they will."

Iris and Saskia sat back in their chairs and stared at each other.

"*Kut.*"

"Jacques de Gardin is married to the daughter of the founder of the group that controls *Revue*," Iris said. "Let's pretend for now that we didn't see this, 'K?"

Iris took a picture of the screen. "How do these guys get away with their abominable behavior?"

"Money, power . . . the usual." Saskia continued to click on the thumbnails, then she dragged the picture into her folder.

Iris went to the kitchen and percolated coffee as the atelier became dark. She looked out of the high window at the last rays of the setting sun. Shaking her head, she tried to erase the images of Jacques de Gardin that she had just seen.

"Saskia, I'm starving, I can't think anymore. I'm going to Chez Coco. Want something?"

"Yeah! *Merguez* and a couple of beers, please."

Iris locked the gate behind her. Jean Marc's atelier was the only building that was still lit in the long alley.

She turned on the harsh lights by the atelier gate. Where the passage hit Faubourg Saint-Antoine, there was the side door to the couscous restaurant. Its small *terrasse* was full of customers. She walked up to the counter and recognized Ahmed.

"*Comment ça va, ma gazelle?*"

"Good, thank you, Ahmed. Kind of busy, no?"

"We're always busy, always. Monsieur Jean Marc, that is *terrible*...the ambulance come, they take him out in a stretcher. Is he all right?"

"No, Ahmed. Bertil is at the hospital with him now, he's in a coma."

Ahmed shook his head. "Oh no! *Pas vrai!* Please give Monsieur Bertil my *bonjour.* Tell him we all think of his *papa* here at Chez Coco."

"Thank you, Ahmed. Can I order some food?"

"For here or you take away?"

"Take away. Six *merguez*, one *frites*, and four beers."

"*Ça marche.* Five minutes. You sit here at the counter? I give you the house red while you wait."

Iris smiled and nodded, welcoming the break. It was early evening and her eyes burned from having spent hours staring at Saskia's screen.

She looked around her. The place was small but cozy, and the walls were covered with North African memorabilia: a collection of flags, vintage hand-tinted postcards of young couples, bright plastic flowers in mismatched vases, gaudy souvenir ashtrays, and a map of Algeria. A few wooden chairs faced an old television. Sticky pastries made of dates and nuts sat oozing honey on two metal trays on the counter. Then her gaze turned to a greenish screen by the kitchen door. It was a monitor for surveillance cameras. The screen was split into four small squares, one of which showed the entrance to Jean Marc's alley.

Ahmed was behind the small counter washing glasses and gazing at Iris with love-struck eyes.

"Ahmed, could I ask you for a big favor?"

"*Oui, ma gazelle.* Anything for you. Will you marry me? I take you back to Algeria, you will be very happy with me."

"Thank you, Ahmed, I would love to go to Algeria with you, but I'm half *gringa*, and I live in America."

Ahmed sighed loudly. "*Tant pis.* My loss. America? I won't come to marry you then, they don't like us in your country."

"No, some people don't." Iris sipped her wine. "Ahmed, do you have the security camera recordings of three days ago?"

"Monday? Tuesday? Yes, why?"

"It's just a feeling, but don't tell Bertil. He'll worry if I'm worried."

"Someone try to steal in the ateliers?"

"Yes."

Ahmed cussed under his breath and shook his head. He clicked on the remote and rewound.

"Here, come in behind the bar."

Iris squeezed past him. He handed the remote to her.

"You are now in the morning of Monday, you fast-forward like this until the evening, the hours are at the bottom of the screen. There, you see?"

Iris nodded and fast-forwarded, stopping every now and then to observe the comings and goings in the alley. The motion detector had been set off by a trickle of delivery boys, customers of the ateliers, a bike messenger, an enormous cat, an old man with a protective mask whose overalls were covered in paint, Jean Marc and Bertil walking toward the camera . . . then it was dark in the passage.

The digital clock on the screen indicated it was a little past midnight. Two figures walked down the alley: a smallish man and a very tall one. They were both wearing sneakers, the tall one's head hidden under a dark hoodie.

Iris caught her breath, thinking she recognized Clemente's strut. A chill ran down her spine and the hair on the back of her neck bristled.

As soon as they disappeared out of the frame, she wrote down the exact time and then fast-forwarded.

Twenty minutes after the men entered the alley, they walked out again, this time much faster. She stopped the image and peered into the screen. It was Clemente all right. With him was a tall skinny man in a tracksuit.

Her hand shook as she took a picture of the screen with her phone. She replayed it and filmed it.

Iris begged Ahmed not to erase the recording. Ahmed called over his cousin Hakim, who promised he would email her a file with the recording, which was "in the clouds."

Iris took the food and walked back to the atelier. The greasy smell of the fries and *merguez* was making her nauseous.

Her heart stopped. In the shadows at the end of the alley a shape moved.

CHAPTER 72

"Mom?" I come into the light, and she stares at me as if I am a ghost. She carries two plastic bags. She drops them and runs toward me.

Her eyes are wide open, I have never seen her that shocked before. "What the hell . . . what on earth—Lou?"

I crush myself against her and let her hold me very tight as I sob.

"Mom, Mom, I needed to see you, Mom, I was so scared."

My mother pulls away from me and holds my face; she is crying too.

"Is Maca with you? Where is Maca?"

I cannot reply.

"But how? Did you run away? Lou, what the hell were you thinking?"

"I have something to tell you, Mom."

Mom is staring at me, shaking her head.

"Lou—"

I cannot stop crying with relief. Mom wipes a tear off my chin. "Let's go inside."

Mom picks up the bags, and I can hear the tinkling of broken glass. One bag is dripping. I can tell that she is calming down by the way she is looking at me. She is still bug-eyed but not giving me the death stare anymore.

I tug my small bag from behind the trash cans and follow her down the alley to Jean Marc Firmin's atelier.

The tall blonde I had spied through the windows opens a clanking gate and helps Mom with the bags.

"Look who I found in the alley," Mom says. "A runaway."

The woman's mouth and eyes open wide. "Oh my God!" Then she starts to laugh, a loud, funny belly laugh.

"Lou, this is Saskia."

Saskia gives me a hug and kisses both my cheeks loudly. She is so beautiful; she is very tall and modely. She observes me with strange slanted eyes that shine like the snake's eyes in *The Jungle Book*. I love her already. She takes the food to the kitchen and throws away the shattered bottle. After laying everything out on the counter, she opens a beer and sits on a stool facing me.

"Hey, Iris, need some alone time while you yell at her?"

"Not gonna yell at her now but, oh boy, she's gonna get yelled at later in a major way. Lou, call Maca right now and tell her you're here and then pass her on, please," Mom says.

I pull out my phone; Saskia gives me the Wi-Fi code. I see Maca is online. I hate to make this call. Maca is always chill, but I am sure she is going to lose her shit over this.

Maca answers on the first ring. "Put it on speaker, Lou," Mom says.

"Hey, bunny. I was about to check in. All good at Amy's?" Maca says.

I gulp and clear my throat. "Maca, I'm not at Amy's, I'm with Mom in Paris."

There is a long silence. "Say that again?"

Mom sticks her face in my phone. "Maca, it's me. Lou just turned up on my doorstep. I'm so sorry for this. I can't believe she would do such a thing."

Maca is silent. I keep my eyes on my phone, avoiding Mom's assassin glare. Then Maca says, "Young lady, you and I will discuss this when you come back. I don't even want to know how you got to the airport. I'm *very* cross with you, you were *my* responsibility. You tricked me."

"I am so sorry, Maca, I really am, I just needed to get here immediately. I'll explain."

"How. Did. You. Get. There?" Maca asks.

"Lyft," I said.

"I didn't know you had an account."

"I don't. I used Amy's."

Mom is staring at me. Maca is silent. Saskia is pretending to look serious, but her eyes glint. She takes a swig of beer and winks at me.

"And your ticket?"

"I used Mom's Amex award points."

Oh boy, is Mom angry. She grabs my phone and says, "Maca, I swear to God this is not going to go unpunished. I'm going to give her up for adoption."

"So, Amy was in on this too?"

I don't reply.

"Lou?"

"Well, no. Not until yesterday. I panicked. I had to come help Mom. I had my passport already with me thinking that she would ask me to come after my exams. I begged her a thousand times, but she didn't say I could come, so . . ."

Mom pounces on the phone again. "Maca, I am so sorry, desperately sorry. I'll call you when I've calmed down and gotten to the bottom of this."

"Okay, darling. Have fun," and she clicks off.

Mom is glaring at me with a look that could kill. "Lyft? Amex? How did you get here from the airport?"

"Air France bus and then the subway. I figured it out, it's easy."

"And Chuck? Does he know?"

"Chuck is away. I would have asked *him* for help had he been around, Mom, he would have understood. He would have helped me too . . ."

Saskia is looking at me, amused. "Are you hungry?"

"Starving," I say.

Mom sits on a stool and opens a bottle of beer. Then she starts laughing and says, "I'm happy you're here. But La

Arboleda to Paris alone, are you out of your mind? I still cannot believe it, I am *so* mad at you." She shakes her head.

"*What*, Mom? You went to Milan and Paris alone, without internet or a smartphone, and you were my age, so what's the big deal?"

Saskia snorts loudly. "I love her, she has a point. Here, eat my *merguez*. I think I need more beer."

I chomp on the spicy meat and scarf down the fries. I look around the space. This is my kind of place, it looks sick. I can't wait to snoop around. The *merguez* is delicious, and I start to feel less tense, but also very tired. I look at my phone. I have been awake for over twenty-four hours.

Mom calls Joan and speaks to her in a hushed voice, walking to the end of the space. She gives me side-looks, most likely discussing my fate. Joan must be very cross too.

I eat my fries. Mom comes back and moves the stool closer to mine.

"What happened, Lou? Why did you panic?" Mom asks gently.

I glance at Saskia.

"It's all good, you can talk," Mom says.

"Mom, I talked to Dad's agents, Peggy and Molly, and they told me that Campisi had pulled a knife on Dad and on Ilaria."

"Ilaria? Peggy? Molly? A knife? Hold on, hold on, go slow, Lou."

Mom and Saskia are now leaning toward me, hanging on my every word.

I recount in detail my emails and my conversation with Peggy and Molly and how that ended with Campisi's fight over Dad's archives, Ilaria, and the knife episode in Berlin. I do not tell them about Dad's last days. I am not ready for that yet.

"And on Dad's—"

"And what? Where?" Mom said.

"Nothing. Not important, Mom."

"You said *Dad*. Look at me, Lou, in the eyes. What is it? You're hiding something, I can tell." Mom is in my face now. I am going to get so punished for this, like grounded for a year and my phone and computer confiscated.

"I have Dad's phone, and it still works, and I read Ilaria's messages to him. She was worried about Campisi, he was harassing her. Dad was furious. She had talked to an Italian lawyer who did not want to get involved because he was dangerous." I blurt out, "Mom, Campisi is out to get you—"

"Get *me*? What do you mean?"

Mom's eyes are like steel, and Saskia looks like she is ready to pounce on someone.

"Mom, I just spoke to Ilaria—"

"When?"

"I called her from the airport when I landed in Paris. She says that Clemente has been out of control because you have something on him. He's been going insane in the office, and Ilaria was so scared she left Paris. She said she will send us something that will help . . ."

"Help how?"

"She says you will know what to do with it."

I look at Mom, and her steely look has softened.

"Give me Gus's phone," she says.

I dig around in my backpack and pull out the phone.

Mom gives Saskia a side-look as I pass it to her.

Saskia says, "*Kut*, I need a smoke and another beer, come with me?"

I am grateful for Saskia. I want to leave Mom alone with Dad's phone.

As I leave with Saskia, Mom calls out, "Saskia, I have to tell you something important. Clemente tried to break into the atelier Monday night. It's all on Ahmed's surveillance system at the couscous place."

"You gotta be fucking kidding," Saskia says, freezing in her tracks.

Mom does not even scold her for swearing in front of me. She looks very serious. "Just make sure you two stay right by the gate."

CHAPTER 73

My eyes are closing and I fight to keep them open as I lie on the couch while Mom and Saskia work. They are selecting pictures for Saskia's interview, something about the girls they knew when they were modeling. They have nearly finished but cannot leave until Jean Marc's son comes back from the hospital.

I had stood outside with Saskia while she smoked. She was very nervous and angry; her hands were shaking. She kept on clenching and unclenching her jaw. She looked like she wanted to rip someone to pieces.

"It's a good thing you came, Lou. Your mom missed you a lot."

"Are you sure?"

"Fuck yeah, she told me all the time, every single day."

My head exploded when I heard that. I digested this piece of information. I have been resenting Mom since forever because she had deleted Dad from the equation. I'm sure Dad tried to reach out to her many times but she turned him away. Why didn't she think of me? I wanted to meet him, I don't care if she didn't. She has never wanted to speak about him or contact him, and every time I tried to bring up the subject, she went weird and retreated behind her wall. It's like she had shut down that part of her heart and her brain, shutting me out in the process, neglecting my needs. It was as if Dad had never existed, ever. I'm an idiot. I should have made contact with him regardless. I thought I had time. Now it's too late and I feel this unbearable pain in my chest, but I have to be strong for Mom. Dad did say to me in his letter to take care of her, and a whole bunch of other things, so whatever. I think I kind of understand Mom, and I know that I have to look after her. She's in deep shit with this Clemente dude.

When Saskia had finished her cigarette and we went inside, I saw that Mom was crying. Saskia went up to her and took Dad's phone from her hand, then she sat by her while Mom sobbed. I had never seen Mom cry.

After Saskia returned to her laptop, I kneeled by Mom and put my head on her lap. She caressed my face in silence.

I wake up to a man's voice. I sit up on the couch and see a tall, cute guy with long hair and cool sneakers.

"Bertil, this is my daughter, Lou."

The guy comes up to me, and when I stand, he kisses me on both cheeks. He smells of disinfectant.

I hear Mom and Saskia talking to him. I only catch a word here and there: *Jean Marc, hospital, surveillance camera, Campisi, photo selects . . .*

Saskia's phone rings. "Hey, Prosper, 'sup?"

Saskia's face doesn't sound good. We all stare at her, worried.

Saskia clicks off. "*Kut. Kut. Kut.* Motherfucker."

Bertil calls us a taxi. He waits with us at the entrance of Chez Coco, under the bright neon lights.

I fall asleep in the taxi until we get to Saskia's. She and Mom get out, and I wait in the car until a big guy who looks like a mod comes out of the building. Mom tells our taxi driver to turn off the motor. Mom, Saskia, and the big guy with the wide, turned-up jeans and Perfecto jacket talk on the sidewalk. All three now face me. I slink low into the back seat. After what seems like forever, I hear a greasy rumbling sound and another guy built like the Hulk arrives on an old Triumph. Saskia and the Perfecto guy go inside her building. Mom and the second guy stand by the door and watch me in the taxi. He has a sick pair of lace-up Dr. Martens boots and a fitted short-sleeved shirt that is tight across his chest. Ten minutes later, Perfecto guy comes out of the building dragging a tall, skinny man by the scruff of the neck. He shoves the man, who stumbles and falls. Perfecto guy yells something at him. The man cowers, his tracksuit pants have ripped. Then the Dr. Martens guy puts Mom in the taxi and we drive off. I turn to see Perfecto guy lifting the man off the sidewalk and dragging him down the street. Saskia follows. She is on the phone. The Dr. Martens guy walks back into the building.

Mom is shaking. Our driver glances at her in the rearview mirror. "*Vous voulez une clope?* Cigarette?"

"*Non, non merci,*" Mom replies. She is freaked out, I can tell.

"*Ça vous derange?*"

"*Non, non, pas du tout.* Go ahead."

The driver opens the window and smokes while he drives.

"Not one word about this to Joan or Othilia. Understand?"

I nod. What is there to say? I don't even know what the hell I just saw.

After that, I sort of doze off again and then we arrive at Joan's. I remember being introduced to her and Othilia, and Othilia taking me up to her room.

I am so tired I am about to faint. I shower and go to bed.

CHAPTER 74

"*Quelle histoire,* Iris. Lou has balls, excuse *mon français,* you should be proud of her . . . to pull that off—"

"I'm still in shock, hovering between 'I want to throttle her' mode and 'I want to kiss her' mode, but we should go to a hotel."

"Don't you worry your head with that now, you have enough on your mind. Lou is welcome to stay here. By the way, I've been thinking, Iris . . ."

Iris looked up at Joan as she cleared the plates off the dinner table.

"I have listened to you and Othilia, and I have embraced your vision of my future. It all makes sense. I thank you for that."

Iris smiled at her and toasted with her glass of water.

Joan continued. "I'm going to accept the *Revue* proposal but on my terms, and that is that I will stay for only four years and only if I can pass Delfine's legacy on to the next generation. I want *Revue* to be what it was when your mother was at the helm: a fashion magazine for smart women, and once again *the* place to discover new talent instead of deferring to those entrenched in their comfortable ways." Joan rinsed the plates and placed them in the dishwasher.

She turned off the water and faced Iris. "I want a new section with political reporting about women's issues."

"Wow! Yeah!"

"And, I want to give the next generation the template and tools to catapult the magazine into the future, digital content included, using the old *Revue* archive as inspiration. I want to harness their passion and enthusiasm and guide them through the process. After four years I want to retire and dedicate my time to my family, my Gaston and Othilia, before I hit sixty."

Iris grinned. "Delfine would have been thrilled. I am moved, thank you."

Iris's phone started ringing. It was Bertil.

"Bertil? How is Jean Marc?"

"Good news, Iris, he woke up! The hospital called me and I rushed back."

Iris closed her eyes as a wave of relief washed over her. "I am so happy, you have no idea."

"Iris, Clemente pushed him off the mezzanine."

Her heart stopped.

"I have to go, I'll call you tomorrow. My father needs me."

Bertil hung up. Iris stared at her phone, unable to utter a sound.

Joan was looking at her.

"It was Bertil, Jean Marc Firmin's son. Jean Marc had an accident. He was in a coma, but now it seems like he will be okay."

"Jean Marc? I didn't know. That's dreadful. I just saw him at Hyères. He's a legend. His retrospective was beautiful."

"Did you know that Ada did not renew his contract last week?"

Joan frowned. "No. Why would she do that? Jean Marc has been with *Revue* forever. Talk about a legacy . . . we are lucky to have him in our roster."

"Clemente told her to do it, to cancel it."

Joan shook her head. "Darling, I think you're tired and need some sleep."

"I am not delirious, Joan, I am not making this up. I am dead serious. People are not who you think they are. Clemente has powerful criminal connections—"

"Oh, Iris . . ." Joan sighed.

"You must renew Jean Marc's contract, promise?"

"Of course I will, *chérie*."

Iris went up the stairs to Othilia's room. She peeked in through the door and saw Lou asleep in her old bed. She brushed away a tear.

Her phone rang. "Iris?"

"Where are you, Saskia?"

"At the police station. Prosper is filing a 'breaking and entering' form. I showed them the CCTV footage from Chez Coco. It's the same guy. They're calling Bertil now."

"Who is he?"

"No idea. He has no papers on him. He has an Eastern European accent."

"You can't go back to the loft, Saskia. Clemente pushed Jean Marc off the mezzanine."

Saskia was silent.

"Saskia? You must move. You can't stay there anymore."

"I've got Prosper with me, and his friend Adam is at the loft. We can't move the archive tonight."

"'K. Be careful, please."

CHAPTER 75

The wooden stairway resonates with the pounding of the heavy black boots. At the fourth floor, they stop.

After ringing the doorbell a few times, the police officer turns toward Clemente's *concierge*. She takes out a set of keys from her bathrobe pocket and hands it to him.

The police officer unlocks the reinforced door and walks in. His four men follow. The *concierge* shuffles behind the men in her woolly house slippers until the *officier de police* bars the way.

She stands muttering by the doorway, trying to peer in.

The policemen walk through the vast apartment. The closets that line the hallway are open, their contents gone. Empty drawers are scattered across the bedroom floor. At the end of the corridor is a small home office. The doors of a metal filing cabinet are ajar, and the men walk around the files strewn on the carpeted floor.

On the wall behind the desk is a garish painting of a sunset over the Bay of Naples. The painting is askew. Underneath it, a wall safe gapes open. Empty.

CHAPTER 76

The smell of coffee wakes me. I look at my phone. It's seven in the morning. I have been out cold for nine hours. Someone has laid a white bathrobe on the bed, and Othilia's bed is empty. I wash up and follow the sound of voices downstairs.

Mom, Joan, and Othilia are sitting at a long bench in the kitchen. They stop talking when I walk in. They are already dressed, and they are very chirpy, or maybe I just think they are chirpy because I feel so shitty.

Othilia jumps up. "Lou, what do you want for breakfast, toast?"

"Toast is cool. Thank you."

That's nice of her. I like the way she looks. She has these girly clothes on, but she wears them in this fucked-up way; her look is tight, she looks fierce. She has a friendly face with eyes that are alive and a big smile.

"I'm having a café au lait, want one?"

"Cool, 'preciate it, Othilia," I mumble, still trying to clear the fog in my brain. I've never had a café au lait before. It sounds very grown-up.

Joan smiles at me. "I was just saying to Iris that Othilia and I are very glad that you came and you should stay with us as long as you want."

"Cool. Thank you," I mumble again.

"My last day of exams is today. We can hang out and do anything you want tomorrow. I can take you around Paris," Othilia says.

"Cool." Is that the only stupid word I can say? I rack my brain for more vocabulary.

"How are you feeling, fugitive daughter?" says Mom.

"As if a bulldozer had run over me."

"Jet lag, you'll get over it in a week."

"A week?" I panic.

"Yeah, at least. Welcome to the club."

I groan.

"What are you up to today?" Joan says, addressing Mom.

"Saskia's doing an interview about the modeling industry, I'm going with her. I'll take Lou." Mom sounds vague.

"Does it concern *Revue*?" Joan inquires.

"No."

"Any luck with Gus's archive? Did you find out more about Finart?" Joan asks.

Mom shoots Joan a look, and Joan changes the subject. "Iris, *chérie*, Lou looks exactly like you but taller, she's divine, *n'est ce pas*? I would love to shoot you two for *Revue*, for our couples issue."

Shoot us? Count me in. But what about Finart? I had heard that name before, but where?

Othilia gets up and kisses Joan and Mom goodbye. She high-fives me. *"À toute a l'heure."* I like her. We all wish her luck.

Joan picks up her plate and slides from the bench with grace. I study the woman who took care of Mom when she was my age. She looks like a star, there is something so slick and poised about her. But she also gives me the impression of being a bit uptight and guarded. I love her skinny skirt and high pumps; how could she walk all day in those? I immediately sit up straight.

I face Mom. We have breakfast in silence; she is sipping strong coffee and looking into space. I devour my toast.

The sun is pouring in through the kitchen window. I can see the magnolia tree she told me about.

"It's strange to sleep in your old room. Was that your bed? The one nearest the door?"

"Yes."

"Have you been to your old room?"

"Yes, last night."

"And?"

"It feels bizarre," Mom says.

Mom is acting weird. I want to distract her from her mood. Is she still mad at me?

"Mom, I'm worried for Ilaria."

"I am worried too."

"Did you read the stuff she sent last night?"

"Yes."

"I didn't understand bits of it, like the laundering bits. Mom, how do you launder money?"

"You disguise where it came from. You take illegal or dirty money and you make it appear to be legal, or 'clean.'"

"How?"

"By passing it through legitimate businesses or through fake corporations. In the end, the money that comes from source A looks like it came from source B."

I ponder this. Mom puts her coffee cup down and looks at me.

"Do you think something is going to happen to her?"

"I don't know, Lou. I have no way of finding out. You were the last one to speak to her."

"Something must be done about that agent . . ."

"Yes, something must be done . . ."

"Did you call Ilaria today?"

"Yes, Lou, but it went straight to voicemail."

Mom is odd. "Lou, want to go for a walk? We can cross the river and be at the meeting by ten."

"I can come to the meeting?"

"I'm not going to leave you alone, am I?"

"I'll be quick." I run down the corridor and bound up the stairs.

"Lou, please hang up your clothes and put everything away. Not taking you anywhere until you do," Mom yells up the stairs.

"Whatever," I yell back.

I make the bed, dump my suitcase on it, and get into the shower. When I come out, Mom is sitting on the bed, folding my clothes.

"Does it look the same as when you lived here?"

Mom looks around the room. "It's very different. I had this cute, flowery wallpaper, only one bookshelf, a small desk, and my bed. It was less sophisticated. It was my home for two and a half years. It feels strange that someone else is living in it."

I detect a hint of nostalgia in Mom's voice. She is being all dreamy as she folds my stuff, which is strange because Mom cuts through the bullshit and is mostly in control of herself. I must have reminded her of her youth.

"Mom, do you think Ilaria is all right?"

"Lou, stop that. You're freaking me out."

"Why do you think she's not answering today?"

Mom puts a pile of folded clothes in a drawer. I can see that she is thinking.

"Peggy and Molly told me that she was Dad's closest friend for years. We should speak to her. I dunno . . . I would like to ask her lots of questions about Dad."

Mom is looking at me funny again. She nods slowly.

The landline rings and I about jump out of my skin. Mom ignores the ringing handset on the desk. The answering machine picks up. There's silence on the other end of the line, then it goes dead.

I throw on some clothes and we walk downstairs to the courtyard. The staircase blows my mind. It has black-and-white stone steps and a winding, polished-wood balustrade, and it ends in an entryway full of arches and white statues. I wish I had brought one of Dad's cameras. Mom then introduces me to Blanca, who is sweeping under the archway.

It's a beautiful, sunny morning, and people are headed to work. Many smoke as they walk. We stop at a café at the corner of a wide street and Mom has another coffee. Her French is flawless. I have a croissant; it is absurd good.

People sit outside and smoke and read the newspaper while they drink their coffees. Girls are biking in dresses and heels. I see many hot boys. Everyone looks so different, they look like *city people*. People in San Francisco and LA look like California people, not urban people. Mom's Paris hood is like a real barrio with a lot of personality. I can't wait to explore it with Othilia.

We continue south, past a Gothic church called Saint-Paul-Saint-Louis. We walk in, and Mom shows me the beautiful dome. A few people are sitting in the church praying. It feels sacred, special, also because it is massive and dark.

We keep on walking south. Mom points out to me the Maison Européenne de la Photographie, a cool center for contemporary photography where some of Dad's pictures are. I really want to visit, but we have no time.

After a few minutes, we arrive at the Seine and I dash across the road to peer over the edge of the stone walls. At the bottom runs a wide riverbank, cobbled and decorated with flowery shrubs and trees in wooden planters. Farther down the river, houseboats are bobbing in the ripples. I beg Mom to go below, and we find some stairs that take us down to the river level. We cross the Île de la Cité and walk on the left bank for a long time until we reach the quais with the mad traffic. Then we climb up the stairs to the main road and zigzag through an area with narrow streets and shops full of beautiful antiques.

We arrive at a big café with a glassed-in terrace, and Mom goes inside the packed room and kisses everyone. The floor manager makes a big fuss over me, kissing me many times and telling me how I look like Mom. I guess that's what he's saying because I understand some French, even though I can't speak it.

Mom and I go upstairs to a room with windows full of red geraniums through which the sunlight pours in. It is quiet, only a few tables are busy. Mom walks to the end of the room and sits at a table around a corner, hidden from view. Saskia arrives two minutes later. She has her laptop with her, and dark circles are under her eyes. She looks very serious and barely smiles at me. After ordering an orange juice, she exchanges a long look with Mom. We wait for a journalist named Amanda from the *Daily Stand*.

I see a lady at the top of the stairs talking to our waiter and he points in our direction. She is carrying a heavy bag and looks kind of flustered. I jump up and take the bag from her. We walk toward the table in the corner.

"Thank you, dear, you must be Lou, Iris's daughter, what? You look like her clone. Are you a model?"

Mom and Saskia stand up and shake hands. Amanda hands each one of us her business card: *Amanda Greenwood, Senior Reporter, The Daily Stand Media Group.*

Mom, Saskia, and Amanda sit at one table. I sit at another table right next to them.

Amanda looks at Mom as if saying, *Should she be here?* I know that look by now, there have been a few of them between Saskia, Mom, and Joan since I arrived.

I watch Amanda heave her bag onto the leather banquette and unbutton her coat. "Bloody weather, never know what to wear. It was pouring in London."

"Did you have a nice trip?" Mom asks.

"It was quite all right, what? Too early, though." Amanda looks around her and sighs. "I love the Café de Flore. It's funny, I interviewed Madame Rykiel right here, at this very seat, a decade ago. She came every day for lunch, she even has a club sandwich named after her. Bless her soul, may she rest in peace."

Our waiter appears, and Amanda orders a runny omelette and *"beaucoup de café et de pain,"* and I ask him for the Wi-Fi password.

I try to figure out how old she is—midforties perhaps? She wears a wedding band, she has shoulder-length brown hair, a big, animated face, and lumpy features. I can't stop staring at her nose; it is round at the end and it wobbles when she speaks. I'm sure that if she made an effort, with a proper hairdo and makeup, she would look prettier. Amanda has two pairs of reading glasses hanging from chains around her neck. Her long legs are hidden in black slacks, and the rest of her body is camouflaged under a shapeless shirt, which does nothing for her, and a shapeless raincoat. But when she looks at you, her eyes are razor sharp. Maybe that's the point of her outfit, she's a detective in disguise, a female Columbo? I've seen his picture, solid. I laugh on the inside thinking of this.

Mom leans back in her seat, and Saskia sits up straight, very close to Amanda's face.

"How old are you?" Amanda asks me. "Sixteen? Seventeen? I have daughters your age, and a son who's a bit older."

I smile at Amanda, I get a good vibe off her. I think she acts hurried and to the point, but she seems like a nice lady. Mom had told me this morning that she was a pain in the ass, that she had hounded her for days and days to get a story on Dad, but isn't that what reporters should do? Mom tells me not to let my guard down and let her trick me into saying anything. I sit back in my seat, clamp shut my lips, and nod silently when anyone looks in my direction.

Amanda takes out a recorder and puts it on the table where I am sitting. She turns it on, then takes a thick notebook from the bag along with many pens, which she lines up in a row next to her plate.

"This is now on the record. Saskia dear, introduce yourself, give us a bit of backstory and tell us what your project is about."

I listen intently to Saskia talk about her platform. Saskia then explains how she got started in the business when she was only fifteen, scouted at a shopping mall, and so never finished high school. She had gone straight into modeling, moving from a quiet hamlet on the outskirts of Amsterdam to a model apartment in Tokyo with six other teenaged girls. Saskia tells her story in a dispassionate way, without self-pity, talking about the travel, the loneliness, the exhaustion, the hunger. She tells Amanda how she dealt with puberty on the job and how her booker sent her to an old male doctor who put her on the pill and never discussed the dangers of casual sex.

Amanda makes clucking noises every now and then and appears sincerely concerned.

Saskia then tells her about arriving in Paris and landing the editorials that launched her career, being the one in a thousand girls that made it. Most of the girls she had been with in Tokyo and Milan did not make it and had either dropped out or looked for other, faster ways to make money, getting more and more into debt with their agencies. In Paris, Saskia made a lot of money and met my mom. They became best friends and partied together a lot. Mom listens, nods, but does not speak.

Amanda says, "When you say a lot of money, what kind of money are you talking about, dear?"

"My last year modeling I cleared one and a half million dollars after the agency's commission and my living expenses. I did a perfume campaign. The usage was worldwide, all rights, for five years. I also did cosmetics, a car ad, lingerie, and a luxury watch ad, amongst other campaigns. I did a ton of runway too. Before that I was making around a quarter of a million, net in my pocket. I was twenty when I stopped. I would have made two to three mil a year had I continued. I was working all over the world."

"Why did you stop?"

"First I got addicted to diet pills, which were really just speed with diuretics. Then I started doing other drugs. I partied a lot, I lost my mind. I was sent to a mental hospital and did drug rehab for many years."

Amanda makes clucking noises again. "It must have been hard . . ."

"I survived. I had a guardian angel watching over me."

Amanda peers at me from the corner of her eye. I stare back.

Saskia then explains in detail how the profession works and who some of the players were.

"Did your parents visit you? Check in with you?" Amanda asks.

"No," Saskia says.

"What are the most common dangers that a young model can encounter?"

"Eating disorders, exhaustion, depression, and other mental illnesses that go untreated. Even the most basic things can become a problem when you are that young and without parental guidance. Many of the girls haven't a clue about personal hygiene, diet, and . . . I don't know, man, like going to a dentist every so often to check on your teeth. Then . . . the drugs you're exposed to: speed, cocaine, and a myriad of other over-the-counter meds like Adderall to keep you going during the day. Unhealthy lifestyles with too much partying, alcohol, Red Bulls, and no sleep . . . and the predators . . . the guys that take advantage of the girls' youth, of their innocence. There're lots of them around young models."

Amanda looks at me again. She shifts in her seat. Saskia turns to my mom.

"It's okay," Mom says. "She should listen."

"And these men . . . they are professionals in the business?" Amanda says.

"Yes. Photographers, agents, bookers, a couple of designers, advertising people, their clients . . . but also the hangers-on, the parasites. Party boys who hire girls to go to clubs, promoters that pay girls to go to parties, venture capitalists investing in modeling agencies to secure access to beautiful young girls—the girls that end up as deck candy on the yachts during the Cannes Film Festival . . . and then they accept money for sex or drugs for sex," Saskia continued. "The girls get hundreds of offers and their bookers should screen these, but they don't because their client relationships are more important than protecting their girls. The bookers even push the girls to go to industry parties, saying it will advance their careers. I'm *not* saying that all agencies are bad. I *am* saying that a few of them don't care that their girls are at risk. Audrey was our friend, she was a darling girl. She never should have died, and I never should have wasted ten years of my life in and out of hospitals."

Amanda asks Saskia about the girls in her gang. I listen to stories about girls named Audrey, Billie, Nastasia . . . it makes me sad and scared, and also a bit ill. Saskia opens her laptop and shows Amanda the pictures she and Mom had selected from the archive last night. They keep me away from the laptop. Saskia says that she is interviewing girls here in Paris and that things are still the same, nothing has changed. There are still no strict laws protecting these girls, no one checking on their work conditions.

"There was an American model in the early eighties, Terry Broome. Her boyfriend was an Italian playboy. Terry was kept high on cocaine all the time. She was forced to have sex with his friends at parties. Then one day in Milan when she was high, something snapped and she shot and killed him. There are so many stories like these . . . the men that morally obliterate their victims . . . when I arrived in Milan, we were told Terry's story by the other girls. It gave us the shivers and then what? We were at those same parties, at those same castings, exposed to all of that like Terry Broome." Saskia shrugs. "But nothing's been done to address sexual harassment, to reveal the other problems, the drug use, the mental health issues. Any girls who speak up or point fingers are simply told to shut up. It's fashion's dirty little secret."

Amanda, Saskia, and Mom go quiet.

Saskia sips her orange juice, and Amanda scribbles on her pad. Mom stares at her coffee cup. Amanda clicks off the recorder while she reads over her notes. This takes forever.

I pull out my phone under the table to check on Ilaria, but she's offline. Is her phone disconnected? Why is she not answering? My heart is beating very hard.

Amanda looks up from her note-taking. Her glasses are perched on the end of her nose. "Are you going to give me some of those names?"

"Names?" Saskia says.

"The predators. They have names, don't they?"

Saskia and Mom look at each other, and then at me. Mom sits up straight and holds Saskia's hand. A current passes between them, a wordless pact, a tension so tangible that it becomes an aura around them. We can all see it. Saskia's lips have lost their color.

Amanda goes back to her notes to give them space.

Mom speaks out for the first time since the beginning of the interview. She looks very pale. Her voice hardens. "You can turn your recorder back on, Amanda."

I shrivel in my seat.

CHAPTER 77

Iris and Saskia stopped at a *quincaillerie* and bought a large wire cutter. It was early afternoon by the time they dropped Lou off with Othilia and returned to Saskia's loft.

Saskia knocked three times. "Open up. It's me."

The door opened and Iris recognized the big man in the motorcycle jacket. He nodded to her and retreated to the back of the room.

"Prosper is moving in for a while. He'll help me look after the archive."

"Thank you for this, Saskia." She picked up the canvas bag from the stack of boxes. Saskia cut through the wire lock and gave the canvas bag to Iris.

Iris rummaged through the many flaps. She found a brown manila envelope in the last pocket. From it she pulled out a file. It was a medical file from the American Hospital in Paris.

"I'll make coffee."

"Saskia, please stay here."

Saskia sat near Iris as she went through the papers in the file. Iris read slowly.

She put the file down.

Saskia observed her.

Iris's voice caught in her throat. "Gus had a mental illness."

"What?"

"Here, read for yourself. This is from 1996, from a Dr. McCormick, a psychiatrist. He lists Gustavo de Santos's symptoms: *emotional highs, deep depression, euphoria, dysphoria, irritability, grandiosity*—it says that the patient is on nine hundred milligrams of lithium carbonate a day but is not following his treatment because he feels *dulled, numbed, lethargic, flattened, like swimming in mud, emotions are too distant, robbed of creativity.*" Iris handed the papers to Saskia.

"Oh crap," Saskia said as she read.

Iris lay down on the floor near Saskia and gazed at a spot on the high wooden beams where patterns of light and shadow made eerie shapes. "Gus had a mental condition but never told me. He wanted me to find the medical file, didn't he? All those times he went inside himself or just disappeared were not because he didn't love me anymore."

"He was self-medicating, a manic-depressive on drugs and alcohol . . . I met a few of those when I was locked up, artists who didn't want to be on lithium. They couldn't create, many went crazy, tried to commit suicide," Saskia said.

"Why didn't he tell me? I would have done things differently. I would have supported him more, I would have forced him to work less . . . I would have fired Clemente . . . I would have understood many things . . . my poor Gus, how can I be angry at you anymore?" Iris's voice broke.

"Years ago, people didn't come out with their mental illnesses as they do today . . . there was a stigma attached to it. And there still is, even if some of the world's most creative geniuses are bipolar. Now there are meds that allow you to live a normal life," Saskia said.

"I am so angry with myself, I should have suspected something. Gus didn't tell anyone about his cancer either. That's the way he was—he didn't want people to feel sorry for him, to take care of him. How would his parents have coped with this news?"

"Do you believe in expiation?" Saskia said.

"Expiation?"

"Yes, gaining forgiveness."

"Atonement," Iris said.

"I think that Gus's suffering was meant to cure you of what he did to you. He imagined you getting the archive one day, then looking at it. You would see how much love he had for you; you would see the pain he suffered after you left him. He didn't want to excuse his behavior, but he needed you to be aware of his pain. That's my take on it."

Iris did not speak.

"There's another thing in the bag." Saskia pulled out a black cardboard folder. She peeked inside, then passed it to Iris. "I think you should see this."

Iris sat up and opened the folder. It was a small close-up of her laughing as she held a tiny frog in her cupped hands. Her eyes crinkled at the corners, shining with joy; her smile was pure, full of trust. On the bottom right of the print Gus had written, *Innocence.*

She looked at the date. It was the day she had left Paris.

On the back of the print Gus had written, *Today I lost my love.*

EPILOGUE

Mom cried when she read the pile of letters from Dad that Chuck found in my desk. Dad had written her a letter every week for years. Mom said it was like in the book *Letters to Lou*. But unlike the book, Dad never sent them, he just put them away one by one in the drawer. It made me so sad to picture him doing that.

Dad's archive is now all over the floor of Mom's studio. It's sick to see my father's work up close. It's a treasure trove for an amateur photographer like me, to be able to study the quality of his vintage prints, his beautiful retouching . . . I can't look at them enough.

Chuck knocks on the door. "May I come in?"

"Please do."

Mom smiles up at him and reaches for his hand.

Chuck drops a skinny Russian Blue cat on my lap and sits on the sofa next to Mom.

"Yo, Virgil." I tickle his chin. Virgil starts to purr.

Mom caresses my hair and tugs on my ponytail. "What are you thinking?"

I go back to Dad's pictures. Mom looks like an angel in some of them. Her gaze is so limpid, she is like a fragile bloom. I had cried at the massive love between Mom and Dad in those shots. In some of them there was a lot of sadness, some were very tough, and most were extremely intimate and made me a bit uncomfortable. I don't know why Mom waited all this time to tell me about recovering Dad's archive. I think that she had wanted to hide them away forever but somehow changed her mind.

Chuck rises and walks toward the door, never taking his eyes off Mom. She smiles at him as he leaves.

Mom lifts my head and holds my chin. She looks straight into my eyes. "Do you think these should be shown?"

"Yes. Some of them, Mom, not all."

"Do you still want to be a model?"

I hold her gaze and do not answer.

ACKNOWLEDGMENTS

I would like to thank the many whose help and friendship made this book possible.

First of all, Paul Zaentz, whose support allowed me to focus on *Wildchilds* for these years. Without you, this novel would not exist.

To my sister Sylvia Melián, for forcing me to start a blog where I could tell my stories.

To my friend Nicanor Cardeñosa Monzón, who edited from the very first draft. Always there for an urgent question, a long call, a doubt. Nicanor: your brilliance has been essential to *Wildchilds*, your mind is so acute, your eye so sharp. Thank you for pushing me so hard.

My heartfelt thanks to my readers who were so serious in executing their job: Lucinda Chambers, for your thorough notes—is there anything you can't do? Kristen Vallow, your knowledge of books is thrilling, your advice precious. Katie Knab, your enthusiasm and OMFG's helped me through moments of doubt. Andrea Puig Baselga, your detailed observations made me cry in despair. Martin Paul Smith, yes, it really needed that extra scene. Val Aikman-Smith, for reading a draft in thirty-six hours and not wanting to kill me afterward. I listened, I added. Yasmin Sabet, you were so right, I listened too.

I bow down to Ethan James Green for the stunning cover shot and Shawn Stussy for the fierce cover design. You have given me so much. And my beautiful models Dara Allen and Fernando Cerezo III for working it so hard and being so involved.

An enormous thanks to the team of knowledgeables that I consulted to keep *Wildchilds* real: Ignacio Garza for the songs and saints of Mexico and Luciano Concheiro for the popular culture. I love your country. My brother, Cristobal Hara, and Peggy Sirota, Hellen Showalter, Chrissy Olson, and Penn Stussy; because shooting and printing is a complex and technical art. Piero Biasion in the photographers' pit: we go back thirty years. Christabel MacGreevy, I loved interviewing you. Emile Ferreux for the science and biotech bits. Matthew Vafidis: where there are lawyers there needs to be credible language and legal terms. Ps, I turned you into the debonair one, by the way. Matt Sachs: you know what you consulted in, let's leave it at that.

Huge shout-out to my beloved friend Susi Wyss, *Guess Who Is the Happiest Girl in Town*. You are so much part of this story and my life; Kitti wouldn't exist without you. And to Lola, A.K.A Laurent Mercier, you have inspired so many of my Paris nights.

To Jane Burack, for the first proofread and fixes—that must have been a pain.

To my precious team at Girl Friday Productions who held my hand and guided me seamlessly through the whole process: Christina Henry de Tessan, the amazing Emilie Sandoz-Voyer, Amara Holstein, Meghan Harvey, Georgie Hockett, Rachel Marek, Laura Whittemore, Carrie Wicks, Paul Barrett. You rock!

Always there: José Sainz de Vicuña, Joan Juliet Buck, Carol Ann Emquies, Jessica Bendinger, Cristina Malgara, Karla Otto, Victoria Melián, Blanca Trueba, Florence Maeght.

To the kids whose passion for the art of fashion made me believe in the magic again: Dara Allen @dara._, Fernando Cerezo @fern.ando, Marcs Goldberg @tuna.bird, Cruz Valdez @cruzcvaldez, Marcus Cuffie @marcus.cuffie, Jesús Medina @justchuythings. Thank you Ethan James Green for the introduction.

Thank you to Young Kim, Estate of Malcolm McLaren for *II Be Or Not II Be* by Malcolm McLaren.

Thank you to Luis Aguilar Montes at PHAM, Aimee-Leigh Lerret at Hal Leonard LLC, and Michael Degen at Alfred Music.

And to my readers, this one is for you.

BOOK CLUB QUESTIONS

1. If you had to describe *Wildchilds* in a tweet, what would you write?
2. How realistic did the main characters' world feel? Did you get drawn into it? Or were you repelled by it? Did it make you feel like an insider? Were you interested?
3. If you could ask the author one question about *Wildchilds*, what would it be?
4. What are the main themes of *Wildchilds*?
5. Did you feel for the characters? Did you have empathy with their flaws? Who was the character that you related to most?
6. What did you think of the muse-artist relationship? Was it inspiring? Frightening? Frustrating? Why? Did it make you understand better the creative process between a fashion photographer and a model? The creative chaos? The vulnerability?
7. Did *Wildchilds* upset you? Did it make you feel understanding? Angry?
8. Did *Wildchilds* make you change your mind about something?
9. Both Iris and Lou have created armor and barriers to protect themselves. Did you have empathy or hope for the mother-daughter relationship and dynamic? Would you have done things differently? If yes, what?
10. *Wildchilds'* characters are damaged. As the book progresses and we see more flashbacks to Iris as a young woman, what happens to how we view Lou? Does our understanding of

her change? Did it make you want to find out what Iris had kept from her in order to shield her?

11. *Wildchilds* is a coming-of-age story. In an industry where children are treated as adults and are on their own, what does it say about the role of family in reaching adulthood unscathed? Is it okay to let your children fend for themselves? Or is it better to protect them? When does a child reach adulthood? Would you let your child work in the industry like Delfine and Ludo did with Iris?

12. Does being an exceptional artist forgive that person's sins? Does knowing about a person's transgressions make their art less beautiful or important?

13. What do you think Lou chose in the end?

ABOUT THE AUTHOR

© Ethan James Green

Eugenia Melián is a former model, fashion photographers' agent, producer, and music supervisor who was born in the Philippines to a Spanish father and an American mother. In Paris in the early 1980s, she discovered and launched the career of the groundbreaking iconic fashion illustrator and photographer Tony Viramontes. Since that time, and working out of Milan, Paris, London, New York, and Los Angeles, she has managed, art directed, and produced some of the most talented artists of our time, including Malcolm McLaren, David LaChapelle, Blanca Li, Matthew Herbert, Peggy Sirota, and many others. This is her first novel.

CPSIA information can be obtained
at www.ICGtesting.com
Printed in the USA
FSHW011833080119
54871FS